"Fast-paced and exciting . . . Berry has a knack for presenting alternative history that seems as though it might be true."

—*Library Journal* (starred review)

"Berry mixes historical facts with his own fictions in a manner that readers of this terrific series have come to love. *The Bishop's Pawn* . . . keeps the suspense building until the final pages."

—*Connecticut Post*

Praise for Steve Berry and the Cotton Malone Novels

The Warsaw Protocol

"Berry builds suspense nicely, allowing readers to anticipate the violence that eventually comes. To a great extent, the novel is a richly detailed homage to Poland, its culture, and its ability to survive so many invasions over the centuries. . . . An enjoyable read. Berry's fans won't be disappointed."
—*Kirkus Reviews*

"Berry has called Dan Brown and raised him, taking the lead in the big-money game of the religious-relic thriller."
—*Booklist*

"Packed with plenty of action, historical detail, and enough suspense to keep readers on the edge of their seats from start to finish, Steve Berry delivers another conspiracy-laden thriller that his fans will surely devour."
CrimeReads

"I love chase scenes and Berry provides the most exciting and complicated that I have read for a long time. So the history lessons about a country that most of us know little about, and Cotton Malone's ability to find his way through all the mazes in Poland, will remain with me for a long time."
—ReviewingtheEvidence.com

The Kaiser's Web

"Another thrill ride, with lots of twists and turns that keep the reader on their toes."
—Red Carpet Crash

"[Berry's] most ambitious and relevant thriller to date. A no-holds-barred, high-stakes romp with echoes of class spy novelists like John le Carré, Len Deighton, and Alistair MacLean . . . This is a dream read for the unabashed thriller aficionado, a story stitched along classic lines that never disappoints in laying out a riveting and relentless tapestry."
—*The Providence Journal*

"Ominously up-to-date."   —*Kirkus Reviews*

"Berry skillfully lays out yet another tantalizing historical what-if."
                                                        —*Publishers Weekly*

"Berry keeps finding enticing alternate-history mysteries for Malone to
solve. . . . Keep 'em coming."   —*Booklist*

The Malta Exchange

"The result is a thriller that intrigues and provides historical context. Berry
is the master scientist with a perfect formula."   —Associated Press

"This one will appeal to Dan Brown fans and anyone else in the mood
for a page-turning yarn."   —*Kirkus Reviews*

"Enthralling . . . Fans of Dan Brown will have fun, and some may
even prefer Berry's action-oriented hero to Brown's cerebral Robert
Langdon."   —*Publishers Weekly* (starred review)

"Berry has the lock on making history zing with breathless suspense and
galloping action."   —*Library Journal* (starred review)

"[Berry] really is very good at the historical-conspiracy thriller; he's a skilled
writer—much more so than Dan Brown, to whom he's often compared—
and a more dexterous plotter than many of his contemporaries. Fans of the
Malone series will give this one an enthusiastic thumbs-up."   —*Booklist*

"Berry has built a career exploring historical fact through the lens of
fiction."   —*Mystery Scene*

"Steve Berry has mastered the art of page-turning."   —*BookTrib*

The Bishop's Pawn

"Berry's most personal novel to date."   —Associated Press

THE
WARSAW
PROTOCOL

STEVE
BERRY

MINOTAUR
BOOKS
NEW YORK

Published in the United States by Minotaur Books, an imprint of St. Martin's Publishing Group

THE WARSAW PROTOCOL. Copyright © 2020 by Steve Berry. All rights reserved. Printed in the United States of America. For information, address St. Martin's Press, 120 Broadway, New York, NY 10271.

www.minotaurbooks.com

The Library of Congress has cataloged the hardcover edition as follows:

Names: Berry, Steve, 1955– author.
Title: The Warsaw protocol / Steve Berry.
Description: First edition. | New York : Minotaur Books, 2020. |
    Series: Cotton Malone ; 15 |
Identifiers: LCCN 2019043232 | ISBN 9781250140302 (hardcover) |
    ISBN 9781250768612 (signed edition) | ISBN 9781250140319 (ebook)
Subjects: LCSH: Malone, Cotton (Fictitious character)—Fiction. |
    Political fiction. | GSAFD: Suspense fiction. | Spy stories.
Classification: LCC PS3602.E764 W37 2020 | DDC 813/.6—dc23
LC record available at https://lccn.loc.gov/2019043232

ISBN 978-1-250-14033-3 (trade paperback)

Our books may be purchased in bulk for promotional, educational, or business use. Please contact your local bookseller or the Macmillan Corporate and Premium Sales Department at 1-800-221-7945, extension 5442, or by email at MacmillanSpecialMarkets@macmillan.com.

First Minotaur Books Trade Paperback Edition: 2021

10 9 8 7 6 5 4 3 2 1

For Frank Green,
A Man of Inspiration

ACKNOWLEDGMENTS

Again, my sincere thanks to John Sargent, head of Macmillan; Sally Richardson, who serves as chairman of St. Martin's Publishing; Jen Enderlin, who captains St. Martin's Press, and my publisher at Minotaur, Andrew Martin. Also, a huge debt of gratitude continues for Hector DeJean in Publicity; Jeff Dodes and everyone in Marketing and Sales, especially Paul Hochman and Danielle Prielipp; Anne Marie Tallberg, the sage of all things paperback; David Rotstein, who produced the cover; and Mary Beth Roche and her innovative folks in Audio.

A huge bow goes to Simon Lipskar, my agent and friend, and to my editor, Kelley Ragland, and her assistant, Madeline Houpt, both of whom are wonderful.

A few extra mentions: Meryl Moss and her extraordinary publicity team (especially Deb Zipf); Jessica Johns and Esther Garver, who continue to keep Steve Berry Enterprises running smoothly; Anna Slotorsz, for making our trips to Kraków so much easier; Patrycja Antoniak, who twice guided us through the Wieliczka salt mine, answered my endless inquiries, then read the manuscript looking for errors; Jan Kucharz, one of the salt miners who showed us the hidden treasures; Iwona Zbela, for extending some great hospitality while we were in Wieliczka; Jolanta Pustuła Szeląg, who possesses an encyclopedic knowledge about the Spear of St. Maurice; and Father Simon Stefanowicz for the wonderful tour of Jasna Góra.

As always, though, my wife, Elizabeth, remains the most special of all.

Twenty-nine years ago a man at a local community college asked me to join his creative writing group. I did, and so began a relationship that altered the course of my life. Here's a fact: No one can teach anyone how to write. It's impossible. But there are people who can teach you how to teach yourself to write.

Frank Green was that for me.

He was a tough taskmaster, but I would not be published if not for him.

Thankfully he's still there.

In my head.

Every day.

Poland has not yet perished,
So long as we still live.
What the foreign force has taken from us,
We shall with sabre retrieve.

*—*POLISH NATIONAL ANTHEM

PROLOGUE

MONDAY, AUGUST 9, 1982
WARSAW, POLAND
3:45 P.M.

JANUSZ CZAJKOWSKI WANTED TO LOOK AWAY FROM THE GRUESOME scene before him, but he knew that would be worse.

He'd been brought here to Mokotów Prison for the express purpose of watching. This place had a long and storied history. The Russians built it in the early 20th century. The Nazis used it extensively, as did the communists after the war. Since 1945 this was where the Polish political underground, the intelligentsia, and anyone else considered a threat to the Soviet-controlled government was held, tortured, and executed. Its heyday had come during Stalin's time, when thousands had been held at Rakowiecka Street Prison, which was how most Poles referred to it then. Sometimes, though, they spat out the German label: Nacht und Nebel. Night and Fog. A place of no return. Many were murdered in the basement boiler room. Officially, such atrocities had ended with Stalin. But that was not actually the case. Dissidents for decades after had continued to be rounded up and brought here for "interrogation."

Like the man before him.

Middle-aged, naked, his body bent over a tall stool, his wrists and ankles tied to the bloodstained wooden legs. A guard stood over him with legs spread across the prisoner's head, beating the man on his back and bare ass. Incredibly, the prisoner did not make a sound. The guard stopped the assault and slipped off the bound man, planting the sole of his boot into the side of the man's head.

Spittle and blood spewed out.

But still, not a sound.

"It's easy to manufacture fear," the tall man standing next to Janusz said. "But it's even easier to fake it."

The tall man wore the dour uniform of a major in the Polish army. The hair was razor-cut in military style, a black mustache tight and manicured. He was older, of medium build, but muscular, with the arrogant entitled personality he'd seen all too often in the Red Bourgeoisie. The eyes were dark points, diamond-shaped, signaling nothing. Eyes like that would always hide much more than they would reveal, and he wondered how difficult maintaining such a lie must be. A name tag read DILECKI. He knew nothing about this major, other than having been arrested by him.

"To manufacture fear," Dilecki said, "you have to mobilize a large portion of the people to accept it exists. That takes work. You have to create situations people can see and feel. Blood must be shed. Terrorism, if you will. But to counterfeit fear? That's much easier. All you have to do is silence those who call fear into question. Like this poor soul."

The guard resumed beating the naked man with what looked like a riding crop, a metal bearing hanging from its tip. Welts had formed, which were now bleeding. Three more guards joined the assault, each delivering more blows.

"If you notice," Dilecki said, "they are careful. Just enough force to inflict pain and agony, but not enough to kill. We do not want this man to die. Quite the contrary. We want this man to talk."

The prisoner clearly was suffering, but he seemed unwilling to allow his captors the satisfaction of knowing that fact.

"You've forgotten the kidneys," Dilecki called out.

One of the guards nodded and began to concentrate his blows to that area of the body.

"Those organs are particularly fragile," Dilecki noted. "With just the right blow, there's no need to even bind or gag people. They cannot move or utter a sound. It's excruciating."

Not a hint of emotion laced the shrill voice, and he wondered what it took for someone to become so inhuman. Dilecki was a Pole. The guards were Poles. The man being tortured was a Pole.

Madness.

The whole country was being held together by force and propaganda. Solidarity had risen from nothing and tried to eliminate the Soviets, but eight months ago Moscow finally had enough of concessions and ordered a crackdown. Overnight tens of thousands had been jailed without charges. Many more were seized, then bused out of the country. People simply vanished. All pro-democracy movements were banned, their leaders, including the famed Lech Wałęsa, jailed. The military takeover had been quick and coordinated. Soldiers now patrolled the streets of every major city. A curfew had been imposed, the national borders sealed, airports closed, road access to main cities restricted. Telephone lines were either disconnected or tapped, mail subjected to censorship, and classes in schools and universities suspended.

Some had even died.

No one knew the exact count.

A six-day workweek had been ordered. The media, public services, health care, utilities, coal mines, ports, railroads, and most key factories were placed under military management. Part of the crackdown involved a process that examined everyone's attitude toward the regime. A new loyalty test included a document that pledged the signer would cease all activity the government even thought might be a threat. Which was how many had been netted, including himself. Apparently his answers had not been satisfactory, though he'd lied as best he could.

The beating stopped for a moment.

He forced his brain into action and asked, "Who is he?"

"A professor of mathematics. He was arrested leaving a Solidarity meeting. That makes him, by definition, *not* innocent."

"Does he know anything?"

"That is the thing about interrogation," Dilecki said. "Many times it is merely a search for useful information. So what he knows remains to be seen."

A pause hung in the air.

"Interrogation also has other purposes. It can frighten those not being tortured, allowing us to break down their resistance and rebuild them in more . . . pliable ways."

Now he understood why he was here.

Dilecki's eyes narrowed as his gaze focused. "You hate me, don't you."

No sense lying. "Absolutely."

"I don't care. But I do want you to fear me."

His legs began to tremble.

Dilecki turned his attention back to the prisoner and motioned. One of the guards kicked the stool over, tumbling the beaten man hard to the concrete floor. The wrists and ankles were untied, and the man's bleeding body folded in pain. Still, though, he'd neither cried out nor said a word.

Which was impressive.

More so, in fact, than Dilecki's counterfeit fear.

So he drew off that courage and asked, "What do you want with me?"

"I want you to keep your eyes and ears open and tell me what you see, what you hear. I want you to report all that you know. I want to know about our friends and our enemies. We are facing a great crisis and need the help of people like you."

"I'm nobody."

"Which makes you the perfect spy." Dilecki laughed. "But who knows? One day you might be a big somebody."

He'd heard what the instigators and supporters of martial law liked to say. Poland was surrounded by the USSR, East Germany, Czechoslovakia, Ukraine, and Belarus, all Soviet-controlled. Martial law had been implemented to rescue Poland from a possible military intervention by those Warsaw Pact countries. Like what happened in Hungary in 1956 and Czechoslovakia in 1968 when the Soviets crushed all opposition. But no one seriously believed such nonsense. This was about those in power keeping power.

Communism's entire existence depended on coercion.

Polish communism seemed an odd mixture of socialism and fascism, where a small group controlled everyone else, along with all of the resources, while the vast majority lived in hunger and poverty.

The prisoner on the floor stirred, his frail body twisted as if gripped by a terrible arthritis. One of the guards kicked him in the midsection.

Vomit erupted from the man's mouth. One part of Janusz desperately wanted to help the man. The other just wanted to flee, doing, saying whatever was necessary to make that happen. Dilecki, like an exacting schoolmaster, was challenging every conclusion, every statement, keeping him in confusion. With no choice, he said what was expected, "All right. I'll do as you ask."

Dilecki stood, hands lightly clasped, the shrewd eyes steady. "I want you to remember that if you lie to me, or try to trick me, or hide from me, you will end up tied to a stool, too." The thin lips curled into the faintest of smiles. "But enough threats. You have done right, comrade. As the song proclaims. *Poland has not yet perished, so long as we still live.*"

"And what . . . the foreign force . . . has taken . . . from us, we shall . . . with sabre . . . retrieve."

The words came from the prisoner on the floor, lying amid his own vomit. Beaten. Bleeding. Making no attempt to conceal the triumph in his voice as the second line of the national anthem was repeated.

Sacred words to every Pole.

And ones Janusz would not forget.

PRESENT
DAY

CHAPTER ONE

Cotton Malone hated when two plus two equaled five. Over the course of his former career as an American intelligence officer, that troubling result had happened far more often than not. Call it an occupational hazard or merely just plain bad luck. No matter. Nothing good ever came from fuzzy math.

Like now.

He was standing inside what the Belgians called Heileg Bloed Basiliek, the Basilica of the Holy Blood, a foreboding 12th-century edifice, home to one of Europe's most sacred reliquaries. The ancient church was tucked into a corner of the castle square, squished between the old city hall and a row of modern shops. He'd traveled to Bruges for the largest antiquarian book fair in Europe, one he'd attended several times before. In fact, it was a favorite. Not only because he loved the city, but also thanks to the best dessert in the world.

Dame Blanche. White Lady.

Vanilla ice cream, drenched in warm Belgian chocolate, topped with whipped cream. Back in America they called them sundaes. Fairly ordinary. Not here. The locals had elevated the treat into an art form. Each café possessed its own version, and he'd definitely be enjoying another incarnation after dinner tonight.

Right now he'd come to see a spectacle. One he'd never witnessed before, but had heard about. It used to happen only once a week. Now it was every day, either mornings between 11:30 and noon or 2:00 and 4:00 in the afternoon, according to the placard out front.

It even had a title.

The Veneration of the Precious Blood.

Legend said that, after the crucifixion, Joseph of Arimathea was granted Christ's body. With solemn devotion he cleaned the corpse, catching all the blood flowing from the wounds into a sacred vessel, which he supposedly passed down to his descendants. Depending on which version was to be believed, drops of that blood made their way to Bruges either in the 12th century by way of Jerusalem or in the 13th century through Constantinople.

Nobody knows which tale was true.

But here that blood had stayed, occasionally hidden away from Calvinists, revolutionaries, and invaders. Pilgrims had come for centuries to see it, encouraged by a papal bull from the 14th century that granted indulgences to all who prayed before the relic. The whole thing ranked as beyond strange given that the Bible mentioned nothing about any of Christ's blood ever being preserved.

Yet that had not deterred the faithful.

The basilica consisted of two chapels. The lower dark and Romanesque, and the upper bright and Gothic. Twice destroyed, each time rebuilt. He glanced around at the upper chapel. The soaring ceilings of three richly embellished naves drove the eyes heavenward. Impressive stained-glass windows allowed golden rays of afternoon sunlight to seep inside. An elegant ceiling, like an upturned boat, stretched overhead, all in stunning polychrome woodwork. A bronzed pulpit hung high on one wall, shaped like a globe. A gold-laden altar stood before a series of ascending murals, rich in color, that, appropriately, depicted Christ shedding blood. Tourists filled the rows of wooden chairs before the communion rail, and even more loitered about snapping pictures.

But back to that weird math of two plus two equaling five.

Starting with three men.

Different from the other visitors. Young, cautious, unshaven for a few days, with plain, even features. Their faces also wore a different expression from those surrounding them, as if they had a more urgent reason to

be here than mere sightseeing. Their alertness bothered Cotton, projecting a tension that said these were not tourists. A final red flag came from
their positions, strategically around the chapel, near the exterior walls,
their focus more on one another than the reverent surroundings.

He glanced at his watch. 2:00 P.M.

A bell sounded.

Showtime.

In the side nave, beyond the arches, a door opened and a priest
emerged.

The veneration had begun.

A robed prelate carried a rectangular-shaped, glass-sided box. Inside,
atop a red velvet pillow, lay the reliquary. The phial itself, which harbored
pieces of sheep's wool clotted with blood, was about six inches long and
two inches wide. Mainly rock crystal of a clear Byzantine origin, the neck
was wound with golden thread, the end stoppers sealed with wax. It lay
inside a larger glass cylinder with golden coronets ornamented by angels.
He'd read enough about the outer cylinder to know that engraved on the
frame was a date in Roman numerals.

May 3, 1388.

The priest paraded across the chapel, his face an expression of great
piety, to what was known as the Throne of the Relic, a white marble
Baroque altar, its top covered by more red velvet. The prelate gently laid
the glass-lined box atop the platform then sat in a chair, ready for the
faithful to pray before the relic.

But not before they each made a donation.

A line formed to the left where another priest stood before a collection bowl. People dropped euros into it before stepping up the short stairs
and spending a few moments in silence with the relic. Cotton wondered
what would happen if someone failed to drop a coin but still wanted to
venerate. Would they be turned away?

The Three Amigos had shifted position and, along with everyone
else, moved from the main nave toward the side chapel. Several attendants shepherded the crowd and shushed any voices that rose too loud.
Pictures, pointing, videos, gawking, and donating were allowed.

Talking, not so much.

One of the Amigos worked his way into the veneration line. The other two stayed back, near the archways, watching the spectacle from twenty feet away. A bank of devotional candles separated the Throne of the Relic from the crowd, a couple hundred little glass sockets, many of them flickering with flames. Several of the visitors approached and lit a candle of their own. After, of course, dropping a coin into a metal container.

People continued to step up to the reliquary, pausing a few moments for prayer and a sign of the cross. The pair of Amigos who'd stayed back both toted knapsacks. Though many of the others present also carried them, something about these two shouldering them didn't seem right.

Twelve years he'd worked for the Justice Department at the Magellan Billet, after a career in the navy and time as a JAG lawyer. Now he was retired, opting out early, the owner of a rare-book shop in Copenhagen, occasionally available for hire by governments and intelligence agencies. He made a good side living from freelancing, but today was no job. Just sightseeing. Apparently in the right place at the wrong time.

Something was happening.

Something that every instinct in his nearly fifty-year-old body told him was not good. Old habits were truly hard to break.

The Amigo in line approached the collection bowl, dropped in a coin, then climbed the short steps to the marble table where the stoic priest remained on guard. The two other Amigos slipped off their backpacks and unzipped them. The clangor of alarm bells inside Cotton's head took on a shriller tone. He could hear the robot from *Lost in Space,* the old sci-fi show. *Danger, Will Robinson.*

One Amigo removed a gun, the other held what appeared to be a metal cylinder. He pulled the pin and tossed the canister into the side chapel.

A grenade?

Smoke immediately billowed out.

No.

A diversion.

Cotton's thoughts were shattered by the sharp report of the gun being fired twice into the ceiling. Plaster and wood splinters showered down. A wave of panic spread fast. A woman shrieked. Voices were raised. More screaming. People moved in a herd toward the only exit, a richly decorated circular staircase that led down. Maybe a hundred, all rushing out, creating pandemonium.

Another shot rang out.

A thick cloud of gray smoke billowed into the main nave, obstructing the view into the side chapel and reliquary. Cotton pushed through the crowd and headed for the smoke. Through the growing haze he saw the Amigo who'd been in line shoving the priest aside. Another wave of excited visitors formed a wall between where he stood and the Three Amigos, who were moving farther against the grain of the exodus. He pushed his way forward, the two other Amigos angling toward the third, who shattered the glass case holding the reliquary. The priest lunged, trying to stop the theft, but one of the Amigos planted a fist in the older man's face, sending him down.

What was this?

A classic flash-and-bang robbery?

Sure looked like it.

And it was working.

Big time.

The Three Amigos moved toward the side door from which the priest had first entered, which surely led into the back bowels of the basilica. Probably another way down, too. Which meant these guys had done their homework.

Cotton cleared past the last of the frantic tourists and stepped into the side chapel. He was having trouble breathing, coughing out smoke, his eyes watering. The priest was a concern, so he made his way to the altar and found the older man lying on the floor.

"You okay?" he asked.

The guy was groggy, his right eye red and swollen. But the priest grabbed Cotton's right arm in a tight clamp. "Need to . . . get it back."

The Three Amigos were gone.

Surely the police were on the way. Somebody had to have alerted them. But they'd be little help in finding the thieves, who were about to dissolve into the busy streets of Bruges.

He galvanized himself into action.

Sightseeing over.

"I'll get it back."

CHAPTER TWO

SLOVAKIA

JONTY OLIVIER HATED THE INTIMIDATION ASPECT OF HIS BUSINESS. He considered himself a refined gentleman, a man of distinguished taste, a connoisseur of aged wine and good food. A learned man whose studies of the classics dominated his spare time. Even his name conjured up movie royalty. *Olive-ee-ay.* As in Sir Laurence Olivier. Above all, he was a consummate professional. His specialty? Information. His reputation? One of a man who could provide exactly what someone needed to know.

Interested in the hidden net worth of a potential business partner or a possible buyer? No problem. How many automatic rifles and how much ammunition had the Boko Haram imported into Nigeria last month? Easy. What will the Revolutionary Armed Forces of Colombia press for at the coming bilateral talks? A bit more difficult, but doable. What were the Hizbul Mujahideen up to in Kashmir, or how will the EU foreign exchange markets value the euro at the close of business today? Both tricky, but the answers would be close enough. Besides, he gave a discount if he wasn't 100 percent sure, since by and large partial information was far better than none at all. His motto? *Scientia potentia est.* Sir Francis Bacon had been right.

Knowledge is power.

But its acquisition came with challenges. Greed remained a universal motivator, so money usually worked. Bartering also brought results. He didn't even mind a hard bargain, as that was the nature of the game.

But spies? Those he detested.

The arms and legs of the man sitting before him were taped to a metal chair. A wire snaked into the mouth and down the esophagus, its gauge carefully chosen, fine enough not to trigger any gagging reflex, but thick enough to do the job. At its end hung a metallic, conductive beak, while the other end connected to a DC transformer. Amateurs would have worked on the exterior, prying, twisting, beating, or kicking the information out. He preferred a more refined approach. This technique administered a much deeper and more painful discomfort, and came with the added benefit of not leaving a mark.

He pointed. "Who sent you?"

No reply.

He glanced at his associate. Vic DiGenti had worked with him a long time. Their paths had first crossed in his former line of work, where he'd learned that Vic could handle almost anything. And thank goodness. Everyone needed a sidekick. Laurel had Hardy. Martin, Lewis. He had Vic. A thin, gnarly man with straight black hair and narrow gray eyes. A person of few words, but with great discretion and absolute loyalty, all with a total lack of greed.

He motioned and Vic twisted the transformer control.

The eyes of the man bound to the chair went wide as electricity surged through the thin line and down his throat. The body convulsed against the straps. Not a sound was made, as one of the side effects of this particular method of persuasion was an inability to scream. Vic knew when to stop and, after five seconds, he switched off the current.

The convulsions ended.

Spittle drooled from both corners of the man's mouth.

A bit disgusting, but expected.

"Do you require another demonstration?" he asked. "I can certainly provide it. But I beg you, please don't make that necessary."

The man's head shook from side to side, his breathing hard and labored.

The whitewashed walls around him smelled of damp and rot, and he wanted to be gone. "I'm going to ask my question again. It's vitally important that you answer. Is that clear?"

The man nodded.

"Who. Do. You. Work. For?"

More silence.

He let out a long exhale of exasperation.

Vic sent another five seconds of electricity through the man's body. They had to be careful since DC current, if not delivered correctly, killed.

This spy had been caught yesterday in Bratislava. He and Vic had been there, ironing out a few last-minute details. They'd both noticed the attention, then used reflections off cars and an occasional glance to identify the pursuer. They then joined a throng of window-shoppers and confirmed that they had a tail. Vic, being ever vigilant, managed to snag the problem without drawing attention.

"Surely you must see that you're on your own here," Jonty pointed out. "No one is coming to save you. Do I have to give you another demonstration?"

"I was there to check on . . . you. To find out . . . what I could."

The words came out choked from the wire down his throat, and with an Eastern European accent to the English.

"That's obvious. What did you discover?"

"Nothing . . . at all."

He doubted that. "Did you report your finding of nothing?"

"Not yet."

All lies, surely.

"Who do you report to?"

No answer.

This one was stubborn.

He motioned and Vic again turned the knob. The body pulsated hard against the restraints, bucking and stiffening. He allowed the agony to linger a few seconds longer this time, but not enough to paralyze the heart. He nodded and Vic killed the current. The man went limp in the chair, unconscious. Vic brought him around with two hard slaps to the face.

So much was about to happen. Seven invitations had been extended. Nearly all the invitees had shown interest. Only three RSVPs were outstanding. And the deadline loomed at midnight tomorrow, a little over twenty-four hours away.

"I don't like spies," he said to the man. "They obtain information, then simply give it to their employers. They are my chief competition. Thankfully, you're not a good spy. I've asked three times. If you force me to ask who you work for again, I will leave the current on until you are dead."

He allowed his bluff to take hold.

One rule he always adhered to, though never advertised, was that he killed no one. But he would make this man wish he were dead.

The coming operation was the most complicated he'd ever undertaken. Two in one, actually. Both intricate, with lots of moving parts, the one dependent on the other. But the rewards? Oh, the rewards. The one deal could yield twenty million euros or more. The other? Hard to know for sure, but it could approach a hundred million euros. Enough that he could do whatever he wanted for the rest of his life. But everything could be in jeopardy thanks to this spy.

His eyes met Vic's.

"No. Please. Don't," the man begged.

His gaze shifted back to the spy. "Answer my question."

"Reinhardt sent me."

The name sent a shiver down his spine.

His nemesis.

The last person he expected to be watching.

His gaze caught Vic's.

And the knob was turned again.

CHAPTER THREE

COTTON FLED THE SMOKY CHAPEL THROUGH THE SIDE DOOR AND entered a small anteroom. Ecclesiastical robes hung on a rack, which meant this was where the priests dressed before mass. He'd been an altar boy himself until age thirteen, when all of his questions surfaced. Catholicism was really good at explaining what, but not so much on why. Teenagers were full of questions, and when the answers never came he decided that being Catholic was not for him. So he drifted away. Now, when asked about religion, he always said he was *born Catholic but not much of a practitioner.* Maybe that explained why he'd jumped into the middle of this mess.

Did he owe the church one?

Not necessarily, but he'd jumped in anyway.

He fled the anteroom into a short hall that ended at another staircase down. This one was nothing like the elaborate main entrance that the crowd had poured toward when the commotion started. Just narrow wooden risers here. He pounded down, found a door that opened outside, and squinted in the afternoon sunlight. A sea of people filled the square that stretched out before the old city hall. Scared tourists from the upper chapel clung together in a nervous knot. His eyes raked the crowd, searching for signs of the Three Amigos. He spotted them at the far end of the cobbles, about to turn a corner and disappear. The reliquary was not in sight, most likely inside one of the backpacks.

Bruges was a Gothic gem, its egg-shaped historic center light on cars, heavy on people and bicycles. A ring road kept traffic away, but a series of canals crisscrossed the city and gave the place its nickname. Venice of the North. It was Belgium's number one tourist attraction, with a broad tangle of crooked streets lined with colorful guild houses. The old marketplace once hosted trade fairs, medieval jousts, even executions. Many of the multistory polychrome façades remained. Block after block, in fact, formed a living museum that had earned the distinction of a World Heritage Site designation.

His record with those was not good.

Not that he intentionally tried to wreak havoc.

But crap just happened.

He took off after the Amigos and turned the same corner. They were nearly a hundred yards ahead, moving between two more rows of gabled houses. Believing they'd escaped they seemed less panicky, more casual. He decided to close the gap and started to run. There weren't many people on this side street, because it led away from the main attractions, toward the outer ring road.

He managed to close the distance to fifty yards.

One of the Amigos caught sight of his pursuit. The guy grabbed the other two and let them know their escape had been noticed.

They broke into a run.

Great.

He bounded forward.

The street ended at one of the arched bridges, which meant there was a canal coming up. The Amigos made it to the other side and vanished to the right. Cotton bolted into a faster pace and saw that they'd descended a set of stone steps to a quay where a boat waited. The three thieves hopped in and sped off, passing under the bridge beneath him and disappearing out the other side.

Two of the Amigos tossed him a casual wave.

On his side of the canal he spotted one of the many open-topped boats with twenty empty seats, waiting for another group of tourists to buy tickets and make their way down for a water tour. A line had formed at the booth, the sales not yet started. He shouldered his way to its head, then kept going. The attendant inside the booth called out. He ignored the command to stop and hustled down clammy stone steps that smelled of mold. A man waited at the bottom, most likely the tour boat's operator, who reacted to the unauthorized approach by holding up his hands, signaling halt. Cotton brought a knee into the man's gut, doubling him over.

"Sorry about that," he muttered.

He hopped into the boat, whose engine was idling, and released the two mooring lines. He gripped the throttle and shoved it forward, bringing the diesel's throaty *chug-chug* to life. The boat lurched forward and he twisted the wheel, aiming the bow in the direction of the Three Amigos. He'd been on one of these before, having taken a couple of canal tours of Bruges. They usually tooled along at a snail's pace, seeing the sights, and he'd always wondered if there was more bark under the hood.

And there was.

He maxed out the throttle.

The prop bit and the bow rose, cutting through the brown water of the narrow canal, tossing up white foam in its wake. He passed under the same footbridge, emerging on the other side where the canal doglegged left and wound its way around a stretch of gray-stone buildings softened by clingy vines. Another sharp turn right and the waterway straightened, the stretch ahead flanked by more vine-covered houses and timber façades.

He passed under the rusted scrolls of another arched bridge.

The Three Amigos had a solid head start but apparently were not using excessive speed, thinking they were finally in the clear.

And that was allowing him to gain ground.

The canal was about fifty feet wide, flanked on both sides by tall stone walls and leaning trees. Another of the tour boats suddenly appeared from the right at a junction. He veered left and passed close to the other boat's bow. Few of the other occupants escaped a bath from his wake. He waved an apology but kept going, straightening out the wheel and focusing on where the route widened into a large basin at another T-junction. The Three Amigos were waiting in the basin, their boat perpendicular to his approach, two of the men with guns aimed his way.

They started firing.

He was headed right toward the bullets at nearly full throttle, the gap closing fast. He ducked below the windscreen and the rounds whined by. The Amigos' boat jolted forward, blocking any turn to the left. The guns also kept firing. Too late to go right. Not enough room in the long rectangular basin to make the turn without hitting the barrier wall.

No choice.

He leaped into the water.

The boat sped on, pilotless, but only for another twenty yards before slamming into the stone wall and exploding. He ducked beneath the surface, mindful of something he'd once read. Until the 1980s raw sewage had been dumped into the canals. Hopefully four decades of cleansing had eliminated any hazards.

He popped his head from the water.

The Three Amigos were gone.

Getting out of the canal could prove a problem. He saw no ladders or steps up along the walls that encased the waterway.

He heard a siren and swiveled around.

A police boat was racing his way, blue light flashing. His own boat was a burning hulk, sinking into the canal. The police boat swung up alongside. Two uniforms had their guns out and aimed. Neither looked friendly.

Getting out of the water was no longer an issue.

But where he would end up?

That could be a big problem.

CHAPTER FOUR

Jonty poured himself a generous splash of Krupnik. He'd always liked the drink, a unique combination of honey, herbs, and spices, diluted, boiled, then strained before being added to a vodka base. Legend said the recipe was created by Benedictine monks in Belarus and eventually traveled to Poland. Usually it was served warm, but he preferred his at room temperature.

He sipped the concoction, the strong liquor soothing in a way that seemed to brush away any rough edges. He was still unnerved by the unpleasantness that had happened in the basement. The nosy spy was tied up and would stay there until Thursday. After that, they'd let him go. The information he'd learned was disturbing on a number of levels, and Vic was going to turn his attention to the matter.

Reinhardt.

Of all people.

Gandhi said it best. *There is a sufficiency in the world for man's need but not for man's greed.*

That explained his archrival.

He stared around at the old library.

Sturney Castle seemed perfect. A 13th-century neo-Gothic fortification, it featured three wings situated around a pentagonal courtyard, enclosed on the fourth side by a stately main gate. It occupied strategic real estate, built into a rolling rock formation close to the River Orava, fifty kilometers south of the Polish border, safe within Slovakia. Five towers, each crowned with a cupola, topped the corners, a balcony ringing the highest conjuring images of a princess in peril. It had been able to resist the attacks of Turks, Cossacks, and Hussites who'd swept in regularly for centuries. It seemed a place that had never known poverty, as every room was chock-full of tapestries and antiques from its prosperous past. The Polish crown jewels had been hid here when the Swedes invaded in the 17th century. Then, in the 18th, the future king of Madagascar had been imprisoned here. Once owned by local aristocracy, it was taken over by the communists in the 1950s as part of a land reform policy. Thankfully, documents in the official registry were never changed, so after democracy was restored the property was returned to its former owners, who proved incapable of maintaining it. Now it was a high-end rental, with a staff and caterers, available to corporations and individuals who could afford the hefty price tag.

He walked over to the French doors and stepped out onto an upper terrace. Potted plants, full of color, lined the outer half walls. Birch, fir, pine, and spruce trees stretched as far as he could see through an ancient Jurassic valley. Northern Slovakia was spectacular. The Tatras, the highest range in the Carpathian Mountains, touched the northern sky, snow dusting the highest peaks, a mecca for hikers and skiers.

Out of necessity he lived a solitary life. He was philosophical about his failure with women, which seemed a recurring theme, and men did not interest him. Finding the hard to find? Then making a sale? That he loved. And unlike Reinhardt, he preferred to manufacture his own business opportunities instead of preying off others. There'd been too many deals to count, each one profitable in its own way. He skirted the law, for sure, but never had he been considered an official threat. He tried hard to stay apolitical, taking no sides, harboring no ideals. He was the embodiment of Switzerland. Neutral in all that mattered, save for profit.

He'd definitely come to enjoy the finer things of life. Never having to worry about money, buying what he wanted, when he wanted? Going wherever? Francis Bacon had been right. *Money was a great servant, but a poor master.* And now he was about to close the biggest deal of his life.

A soft jangle signaled an incoming call. He found the phone in his pocket. Today's cellular unit. He changed every three days, all part of an institutionalized paranoia and the embodiment of a maxim he'd long lived by. *Nobody really needed to find him unless he wanted to be found.*

"The Holy Blood was taken earlier," Vic said to him. "I have a confirmation email from the Russians."

He smiled.

Another RSVP. That made five. Only the Americans and the Germans remained.

"Any issues?" he asked.

"It seemed to be a clean theft in Bruges."

Good to hear.

"We need to make sure that nothing has been compromised," he told Vic. "I'm concerned about our guest in the basement and who sent him."

They'd been extra careful leaving Bratislava, with the spy tied and gagged in the rear seat, ensuring that they were not followed and that their car had not been electronically tagged.

"Be right on this, Vic," he said. "Reinhardt is way too close for my comfort."

"I understand. I'll have more information shortly."

"And what of this evening?"

"It's all arranged. I'm headed north in a few hours."

That was good to hear.

He ended the call and returned inside, depositing his empty glass on the walnut sideboard. He'd chosen this locale for a variety of reasons. First, it was gorgeous. Second, it was within two hours of Kraków, but safely over the border in another sovereign state. Third, no one lived within ten kilometers. And fourth, it came with lots of space. A ballroom with an upper gallery, dining hall, a dozen upstairs bedrooms, an ample kitchen, and, most important, servants' passages that offered a concealed way to move from one room to another.

He loved secrecy.

What a thrill to know things others did not. And here he knew something nobody else in the world knew. All others privy to the information were long dead. A fortuitous piece of knowledge that had dropped into his lap. Unimportant at first. Beyond value now. Living by his wits had always intrigued him, as did the danger and glory that intrigue spawned. Not to mention the rewards. But the clammy, tight band of fear that could sometimes encircle his gut like a snake? That he hated.

Reinhardt.

A problem.

One he'd deal with, if necessary.

But first he had to destroy the president of Poland.

CHAPTER FIVE

PRESIDENT JANUSZ CZAJKOWSKI FLED THE PALACE AND HEADED for a waiting car. He'd timed this excursion carefully, freeing his calendar for the rest of the day on the pretense of a rare evening off when he could have dinner and retire early. Consequently, no coterie of self-important aides accompanied him. No media. No one, other than his security detail, all agents of the Biuro Ochrony Rządu, the BOR, Government Protection Bureau. He'd been assigned two armed men and a nondescript Volvo for the off-the-books trip.

The latest incarnation of the Republic of Poland came about in 1989. So as far as countries went, this one was relatively young. There'd been a previous version, but World War II and the Soviet occupation interrupted its existence. Since its rebirth there'd been nine heads of state. The constitution provided for a five-year term with the possibility of a single reelection, but only one of his eight predecessors had managed a second term.

Polish politics, if nothing else, stayed fluid.

Most of the everyday work was done by a prime minister, usually the head of the majority party in Parliament—but in theory it could be anyone. The national constitution provided the president with an executive veto, which could be overridden by a three-fifths majority in Parliament.

The president served as the supreme commander of the armed forces, able to order a general mobilization. He nominated and recalled ambassadors, pardoned criminals, and could override certain judicial verdicts. Pertinent to the current predicament, the president was also the supreme representative of the Polish state, with the power to ratify and revoke international agreements.

Lucky him.

He climbed into the car and they motored away from the palace, leaving through a side exit.

His first term was drawing to a close.

The qualifications for president were simple. Be a Polish citizen, at least thirty-five years old on the day of the first round of the election, and collect the signatures of one hundred thousand registered voters. The winner was chosen by an absolute majority. If no candidate achieved that threshold, a runoff was held between the top two. He'd won his first term after a close runoff and another battle loomed on the horizon, as various opponents were emerging. A former prime minister. A popular lawyer. Three members of Parliament. A punk rock musician who headed one of the more vocal minor political parties. A former government minister who'd declared he would run only if Czajkowski pissed him off. Apparently that was now the case as the loudmouth was gathering his hundred thousand signatures.

The coming political season looked to be a lively one.

Thankfully, he was somewhat popular. The latest opinion polls showed a 55% approval rating. Not bad. But not overwhelming, either. Which was another reason he now found himself in a car, watching the kilometers glide by, as he was driven west toward the village of Józefa. After three weeks of searching the source of the problem had been found. A former communist-era loyalist who'd been dead for over a decade. It had been too much to hope that he took whatever he knew to the grave. Instead, some old information had surfaced. And not just random facts and figures. This was something that directly affected him. In fact, it could ruin him. Especially with a hotly contested election on the horizon.

Foolishly he'd believed the past dead and gone.

But now it seemed to be threatening everything.

Time for him to deal with it face-to-face.

The car passed through Józefa, perched on a cliff overlooking the River Wisła. It had a long history and an attractive old center, boasting a castle ruin and a cathedral, but its main claim to fame was a nearby refinery that employed hundreds. The house he sought was south of town, on a side road that led away from the river. His driver parked to one side, away from the street, among the trees, where the car would not draw attention. He stepped out into the warm evening and walked toward the front door. A man waited, dressed in a black suit and black tie, with an inscrutable expression that was proper but cold. Michał Zima. The head of the BOR.

He entered the house.

A simple place, similar to the one in which he'd been raised in southern Poland, close to Rzeszów, his parents farmers, not revolutionaries. But that all changed in the 1980s. Private landownership had never been allowed. To appease a growing unrest, everyone was promised ownership through purchase or inheritance. But it was all a lie. Eventually his parents and most of the other farmers rebelled and refused to sell food at the undercut government-set prices, instead donating their crops to strikers.

A brave act that had made a difference.

"Where is she?" he asked.

"Out back."

"And the other?"

Zima motioned. "In there."

"Tell me how you found this place?"

"A bit of luck, actually. But sometimes that's all you have."

He caught the message. *Don't ask too many questions.*

His gaze raked the room and he noticed an array of framed pictures on a table. One caught his eye. He walked over and studied the image of a man dressed in a uniform. A major in the Polish army, with the insignia of the SB, the Security Service, on his shirt. He recognized the nondescript face, with razor-cut hair and manicured mustache, the same man from Mokotów Prison.

Aleksy Dilecki.

He'd neither seen nor heard anything of the man in decades.

World War II destroyed Poland, everything bombed and gutted to oblivion with no resources and little manpower left to rebuild. The Soviets promised a rebirth and many believed them. But by the late 1970s, the lies were evident and the country's patience had come to an end. By then everyone worked long hours, found little food in stores, and was constantly cold from a lack of coal and clothing, including coats. They were spied on all the time, fed propaganda, their children brainwashed. The threat of force never ended. Nor had hunger, with the government even dictating how much a person could eat through ration cards. *We all have equal stomachs.* That's what many had echoed. And when people were hungry, when their children were hungry, they would do anything to calm the pain.

And they did.

He liked what Orwell wrote.

All animals are equal, but some are more equal than others.

That had been Aleksy Dilecki.

Politicians and police were always favored. They received more rations. They shopped at special stores. They lived in better housing, with more privileges. They even had a name. Nomenklatura, a Soviet term for the list of government jobs always waiting to be filled. People were selected not on merit, but solely on loyalty to the regime. They became an informal ruling class unto themselves. The Red Bourgeoisie. Corruption and cruelty were constant means to their ends.

And he was staring at one of the participants.

He remembered what was said, all those years ago, in Mokotów Prison.

Who knows? One day you might be a big somebody.

He shook his head at the irony, and liked the fact that Dilecki was dead.

"Do you know him?" Zima asked.

He'd only briefed one person on the relevant history, and it wasn't Zima. So he ignored the inquiry and said, "Show me what you found."

And he replaced the photo on the table.

He followed Zima into a small storage room, the space cluttered with remnants of a family's past. He saw the two rusted filing cabinets.

"They're filled with documents," Zima said. "Reports, correspondence, memoranda. All from the late 1970s to 1990. Scattered dates and incidents. No real pattern to anything. Dilecki worked for the Security Service a long time. He would have been privy to many secrets. Apparently, he removed some of those when the communists fell."

So much had been lost during that chaotic period after the Soviet Union collapsed and Poland reemerged. Today few cared about the past. Everyone was just glad it was over. The future seemed to be all that mattered. But such shortsightedness was a mistake.

Because history mattered.

"Has anyone examined those files?" he asked.

"Only me. And my review was quick and cursory. Just enough to determine that it might be what you are looking for."

He was curious. "How do you know I'm looking for anything?"

"I don't. I'm merely assuming, based on what I know so far."

He should inquire about the extent of what this man knew. But not now. "Have everything in those two cabinets loaded into the trunk of the car I came in."

Zima nodded his understanding.

"Did Dilecki's widow sell any of the documents?" he asked.

"No. Their son did. We have him in custody."

That was new information.

"We arrested him a few hours ago." Zima motioned and he followed him back to the parlor. A blue nylon duffel bag lay on the sofa. Zima unzipped the top to reveal stacks of zlotys. "Half a million. We recovered it from the son's house."

Now it all began to make sense. The parents were good, loyal communists, the son not so much. Decades had passed. The father was gone, the mother aging. Two file cabinets might hold the key to changing everything, especially when some of those documents mentioned the name Janusz Czajkowski. All you had to do was find a buyer.

"Has the son admitted to anything?"

Zima nodded. "He made a deal with a man named Vic DiGenti, who is a known associate of Jonty Olivier."

"You say that name as if you know him."

"We do. He peddles information. Somewhat reliable, too. Our intelligence services have used him on occasion. The mother was totally unaware of what the son did. She only found out last evening, when he offered her some of the money. She was not happy. They had a bitter fight, just a few hours before we arrested him."

"Show me the rest," he said.

Zima led him out the back door to a small corrugated-roof barn. Trees and shrubs shielded the structure from the nearby highway. Its door hung open and he entered. A weak electric lantern dissolved the shadows. Not much there. A few tools, a wheelbarrow, an old rusted car, and a woman, hanging from the rafters, her arms limp at her side, the neck angled over in death.

"She did it during the night," Zima said. "Perhaps after learning of her son's arrest. Or maybe out of a sense of loyalty to her husband. We'll never know."

She'd apparently climbed atop the old car, tied off a short length of rope, then stepped off to oblivion.

He shook his head.

Now everything depended on Belgium.

CHAPTER SIX

COTTON SAT IN THE CELL, STILL DAMP FROM HIS CANAL SWIM. He really should take a shower, though this wasn't the Four Seasons. But as far as cells went, it wasn't so bad. Roomy. Clean. With a toilet that worked. He'd been locked inside far worse.

So much for owing the Catholic Church one.

It was nearly 7:00 P.M. He'd been here alone for several hours. The Bruges police had not been in the best of moods when they fished him from the canal. They'd promptly cuffed his hands behind his back and tried to question him. But he knew when to keep his mouth shut. Of course, at some point he was going to have to explain things. Hopefully the priest from the basilica would tell them that he'd been the one to ask him to go after the reliquary. So far all they knew was that he'd stolen a boat and crashed it in the canal. By the time the cops arrived the shooting had stopped and the Three Amigos were gone.

He was the only problem.

The police had taken his wallet. His passport was back at the hotel. They at least knew his full name, Harold Earl Malone. The nickname Cotton was nowhere on his Danish driver's license, or anything else official. People liked to ask where the label came from and his answer was always the same. *Long story.* And it was, one that involved his father. He still recalled the day when he was ten years old and the two naval officers came to the house and told him and his mother that his father's submarine had sunk, all hands lost. No body. No funeral. Everything classified. It took him nearly four decades to discover the truth, and the whole experience had bred an extreme distrust for government, no matter the level.

Which further explained why he hadn't spoken to anyone.

When the time came he hoped the truth would work best—after all, that was all he had to work with. Surely, by now, the Bruges police knew of the theft. The Holy Blood was the most important object in the city. Hundreds of thousands came every year to see it. Since the 14th century, they'd paraded it around the town in a huge annual celebration. But if they knew it was gone, why had they not come for a chat? Seems they'd want to know what he knew.

Or maybe not.

A clang disturbed his thoughts.

One of the metal doors down the hall opened, then closed.

Footsteps echoed as they approached. A slow and steady clack.

He looked up and spotted a woman.

Petite, with a confident face and dark hair streaked by threads of silver. She was in her mid-sixties, though he knew Justice Department personnel records, which he'd once seen, contained only N/A in the space reserved for date of birth. Everybody was touchy about something. For her it was age. Two presidents had tried to make her attorney general, but she'd turned down both offers. Why? Who knew? She tended to do what she wanted. Which made her really good at what she did.

He stood and approached the bars. "Isn't this how we first met?"

Stephanie Nelle smiled and nodded. "In the Duval County jail, as I recall."

He grinned. "I was a hotshot navy lawyer."

"Who'd just shot a woman."

"Come on. She fired first, trying to kill me."

"And here we are, so many years later, and you've crashed a stolen boat into a canal. Trouble does seem to follow you."

"What about the three thieves and the reliquary they stole?"

"That's the thing, Cotton. There's no theft."

The revelation surprised him. Then he realized. "You put a lid on it?"

She nodded. "I was in Brussels, at our embassy, when the call came from the police. They learned you were once one of ours and made inquiries through Atlanta. The office contacted me. I, of course, had no idea you were here. But I claimed you, nonetheless."

He shrugged. "Wrong place, right time. I just happened to be there. But those thieves knew exactly what they were doing. The whole thing was planned."

"Tell me more."

He explained what had happened in the basilica and after. She on one side of the bars, he on the other. When he finished he asked, "What are you doing in Brussels?"

"The answer to that question will cost you."

He understood. She'd left him in the cell for this conversation for a reason. A few years ago, when he'd retired early from the Justice Department, he'd thought seeing Stephanie Nelle again would be a rarity. One of the reasons he'd quit was to escape the risks and try his hand at something different. He'd been a committed bibliophile all his life. Now the owner of his own shop in Copenhagen, his primary profession *was* books. He'd come to Belgium on the hunt for some rare tomes a few of his regular customers had expressed an interest in owning. An 1897 printing of *Dracula*. A 1937 first edition of *The Hobbit*. And a 1900 original of *The Wonderful Wizard of Oz*. All expensive and hard to find. He'd made a name for himself as a guy who could locate what collectors wanted. But instead of being at the book fair, he was in jail, his former boss apparently holding the key to the door.

"What do you want?" he asked.

"I always liked your directness. It saves a lot of time."

While Danny Daniels had served as president, the Magellan Billet had been the White House's go-to agency. Stephanie had not always enjoyed such a chummy relationship with the executive branch. In fact, most presidents hadn't really cared for her. She and Daniels had not gotten along at first, either. But she'd earned his trust. Daniels' two terms had ended and he was now the junior U.S. senator from Tennessee. Divorced, he had cultivated a personal relationship with Stephanie that, if the rumor mill was to be believed, had blossomed into love. He was glad for her. She deserved happiness. Work should not be what defined a life.

Or at least that's what he kept telling himself.

Stephanie was one of a handful of people in the world whom he called a friend. One of his closest. They'd been through a lot together. His entire professional career as an intelligence agent had happened thanks to her. She took a chance on a young navy lawyer and gave him the opportunity to become really good at what he did. So much so that she kept coming back to him for help, even in retirement.

"You haven't answered my question," he said. "Nor have you offered to get me out of here. I'm assuming the two are related? So let's cut to the chase. How much you offering?"

"Can this one be a favor?"

Now it was his turn to toss her a quizzical look. "I have bills to pay. I'm here to buy books for people who are paying me to do it. A lot of money, I might add. I do have a business—"

"A hundred thousand," she said.

"How long?"

"A few days. To Thursday evening, at the latest."

"The threat level."

"This one could be tricky."

Stephanie was not noted for exaggeration or underestimation. So if she attached the adjective *tricky*, that warning could not go unheeded. But as he'd learned through the years, sure things hid the most danger. *Tricky* might be better.

"A hundred and fifty," he said. "A little extra for the tricky part."

She nodded. "Okay. I have big problems."

"Get me out of here and I'll help you solve them."

CHAPTER SEVEN

COTTON FOLLOWED STEPHANIE AS THEY LEFT THE JAIL AND STEPPED back onto the streets of Bruges. A flood of tourists was out enjoying the beautiful evening. The police had not been happy to see him go, but no one challenged Stephanie. Her authority came straight from Brussels, far higher on the food chain than any local police chief.

Though his clothes had begun to dry from the dunking, his sandy-blond hair was still a mess. He was coming down off the high that action always gave him. He told himself over and over that he didn't miss it. But that was a lie. He seemed at his best when the pressure was on, though his attempt to catch the Three Amigos had not been one of his finest moments. Stephanie's sudden appearance, however, had placed a new light on things.

Something big *was* happening.

And who didn't like being a part of that?

They made their way into the crowded central square.

Bruges began as a 9th-century fortress, built to defend the coast from Vikings. Back then the town faced the sea. But slowly, over the centuries, the ocean withdrew and the remaining mudflats evolved into dry, fertile soil, transforming the town into a major medieval trading hub. People had gathered in its cobbled main square since the 10th century, and standing there now he envisioned fishermen selling their wares, farmers hocking produce, Flemish cloth being inspected by foreign buyers, and the many fairs and festivals that drew crowds from all over Europe. This was the New York City of its time. The center of social, political, and economic life for the entire province.

He stared at the square.

Most of it, he knew, came from a 1990s renovation that retained the feel of a bygone era while making it more pedestrian-friendly. No billboards, neon, or high-rises existed then or now. Its charm oozed from an unpretentious simplicity, the aging hand of time dominating with not a hint of neglect. The rows of step-gabled houses were full of hotels, banks, souvenir shops, retailers, bars, and cafés, everything put to good use as though it were not a priceless relic from another epoch. The trademark belfry cut a path high into the evening sky. Nearly three hundred feet tall and, as he'd found out a few years ago, worth a climb. On a clear day the Flemish coast could be seen miles in the distance.

"I'm listening," he finally said to Stephanie, who'd been quiet on the walk. Time for her to ante up.

"Washington's in upheaval," she said.

He smiled. "What else is new?"

Every day there were press reports on the Warner Fox administration, detailing one misstep after another. Policy shifts and staff changes occurred constantly, all with little to no consistency. Fox would say one thing, his advisers and cabinet officers another. Everything seemed rudderless, adrift, lacking direction. Hit or miss. Mostly miss.

"How bad is it," he asked.

"They're idiots. They have no clue what they're doing. A band of arrogant, stupid imbeciles who managed somehow to get a grip on power."

He chuckled. "Tell me how you really feel."

"The attorney general has never been inside a courtroom. Never served in public office. He was a Wall Street corporate lawyer who graduated from Yale 145th out of a class of 152. His only saving grace is that the guy at number 133 in that same class was Warner Fox. They were roommates in law school. He's absolutely loyal to Fox. Never questions anything. He just does what he's told."

"Are you still being frozen out?"

He'd been there on Inauguration Day, seen the early ineptness for himself. But Fox had been conciliatory, promising to be more open-minded and agreeing to keep Stephanie on as head of the Magellan Billet, though the new president had initially tried hard to eliminate both her and the agency.

She shook her head. "Even our successes have been met with skepticism. My budget has been hacked by a third, which has handicapped what I can effectively accomplish. But that's the whole idea. They want me gone."

He got it. "But they're afraid of Senator Danny Daniels."

"He's a force to be reckoned with. A bad enemy to have, but a good ally."

"And boyfriend?"

She smiled. "That too."

"He makes you happy?"

"Every day."

"That's good to hear."

And he meant it. Stephanie had lived a solitary life. Her husband died long ago, and her son lived in France fairly inaccessibly. He knew of no close personal relationships, until Danny came along. Cotton firmly believed there was somebody for everybody. His own life seemed proof of that. He'd been divorced from his first wife for a number of years and thought love something of the past. Then Cassiopeia Vitt came along and changed everything.

"How is Cassiopeia?" she asked, seemingly reading his mind.

"Feisty, like always. She's coming to Copenhagen this weekend."

"So you need to be done by Friday?"

"Something like that."

People filled the square, out for an early dinner or finishing off a day of sightseeing and shopping. He scanned the faces and tried to assess threats, but there were simply too many to know anything for sure. This wasn't like inside the cathedral where things had been more contained, the people easier to compare and contrast.

"Something strategic is occurring," she said. "What you saw in the basilica is not the first theft of a holy relic."

He waited for more.

"There have been four others."

Interesting.

"All have been kept secret," she said. "For the record, I didn't agree with that tactic, but chalk it up to the all-knowing Fox administration, which stepped in and imposed that strategy."

"Did other locations with relics at least beef up security?"

She shook her head. "None were advised. The know-it-alls decided it would only attract more attention."

"Obviously not a smart decision, given what happened today."

"There's been a lot of those made lately in Washington."

He could see she was frustrated, which was not normal. This woman was usually a model of self-control. Direct. Pragmatic. Truthful to the point of pain. Honest to the point of nuisance. She almost never lost her cool. And there wasn't a political bone in her body, which could be both an asset and a liability.

"What's going on here?" he asked.

"What do you know about the Arma Christi?"

CHAPTER EIGHT

JONTY ENTERED THE CASTLE'S DINING HALL AND SAT AT THE STOUT table. The room stretched in a long rectangle, facing west and the vanishing sun. The table was an oak monstrosity that could accommodate at least twenty people. He loved the ornately framed, brilliantly colored paintings that adorned the walls. Lots of warriors, holding swords and spears, fighting epic battles. The rich colors conveyed strength, the free and forceful sweep of the brush illustrating a sense of exuberance. Sadly, no one was joining him for dinner. Nothing was more pleasurable than sharing conversation during a meal. But he had to maintain a low profile until the weekend, and part of that involved eating alone.

The chef had prepared a lovely dish of roasted pork and boiled red potatoes. Much more Polish than Slovakian. But here, so near the border, the cultures mixed. The damn communists had nearly destroyed Eastern European cuisine. What a horrible time. Everything had been rationed. Waiting in long lines became a way of life, hoarding an art form. No one ever knew when food would be available, or if anyone would be allowed to buy it. Restaurants were issued compulsory menus that never changed and deviations were not allowed. Government cooking manuals specified the exact amount and number of ingredients for each dish. Needless to say, creativity was stifled.

Thank goodness things had changed.

He sat and spread a black linen napkin into his lap. A glass of red wine had already been poured. With the right prompts, food and drink being two of those, people would tell a stranger nearly everything. Nothing seemed sacred anymore. Facebook, Twitter, and every other social media site seemed proof positive of that. What no one would have ever yelled from their front porch to neighbors across the street was now posted for billions to see for all eternity. Still, he loved the internet. So much could be learned so fast with little effort and no fingerprints.

He ate his pork, which had been cooked to perfection. He'd already supplied the staff with the hors d'oeuvre menu for Thursday. An elaborate international array of sweet and savory, all fitting for the guests, who would come from around the world. He'd also bought an expensive variety of liquor, wine, and champagne, anything and everything the guests might enjoy. Food and drink went a long way toward enhancing a deal. As did ambience. Which was another reason he'd selected this olden fortress in the woods of northern Slovakia. Everything about it reeked of resolution.

He finished the entrée and hoped there was more. Being a man of the world, he'd made a point of becoming familiar with the finer things. Sadly, the ones he favored most carried a wealth of calories, which all seemed to go straight to his ever-expanding girth. Weight had become a problem of late. His tailor had been kept busy altering his many suits. He was far too heavy for his height, all thanks to a horrible diet and a hatred for exercise. Physically he'd never been all that much. Flaccid, fleshy lips, a wide nose, and the bright eyes of a man who lived by guile, not brawn. His hair was cut simply and parted in the middle, squared off to either side of his perpendicular temples and whitening prematurely. He was beginning to show his fifty-three years.

He'd lived an interesting life.

His childhood was steeped in poverty. His mother, God rest her soul, cried a lot, so much that he began to believe that he was the reason. She also constantly talked about dying, or leaving. He always wondered if she'd be there when he came home from school. Eventually, maturity taught him that she'd used all that as a means of control over him, his brother, and his father.

And the tactic affected him.

If his own mother didn't care for him, why care about anyone else? If she'd leave, anyone would. So his relationships, whether business or personal, had all been superficial, mainly his fault as he preferred to remain obtuse and uninvolved.

Life, though, had definitely treated him as a favored son, the future an inviting, well-paved highway of opportunity. He liked to think of himself as noble in bearing, virtuous in character, cultured, sophisticated, and charming. But that was all part of the wall of bluff he'd built around himself. He'd grown to love the romance of being hunted, then becoming the hunter. He'd long ago dismissed any definition of goodness that society liked to frame. Instead, he applied a code learned from bitter experience where *good* meant fighting the odds, clawing upward, spitting in the eye of your enemies, and not asking for help or pity. He'd never been a whiner and never would be. His mantra was simple. Do what was necessary, then force a smile onto your face and take another crack at whatever. Buddha said it best. *There is no wealth like knowledge, and no poverty like ignorance.* But Einstein added a great caveat. *Information is not knowledge.* Absolutely true since the most successful person was the one with the best *knowledge.*

And an investment in knowledge always paid high interest.

He liked to tell prospective clients that the price of light was far less than the cost of darkness. Information was like money. To be valuable it had to circulate, which increased not only its quantity but also its worth. Holding information only eroded its value. But thank goodness ready, willing, and able buyers existed for nearly everything.

He finished his dinner and rang the silver bell that sat next to his wine goblet. One of the uniformed staff appeared, and he asked that the plate be removed and a fresh one brought with a second helping of pork. While he waited, he sat in the high-backed, gilded chair and considered the next two days. Nearly everything was ready. But the unexpected was what worried him. Like the man tied up in the basement.

And Reinhardt.

He heard footsteps and assumed the server had returned with his food, which was damn quick. Instead Vic entered the dining hall and walked over to the table.

"Do you want some dinner?" he asked Vic.

"No, thank you. I'll eat later."

The server returned with his plate.

"Oh, sit down. Eat. Bring my friend here some pork," he said, glad to have the company. "Along with wine."

He and Vic had shared many meals together, so he knew his acolyte would not argue.

"So much is at stake on this deal, Vic. More so than on any we've ever had. It is all so exciting, wouldn't you say?"

He made a point to always use the plural *we*. Never the singular *I*. It connoted a team, which made everyone feel included. He amplified that feeling by always sharing generously with the help. That was why so many loved to work for him, and were so loyal. He was especially generous to Vic, whom he counted on in many ways. One of those was as a handy forum upon which to test new ideas.

"I made a mistake thinking we could keep this venture quiet," Jonty said, his voice low. "But I truly thought we had everything under control."

"If Reinhardt knew we were in Bratislava, he knows we're here."

"I agree. Which is disturbing. So what is he waiting for?"

"Probably for his man to report in."

Good point. "So he'll soon be wondering what happened to him."

Vic nodded. "And there will be others coming."

The server returned. He motioned for Vic to eat, but Jonty's appetite had waned. Assurance was what he needed, and that could not be brought to him on a plate.

"There are two relics of the Arma Christi left," he said. "And less than twenty-four hours to RSVP. One of those involves the Americans. What if they refuse to participate? I took a chance making personal contact and extending them a special invitation. Maybe that was foolish."

He wondered if Washington was responsible for Reinhardt's presence. But how could that be? A leak? That was possible. An old Persian proverb came to mind, one he'd come across in his readings. *The man who knows not, but knows not that he knows not, is a fool. Shun him.* A wise precaution. *The man who knows not, and knows that he knows not, is a student. Teach him.* Definitely.

The man who knows, but knows not that he knows, is asleep. Awaken him. That was where he currently found himself. But *the man who knows, and knows that he knows, is a teacher. Learn from him.*

Absolutely.

"When do you leave to head north?" he asked Vic.

"Shortly."

Originally, Vic would have handled things tonight alone.

But Jonty decided on a change in plan.

"I want to go with you," he said.

CHAPTER NINE

The accumulation of holy relics started with Helena, the mother of Constantine the Great. She was granted the high title of Augusta Imperatrix and allowed unfettered access to the imperial treasury so she could secure the precious objects of the new Christian tradition.

To fulfill her mission, in A.D. 326, at the age of eighty, she traveled to Palestine as the first Christian archaeologist. In Jerusalem she ordered a temple that had been built over the site of Christ's tomb near Calvary torn down and a new church erected. According to legend, during the construction, remnants of three different crosses were discovered. Was one the cross upon which Christ died? Nobody knew. To find out, the empress commanded that a woman who was near death be brought to the site. When the woman touched the first and second crosses her condition did not change. But when she touched the third she immediately recovered. Helena declared that to be the True Cross and ordered the building of the Church of the Holy Sepulcher at that spot.

And so began the veneration of objects.

From its inception Christian belief depended on the miraculous, with Christ rising from the dead. Relics became a part of that belief, filling a void after pagan idols were banned. They were common prior to A.D. 1000, but the Crusades brought a new wave of relics into Europe. Thousands of objects, everything from teeth to appendages, bones, blood, even entire bodies. For a church to possess a relic meant that pilgrims would come, and with them a constant revenue stream. Not surprising then that so many faux relics appeared, as it was much easier to create your own than travel to find one.

The Protestant Reformation brought change, as relics horrified the reformers. John Calvin said that if all the fragments of the True Cross were gathered together they'd fill a large ship. Yet the gospels testified that a single man was able to carry it. After 1517 Martin Luther relics lost much of their importance, but eventually seven attained special status.

The True Cross, the Crown of Thorns, the Pillar of the Flogging, the Holy Sponge, the Holy Lance, the Nails, and the Holy Blood.

The Arma Christi.

Weapons of Christ.

Instruments of passion.

According to Corinthians, to those who renounced the "weapons of this world," the Arma Christi *were a great protection against temptation.*

Cotton listened as Stephanie explained.

"The Arma Christi still exist, though there is debate as to which are the true relics and which are fakes. But the Vatican solved that problem by compiling its own official list."

Pieces of the True Cross were everywhere. The largest, and most notable, sat in the Monastery of Santo Toribio de Liébana in Cantabria, Spain. The Crown of Thorns seemed equally scattered, many claiming that their thorn was authentic. But the one in St. Anthony's Chapel in Pittsburgh, Pennsylvania, had acquired a stamp of authenticity. A segment of the Pillar of the Flogging, supposedly retrieved by Helena herself, remained in Rome's Basilica of St. Praxedes. The Holy Sponge moved from Palestine, to Constantinople, to France, ending up in Notre-Dame.

Whether Christ was crucified with three or four nails had been long debated. But legend said that Helena, while in Palestine, found four Nails. She supposedly cast one into the sea to calm a storm, a second was mounted into Constantine's battle helmet, a third was fitted to the head of a statue, and a fourth was melted down and molded into a bit for Constantine's horse. Yet there were dozens of Nails scattered across Europe.

The Vatican ended the debate by blessing the one on display at the cathedral in Bamberg, Germany, as authentic.

"The sixth relic, the Holy Blood, was here in Bruges," Stephanie said. "Or at least it has been for the past nine centuries. The seventh is the Holy Lance."

"People are stealing these relics?" he asked.

She nodded. "Over the course of the last three months five have been taken. Two remain. The Nail and the Holy Lance."

What had Ian Fleming written? *Once is happenstance. Twice is coincidence. Three times is enemy action.*

"We need to go," she said, and they left the market square, walking back toward where the Basilica of the Holy Blood stood. From there Stephanie led him down an enclosed path identified as Blinde Ezelstraat, Blind Ass Street, which emptied into a small plaza that accommodated a columned, concrete arcade.

The fish market.

He knew the story. For centuries fresh saltwater fish had been sold in Bruges' main square. Centuries ago the delicacy was expensive, available only to the rich. The common folk complained about the stench, so in the early part of the 19th century the merchants moved here, away from the crowd. It remained in use to this day, but no one was hawking their catch this evening. A placard informed them that the market was only open a few days a week from eight until noon. A crowd had collected beneath the colonnade, taking advantage of the empty concrete tables. Children played on the cobblestones beyond.

"Are we going somewhere in particular?" he asked Stephanie as they walked.

She stopped near the pavilion. "We have a serious situation developing in Poland."

He heard the concern in her voice.

"The Fox administration wants to bring back the European Interceptor Site."

He shook his head in disbelief.

In 2007 the United States opened talks for a missile defense system to be located in Poland. It would consist of ten silo-based interceptors to be used in conjunction with a tracking and radar system to be located in the Czech Republic. The idea was to protect against missiles from Iran, but Russia strongly objected, interpreting the move as a test of American strength. In retaliation the Russian president threatened to deploy short-range, offensive missiles in Kaliningrad to counter any supposed defense system. Europe likewise expressed deep reservations. France, Germany, and Italy all opposed the move, thinking it more provocative than strategic. The uproar continued until the Obama administration finally canceled the proposal.

"They really want to step into that ant pile again?" he asked.

"They definitely want to go there. The thinking is to send a message to Moscow that there's a new sheriff in town. Things are going to be different. A way to show the world that Fox is a man to be reckoned with."

"Talk about poking the bear. As I recall, the uproar against the missiles was nearly uniform. Nobody thought it was a good idea."

"Fox hates the European Union and NATO. He's spent the last few months antagonizing nearly every ally we have. He doesn't give a damn what the EU or Russia wants."

They stood on the backside of the high-pitched roof of the old town hall, its pinnacles, turrets, and spires giving play to fanciful light and shade. The path ahead, past the fish market, was lined with bars and cafés preparing for another night's business. Tables dotted the cobbles, many already filled with folks enjoying supper. The time was approaching 8:00 P.M., and he was a little hungry himself.

"The key to everything this time," Stephanie said, "is the president of Poland. He alone will make or break any decision about the deployment of those American missiles."

"He wants them?"

"That all depends," she said.

An odd answer, so he tried, "What do missiles in Poland have to do with the Arma Christi?"

"Quite a bit. Those thefts happened for a reason. A rather strange reason, but definitely a reason."

He could tell that there was more to the story. "When are you going to tell me?"

"Right now. Follow me."

CHAPTER TEN

COTTON WALKED WITH STEPHANIE PAST MORE CAFÉS WITH TABLES and wicker chairs under colorful awnings. She avoided all of them and headed for one of the ivy-clad buildings that fronted a canal. An iron sign attached to the brick façade read LA QUINCAILLERIE. Hardware store. An odd name for a restaurant.

Inside was strictly Old World with smoke-blackened beams, marble-topped tables, and waiters in starched black aprons. The rough-brick walls were adorned with prints and mementos collected over the generations. The windows were open to the evening, facing the same canal he'd sped down earlier. Across the water were more brick buildings with terraces and diners.

A man waited at one of the window-side tables. Medium height with a thin, quiet, clean-shaven face, sallow skin, and modest brown hair. He wore a dark suit and tie and stood as they approached.

"Cotton," Stephanie said. "This is Tom Bunch. He works with the White House."

Handshakes were exchanged and they sat.

"Tom is the deputy assistant to the president and the deputy national security adviser," Stephanie said.

Cotton caught the emphasis on the word *deputy*, repeated twice surely on purpose, knowing how she felt about that label. The Magellan Billet's bureaucracy was simple. She had total control. No deputies. No seconds in command. All decisions from one source.

"Tom is the reason I'm here in Belgium," she said. "The Justice Department was asked to assist the White House with this matter, and the attorney general delegated it to the Magellan Billet, with specific orders to work with Tom."

That meant the president had wanted the task given to the Billet. The more important question, which Stephanie surely had asked herself, was why, considering how Fox felt about her and the Billet.

A waiter appeared with menus and asked for drink orders. Bunch requested a rather expensive French red wine. Stephanie opted for sparkling water. Cotton chose the still version. Carbon dioxide immersed in liquids had never been his thing. Alcohol was also something he'd never acquired a taste for, along with coffee, cigarettes, or almost anything that came from a pharmacy.

Bunch scanned the menu, so he decided, what the heck, why not. He was hungry, and the offerings appeared robust and filling. No gourmet fare. Thank goodness. The kalfsblanket, veal in a creamy sauce, caught his eye. He also saw there was a Dame Blanche for dessert. The waiter returned with their drinks, and Bunch asked that they have a few minutes before ordering.

"You look a little wrinkled," Bunch said. "Stephanie said you took a swim in the canal."

"It's part of the tour excursion I booked. A chance to experience the canals firsthand," he said, trying to make light of things.

But Bunch did not seem amused. "I don't know anything about you. But Stephanie says you're the man for this job. I assume you know about Jonty Olivier?"

The question came with an aura of self-importance, as if everyone knew the name.

"Why don't you enlighten me," Cotton asked, and he caught the grin on Stephanie's lips at his self-restraint.

"I'm a little surprised you've never heard of Olivier."

He caught the smugness. This guy wasted little time getting on people's nerves.

"Jonty Olivier," Stephanie said, "is a broker."

"We talking books, art, real estate?"

Bunch chuckled. "You really are out of the loop. How long have you been retired?"

"How long have you been a *deputy* national security adviser? Since January? Six whole months. What did you do before?"

"That's not relevant. I'm now with the White House, and I'm in charge here. That's what matters."

He slid his phone from a pocket—waterproof, so it had survived the swim—and opened to a search engine. He typed TOM BUNCH, WHITE HOUSE and found many references. He decided on the Wikipedia link. Why not? Might as well see what the masses thought of him. He touched the screen and called up the page, which was, not surprisingly, short.

Bunch, throughout the presidential campaign, wrote a number of pro-Fox articles under a pseudonym, E Pluribus Unum. He was critical of the left and right, but never the pro-Fox conservatives. He portrayed the election as a battle to save America, and in one article, described it as the "Flight 93 election," referencing the plane that was hijacked on September 11, 2001 but which crashed after passengers fought back against the hijackers. "Charge the cockpit or you die," he wrote. Then he went on to say, "You may die anyway. You—or the leader of your party—may make it into the cockpit and not know how to fly or land the plane. There are no guarantees. Except one, if you don't try, death is certain." The true meaning of that statement remains unknown. Before coming to the White House, Bunch worked for Burdi Macro LLC, which manages the personal capital of Rich Burdi, a huge financial supporter of Warner Fox during the election.

"What are you doing?" Bunch asked.

"Reading about you."

Bunch glanced at Stephanie. "This is a waste of time. He's unacceptable."

"I was thinking the same about you," Cotton said. "And now I know why."

His eidetic memory kicked in and he recalled press accounts about President Fox's attitude toward the National Security Council. Too big.

Too diverse. Unwieldly. In need of trimming. Fox favored fewer meet-
ings, less input, less paperwork. The pundits had translated that into him
wanting total command of foreign policy, with little to no input from
others. Several senators had publicly proclaimed the White House incompetent, insular, and indecisive. Decision making was slow to nonexistent, and usually wrong. The goal seemed to be to please the boss, not
enunciate and implement clear national security goals. The best explanation for why all of that was happening? Unqualified people, in positions
of authority, kissing ass. A perfect example of which was sitting across
the table.

"Do you have any idea what you're doing?" he asked Bunch.

"I have the ear of the president of the United States. I'm here at his
personal direction. That's all you need to know."

He should leave. Forget the $150,000. Head back to his hotel, take a
shower, go to bed, and attend the book fair tomorrow as planned. This
was not his problem. He'd already done way too much. The older he got
the more he found that he suffered no fools, was impatient with medioc-
rity and disdainful of subtlety. But three things kept his butt in the chair.
First, the look of frustration in Stephanie's eyes. Second, he was hungry
and the veal in cream sauce sounded wonderful, not to mention a White
Lady for dessert. And third. That was the kicker.

But first.

"Tell me about Jonty Olivier?" he asked Stephanie, returning to the
issue at hand and ignoring Bunch.

"He's British, but holds a dual passport with Switzerland, thanks to
a Swiss mother. He was fairly nonexistent until about fifteen years ago,
when he emerged as a broker who accumulates and trades information.
I'm told the CIA and NSA have regularly used him. He's proven both
reliable and reasonable. He has no political affiliations, no personal
causes, no morals, no scruples. He's just a businessman. Buying and selling. Trading. Making money. He deals with people, corporations, governments. Doesn't matter to him. Reports say he's a man of *patrician tastes
and earthy language.*"

He smiled. "Where is he based?"

"He moves around constantly," Bunch said. "He prefers renting luxury condos and staying in five-star hotels to owning mansions. He gener-

ally keeps a low profile and works through the internet, wire transfers, and intermediaries."

Cotton noticed that Bunch spewed out facts about a bad guy the way someone who'd never served in the military told war stories.

"He also avoids breaking laws," Bunch said. "He skirts close, but always stays just on the legal side. Olivier recently made contact with the White House. He and the president know each other from before the election."

Interesting. "They're friends?"

"They've done business in the past. Olivier talked directly with the president about this matter."

"Was that wise?" Stephanie asked, clearly surprised. "This whole situation is just grandiose extortion."

What *situation*?

"The president knows how to make a deal," Bunch said, clearly annoyed. "It was his forte in business. He prefers personal contact and personal assessment."

"You really don't have any idea what you're doing," Cotton declared.

"I resent your insubordination," Bunch said.

He shrugged. "Last I looked, I don't work for you."

"And I doubt you will."

Time for that third thing.

The kicker.

They sat adjacent to an open window. A bronze wind chime just outside sounded a mournful pentatonic. Occasionally one of the tour boats cruised by beneath on the canal, the city's fleet one short tonight. White swans dotted the calm brown water. Long-necked, heavy-bodied, big-footed birds whose gracefulness belied their cantankerous personality.

Across the canal he caught sight of a familiar face.

One he'd noticed a few moments before.

Another swan of sorts.

Slim and lean. Cool and sleek. Sure of herself. Ash-blond hair falling in casual disarray to thin shoulders. Her full mouth was a little wide for her nose, a small imperfection that, to him, only added to her allure. He knew her to be almost wolflike, with the blue eyes to match. In many ways she was a fortress, often scaled and assaulted, but never conquered.

Ivona Novak.

Sitting alone at a terrace table, her gaze locked across the canal, straight at him.

"Hold that thought," he said to Bunch.

And he rose from the table.

CHAPTER ELEVEN

Cotton left the restaurant and turned right out the front door, following the cobblestones over another of the footbridges that ended at the ring road. Cars chugged by in both directions. From there the sidewalk led to another footbridge, back toward old town and the buildings that sat on the opposite side of the canal from La Quincaillerie.

He found an eatery, this one with the more benign name of Le Quai, the quay. A busy tavern that, considering the aromas, specialized in fish. It filled another of the guild houses, diners inside and out. He bypassed the maître d's stand and headed for the terrace. The table he'd spotted from across the canal was empty, its occupant gone. He was about to leave when he noticed a piece of paper tucked beneath a saucer with his name printed on top.

He stepped over and slipped it free.

So lovely to see you again, Cotton.

He smiled at the feminine script and glanced across the water at the open window in La Quincaillerie. Stephanie was staring his way. Only Tom Bunch's hands were visible, moving, apparently talking to her, oblivious to anything happening that did not include him. He sympathized with her predicament, forced to deal with imbeciles. Danny Daniels had understood how to get the job done, which was why he'd been the perfect partner in the White House. Daniels and the Magellan Billet had done a lot of great things together. Of course, Daniels was not a guy who craved credit. Results. That's all he'd ever wanted.

He left the terrace, retraced his route to Stephanie and Bunch, and sat again at the table. "Where were we? I think you said that Jonty Olivier contacted the White House."

Bunch tossed him a quizzical look. "Where'd you go?"

"Bathroom."

Which seemed to satisfy the moron. Stephanie, though, definitely wanted to know more, but his gaze signaled *later.*

"That's right," Bunch said. "Olivier first made contact with us two months ago. He sent a personal message." Bunch found his phone, tapped, and handed it over. On the screen was a photo of an invitation with black-and-gold Edwardian script.

Your Presence Is Requested
For A Sale Of Information
Concerning President Janusz Czajkowski
Of The Republic Of Poland
If Interested Send A Reply To This Address.
missilesornot@de.com

"Seems the sender has something to sell," Cotton said. He faced Stephanie. "Which concerns the European Interceptor Site?"

She nodded. "This came about a month after the White House announced the renewed missile objective. By then half of Europe, China, and Russia had all come out against it. Olivier seems to have seen an opportunity and set up an auction for some damaging information that could affect the decision. As I said earlier, this all seems like just grandiose blackmail against the president of Poland."

"When the White House replied to the email address," Bunch said, "Olivier answered personally."

"Or at least someone using his name answered," Stephanie added.

He caught her tone. The reply had been handled without the appropriate safeguards in place.

"It was Olivier," Bunch said. "He and the president spoke by phone. We want that information."

"What kind of information?" Cotton asked.

"The embarrassing, political-career-killing kind," Bunch said. "James Czajkowski is about to stand for reelection. We need him to win that election, then do exactly what we want. Or to be forced to resign now, since the man who would assume the role of acting president is quite friendly to us. He would be much easier to deal with."

Somebody had been reading their intelligence briefs. Kudos to Bunch. But Cotton noticed how the guy pronounced the Polish president's name. Not *Cha-koff-skee*, like the composer. More *Sha-kow-ski*. And he used the English *James* instead of *Janusz*. It seemed that a "deputy assistant to the president and deputy national security adviser" would at least know how to properly pronounce a foreign dignitary's name.

"What is it, exactly, you want the president of Poland to do?" he asked Bunch.

"That's classified."

"Cotton has the highest clearance," Stephanie noted, irritation in her voice.

"How's that possible? He doesn't even work for the government. Getting that kind of clearance takes credentials."

"Like the kind that come from posting kiss-ass crap on the internet and working as an assistant financial adviser for a rich fat cat?"

Bunch's face went sour. "I don't have to explain myself to you. I currently work for the president of the United States. Maybe this meeting wasn't such a good idea."

The guy stood.

"You're not eating," Cotton asked. "Or at least picking up the tab?"

Bunch pinched back the sleeve of his jacket and studied his watch. "I don't think so. On either count. Stephanie, find help elsewhere."

"No."

Strong. Clear. Emphatic. The tone screaming *non-negotiable*.

"Excuse me?" Bunch said.

"What part of that word don't you understand," she said. "I've retained Cotton's services. We'll be using him."

"Do you want me to call the White House?"

She shrugged. "That's your decision. But you're running out of time and Cotton is the best. We caught a break that he happened to be here today."

"I don't see it that way."

"You don't see much of anything," Cotton said.

Bunch stared at him.

"You have an admirer. Her name is Ivona Novak. She works for the Agencja Wywiadu. The AW."

He could see that Bunch had no idea what he was talking about.

"It's Poland's foreign intelligence agency," he said.

"And she's here?" Bunch asked.

"She was. Gone now." Cotton pointed out the window. "It's where I went."

"She left the table," Stephanie said, "before you made it over there. But not before tossing me a wave. She definitely has style."

"You know this woman?" Bunch asked.

"It's my business to know people like her. Cotton's right. She's an excellent operative. She came along after Solidarity and went to work for the new Polish republic. Her presence here is a message."

Bunch sat back down at the table. "I'm listening."

Cotton nearly smiled. Sure he was listening, since he had no friggin' idea what was happening.

"President Czajkowski has to be aware of the auction," Stephanie said. "He may have even been extended an invitation, too. What better way to up the price than to have the proposed victim bidding. So he sent his number one operative to deal with it. Ivona being here, in Bruges, when the Holy Blood is taken? That's no coincidence."

"Did she steal the relic?" Bunch asked.

Cotton shook his head. "Hardly."

Otherwise she'd be long gone. Incredible this idiot could not put two and two together, since this time it only came to four.

"Obviously," Stephanie said. "Our problem just amplified."

CHAPTER TWELVE

CZAJKOWSKI SAT INSIDE HIS PRIVATE STUDY. HE'D BEEN BACK AT the presidential palace for nearly two hours, secluded. His wife had gone to the opera for the evening. Thank goodness she loved the arts, devoting a lot of her time to their promotion. He had no interest in such things. Sadly, their marriage had failed. Both of them recognized that it was over, but both of them liked their positions. He as president, she as First Lady. So they'd come to a private arrangement. An understanding. Separate private lives. Separate interests. Separate lovers. But always discreet. Never embarrassing the other or jeopardizing their positions. He knew she'd already found someone, and he was happy for her. He, too, had someone special. But it was politics, not love, that seemed to consume him on a daily basis.

And a good thing, too.

Poland seemed overrun by politics.

There were two major parties. The PO and the PiS. But the variety of middling, minor, and other nonsensical groups seemed endless. About forty at last count, scattered across a wide spectrum of beliefs. Anything and everything. Catholics, conservatives, liberals, communists, socialists, corporatists, nationalists, social democrats, feminists, right-to-lifers. You name it, there was a political party representing that interest.

His favorite?

One from the past.

The Polska Partia Przyjaciół Piwa. The Polish Beer-Lovers' Party. Its original aim had been to promote beer drinking in English-style pubs, instead of vodka, all designed to fight alcoholism. It emerged in 1990, right after the communist fall, and incredibly, voter disillusionment led 3 percent of the electorate to vote for its candidates, allowing it to win sixteen seats in Parliament. Its platform of quality beer served nationwide became a symbol of freedom of association and expression, intellectual tolerance, and a higher standard of living. Word of mouth also contributed to its popularity, with many openly saying that *with the PPPP at the helm it wouldn't be better, but for sure it would be funnier.* But as was typical, the party soon split into factions and eventually dissolved to nothing.

That seemed to be Poland's fate, too.

Rise and fall.

One incarnation after another.

The country had always been surrounded by empires. Swedes to the north, Cossacks east, Prussians west, Turks in the south, with no natural borders east or west, allowing for a free flow of invaders.

And they'd come for centuries.

It didn't help that most of the terrain was flat, open plain, ideal for a battlefield, which made it easy for the heel of oppression to always be firmly planted on Poland's neck.

Eventually a defined state emerged, but it was wiped from the political map in 1795, when Russia, Prussia, and Austria divided up the country, the first European nation to ever meet such a fate. A provision of their secret agreement stressed the *necessity of abolishing everything which might recall the existence of a Polish kingdom.* Which was precisely what they did. The Prussians melted down the crown jewels. The Austrians turned palaces into barracks. The Russians stole everything they could. Then they collectively proclaimed that Poland had merely been an uncivilized corner of the world in need of redemption.

A second chance at statehood came in the 20th century, but first the Germans stole it away, then the Soviets finished the task—once they liberated the country from the Nazis, they never left. By 1948 the communists totally controlled Poland. Even worse, the Allies at Potsdam reconfigured the borders, ceding away long-held territory and adding new portions, shifting the entire nation two hundred kilometers to the west, making it a different place from before the war. Its first president supported Stalin unconditionally and imposed harsh and repressive measures to cow the people. Workers supposedly played a vital role in running things but, in reality, had no say whatsoever. The standard of living decreased by the year. Most of the national budget went to the military. Coal and other commodities were shipped free to the Soviet Union. The first seeds of rebellion were planted in 1956, but it took a quarter century for those to sprout, another decade to bloom. Only recently had the communist yoke finally been broken and a republic once again established. But the radical shift from one-party rule to a liberal democracy and pluralism had encouraged new thought. No single party had ever achieved any measure of control. Instead, Poland was governed by ever-changing compromise.

Hence politics consumed his every thought.

He often thought it akin to trying to hold ten balloons underwater all at once. One was always slipping away, popping to the surface. And by the time it was retrieved another managed to break loose. It was a nearly impossible task, but one that had to be tried if you wanted to govern the nation. His current coalition of eight varied parties seemed fragile at best. A nervous collection of hawks, doves, and activists. Now the new American president had decided to force himself upon Poland with another cursed European Interceptor Site. He'd served in the government years back, as undersecretary in the foreign ministry, when the idea had first been proposed, then ultimately rejected by all, including the Americans.

Now the dead had come back to life.

And in more ways than one.

He'd genuinely thought the past gone. It all should have died with the communists. The Institute of National Remembrance and its Commission for the Prosecution of Crimes Against the Polish Nation had spent years investigating both the Nazi and the communist times. He was there when Parliament issued its mandate for full disclosure and for the past twenty years, the commission had collected millions of pages of archival documents, interviewed thousands of witnesses, and convicted nearly 150 people of crimes against peace and humanity.

All well and good.

Since none of it had involved him.

So far.

He continued to chew on his thoughts but hated the bitter aftertaste. He'd not tasted such disgust in a long time. A soft knock snapped his glum reverie. The door opened and his private secretary said that the head of the BOR was ready to speak with him.

Finally. Maybe some answers.

Michał Zima entered, and they were left alone.

"I have some bad news," Zima said. "The son was found dead. He hanged himself."

He was shocked. "How is that possible?"

"We had no indication that he was suicidal. After questioning, I had him placed in a holding cell. He used a bedsheet fastened to one of the bars."

He rubbed his tired eyes. Dammit. He should have some pity for both the mother and son, but it was the son who had brought all their troubles onto them.

"I'm assuming the guilt over his mother's death was too much," Zima said. "He was upset when he was told and asked for some time alone. Nothing indicated that he would hurt himself. I planned to release him shortly."

"Why?"

"He's broken no law. We were pushing things, bringing him in for questioning, but I justified that based on the . . . situation."

"What situation?"

"Whatever it is the son sold. I can only assume it is a direct threat to the presidency."

"Or this nation."

"If that were true, then I would not be kept in the dark. I sense that this is more personal."

True. But he still was not about to explain himself.

The files from the house had been brought into the palace and lay stacked across the study's parquet floor. He'd given every page a cursory look and determined there was nothing that related to him. Which meant the important stuff was already gone. Sold. To a man named Jonty Olivier. Zima knew nothing other than what the son had done.

"Did the son tell you anything about what he sold?"

Zima shook his head. "I had not progressed that far in my questioning. I planned to do that once I returned from meeting with you. But by then he was dead."

Which now seemed like a fortuitous happening. But he did not like people dying in custody. It brought back memories from the 1970s and 1980s.

What a time.

A nationwide labor turmoil had led to the formation of the independent trade union Solidarity, which grew into a powerful, independent political force. To stop its growth, in 1981 martial law was imposed, but two years of oppression failed to quell rising tensions. By 1989 the government was forced to hold the first partially free and democratic parliamentary elections since the end of World War II. Ones they could not manipulate or control.

A year later the Soviet Union collapsed and Lech Wałęsa, the head of Solidarity, won the presidency.

Then, one by one, communist regimes imploded across Eastern Europe and the Cold War ended.

Throughout communist times, the Służba Bezpieczeństwa stayed at the forefront of the authoritarian state's efforts to hold on to power, spreading fear and terror. He knew the numbers. At the end, the SB employed 25,000 agents and had some 85,000 informants. It infiltrated every aspect of Polish life, trying to snuff out dissent. Places like Mokotów Prison flourished. Discontent had always simmered hotter in Poland than in any other Eastern Bloc nation, as there was no socialist tradition here. In fact, the whole concept of *from each according to his ability, to each according to his need,* which Marx proclaimed, was contrary to the fiercely independent beliefs Poles held dear.

All that was gone.

Though tonight a tiny piece of it had resurrected.

And he felt awful.

"I want that man, Jonty Olivier, located," he said.

"We are working on that."

"I want a dossier on him, too. Everything you have. And fast."

Zima nodded. "Of course."

"You can go."

Another privilege of office was the ability to end a conversation whenever he wanted. Zima left.

The evening had turned into a circle of frustration. But he'd fought enough political battles to know that when you gambled, sometimes you lost.

His best hope remained in Bruges.

So he picked up the phone and dialed.

A few moments later Ivona Novak answered.

He said, "Please tell me things are working out there."

CHAPTER
THIRTEEN

COTTON SAT BACK IN HIS CHAIR AND CONSIDERED STEPHANIE'S dilemma. What a tough position. Professionals on one side, idiots on the other. Both dangerous.

Nearly twenty years ago Stephanie had plucked him from the navy and provided him an opportunity to be something more than a lawyer. He'd accepted that offer and risen to the challenge, proving himself more than capable as an intelligence officer. Which resulted in a major career shift to the Justice Department and the Magellan Billet. Stephanie created the unit, a special division within Justice to handle highly sensitive matters. Twelve agents, whom she personally oversaw. He'd stayed for a dozen years, until a bullet tore through his shoulder in Mexico City. He'd managed to take down the shooters, but the resulting carnage had left seven dead, nine injured. One of them had been a young diplomat assigned to the Danish mission, Cai Thorvaldsen. Ten weeks after the massacre a man with a crooked spine appeared at his front door in Atlanta. They'd sat in the den, and he hadn't bothered to ask how Henrik Thorvaldsen found him.

"I came to meet the man who shot my son's killer," Thorvaldsen said.

"Why?"

"To thank you."

"You could have called."

"I understand you were nearly killed."

He shrugged.

"And you're quitting your government job. Resigning your commission. Retiring from the military."

"You know an awful lot."

"Knowledge is the greatest of luxuries."

He wasn't impressed. "Thanks for the pat on the back, and I'm truly sorry for your loss. But I have a hole in my shoulder that's throbbing and a lack of patience. So, since you've said your piece, could you leave?"

Thorvaldsen never moved from the sofa, he simply stared at the den and the surrounding rooms visible through an archway. Every wall was sheathed in books. The house seemed nothing but a backdrop for the shelves.

"I love them, too," his guest said. "I've collected books all my life."

"What do you want?"

"Have you considered your future?"

He motioned around the room. "Thought I'd open an old-book shop. Got plenty to sell."

"Excellent idea. I have one for sale, if you'd like it."

He decided to play along. But there was something about the older man's eyes that told him his visitor was not joking. Veined hands searched a suit coat pocket and Thorvaldsen laid a business card on the sofa.

"My private number. If you're interested, call me."

He'd made the call, then finalized his divorce, quit his job, sold his house, and moved from Georgia to Denmark.

Never regretting a day.

Earlier, in the basilica, memories of that day in Mexico City had come rushing back. People in danger. Him there. Able to act.

Do something.

And he had.

But he'd made mistakes in Mexico City, ones he tried hard never to repeat. Like underestimating the opposition.

"Mr. Bunch," he said. "You have a highly qualified agent of a foreign government who went out of her way to let us know she's here. There's a reason she did that. A reason that obviously concerns Poland."

The restaurant was becoming noisy, filling with diners. Bunch sat oblivious, sipping his expensive wine. Cotton did not like discussing such a sensitive subject in so public a place.

"Should we not leave?" he asked, looking at Stephanie.

She motioned like, *Do you really think I'm in charge.*

"We can talk right here," Bunch declared.

He shrugged, indicating, *What the hell? Why not. More amateur hour.*

"Cotton," Stephanie said. "When we responded to the auction invitation, I'm told that the information sent back via email said the price of admission was us bringing a specific artifact. No artifact, no admission."

Now he understood. "One of the Arma Christi."

She nodded. "Ours is the Holy Lance. The Spear of St. Maurice in Kraków, Poland."

Which might further explain Ivona Novak's appearance.

"Of the seven relics," Stephanie said, "five have already been taken. By who? We have no idea. But they'll be bringing their respective relic to the auction, so we'll learn all that then. There are two left. The Holy Lance, which is our ticket, and the Nail in the cathedral at Bamberg, Germany. We have to have the lance in our possession by tomorrow at midnight. A little more than twenty-seven hours from now. If not, then we can't attend."

"Just wait, then locate and raid the auction," he said.

Bunch smirked. "It's not that easy. No location was provided. That will come after we have the relic."

The explanation came with an as-if-I-have-to-explain-something-so-obvious tone.

"You're telling me you can't find the location?" Cotton asked. "You have the most extensive intelligence network in the world."

"The thinking," Stephanie said, "is that the others invited will have competing interests. Some want the information. Some want it destroyed. It may not be so easy to shut things down. I'm also assuming that this Jonty Olivier will take the necessary precautions against a preemptive strike. He surely knows that there could be trouble."

"And you have no idea what you're buying."

"Not true," Bunch said. "A sample was provided with the invitation."

Cotton was curious. "If I hadn't come along, what were you planning on doing?"

"I had someone else in mind to work with us," she said. "That's what I was arranging in Brussels."

"It's why I'm here, too," Bunch added. "I'll be attending the auction, with the relic, to bid for the information."

That was a bad idea on a multitude of levels.

"Orders from the White House and the attorney general," Stephanie said.

He got the message. No sense beating that dead horse. But he had to say to her, "You do have a lot of problems here."

Bunch seemed irritated. "I get it that you two think I have no business in this. But that's not your call. The president says I do, so can we create a workable plan?"

"Does that mean I'm now acceptable?"

"Sure, Malone. Why not? What choice do I have? Stephanie's right. Time is short."

Who was this guy fooling. "That way, if I fail, you blame it all on her. She picked me."

Bunch grinned. "Something like that."

"Cotton," Stephanie said, "we've already done the preliminary legwork. We know where the spear is being held and how it can be taken."

"I saw the Spear of St. Maurice once, years ago," he said. "It's inside Wawel Castle's cathedral museum."

"Not at the moment, which is to our advantage. The message we received from Olivier indicated that the relic has to be stolen before any further information is provided. I assume the theft itself is some sort of proof. Obviously, we can't borrow the spear from the museum, or ask the Poles to cooperate with us. Why would they? The last person they would want to obtain damaging information on Czajkowski is Fox. With Ivona here in Belgium, that means Poland is now part of this equation. They also would not want that auction to happen. I'm sure Ivona has been charged with stopping it."

"Unless Poland got an invite of their own," he added.

"That's possible," she said. "But my gut says that didn't happen."

"Do you think Czajkowski knows the price of America's admission?"

She shook her head. "Which is probably also why Ivona is here. The

Holy Blood is gone. So she's focused now on the lance and the Nail in Bamberg, waiting for us to make a move."

"For all she knows, we took the Holy Blood," Bunch added.

Which was the first thing this guy had said that made sense. "He has a point."

Stephanie nodded. "It's possible, but you'll need to figure that out."

Obviously the nature of the blackmail was political. And damning enough to attract a lot of interest. But he learned a long time ago to know the stakes of the game before anteing up. "Do you plan to tell me the nature of this information on Czajkowski? You got a sample."

Bunch raised a hand to stifle the question. "I told you that's classified, and it's not necessary for you to know. We just need you to obtain the spear."

He now knew what to say and stood from the table.

"I'll pass."

CHAPTER FOURTEEN

JONTY STEPPED FROM THE CAR.

After dinner he and Vic had driven north from the castle, crossing into Poland, heading toward Kraków. But before reaching the city, they'd veered east and found the town of Wieliczka. He'd always had a tough time with Polish. So many different sounds to familiar letters. Wieliczka was a perfect example, pronounced *Vye-leech-kah*.

The salt mines had always fascinated him. According to legend, in the 13th century Duke Bolesław of Kraków wanted a bride. So he arranged a marriage to Kinga, the daughter of the king of Hungary. Being a practical woman Kinga asked her father for an unusual dowry, something to help build prosperity in her new homeland. So he gave her a salt mine. But it was located in Hungary, a long way from Poland. In a gesture of thanks she cast her engagement ring into the mine's shaft. Years later, once in Poland, she visited Wieliczka where salt had recently been discovered. While there, one of the workers presented her with a lump of salt that contained a shiny object. When it was broken open she saw it to be her engagement ring, which had found its way there underground, all the way from Hungary.

That fanciful tale explained two things.

First, why St. Kinga was the patron of Polish salt miners. And second, why there'd been a salt mine at Wieliczka for the past seven hundred years.

And what a place.

Nine levels, the first one sixty meters down, the last more than three hundred. Two hundred and fifty kilometers of tunnels snaked a labyrinth through the earth, which led to over two thousand chambers hollowed by forty generations of miners. The real credit for its discovery goes to local farmers who found the salt deposits by accident, then started digging. Before that salt either had come from brine or had been imported. But after? A less expensive and plentiful alternative became available.

Salt. Gray gold.

Produced when a base and an acid react to each other. More specifically when sodium joins with chlorine, producing sodium chloride, a staple food and the only rock humans can digest.

And thank goodness.

The body could not produce salt. It had to come externally. And it was vital. Two hundred milligrams were lost by an adult every day and had to be replaced. No sodium? No oxygen moved through the blood. No nerve impulses or muscles moved, including the heart. No digestion. Its perpetual value came from its constant loss and the need for continual replacement. It has always been one of the most sought-after commodities, unique because even dissolved into a liquid it can be evaporated back out.

In Poland the obtaining and selling of salt had always been a royal right, making kings wealthy and keeping the locals employed. During the Middle Ages seven to eight thousand tons of salt were extracted per year from the earth below him, and that continued well into the 20th century.

The time was approaching 8:00 P.M. and the mine was closing down. Nearly two million people visited a year, all on guided tours, the last official one leaving at 7:30, as a nearby wall sign explained. After hours by special appointment, tours were available, which he assumed had been arranged through their contact.

He followed Vic inside an attractive art nouveau building that accommodated the Regis Shaft, sunk in the 14th century and the oldest of the ways down. Once the miners had descended by rope into the deep recesses. Elevators handled the task today, the ones here used by the special tours. Two other sets were in differing locations, one for the horde of daily tourists and the other for miners who still worked below keeping the passages safe and open. A few people were still around inside the building, removing olive-green coveralls and mining hats, talking with excitement, apparently just returned from a trip below.

A man waited for them, also dressed in coveralls, only his were a beige color. A name stitched to the outside read KONRAD. Jonty knew that several hundred guides led groups through the mine. Each one was trained and certified. Most worked only part-time. Konrad was a hybrid, being one of the full-time miners still employed at the site, but assigned to public relations duties for special tours. Thankfully, Konrad was also deeply in debt thanks to two failed marriages and some reckless spending. A few thousand euros had bought his unquestioned loyalty.

It bothered Jonty that an outsider was so close to things, but this situation was unusual to say the least. Timing was everything in his business. Important information today could be worthless tomorrow. The trick was to make a deal while things were hot. That's why he'd been overly generous with this corruptible soul. As a precaution, Vic had kept a close eye on Konrad and nothing unusual had piqued their interest. Of course, the spy's appearance and the mention of Reinhardt had sparked a new wave of paranoia.

"I didn't realize you'd be coming," Konrad said to him.

"Is it a problem?" Jonty asked.

"I had only planned for one for this special tour. But I can make the adjustment. Give me a minute."

Konrad walked off.

Jonty stepped over to a large sign that mapped out the tunnels below and explained what he was about to experience.

Covered in working clothes and armed with mining equipment, visitors to the Wieliczka mine stop feeling like tourists as soon as they descend into the darkness by the oldest existing mine shaft, the Regis. The trail, located far off the busy tourist route, allows visitors to discover the inner workings of the mine. On their own, they measure the concentration of methane, grind and transport salt, set the path, and explore unknown chambers. They also experience the daily routine of underground life and the secrets of mining traditions and rituals, and experience firsthand the real taste of miners' work.

It all sounded so adventurous.

Visitors receive a protective coverall, a lamp, and helmet. Please bring warm clothing. Temperature underground ranges between 14° and 16°C. Wear comfortable, waterproof footwear.

Which he'd done.

He'd come a long way from his beginnings.

He started out as a black-market dealer, mainly fencing stolen supplies acquired from U.S. military bases scattered across Europe. Anything and everything. The supply of buyers had seemed unending. He made a lot of money and managed to stay out of jail. Then he progressed into people, becoming a recruiter. If someone needed an experienced burglar, a qualified arms expert, or a high-tech hacker, he found the right person for the right price. Incredible that no one had started such a service before. Everybody thought criminals either all knew one another or formed their alliances on a whim. Not so. An inability to advertise, the scrutiny of law enforcement, and an overall lack of honesty made it tough to find good help. After all, you couldn't ask for references. He'd solved that problem and made a lot more money in the process. He'd had only one rule. He never worked for murderers, terrorists, or kidnappers. For nearly a decade he was the underworld's number one employment agency.

Then a third shift. Into information.

Another service few had exploited.

Unfortunately, no university offered any degree in his line of work. No trade unions sponsored apprenticeships. No traditions existed upon which to draw. You simply learned as you went. And he had, making mistakes here and there, but never repeating them. His reputation had grown such that he was considered one of half a dozen people in the world who could supply good, reliable information. Now he was on the verge of the biggest deal of all. Provided he could keep everything under control for another two days.

Every life had a turning point. This was his.

Konrad returned. "All is done. I laid out mining kits for you both in the locker room. Slip on the coveralls, then meet me with your helmets and lights over there at the elevator."

CHAPTER FIFTEEN

COTTON LEFT THE RESTAURANT.

Stephanie had offered no argument to get him to change his mind, her eyes signaling that she understood. A hundred and fifty thousand dollars was nowhere near enough compensation to deal with a guy like Tom Bunch. He actually felt for her, but Stephanie was a big girl. She could handle things. Still, whoever else she had in mind to team with Bunch?

God help them.

He wondered why she stayed on the job. Just retire. Find something else to do. She could make a fortune in the private sector. But he knew the answer. The Magellan Billet was her life. She was a loyal soldier, the kind you wanted on your side, and normally he'd do anything for her. But his personal bullshit-tolerance level had long ago dropped to zero and he was simply not the guy to babysit Tom Bunch.

The fading light of a northern dusk had taken hold, the June evening air dry and pleasant. The streets were choked with people, vendor carts, and bicycles that sped along at a fast clip. He'd had an interesting afternoon, to say the least. He missed the job, for sure. But he didn't miss dealing with assholes like Bunch. And he'd had his share of them. He hated leaving Stephanie in the lurch, and knew that her not insisting he stay meant he owed her one.

But that was okay. He'd owed her before.

He kept walking, retracing the route he and Stephanie had taken earlier, past the fish market, the old town hall, and the Basilica of the Holy Blood. All was quiet at the church, the front doors closed for the day, the square out front still dotted with camera-toting tourists. No sign of any police or any other indication something unusual had happened there earlier. He followed another busy street and passed retail stores on both sides, most still trying to lure in a few last customers. The path drained into the central market, his hotel on the far side of the open expanse.

He should call Cassiopeia. They spoke at least once a day. He missed her. Strange to have those feelings about someone else, but he'd come to welcome them. Thankfully, each provided the other a wide berth. No clinginess. Each cherished their own space, but they also cherished each other. He'd even given the M-word a little thought. Marriage would be a huge step. But they both always found a reason to avoid the subject, their relationship a mixture of need, apprehension, and shyness. He'd been divorced awhile, and his ex-wife lived back in Georgia with their son, Gary. All was good there. Finally. But it had taken a struggle.

One he had no desire to repeat.

It was time to get his mind back on why he'd come to Bruges. He had a budget for the purchase of the three books, which should be more than enough. Their resale would entail at least a 25 percent markup, not a bad return on a few days' work. He should be able to make the buys and be back in Copenhagen by tomorrow afternoon. He'd taken the train so his return could be flexible, but he definitely needed to be home by Friday. Cassiopeia was due in Denmark that evening for a few days.

Which he was looking forward to.

A crowd had gathered around the statues of Jan Breydel and Pieter de Coninck. A butcher and weaver, two Flemish revolutionaries who led a 14th-century uprising against the French. He doubted any of the gawkers knew their historical significance. Bars and restaurants dominated the square's perimeter, everything alive with hustle and bustle. He rounded the statues and was about to turn for the side street that led to his hotel when he caught sight of a woman, her long legs, lean figure, and blond hair distinctive. She wore jeans with boots and a silk blouse, and was moving away from a row of flagpoles toward another of the streets radiating from the square.

Ivona Novak.

She'd intentionally revealed herself back at the restaurant. Surely seeing him with Bunch and Stephanie had raised suspicions. Why wouldn't it? But there'd been no opportunity for him to explain. Maybe now was the chance. He kept watching as she dissolved into the crowd. Then something else caught his attention. Two familiar faces. Two-thirds of the Three Amigos. Following Ivona.

Leave it alone.

Walk away.

Yeah, right.

He headed in her direction.

At the junction of the side street and the market square he caught sight of Ivona fifty yards ahead, the Two Amigos in pursuit. Buildings lined both sides, and there were enough people moving back and forth for no one to be noticed. But Ivona had to know she had company, as these guys weren't making any secret about their presence.

She turned and disappeared into one of the buildings.

The Two Amigos followed.

Nothing about this seemed right, but he kept going until he came to a pedimented arch that led through one of the gabled houses, forming an alley about fifty feet long. No one was in sight. He walked through the covered passage into a courtyard flanked by more old houses. Wrought-iron lanterns suspended from the stone façades cast a dim glow. Another covered passage led out on the opposite side. Three doors dotted the exterior walls to his left and right, all closed. Where'd everybody go? He heard a click and turned to see the Two Amigos standing behind him, one of them armed with a gun.

"That way," the guy said, motioning with the weapon at one of the closed doors.

No choice.

He turned.

The door opened and Ivona emerged.

She walked by him and gently stroked his cheek with her hand.

"Sorry, Cotton. It had to be done."

CHAPTER SIXTEEN

CZAJKOWSKI REALIZED THAT HE COULD NOT SIT BACK AND ALLOW things to happen. His whole life was at stake. Perhaps even the entire country's future. Someone named Jonty Olivier was out to destroy him. He'd long expected threats from the various political parties, hostile ministers in Parliament, opposition leaders, even the media—which was not always kind—but never had he thought a foreigner would become so dangerous.

It had been a long time since he'd thought of that day at Mokotów Prison. Many times he'd wondered what had happened to the math professor tied to the stool. The last he saw the man had been forced to crawl on hands and knees from the interrogation room back to his cell. How degrading. He'd been so young then. So afraid. Major Dilecki of the SB had brought him there to make a point.

Do as he was told or face the same consequences.

Countless people had been arrested and tortured. In addition to beatings and burnings, the most popular methods of "interrogation" had been to rip off fingernails, apply temple screws, clamp on tight handcuffs that caused the skin to burst and blood to flow, force prisoners to run up and down stairs, deprive them of sleep, make them stand at attention for hours, reduce their rations, pour buckets of cold water into cells, leave them in solitary confinement, anything and everything imaginable to break a person down. All of it had been applied in a harsh, premeditated manner, without remorse or discrimination. Those who fainted were revived with an adrenaline shot. Before some of the sessions, which could last for hours, many received booster injections to keep them alert. Torturers strictly followed the wishes of interrogating officers like Dilecki.

A damn disgrace.

And for what?

That brave man on the floor that day had been right. *What the foreign force has taken from us, we shall with sabre retrieve.* And that was precisely what had happened. The communists were finally driven away and Poland returned to its people.

But at what cost?

During martial law many had stayed in prison for years, until a general amnesty finally forgave everyone. Till today, he never knew what happened to Dilecki, but apparently the major had kept up with him, secreting documents that should have long ago been destroyed.

One day you might be a big somebody.

What a bastard.

Mokotów Prison still existed, now used by the government as a short-term holding facility. No one, though, had been abused there in a long time. A huge plaque now adorned one of the outer walls commemorating the victims. What happened inside those concrete cells, in unimaginable conditions, had been the subject of books and memoirs. Nobody really knew how many died there, and few paid for those atrocities. Unfortunately, justice back then seemed more like a leaf in the spring air, at the mercy of the twists from an unpredictable wind. Now here he was, decades later, still dealing with it.

How had things come to this?

He was fifty-six years old, a respected citizen of Poland, one who'd managed to attain the highest elected office in the land. His mother had wanted him to become a priest, because back then the clearest path to an education came from the church. All children were taught in school to be subservient to the state and obedient workers to the collective. No mention of individuality ever came. People were helpless in directing their own lives. But he managed to obtain a university degree, eventually heading up, during the time of martial law, a branch of the Independent

Students' Union, the junior arm of Solidarity. That position had been what caught Dilecki's attention, along with his operation of an underground publishing house. He'd been quite the radical. But everyone was back then. The country was changing. The world was changing. And he'd wanted to be part of that change.

He went on to serve in all aspects of government. First elected to Parliament when he was thirty, he served four terms before moving to the executive branch. He'd been an undersecretary of state, the vice minister of national defense, the general secretary of two political parties, then back to Parliament where he rose to vice speaker. He came from a solid, respected family with not a hint of scandal or shame. His grandfather fought with valor in the Polish–Soviet War, his father in World War II.

The Catholic Church meant everything to him.

He remembered vividly the night in May 1981 when word came that John Paul II had been shot. Their beloved favorite son lay fighting for his life. Czajkowski had been on his way to a Solidarity meeting. Instead, he'd wandered into a church where hundreds of people knelt in prayer and a priest said mass. Above the altar hung a dark painting of the crucifixion. He recalled thinking that once again Poles faced a calamity. The life of *their* pope was in peril. Their economy in shambles. Russian tanks were massing at the border. The country seemed on the rack. Yet before him was the strangely calming image of a man splayed by crucifixion. Not only a symbol of the nation's turmoil but a promise of redemption, too. He recalled what someone once wrote. *Poland is the Jesus Christ of nations.*

How true.

And how ironic that the passions of Christ could now be part of his own undoing. He felt like he was about to be crucified, too.

Everyone had been so young back then. The head of the largest Solidarity branch in Warsaw a mere twenty-five. The leader of the Gdańsk Shipyard union barely twenty-one. Most of the high officers in Solidarity were all in their late twenties and early thirties. Lech Wałęsa at the helm had been the old man at thirty-seven. It had been young men and women who'd fought the battle against communism. Youth definitely came with fire and fury, but it also came with bad judgment and inexperience. No one had known where it all was going, or how it would end. Solidarity seemed many times as lost as the nation. The government-controlled media blamed the union for everything, including food shortages. Hearing it so often, people began to believe the lies.

A slogan resonated across the nation.

The government takes care of laws, the party takes care of politics, and Solidarity takes care of the people.

But many times he'd wondered if that was true.

Few had been able to articulate what the nation wanted. But everyone knew what they didn't want.

A distant, arbitrary, central authority full of repression.

Decades of mismanagement and corruption finally caught up with the communists. The Red Bourgeoisie benefited, while everyone else paid the price. The fools overborrowed and overspent, in the end having only enough money left to service the interest on billions in foreign debt. Eventually the economy crumbled, consumer goods vanished, and food went scarce, which allowed a wave of angry young people to mobilize, ten million strong, and bring a government to its knees.

He'd been part of that revolution.

Now he was the head of state.

But for how much longer.

Socialist? Anti-socialist?

It was a question asked many times in the 1980s, but one that disappeared in the 1990s and now no longer mattered.

Poland was free.

Or was it?

The pain in his chest felt like his heart was encased in barbed wire. Not a coronary. Just the past rearing its ugly head and reminding him that it still existed. He had to fix this.

This had to end.

And whatever was required to make that happen—

He would do.

CHAPTER SEVENTEEN

COTTON WAS LED INTO THE BUILDING AND UP A FLIGHT OF STAIRS to a second-floor apartment full of nondescript furniture, the kind bought by cheap landlords who expect the worst from tenants. He caught a strong smell of mustiness and wondered if anyone lived there. A familiar face waited inside, one that ushered him in with a casual sweep of a big paw.

"Mr. Malone. Good see you again."

The feeling was not mutual. "What's it been, three years? Do people still call you Ivan? Or does that change by the assignment?"

"That is my name."

The last time he'd dealt with this devil they'd talked within the shadow of the Round Tower in Copenhagen, then again in Amsterdam, the situation dire. But the rough English laced with a heavy Russian accent remained, as did the man's Cossack appearance—short, heavy-chested, with grayish-black hair. A splotchy, reddened skink of a face was still dominated by a broad nose and shadowed by a day-old beard. No slave to fashion, Ivan wore an ill-fitting suit that bulged at the waist.

Cotton gestured over his shoulder at the Two Amigos standing behind him. "Your people stole the Holy Blood?"

"How is Cassiopeia?"

This guy had loved to ignore questions the first time they'd met, too.

"As I tell you back then, quite the woman," Ivan said. "If I am younger, a hundred pounds lighter?" The Russian patted his belly. "Who knows? But I am dreaming." Ivan paused. "I hope, like last time, you appreciate this problem, too."

"It's the only reason I'm still standing here."

His unspoken message seemed to be received. *Get to the point.*

Ivan chuckled. "You say same thing last time. Like then, you can overpower me. I am still fat, out of shape. Stupid, too. All Russians are, right?"

He had a moment of déjà vu. To Amsterdam. Similar sarcasm. A similar implied threat. Since the two guys behind him then, and now, were not fat and out of shape.

"I hope you still smart," Ivan said. "Years off job have not changed you? Last time, you did good."

That matter involved China, with Russia his reluctant ally. "I seem to be busier in retirement than when I was working for the government."

"That bad thing?"

He shrugged. "Depends. How do you know Ivona Novak?"

"We work together few times. She make good bait."

That she did. He'd willingly taken that bait, though sensing the risk.

"Why am I in the middle of this?" he asked.

Ivan pointed. "That your fault. You go after my men today. Not your business. Or was it?"

Now he understood the curiosity. An ex–American agent in the basilica, at just the right moment, who gave chase, then ended up talking with Stephanie Nelle and Mr. Deputy National Security. That two and two, at least in Ivan's mind, added up to a big fat four. So he decided, *Why not? Play along.*

"You get an invitation to the auction?"

"Me? No. People at Kremlin. They get invite and reply. We told to steal Holy Blood. What they tell you steal?"

"The—"

"Wait," Ivan said, then he motioned at the Amigos. "Leave." The two men withdrew and closed the door. Apparently their clearance level wasn't high enough for that information.

"Go ahead," Ivan said.

"We were told to steal the Nail at Bamberg."

A lie, but hopefully this man had no way of knowing the truth. Time to see if this information route was a two-way street. "Tell me what's up for auction?"

"They not give you taste?"

"I'm curious as to your sample."

Ivan laughed. "President of Poland has many secrets. Ones we were not even aware he had. Bad secrets. Unfortunate for him. Sadly, many of our records are gone. Perestroika. Glasnost. Thieves. Between them we don't have much left."

"What kind of bad secrets?"

"The kind he do not want people to ever know."

"That bad?"

Ivan rubbed his nose between thumb and forefinger, as if easing his sinuses. "Plenty bad."

He got it. Depending on who possessed the information they could get the Polish president to do whatever they wanted, either to place missiles in Poland or not. Certainly Russia was in the NO category, the United States in the YES. That was five of the seven possibilities.

"You know who else was invited?" he asked.

Ivan pointed. "Just you. Rest is mystery."

"You went to a lot of trouble to get me here."

"I want message delivered to your people. One they will understand."

"Ivona can't be your errand girl? I'm retired and have nothing to do with any of this."

"You funny man. For once, Ivona and I find ourselves on same side. We want same thing."

"No missiles in Poland?"

Ivan gestured with his outstretched hands. "Seems like good idea."

And he agreed. But his patience had reached an end. "Look, I just told you I have nothing to do with this. Yes, I was in the basilica today and stuck my nose where it didn't belong. But that was me being the Lone Ranger. The White House just tried to recruit me and I said no. This is not my problem."

"Yet you are here."

Good point. "Okay. What's your message?"

"Moscow not happy. They will not allow missiles in Poland. Whatever that takes. No missiles. Not ever."

The tone had changed. No more frivolity. The mouth twisted into a sour line. This guy meant every word.

"We do whatever necessary to make sure that not happen. Winning auction? Might work. Killing? Might work, too. Tell your people we do whatever necessary. We not start this. Your president start. But we shall finish. I have full authority to do that."

Normally, he'd shake his head and leave. The U.S. government could handle things without his help. And who liked being an errand boy? But Stephanie was riding point on this one, and Bunch had already made clear that she was expendable.

"We not know where auction will occur. But when we do, we will act," Ivan said. "Tell Stephanie Nelle that I do not bluff."

He did not like the sound of that. He'd had enough. "I'm leaving now."

Ivan shrugged, then his hard face split into a toothy smile as he reached beneath his jacket, drew a gun, and fired.

CHAPTER EIGHTEEN

JONTY FOLLOWED VIC AND KONRAD DOWN A BLACK TUNNEL, THE floor a succession of wooden planks, the walls strengthened by a thick timber lining. He understood the liberal use of wood. Plentiful in supply, it flexed with the earth's pressure and never corroded.

The slow elevator ride down the shaft had taken forty seconds, popping his ears. They were now 130 meters into the earth, on one of the mine's lower routes, far past the busy tourist areas higher up on Levels I and II. Up there was a small city with three kilometers of tunnels that accommodated conference facilities, restaurants, bars, chapels, shops, even a sanatorium for chronic allergies, every chamber cut from the surrounding salt. Though not a working mine any longer, the whole place remained full of life. He'd visited all the public areas, but here in the dark solitude the grayish-green salt, more like unpolished granite, seemed far more ancient, the surroundings a warren of tunnels and dangerous pitfalls.

Konrad stopped and faced him and Vic, removing something from his pocket. A piece of paper that he unfolded.

"This is a map for this level."

They were dressed in coveralls. Each wore a carbon dioxide absorber. The only light on the map came from their helmet lamps, which collectively illuminated a printed maze of tunnels and chambers. The routes twisted, curved, and intersected like spaghetti. With so many chambers it would be impossible to keep any of it straight if not for the fact that the vast majority were named.

He noticed five red X's on the map beside labels.

Konrad traced a route with his finger, following the X's. *Gołębie. Barany. Sroki. Szczygielec. Jeleń.* Pigeons. Sheep. Magpies. Goldfinch. Deer.

"The chambers and tunnels are named for animals, birds, famous visitors, cites, provinces, people, even one for a dragon," Konrad said. "Most of the labels are centuries old, attached when they were first hewn from the salt."

And what an endeavor.

Block by block the salt had been removed, starting at the top and continuing down until a vein was tapped out, forming a chamber. Then the miners moved to the next, boring long straight tunnels, called drifts, to connect the chambers, all done for not only excavation but also better ventilation. The result was a maze, kilometers long, apparently made navigable only by the names attached along the way.

"The Barany Chamber is ahead," Konrad said. "It's the only one that intersects with this main drift. Vic said you needed a simple clear path to find the end. Here it is."

Jonty had held off to the last minute with this final detail, now even more important given Reinhardt's presence. "Has anyone else inquired about this?"

Konrad shook his head. "No one."

"Do you know if anyone has been on this level the past few days?"

"Surely some of the miners have. But you can only get down here with a fob that frees the elevator. I have one, and about fifty others do, too. We check every level daily. But if you're asking if anyone has gone to where we're headed? Not to my knowledge. It's fairly remote and inaccessible. There's no reason for anyone to be there."

They continued down the timber-lined drift, the dry salt beneath their boots crunching with every step like packed snow. A steady breeze swept over them from the ventilation system, which helped alleviate any feeling of being entombed. The air was cool but not uncomfortably so.

Vic toted a backpack containing what would make Jonty rich. He'd decided weeks ago not to keep the cache exposed. Better to place it in a secure location and let the high bidder worry about its procurement. All seven participants possessed the resources to make that happen, along with the ability to hunt down and kill him if they did not get what they paid for.

But he had no intention of cheating anyone.

Quite the contrary.

His reputation had been built on dependability, so he planned to offer Vic's assistance, if needed, to secure what they'd paid for. Not quite a money-back guarantee, but close enough.

They kept walking and entered another chamber. This one was huge, at least twenty meters high and more than that long and wide.

He marveled at human industry.

At one point over one-third of the entire royal treasury of Poland had been derived from salt. Twenty-seven million tons extracted over seven centuries, each block hacked from the wall with picks, axes, and wedges. Until the 14th century prisoners of war worked the mine as slaves.

Then free men took over.

And no brutality existed as it did in coal, gold, or other mines. Here there was a much more normal existence, the men living below for weeks at a time, working eight-hour shifts, being paid well, which included a generous salt allowance.

The diggers had been the most important in the social hierarchy, and rightly so. Prospectors found the salt. Carriers moved the blocks from the drifts to the shafts so they could be hauled upward. Penitents had the toughest job of all, guarding against deadly methane gas, which seeped from the rock and accumulated at the ceiling. They wore soaking-wet clothes and held long poles with torches on the end, burning off the gas before it became explosive. Water was the chief enemy, seeping down from above, forming brine, chiseling the salt from the ceilings and walls, crystallizing it into cauliflower-like glazes and stalactites, many visible here on this level, reflecting back from their helmet lights.

"This is Sroki," Konrad said. "It's one of the largest chambers on this level, but it's not in good shape, as you can see. Water is seeping in everywhere. Eventually, the miners will come and make repairs."

Rising on the far side were enormous logs, stacked horizontally onto one another, forming a table-like pillared wall. Cribbing. There to counteract the enormous downward pressure from the rock and prevent a collapse. He noticed the size of the tree trunks and that most bore no evidence of a saw. Instead, they'd been chopped down with an ax from the nearby forests, the hack marks still there, which confirmed they'd been there a long time. Yet they looked relatively recent, proof of the preservation effects a salt mine had on wood. It could last forever. Provided it didn't burn. White paint helped make it more visible and retardant. Fire had always been the greatest threat. For centuries miners worked with open lamps in clay bowls, tallow and oil for fuel. An easy matter for a spark to flare, the fire bringing not only flames and heat but also noxious carbon monoxide. There'd been many fires in the mines over the centuries. Some were deadly and had lasted for months, as there was nothing that could be done except seal the area off and allow the flames to burn themselves out. He noticed that some of the cribbing showed traces of charring.

Konrad led the way down another drift.

Offshoots appeared periodically into more dark passages left and right. Some were labeled, most were not. Then a white sign with black letters noted that an offshoot to the right was named SZCZYGIELEC.

Goldfinch.

"That was marked on your map," he said to Konrad.

"That's right. It will get progressively tighter from here on. This is an area no one visits. It's known only through old charts and records."

Vic turned to face him with a look that asked if he was going to be okay.

"I've never been claustrophobic," Jonty said. "I'll be fine."

They kept going into the blackness, and he felt like he was descending into the abyss. Without their lights they would not be able even to see a finger touch their nose. The passageway narrowed. They found a chamber marked GOŁĘBIE, and finally came to one labeled JELEŃ.

More names from the map.

Ahead the tunnel had fallen in on itself, leaving only a small hatchway through the salt debris, big enough for a man to pass through on his belly. A dark space opened on the other side.

Vic nodded.

Jonty faced their guide. "I need you to wait here. We need to handle this alone."

Konrad had the good sense not to argue and simply nodded.

"I also need that map," Jonty said.

Konrad handed it over.

No sense delaying.

This had to be done.

"Lead the way," he said to Vic.

CHAPTER NINETEEN

COTTON QUICKLY CORRECTED HIMSELF.

Not a gun.

A Taser.

Two barbed electrodes attached to conductors shot through the air. Their needles found his chest. Electricity surged through him. White-hot pain exploded in his brain, leaving a trail of quivering nerves in its path. His muscles overloaded and he collapsed to the floor, his body convulsing into contractions. Like a leg cramp amplified a thousand times. The weapon continued to click as high-voltage current passed through him. The feeling of helplessness and vulnerability seemed overwhelming. He had complete control over his mind, but not his body.

The Taser's clicking stopped.

The whole thing lasted no more than five seconds, but it had been the longest five of his life. He stayed conscious, aware of his surroundings, with only one thought.

For the pain to stop.

And it did.

But he was immobile.

He tried to catch his breath.

Ivan bent down and plucked out the darts. "Pass on message, Malone."

Then the Russian left.

Son of a bitch. That hurt.

He slowly sat up.

His head and mind felt dull and heavy.

Dammit.

He entered the small lobby of his hotel, a fine 18th-century burgher's house converted into a cozy, elegant establishment not far from the central market. On the walk over his nerves had settled. He should call Stephanie and pass on the message. Not because Ivan wanted him to, but because she needed to know the lay of the land. He'd make that call after getting upstairs to his room, where he'd have some privacy. He remained hungry, and his hotel, though quaint and comfortable, provided no room service. He'd have to head back out to find a snack, which wouldn't be a problem given the number of nearby cafés.

He retrieved the room key from the desk clerk and climbed two unbroken flights of wooden stairs to the third floor, pulling himself along on the balustrade. He approached his door and opened the dead bolt. Inside, he tossed the key on the dresser. His room was a small suite with a separate area for the bed, a paneled door in between, which hung half open. No lights were on, the ambient light from outside leaking in through the windows, providing more than enough illumination.

A noise came from the other room.

A squeak.

Then another.

Somebody was there.

He approached the doorway, staying to one side. Only an idiot rushed into the dark, so he reached around the jamb and flicked the wall switch. The room lit with the soft amber glow from two lamps on the nightstands. In the bed, her back propped on a pillow, lay Ivona Novak.

Back when he was still with the Magellan Billet, during the years he lived apart from his wife, Ivona had been quite a temptation, one he'd succumbed to on more than one occasion. Those encounters had not been without passion, though more a uniting of kindred seekers, two drifting souls who took comfort in each other since they both seemed to understand loneliness.

But that was all in the old days. BC. Before Cassiopeia.

Things were different now.

"Ivan asked for a favor and I obliged," she said. "He promised he'd behave. Did he?"

He walked over and sat on the bed, noticing that she'd removed her shoes, her toenails painted blood red. "He Tasered me."

She touched his arm. "Would you like me to make it better? My way of apologizing."

He needed to say something to bridge that clumsy gap between offer and caress. Years ago, as a young navy lawyer, he'd made the mistake of cheating on his wife. Why? Looking back, he had no idea. It just happened. A stupid act, a vain attempt at thinking someone else cared, finding pleasure in them, if only for a moment, regardless of the consequences. He hurt Pam more than he ever thought possible, and she repaid him with a child that he only learned years later was not biologically his. It took more than a decade to end that civil war. He and Pam now got along just fine. Gary, their son, knew the truth, and had come to terms with the fact that though he may not be a Malone by blood he was in every other meaningful way.

More important, his own feelings had finally come into focus.

Cassiopeia was important to him.

She meant something. She laughed at his jokes, admired his intelligence, sympathized with his hurts, and shared his passions. As he did with hers. She was his best friend, and that realization came with a warmth and fullness, a sense of belonging, of a purpose intertwined. He loved Cassiopeia and she loved him. How did that happen? Hell, if love could be predicted it would lose all of its power. All he knew was that he did.

"Sorry, Ivona. I'm not available."

She tossed him a puzzled look. "Has Cotton Malone found someone?"

"You sound surprised."

"I never thought you the domesticated type."

She was gorgeous, with a petite, rounded face, a buttoned chin, and a small, upturned nose that made her far more pretty than glamorous.

Centered between high cheeks was a small but expressive mouth. Her body had not a drop of fat or excess. Her eyes, blue to green, changing with her mood, reflected a lot about her, everything casting an air that was quintessentially feminine. One he knew was somewhat of an illusion, since this woman could definitely hurt you.

"I found someone myself," she said.

"Yet here you are in my bed."

"Fully clothed. This is business." And she smiled, her puckered mouth dimpled at the corners.

"What do you want, Ivona?"

"The United States needs to avoid the auction. Walk away. With America's departure, the value of that information diminishes greatly for Jonty Olivier."

Interesting. She knew the seller. But he understood. "Olivier needs the haves and the have-nots. Both affect the price. And American is the biggest have. Did Poland get an invite?"

She shook her head. "Hence my alliance with Ivan. We needed a little help from someone who thinks like we do on this issue."

"No missiles?"

She nodded.

"What did your president do that's so bad?"

She tossed him a quizzical look. "Tom Bunch didn't tell you?"

He decided to be honest. "Not a word."

She smiled, her teeth white as pearls. "Is it tough being out of the loop?"

"Not at all. The tough part comes when someone wants you in the loop but tells you nothing."

"Are you in this?"

He knew the rules. No information to outsiders. No need. They're not in the game. But players? They were different, and sometimes you had to cast your net wider than usual to see what could be reeled in. "I haven't decided."

"Ivan said you weren't all that receptive."

He smiled. "You and he have quite the relationship."

"Those missiles are a dead issue that your president has resurrected. Russia doesn't want them in Poland. Nor do they want to spend the tens of millions it will take to deploy their own missiles across Central Asia in retaliation. Poland doesn't want the missiles. Europe either. The whole thing is an unnecessary escalation so President Warner Fox can show the world that he's a big man."

He couldn't argue with her assessment. "Bunch is intent on being a part of that auction."

"But first he has to acquire a relic. Which one?"

The lies had to be consistent. "The Nail in Bamberg."

"That will be an easy take. It's just sitting there in a side chapel."

"What do you know about the other relics?"

She shifted in the bed. "Ten days ago a team broke into the Monastery of Santo Toribio de Liébana in Spain and took their True Cross. I traced them back to Iran. Two days after that another team burglarized St. Anthony's Chapel in Pennsylvania and stole their thorn from the crown. The segment of the Pillar of the Flogging, in Rome, was taken last week. The Holy Sponge inside Notre-Dame just two days ago. I've not been able to identify any of those thieves. The Russians took the Holy Blood today. Only the Nail and lance remain."

She cocked her head and leaned forward, her soft lips approaching dangerously close to his. He raised a finger to stop her advance. Once he would have surrendered. When lust took control of good judgment and emotions ran on autopilot, all of it fueled by risk and anxiety.

But he would not make that mistake again.

He stood from the bed. "Time for you to go."

Her restless blue eyes bore testimony to a hit-and-run existence. She'd always been a hive of nerves. What she was doing right now seemed typical Ivona. Playing both ends against the middle. Using every weapon she had at her disposal. But he felt the tense atmosphere that had sprung up between them, as if neither believed a word the other said. They were definitely fencing, each tossing around a measured blend of fact and fiction.

"She's a lucky woman."

"More the other way around."

She rose from the bed, her body just as impressive as he remembered. She slipped on her shoes and headed for the outer room and the door. He stood propped against the dresser, arms folded across his chest.

She stopped and said, "Take Ivan's warning seriously. Stay out of this one. It could get rough."

"As I recall, you liked it that way."

She smiled.

"I do."

And she left.

CHAPTER TWENTY

COTTON ADMIRED RYNEK GŁÓWNY. AT OVER SIX HUNDRED FEET
on each side, the open expanse claimed the title of the largest medieval
square in Europe. Its colorful perimeter buildings were all neoclassical,
filled with every kind of shop, store, and eatery imaginable.

A lot like Bruges, only much bigger.

He'd contacted Stephanie after Ivona had left and told her he'd
changed his mind and wanted in. Call him crazy, but he could no longer
allow her to do this one on her own. So he'd packed his bag, slipped
from the hotel by a back exit, then left in a car waiting at the ring road.
He was driven south into Luxembourg, where he spent the night at an
upscale hotel on the Magellan Billet's dime. He caught an early-morning
flight out to Frankfurt, where he changed planes on a tight connection
to Bratislava. A car had been waiting in the parking lot, keys hidden inside, which he used to drive two hundred miles north, across the open
Poland–Slovakia border, to Kraków. The roundabout route had been for
Ivona's benefit, to keep him off any Polish radars.

Kraków lay in a broad valley nestled close to the River Wisła. For
centuries it was Poland's capital and basked in richness and opulence.
Old and new still mixed there in perfect harmony, with an almost mystical atmosphere, aided by the fact that the city escaped horrific bombing

during World War II. The twin domes of St. Mary's Church rose into the clear late-morning sky. Oddly, one tower was much shorter than the other, different in design and style, too, and he was sure there was a story in that somewhere.

Stephanie had called on the drive through Slovakia and reported that the Nail from Bamberg Cathedral had been stolen last night. That left only the Holy Lance. She'd also gone a bit old school and provided a packet of hard-copy information, waiting in the car inside a manila envelope. He hadn't seen that in a while. Everything today was electronic. Along the way he'd stopped and read what the envelope contained, learning the things he needed to know.

A lance was first described in the Gospel of John. The Romans had wanted to break Jesus' legs, what they called crurifragium, as a way to hasten death during crucifixion. But when it came time they realized Jesus was already dead. To make sure that was the case, a soldier named Longinus supposedly stabbed Christ in the side with his lance.

And immediately there came out blood and water.

Which was why the Catholic mass always included a mixing of the two. Blood symbolizing humanity. Water, Christ's divinity.

The confusion came from the many lances that claimed to be Longinus' original. One was in St. Peter's Basilica, but its provenance had always been suspect, its tip broken off and kept in Paris. Another could be found in Armenia, supposedly brought there by the Apostle Thaddeus. Antioch claimed one, too, found after a monk had a vision that it was buried in a local church. The one that garnered the most attention sat in Vienna, inside the Hofburg. For centuries, Holy Roman Emperors used it in their coronation ceremonies. When the empire disbanded in the early 19th century the Habsburgs incorporated it into their imperial regalia. A legend associated with that lance said whoever possessed it held destiny in their hands. Hence its name. The Spear of Destiny. Charlemagne, Barbarossa, Napoleon, and Hitler had all craved it. Millions came to see it in Vienna every year, but testing in 2003 revealed it to be from the 7th century, not the time of Christ—though an iron pin, hammered into the blade and set off by tiny brass crosses, long claimed to be from the crucifixion, was consistent in length and shape to a 1st-century Roman nail.

The fifth contender could be found in Kraków.

It arrived a thousand years ago, a gift from the Holy Roman Emperor Otto III to the Polish king Bolesław the Brave. Supposedly it was a copy of the original that Charlemagne had possessed. It eventually acquired a name. The Spear of Saint Maurice. When the Swedes invaded Poland in 1655, they robbed the treasury but left the spear. The Prussians and Austrians raided next, but did not take the spear. In 1785 the Germans claimed Poland and stole all of the imperial regalia, melting down the gold, but left the spear. Apparently a simple, black iron lance had no value. But to the Poles it represented their spirit and independence. Hitler seized it in 1940 and had it taken to Vienna for comparison with the Spear of Destiny.

Then something odd happened.

The Spear of St. Maurice was abruptly returned to Poland in 1944.

Which shocked everyone.

Nazis never gave anything back.

One theory hypothesized that the experts in Vienna recognized it as the real spear and returned it, wanting Hitler to have the fake, countering the legend of him holding destiny in his hands. Another story said the spears were switched and the fake was left in Austria, again so Hitler would be denied any mystical powers the artifact might contain. Either version seemed supported by the fact that Hitler failed in his quest, but Poland survived. No one knew anything for sure. Which meant that Ivona might think the Hofburg and the Spear of Destiny to be the target, not Wawel Castle. Of course, he had no idea if her information about the auction was as solid as Stephanie's. But he had to assume that was the case.

His instructions from the envelope were for him to come to Kraków's main square and enter the cloth market. Once the center of the medieval trade, the splendid Renaissance edifice had stood in Rynek Główny since the 14th century. A Gothic rectangle the length of a football field, its inside was lined with stalls that sold every souvenir imaginable while its outer arcades accommodated cafés and bars. Each end was open, people milling about through the covered space. He was told to head for the booth identified as number 135 and wait. He'd be approached and asked if he knew directions to the Kraków Academy. His reply? That it required

a tram or bus, but walking might be faster. More old school. Oral pass-
words. Then counter-passwords.

He hadn't used that one in a long time, either.

He stood outside one of the market's open ends and caught the sound
of a trumpet in the air. The *hejnal.* One of those long-memory things,
dating back to the 13th century when Mongols invaded Poland. A sen-
try on duty atop St. Mary's Church had sounded the alarm to close the
city gates by playing a specific tune on his trumpet. But he was shot with
an arrow in the throat and never completed the anthem. Still, the town
woke from its slumber and repelled the invaders. Ever since, on the hour,
the same five notes were sounded four times, one for each direction on
the compass, from atop the church tower, always breaking off in mid-bar.

Talk about tradition.

He entered the cloth market and noticed that the booths, one after
the other, were clearly numbered. He assumed he was coming to meet
whoever had been doing the preliminary groundwork, preparing for the
spear's theft. Probably the same person who'd arranged for the car and
provided the manila envelope. It would be good to know more details,
particularly since he'd arrived late to this party.

He kept walking, paying attention to the merchandise and the shop-
pers. He seemed to fit right in, dressed in khakis and a button-down shirt
with the sleeves rolled up.

Once again here he was, back in the game.

At the booth marked 135 he slowed his pace and admired the hand-
carved, brightly painted angels for sale. Three men immediately ringed
him, blocking off any escape except through force. They were dressed
casually, too, part of the crowd a moment ago.

A fourth man approached.

"Mr. Malone. Please come with us."

The group stood, like an island on the pavement, streams of people
hurrying by on all sides. A familiar stirring raised his adrenaline. He decided that he could take these four. But first he asked, "And you are?"

"Agencja Wywiadu. We're hoping you'll come along, as a professional
courtesy."

Polish Foreign Intelligence Agency.

The big boys.

Ivona's people.

The guy added a smile to his request.

Now he was intrigued. "Where are we going?"

"Someone would like to speak with you."

So much for staying under the radar. Apparently, Polish intelligence knew everything he was doing.

The smart play seemed the patient play.

"Okay. Who am I to argue with courtesy."

CHAPTER TWENTY-ONE

JONTY MARVELED AT THE CASTLE'S GRAND HALL, A CAVERNOUS space topped by a magnificent timbered roof. Remnants of medieval paintings emerged in shadow all across the gray-stone walls. Tracery windows broke the long expanse, but the ones high up at the two gabled ends, there only to illuminate the ceiling timbers, seemed unique. A railed gallery encased the hall on three sides and, past a thick stone balustrade, exposed the second floor. Seven pairs of chairs dotted the terrazzo floor, each beside a small wooden table. The communicated rules for the auction allowed two representatives for each bidder. Since there was bound to be animosity among the participants, the pairs of chairs were spaced apart. Each station came with a paddle. To further equalize matters, instead of numbers—common for auctions—each displayed the bidder's national colors.

Russia, China, Germany, France, North Korea, Iran, and the United States.

The rules likewise provided that no outside communication would be allowed and that all transmission signals, in and out, would be temporarily blocked. Vic had already installed a powerful jammer that would run all day Thursday, until the auction ended. The event would begin at 11:00 A.M. with heavy hors d'oeuvres and drinks and should be over by 1:00 P.M., with everyone gone by 1:30. He, of course, would depart immediately after payment was confirmed. He'd already determined an escape route through the castle's back passages, where a car could be waiting to whisk him away.

A single, high-backed chair in the center faced the others. His place. He would personally conduct the auction from there. Vic would listen from above in the gallery and verify payment before the winner was declared. The only line of outside communication would be a laptop Vic would man in one of the second-floor bedrooms with a direct internet connection.

A stout oak table stood just inside the double-doored entryway. Empty at the moment but, tomorrow, each bidder would deposit atop it their portion of the Arma Christi. During the cocktail party that would precede the auction, an expert he'd employed, at considerable cost, would verify each of the holy relics. He'd been assured there were markers that could be used to ensure authenticity, and the expert had spent the last sixty days preparing for a quick analysis. He had to guard against one of the bidders swapping out the original relic for a copy. He planned to sell all seven on the black market. He'd already determined a list of potential buyers. Combined, the seven relics could bring as much as twenty million euros. Clearly, somebody had placed a lid over any public acknowledgment of the thefts. Nothing had appeared in the media. Press reports from Bruges had reported only that a fire inside the basilica had caused a panic and required an evacuation. Not a word had come about the loss of the Holy Blood, though it had been noted that there would be no more venerations for the next two weeks while repairs were made. Similar accounts had come from the other four locations, which had closed off the public exhibition of their relics, too.

Vic entered the hall and walked over to him.

"I think we have everything in place," Jonty said, sweeping his arms out to embrace the grandeur around him.

"The arrivals have all been coordinated," Vic said.

To protect the auction site, each bidder had been provided a different path to a different location within two hundred kilometers of where he stood. Seven teams of two people each had been hired to chauffeur each pair of participants. His former profession had aided that recruitment, as he'd been able to locate and retain fourteen highly capable, and trustworthy, individuals. His biggest fear was that one of the bidders would order a preemptive strike.

A risk, for sure.

Killing him before the auction was certainly in some of the bidders' best interests, but it was equally not so with others. The idea was to play those competing interests against one another and keep everyone off center. The instructions to all seven invitees had made clear that nothing they were bidding upon was located on site. The winning bidder would be told where to go to find what they bought, information that would only be provided once payment was confirmed. He wanted this sale to go perfectly, and he wanted to be alive afterward to enjoy the spoils without worry of reprisals.

Germany's loitering was a problem. But the United States' hesitation had become worrisome. Less than twelve hours remained for an RSVP. Weeks ago he'd personally called President Fox, who'd assured him that America would participate. *What's a few million dollars? A small price to pay to bring the Russians to their knees. And besides, it's not my money.* They'd both laughed at the quip. Fox had always been a dealer, really good at using other people's money. They'd done business a couple of times in the past when Fox had needed the kind of close information that helped cinch a tough business deal. Now the man was the president of the United States, calling for missiles to be placed in Poland. What luck. So he'd taken a chance and made personal contact, revealing both himself and some of what he possessed. Fox had been ecstatic and offered to preempt the sale with a fifty-million-euro offer. But he'd declined, knowing the auction would bring more. Had Fox changed his mind on participating?

"The Nail was taken last night," Vic said. "But oddly, the Germans have not RSVP'd as yet."

That was strange. "They have time. I'm sure we'll hear from them."

"Arrangements are in place," Vic said, "for the five invitees already en route to spend the night at their respective locales. I'll deal with the other two when we hear from them. They will all be transported tomorrow morning, simultaneously. Everyone should be here, on site, by 11:30."

"Damn the United States," he muttered.

Vic said nothing, knowing that the comment was not intended to elicit a reply. He worked hard to keep his good-mannered poise, but a powerful nervous energy had taken hold of him. Usually he could control it with harmless outlets, like reading. And he prided himself on being able to pace his emotions, whatever the pressure. But this was different.

Really different.

"Is our guest below quiet?" he asked, referring to the spy in the basement.

"I had to gag him."

"Probably better. We don't want the staff knowing he's there."

"All have been told that the basement is off limits. Luckily, these people ask few questions."

"With what I'm paying, they should be discreet. We're going to have to be extra vigilant, Vic."

"We will be. I have video surveillance set up outside to watch the main entrance. Each team of drivers bringing the bidders will make sure they come with no weapons, electronic devices, or GPS tags."

"None of which will help us if there's a damn drone in the air, following those cars," he said.

"None of these participants have the ability to deploy a high-altitude drone within the sovereign airspace of Slovakia. Not even the U.S. That doesn't mean they won't try, but the mountains and hilly terrain should work to our benefit. And we've set up some surprises along the way to deal with the possibility."

Good to hear.

His cell phone vibrated.

"Keep at it," he said to Vic, motioning for him to leave.

He answered the call.

"Good day, Jonty," the voice said.

Oh, no.

Reinhardt.

CHAPTER TWENTY-TWO

Cotton stared at the Monastery of the Camaldolese Monks. The white-limestone building, topped by spires and a green copper roof, sat on Srebrna Góra, Silver Mountain, a few miles west of Kraków, amid trees and vineyards overlooking the River Wisła. Monks had lived here in solitude for nearly five centuries.

But what were he and his Polish escorts doing here?

They'd parked at the bottom of the hill, a solid two-football-fields walk up an inclined road, both sides walled. The path ended at an arched doorway flanked on both sides by two tall towers topped with more green copper spires. He'd decided that since his entire presence had been compromised, nothing would be gained by resistance. Better to see where this trail led. So he'd come along willingly, curious about who wanted to have a chat. Apparently it was also to be a private talk, as this place was about as secluded as they came.

One of his minders stepped up to the portal and pulled an iron ring attached to a long chain. A few moments later the stout plank door opened. A man appeared, dressed in a hooded white robe and sporting a long, bushy beard. He appraised them, nodded, then indicated they could enter. Not a word was spoken.

They passed through the gatehouse and entered a grassy courtyard with no trees or adornments. A concrete path led to the main doors of a huge church. At least a couple of hundred feet stretched to the top of its copper spire, the pristine limestone walls bright in the midday sun. Another white-robed monk waited at the doors. Cotton's two escorts stopped and gestured that he should continue alone.

He entered the church and the monk left, closing the door behind him. The interior was a spacious single nave with a barrel-vaulted ceiling. A true Catholic sanctuary, rich in style, both sides lined with impressive Baroque chapels. The main altar at the far end was spectacular. Bright sun broke through the windows in fine streams of dusty light. No one was inside, save for one man, kneeling in the first pew, facing the altar. An eerie figure, backlit by candles, the whole scenario, he supposed, an attempt to deepen the hush and tighten the nerves. The man crossed himself, then stood and calmly walked down the center aisle. He was tall, heavy-chested, and handsome, in his fifties, a thin mat of brown hair brushed straight back from a wide forehead. He was clean-shaven, with a jawline tight as a clamp, dressed in a finely cut blue-gray suit.

"Mr. Malone. I'm Janusz Czajkowski."

A hand was extended, which he shook.

"I thought it best we speak in person," the president of Poland said in perfect English. "And this place offers us absolute privacy. You can't say that about many spots in this world. By the way, you don't speak Polish, do you?"

He shook his head. "That's one language I never mastered. Italian, Danish, Spanish, Latin, German. I can handle those."

"I was told you have a perfect memory."

"I don't know about that, but details do stick with me. *Eidetic* is the term used to describe it. Are you friends with the monks?"

"I like to think so. They are a most impressive people," Czajkowski said, staying with English. "They follow a severe code of self-imposed principles, all governed by *Ora et labora* and *Memento mori*."

He translated the Latin. "Pray and work. Remember you must die. How practical. And depressing."

"It works for them. They only talk to one another three times a week, and interact with the world beyond this monastery just five days a year."

"Except when the president of the country comes for a visit."

Czajkowski smiled. "That title does open doors. The prior and I are old friends."

"That helps, too."

"Life here is simple. Between prayer and work, they consume only vegetarian meals eaten in the solitude of their own small hermitage, where the only piece of décor is the skull of the previous prior. Can you imagine that? But I know for a fact that it is true."

This man was clearly leading to something, so he let him stay at the head of the parade.

"We don't know each other, Mr. Malone. But I'm told you're a reasonable man. I want you to take a message back to the people in Washington."

There it was again. Errand boy. But an interesting choice of words. Not to the president. Or the White House.

To the people in Washington.

"When I was a child," Czajkowski said, "one day my mother received a phone call. It lasted only a few seconds, but after she hung up she told me and my brother to get our coats. While we did, she grabbed some rope and a few cloth bags, then we headed into town. She took us to a local store where we found a big stack of toilet paper. Rolls and rolls of it on the floor. We had not seen so much toilet paper in a long time. She grabbed as many rolls as she could, threading the rope through the center, tying the ends, and draping them around my and my brother's necks. She was hurrying as fast as she could, before others arrived. Once that happened, it would not be long before all that toilet paper was gone. We called it hunting. Not shopping. Hunting. Because you never knew exactly what you'd bring home. Toilet paper was rare, Mr. Malone. A precious commodity. When it became available you had to secure all you could. We had a small bidet in our bathroom and, when we were fortunate enough to have running water, we could clean ourselves. If not?" The president paused. "I'll leave that to your imagination. That was life under the communists, where even toilet paper was rationed. That was Poland before 1990."

He could see the pain in the man's eyes as he remembered.

"Shortages were a way of life. Sometimes they were real, just a scarcity of goods. But most times, and this is important, most times they were engineered by the government as a means of control. You could not buy anything without ration cards. And you could only get ration cards if you registered your identity with the government. Later on, the shortages were blamed on Solidarity and their strikes, as a way to turn the people against the movement. But by then, we all knew the truth."

Which all had to have been horrible, and he sympathized. Still, "Why am I here?"

"An excellent question. Why *are* you here, in Kraków?"

"You know the answer."

"That's right, I do. You've come to gain your way into an auction, where you want to buy damaging information about me."

As sleazy as that sounded, the man was right. But there was a little more to it. "I'm here to help a friend."

Czajkowski appeared puzzled. "Who?"

"An old friend who's in a tight situation."

"Lucky for her she has you."

"Did I say it was a her?"

"No, you didn't."

"You're well informed."

"I try to be. And what of me, Mr. Malone? Do I pay the price for you helping your friend?"

"I suppose you would."

He hated saying it.

Czajkowski paced a moment. "I told you about the toilet paper so you would know that my parents were loyal to the government. But it was not out of any love or support. My parents were loyal out of fear. They realized something vitally important to surviving in the Poland of their day. A simple maxim. *The law is whatever the government says it is.* Not what is written. Not what is known. But what they *say* it is. Period. No discussion. No appeal. Many of their friends, who never realized that truth, disappeared in the night. Taken by the government. Gone. It happened all the time."

He could only imagine the horror that life had been.

"But I survived. And here I am, president of the nation."

"Why am I here?" he asked again.

"I thought that was obvious. I don't want you to complete your mission."

"Which apparently has been severely compromised. I'm curious. How did you know where to find me?"

"That's easy," a new voice said.

He turned back toward the altar and saw a man enter the nave.

"I told him," Tom Bunch said.

CHAPTER TWENTY-THREE

JONTY WAS TROUBLED BY THE CELL PHONE CALL, SINCE IT CAME from the one man he'd been hoping to avoid. With no choice, he'd left the castle with Vic, driving south to Košice, Slovakia's second largest city.

The town was a gem. Its main street lined by colorful burgher houses and palaces, the cobbled square one of Slovakia's most beautiful, dominated by the Cathedral of St. Elisabeth. The caller had requested a face-to-face meeting, instructing that they connect at a hotel just off the square.

He entered the building and headed for a small restaurant. Vic waited in the lobby to make sure that there were no more surprises. The man he sought sat at a table alone, the café a dim, inside room with no windows.

He stared at Augustus "Eli" Reinhardt V.

What a name. Sounded like a crown prince. He lived, of all places, in Liechtenstein, a tiny principality landlocked in Central Europe, squished between Switzerland and Austria. It had one of the highest gross domestic product per person ratios in the world, its claim to fame as a tax haven for rich people.

Like Reinhardt.

His competitor was in his early sixties but looked younger, an utterly punctilious individual with a clipped mustache and a knife-edge crease in his trousers. He wore a pressed blazer over a starched white shirt with no tie. Jonty's well-trained nose caught the waft of expensive blue tobacco mixed with sweet cologne. A Montblanc pen rested in the shirt pocket, and he noticed the distinctive top. A 1998 Edgar Allan Poe Writers Edition. Midnight-blue marble resin base with gold-plated mountings and a gold nib. Eighteen karat, if he wasn't mistaken. A collector's piece, worth several thousand dollars. And this guy carried it around like a cheap ballpoint.

Reinhardt stood as he approached the table. They gazed at each other with open curiosity—gauging, judging, wondering—before each cautiously offered a hand to shake. They'd only actually come face-to-face about a dozen times over the past decade. None of those encounters particularly pleasant.

"So good of you to come, Jonty. And on such short notice."

The tone was soft and polite.

"Was there an option?" he asked.

"Oh, let's not look at it that way. That seems so coercive. Please, have a seat. Would you like anything to drink?"

He waved off the offer. "Get to the point, Eli."

They both sat.

"I want in."

Those were the three words he'd most dreaded.

There were, perhaps, half a dozen legitimate information brokers in the world, including himself and Reinhardt. If they were ranked, he liked to think of himself as the best, with Eli a distant second. Of course, the man sitting across from him would have a different opinion. Regardless, Reinhardt knew the business, and clearly possessed some excellent intel as to what was about to happen. But he decided to stay coy nonetheless.

"In on what?"

Reinhardt reached down to the floor and brought up a small leather case. He unzipped the top and removed a battered iron spike a few centimeters long. "I had this stolen from the Chapel of the Holy Nail in Bamberg Cathedral last night. The reliquary there is now empty. They are really quite careless in how it's displayed. Just sitting out in the open, waiting for someone to take it. I believe they have closed the chapel for . . . renovations."

So much for hoping this was all a bluff.

"You were counting on the Germans stealing this spike, then responding to your invitation. That won't be happening. They opted not to participate in your auction and graciously allowed me the opportunity to take their place."

"And why would they do that?"

"Because I supplied them with some information that they desperately wanted. In return, they provided me with information on your auction."

"They don't want to participate?"

Reinhardt replaced the Nail into the leather bag. "They have greater interests, at the moment. So they were more than willing to offer their spot to me."

"Proxies aren't allowed."

"I'm not a proxy. I'm taking their place."

"This is my deal, Eli. Not yours. Leave it alone."

"It *was* your deal. Now it's *our* deal."

This couldn't be happening.

Everything he'd planned depended on motivations. He'd chosen the seven participants with great care, intent on playing one off the other. The U.S. and Russia were simple. Opposite sides to the same coin. Iran was with Russia, since they would be the target of any missiles. China and North Korea had been included since each wanted leverage on both Russia and the United States. That left Germany and France. Both had previously opposed any missiles in Europe and both were now engaged in open political conflict with the United States. The new American president had gone out of his way to antagonize them. Relations among the three nations had turned frosty, with a trade war looming. He assumed that having something to bargain with would be a good thing for either government, enough that they'd be willing to pay. Not as much as the others, but enough to help drive the price higher.

"How is this now *our* deal?" he asked.

"We'll get to that. First, I sent a man to check on you. His name is Art Munoz. He disappeared. Do you, by chance, have him?"

"I do."

Reinhardt pointed. "You're a clever one, Jonty. As is Vic DiGenti. I told Munoz to be careful. I assumed you took him. That's why I decided to come in person."

"Please, Eli. I'm asking as a colleague that you leave this alone. It's my deal and mine alone."

Reinhardt had interfered before, undercutting his arrangements with potential clients, selling information cheaper, even sabotaging three deals that he knew about. Given the clandestine nature of their business, a certain amount of aggressive competition was to be expected, but Reinhardt had a habit of taking it to an extreme. Jonty had tolerated the prior interference since there was plenty for everyone. But this was different.

"I'll admit, when I first heard of your auction, I was jealous," Reinhardt said. "Quite a thing you managed to orchestrate. Bold. Unique. The potential for an enormous profit. But it's shortsighted, Jonty."

"How so?"

Reinhardt sat back in his chair. "My German friends alerted me to something you apparently do not know."

Now he was intrigued.

"Ever heard of the *Spiżarnia*? It's Polish for 'the pantry.'"

"I have no idea what that is."

"Then today is a good day for you, Jonty. Like Christmas in June." Augustus "Eli" Reinhardt V's lips broke into a big smile. "I've come bearing gifts, my friend. Gifts that will make us both quite wealthy."

CHAPTER
TWENTY-FOUR

COTTON HELD HIS TEMPER AS TOM BUNCH MARCHED DOWN THE center aisle, as if headed for a coronation.

"You set me up?"

The annoying little creature shrugged. "It had to be done."

He'd deal with this imbecile later. Right now he had the president of Poland to contend with.

"A short while ago I spoke with President Fox," Czajkowski said. "I explained to him I do not want American missiles based here. I told him I would never approve such a measure. I asked him politely not to force the issue. Do you know what he said to me?"

He could only imagine.

"He told me that he fully understood my reservations and that he would not pressure me."

A surprising comment, considering what had been said by Bunch in Bruges.

"President Fox also informed me that you were headed to Kraków and told me the rendezvous point."

"Which I provided to President Fox," Bunch added.

"That's how we knew to be in the cloth market at booth 135," Czajkowski said. "I told President Fox that we would deal with you. He had no problem with that, and his personal envoy has been of great assistance."

Bunch pointed. "Poland has been informed that you are working independently, for a division within the Justice Department that has no authority to be here. That division, the Magellan Billet, has embarrassed the United States with its unauthorized actions relative to any supposed auction of information. The White House was unaware of all this, until today. Once we learned of the situation, we intervened to stop what's happening."

He sucked a few deep breaths and kept his cool at Bunch's lie.

"And the auction?" he calmly asked.

"America will not be participating," Bunch said. "That's not the way we do things. Of course, the people who sent you think differently. But we'll deal with them shortly."

Doubt and suspicion surrounded him like an aura.

Everybody here was lying to one another.

"Are you satisfied with those assurances?" he asked Czajkowski.

"I am. President Fox was emphatic and apologetic. He told me he will be withdrawing his missile proposal within the next forty-eight hours. He asked for a little time to deal with his military, who want those weapons here. I understood that reservation and agreed to that time."

Forty-eight hours? Past the auction. Just enough time to rock this man to sleep.

"Where's Stephanie?" he asked Bunch.

"On her way back to the United States. She'll be fired tomorrow, since she's the one who sent you here, unauthorized. We've given President Czajkowski our personal assurance that she will no longer be a part of the American intelligence community, in any way whatsoever."

Two birds with one stone? Absolutely. Not only were they lying to a head of state, but they were going to sacrifice Stephanie to prove the point. That way Fox got everything he'd wanted on Inauguration Day. No Stephanie. No Magellan Billet.

"That auction will go on, with or without the United States," Cotton said.

"That's true, and we will deal with that," Czajkowski said. "It is a Polish matter, for our resolution. But thankfully, the value of the information being offered for sale will be greatly diminished with America's withdrawal. I'm grateful to Mr. Bunch and to President Fox for making that happen."

He knew little to nothing about Czajkowski. But anyone who managed to win a national election, especially one in volatile Poland, could not be as naïve as Bunch and Fox thought him to be. Especially with someone as smart as Ivona Novak working for him. Cotton realized that Czajkowski might be playing along in this game, his acquiescence all a façade. But Tom Bunch's face and squinty eyes telegraphed that he believed the Poles had been placated.

"What now?" he asked.

"You're going back to Denmark," Bunch said. "I'll personally escort you. Hopefully, our friends here in Poland will forgive this transgression and we all will move on."

"I have assured President Fox," Czajkowski said, "that all will be forgiven. I appreciate his candor and discretion in this matter of the auction, and his decision to not pressure Poland on the missiles."

"He's a great guy," Cotton said, his sarcasm evident. "What a pal."

Bunch frowned. "I apologize, Mr. President. This man does not know his place, or how to show proper respect. We'll leave you now, with the United States' sincere thanks for your understanding."

CZAJKOWSKI STOOD IN THE CHURCH AND WATCHED AS TOM BUNCH and Cotton Malone disappeared out the main doors, which one of the robed brothers closed as he left, too.

"What do you think?" he called out.

"I think Bunch is a terrible liar," Ivona said.

She'd been secluded inside one of the confessionals, out of sight, but able to hear everything.

She stepped out.

"As is the president of the United States," Czajkowski said. "No better than the damn communists."

"Cotton is being used. He won't like that. It's not his nature."

He was curious. "How well do you know Malone?"

She grinned, her teeth like a row of pearls. "Are you jealous?"

"Should I be?"

"It was a long time ago. Before you."

He stepped close and took her into his arms, kissing her softly on the lips. "I just might be a little jealous."

"That's something new from you. I like it."

"I need you on this," he whispered to her. "You're the only one I can trust."

"I'm the only one you have."

That was true. His wife would be the last person he'd involve. And there was no way he would recruit Michał Zima and the BOR, beyond what he'd already had them do. Too many people to trust with too much that could go wrong.

He and Ivona had carried on a private relationship for over a year, one that had grown increasingly close. He loved her flashing wit, quick apprehension, and genuine affection. She was a smart, dynamic woman who challenged him in every way. He understood he had no right to demand anything from her, given he was still married, but she'd knowingly offered her love and emotions. She was regarded as the AW's best operative, her abilities and discretion never in question. Nor was her loyalty. If he didn't know better, he'd swear she loved him.

"What will they do?" he asked, still holding her.

"Bunch thinks you're satisfied. A personal assurance from the president of the United States is enough to calm your fears. So he'll have Cotton go after the relic tonight."

There was only one relic left to claim. With Malone in Kraków, America's ticket into the auction had to be the Spear of Saint Maurice.

"The Russians still don't know the auction location," she said. "It will take place tomorrow and their two representatives are en route. But it appears to be a roundabout method. A stopgap location. They're headed for Bratislava, told they'll be transported elsewhere tomorrow. If America is going to get in, Cotton has to move fast."

Czajkowski had known from the start that his options were limited. The Polish constitution provided no directly elected presidential line of succession. If the president died or resigned, then the marshal of Parliament became acting president for sixty days until elections were called. The current marshal was a weak and ineffective man, the type of leader Poland spawned all too often, ones who sought far too much outside help to make themselves strong. That had never worked before, and would not now. If a resignation was forced, his immediate successor would do exactly what Fox wanted, no question. Once done, it would be hard to undo. So anyone who came after that might continue to placate Washington. That meant he had to deal with the problem here and now.

But his past stood in the way.

"How do you know Malone will still steal the spear?"

"Because of Stephanie Nelle. He's loyal to her. He'll do whatever is necessary to protect her. That's his nature. Like he said, he's here to help a friend."

"You sound like you admire him."

"I do. Men like that are a rarity."

"Should I be insulted?"

"Not at all. You're at the head of that rare list. Poland is fortunate to have you as its president. We need to keep you there." She paused. "Whatever it takes."

He smiled at her confidence. "What will you do?"

"Our Russian associates were forthcoming in Bruges to get my help with Cotton. But they've told me little since. They don't want us anywhere near that auction."

"But we need to be there."

"And Cotton is our way in. So I'll be there, tonight. Waiting for him."

CHAPTER TWENTY-FIVE

JONTY COULD NOT DECIDE IF ELI WAS BEING SERIOUS OR WORKING him. His competitor had the resources to learn whatever he wanted, definitely comparable to his own, along with the nerve to explore dark corners where others might hesitate to tread. Eli being here, in Slovakia, was proof positive of that. But was this offer simply more drama?

"What are you talking about, Eli? What kind of gifts do you have?"

"The *Spiżarnia*. I learned about it from my friends in the German government. It was a precautionary measure, taken by Moscow, in the 1990s, when Soviet rule ended and the Polish republic reemerged."

"A precautionary measure against what?"

"Hypocrisy, I'm told."

An odd reply. But he could see that Eli was enjoying himself.

"Jonty, you have incriminating information on one man. The current president of Poland. Information that relates back to his time as a young Solidarity worker. It clearly has blackmail value. But imagine if you had that same kind of information on other people, many of whom, like Czajkowski, have risen to positions of influence. Some in government. Some in private industry. How much would the Americans pay for that? Or the Russians? How much would the people involved pay for it to stay secret? The Pantry offers us an opportunity to find out."

Now he was curious. "What is it?"

"Not so fast. I came here to make a deal. And contrary to what you might think, I actually want to make a fair deal."

He doubted that, but he was listening.

"You have something you want to auction," Reinhardt said. "Do it. Keep whatever you derive from the sale. Then auction off what I have, and I keep whatever is derived from that. A two-in-one event, so to speak. I just want the opportunity for your buyers to bid on what I have."

"I conduct both sales?"

"Absolutely. No need to interject any element of confusion. I'm sure you've invited ready, willing, and able buyers. All governments, I assume. Now you have an additional item to sell. Lucky for us, these buyers have unlimited resources."

As much as he hated to admit it, the proposal sounded reasonable. But he still wanted to know "What is it you have?"

"Let's be candid, Jonty. I could ruin your entire sale. The whole thing depends on secrecy. I wonder, were the Poles invited? I wouldn't think so. I would not have, if I were in your shoes. So I wonder what a call to Warsaw would accomplish?"

He kept his face stoic. But the threat worked. "Okay, Eli. I under stand. You can wreck the whole thing, and that potential gives your presence here value. So I'm listening."

"And if you are thinking about secreting me away with Art Munoz, know that if I don't call in every three hours, contact will be made to Warsaw by some associates I've employed."

He doubted that was a bluff. A wise precaution. One he himself would have taken, if the roles were reversed. "Okay, we have a deal. What's your gift?"

Reinhardt smiled at his success. "Toward the end of Soviet domination, around 1991 is the best guess, the Służba Bezpieczeństwa hid away a huge cache of documents. By then the SB had amassed thousands of informants, many of whom had risen to high positions within Solidarity and the emerging political parties of the time. Some of them volunteered to be spies, others did it for money, others were coerced or blackmailed. Many had no idea they'd been classified as informants—their information came to SB headquarters via a friend, colleague, or family member who'd turned collaborator and sold them out. As insurance, perhaps something to be used in the future, the SB hid away documents relative to those informants. The place where they are stored is called the *Spiżarnia*."

His mind raced.

He knew that Poland had, for years, dealt with the lingering pain of both Nazi and communist rule. The Institute of National Remembrance and the Commission for the Prosecution of Crimes Against the Polish Nation had been around for decades, amassing a huge archive of information that had been used in prosecutions. Most of that happened in the 1990s, in the years right after the Soviet collapse. Never, though, had any great stash of Soviet-era documents been discovered. Most of the revelations trickled in from old government warehouses, offices, and private stashes. He'd managed to stumble onto a stack of 147 pages that dealt with a young Solidarity activist named Janusz Czajkowski. A former SB major had kept a trove of documents from his time in government. That man was long dead, but his son had recently tried to find a buyer. A friend, whom Jonty had done business with before, learned of the effort and five hundred thousand zlotys had completed the sale. He'd originally planned to hold on to the information and explore ways to maximize its value. Then the United States announced a renewed effort to locate missiles in Poland.

Perfect.

Exactly what he'd needed.

The barely meaningful became vitally important.

Now this. A partner.

Something new to the mix.

"What does the Pantry contain?" he asked.

"My German friends speculate that the documents detail thousands of names of people who acted as Soviet informants. Probably reports, correspondence, affidavits, all sorts of information, stored away for safe-keeping."

"Has someone seen this cache?"

Eli shook his head. "The Germans never went after it, and it was largely forgotten until they received your invitation. Fortunately for me I was in the midst of another deal with them. Something of much greater importance, from their standpoint. So we modified the terms to include their invitation to your auction and this lost cache, both of which are now mine."

A thousand questions raced through his brain. But one overcame all the others. "That was quite generous of them."

"I assure you, what I provided to them was worth far more."

That was saying a lot. Maybe even too much. "Are you sure this cache is real?"

Reinhardt sat back in his chair. "That's the thing, Jonty. I'm not. My friends in Berlin were clear. None of this has been verified."

"You made a deal on something that might not even exist?"

Reinhardt smiled. "Your auction is real. I reasoned that, at a minimum, I could extract a payment from you not to interfere with that."

He was cornered and did not like it.

"We need to find out if the Pantry is real," Reinhardt said.

"What do you propose?"

"That we have a look."

He hated that word *we*. This was his sale. His venture. But his choices seemed limited. Reinhardt could surely disrupt things. And why not? He had zero to lose. So he did what he did best and made a bargain. "I want a cut of whatever you receive on your portion of the deal."

Reinhardt grinned. "How much?"

"Twenty percent."

"That's quite a cut."

"I have expenses on the auction that you would need to contribute toward. A lot of money has been spent on privacy and security. Which raises a point. How did you find me?"

"Once the Germans showed me your invitation, I sent men out to track you down. I know your haunts, as you probably know mine. When Munoz disappeared, I assumed I'd found you."

"And how did you know how to call me?"

Reinhardt smiled. "It wasn't all that hard. Like you, I have friends with capabilities. You left a contact number with the agency that handles Sturney Castle. It's the only fortress like it, available for rent, in Slovakia. Lots of privacy."

He cursed himself for being so careless. If he'd made that big a mistake with Eli, what others had he made? Were some of the potential buyers closing in? Had the auction site been compromised? Thank goodness last night he'd taken those final precautions. Then a frightening thought occurred to him. "You followed me last night, didn't you?"

Eli nodded again. "And when you drove north to Kraków, then to Wieliczka, my heart leaped."

He waited.

"The Pantry is hidden away inside that salt mine."

CHAPTER
TWENTY-SIX

COTTON KEPT HIS MOUTH SHUT AND HIS TEMPER IN CHECK UNTIL he and Bunch were in a car, alone, driving away from the monastery, Bunch behind the wheel.

"That should buy you some time," Bunch finally said. "The president himself told Czajkowski that we were backing off, that there'd be no American presence at the auction. Him hearing that directly should do the trick."

"So Fox flat-out lied to a head of state?"

Bunch waved off the accusation. "He merely misdirected him. I simply reinforced that misdirection."

He shook his head. "Both of you are idiots."

"That's the president of the United States you're talking about."

"Yeah. That's the scary part."

They were on a two-laned highway, paralleling the River Wisła, headed back toward Kraków.

"You should have a clear path to the spear now," Bunch said.

"Tom. Can I call you Tom?" He didn't wait for a reply. "I make it a point not to say things I might regret later. Especially to people who work for the White House. But with you, I'll make an exception. How about you go f—"

Bunch pointed at his cell phone.

Odd.

It rested in the center console between their seats.

He'd already noticed it, but had not paid much attention. He lifted the unit and saw that it was on a live call, the setting to SPEAKER.

"Mr. President," Bunch said. "Malone knows you're listening."

He shook his head. This was beyond belief.

"It's good to know what you really think of me," Fox said.

"I didn't know that was a secret, given our first encounter. You apparently didn't learn a thing from almost being blown up?"

"I actually did. I learned that I want my own people handling things. No more of Danny Daniels' leftovers."

"Your people are incompetent."

"As am I?"

He had zero intention of backing down. "You're at the head of the line."

Bunch's face carried a smug grin, clearly pleased with the disrespect being shown.

"Ordinarily, Cotton—I can call you that, right?" Fox said through the phone. "I'd just tell Tom to fire you, hang up, and move on. We can hire other people. But you're there, on the ground, ready to go, and time is really short. We only have until midnight to steal that spear."

"The only reason I might is so I can shove it—"

"Cotton," Fox said, interrupting. "Just steal the spear. Then I want you and Tom to go to the auction and buy whatever information Jonty Olivier is selling."

These two were bold SOBs. He'd give them that.

"I was elected president," Fox said, "because I had the balls to go out and ask people to vote for me. I think big. The problem with most people is they don't think big. They're afraid to think big. So they latch on to people, like me, who think big. I'm not scared to win. I like to win. I do what I have to do in order to win."

"I don't really give a crap," Cotton said to the phone. "I don't have a dog in this fight."

"Except for the $150,000 Stephanie Nelle promised you."

"I can live without it."

Fox chuckled. "I'm sure you can. But I want those missiles in Poland

and if you don't help me out, I'm going to do what I told President Czaj-kowski I would do. I'll fire Stephanie Nelle and the Magellan Billet will be disbanded. All of the American intelligence divisions will be told not to hire her. She will be persona non grata. If anyone in the private sec-tor wants to hire her, she won't receive any positive references from this administration. Quite the contrary, in fact. Her career choices will be limited to going to work for one of my enemies."

He hated bullies. And that's exactly what he was dealing with. And the best way to handle bullies was to get right in their face because, at their core, they were cowards. Right now, though, he had little to nothing to bargain with.

But if he had the spear?

They were beginning to enter Kraków's outer suburbs, coming in from the west, and ahead across the river he spotted Wawel Castle. Its tawny defensive walls rose nearly a hundred feet above the water, at once mas-sive and slender, topped by domes and towers. The seat of Polish kings for more than a millennium, though now only their tombs remained. It was both a museum storing precious objects and a work of art itself.

The symbol of Poland.

And where the Spear of St. Maurice waited.

His best bargaining chip.

"Did you hear me, Malone?" President Fox said.

"You really are a prick."

"Like I care what you think. If I wanted a conscience, I'd buy one. What I want is those missiles in Poland. More important, I want Russia to know that the days of rolling over the United States are through."

"I think Danny Daniels might disagree with your assessment of his eight years in office."

"I'm sure he would, but I'm going to do what it takes to get the job done."

"When you mess with Stephanie, you'll be messing with Daniels."

"I doubt the junior senator from Tennessee could do much to harm me."

No sense arguing with a fool who clearly underestimated his oppo-nents.

"Just steal the spear, Malone, and win that auction."

"And if I do, what happens to Stephanie?"

"Not a thing."

"You do know that you're not the most trustworthy person."

"I'm all you have. Take it or leave it."

Normally, he'd leave it. But two factors urged otherwise. One, he did not want Stephanie to experience the misery Fox would enjoy heaping on her. And two? Janusz Czajkowski was not the fool he wanted people to think he was. The U.S. announces a missile initiative then, because Poland simply doesn't want it, they reverse course? That might happen, as it did years ago, when a bunch of time had passed so everyone could save face. But not this quick. Not by a long shot. Czajkowski was up to something, too, in playing along. And he suspected what that might be. But neither the moron driving the car nor the one on the phone had a clue.

Which almost made him smile.

"Do you have any assistance from American intelligence on this operation?" he asked Fox.

"Only the great Stephanie Nelle and her wonderful Magellan Billet."

"Besides that."

"That's all. This is a White House–based initiative, everything held close."

As he suspected.

Which clinched the deal.

"I'll get the spear," he said.

He was driven back near the cloth market, Bunch leaving and providing a cell phone number for contact. He walked to where his own vehicle was parked and called Stephanie, reporting all that had happened.

"I should resign," she said. "I can't work for these people."

"I hate that I'm even about to say this, since it's not my problem. But if we walk away, America could be in real trouble. The Russians are heavy into this, along with the Poles, and they're not fooling around. This could take a bad bounce."

"I agree. I've had an awful feeling from the start. I can't tell you how relieved I was when they told me you were in Bruges."

That was about as close to warm and fuzzy as she would ever get, and he appreciated the sentiment.

"I'll get the spear," he said. "Then we'll decide what's next for both you and the country."

"I'm in Warsaw, at the embassy. But I'm headed south for the consulate in Kraków. I'll be there in a few hours."

He'd assumed she hadn't left, or had even been ordered away. "I'm going to do a little recon, then handle things tonight. The info you've already provided was helpful."

"You think the Poles will be waiting for you?"

He'd told her his hunch. "There's no doubt in my mind."

"Then why go?"

"Because they need me to do it, too."

CHAPTER
TWENTY-SEVEN

JONTY ARRIVED BACK AT THE CASTLE, STILL SHAKEN BY THE MEET-
ing. He could not decide if Reinhardt was being truthful or merely pos-
turing, trying to edge his way into a deal that he had no part in making.
Prior to obtaining the evidence on Janusz Czajkowski he'd done some
extensive research, all designed to ascertain if what he'd been offered was
real.

That was where he'd come across what happened to Lech Wałęsa.

An electrician in the Gdańsk Shipyard, working long hours for
little pay like everyone else, Wałęsa became a trade union advocate
and one of the co-founders of Solidarity. Images of his mustachioed
face, being borne aloft by workers, became an inspiration for anti-
communist movements across the Soviet bloc. He was arrested many
times and imprisoned, but eventually led the charge to end communist
rule, winning the Nobel Peace Prize. But he did not travel to Oslo to
get it, fearing he would not be allowed back in the country. He was the
first to be elected to the renewed position of president of Poland. But
his popularity waned, and he was defeated for reelection in 1995 after
only one term.

Charges of collaboration had long dogged Wałęsa.

Two hundred and seventy-nine pages of documents eventually surfaced, all from the widow of a former communist interior minister,

who'd tried to sell them. The similarities with what was happening here, with Czajkowski, were frightening. The difference being that Wałęsa's dirt went public. The Institute of National Remembrance studied it in detail, hiring experts who concluded that the documents were authentic. The story they told was of a Wałęsa who led protests and strikes that shook communist rule in the 1980s, but had also apparently been a paid informant for the secret police in the 1970s. Wałęsa claimed fraud, saying they were created by the government to discredit him. A valid charge, considering the parties involved, and a court exonerated him.

Questions remained, though.

The issue of collaboration recurred when the conservative Law and Justice party, run by a former anti-communist activist, an enemy of Wałęsa's, assumed power. Eventually, Wałęsa admitted signing a commitment to inform for the SB, but denied ever fulfilling it. There were at least thirty reports bearing the signature of "Bolek," the code name assigned to Wałęsa, all deemed authentic. In addition, there were cash receipts for payments to him that also bore his verified signature.

Quite the PR disaster for a legend.

One Wałęsa never really recovered from.

Enough, Jonty had hoped, to scare Czajkowski into not tempting fate, making him willing to do whatever the holder of the information on him might want.

He entered the castle and told Vic, "Let the man in the basement go." He'd already explained on the drive back what had happened inside the restaurant. "We need to go back to the mine. Eli included. Can you arrange it?"

Vic nodded.

"Please do it fast. I want this matter resolved in the next few hours."

He'd made a deal with Reinhardt on the condition that the cache still existed and was marketable. If so, there'd be a joint auction. If not, he'd agreed to pay twenty million euros for his competition to stay out of the way. The Arma Christi should bring that amount. The rest from the auction would be all his. He had not liked making the deal, but there was plenty of money to go around, so he decided to spend what it took to keep Reinhardt at bay. Of course, if the cache was there, and relevant, many more millions could be made.

By them both.

So what did he have to lose by taking a look?

CZAJKOWSKI SAT INSIDE THE ROYAL WAWEL SUITE AT THE SHERATON Grand Kraków. The hotel, a modern precast-concrete-and-steel structure, faced the River Wisła, within the shadow of Wawel Castle, displayed in all its glory beyond the room's east windows. He'd decided to stay over for the night to be close to what was about to happen, the move camouflaged by a meeting arranged with local officials, many of whom had been clamoring for a moment of his time. He'd managed to contain his anger with both President Fox and Tom Bunch. Both were treating him like a fool and Poland like a second-rate nation.

Which was nothing new.

Kings, queens, emperors, and premiers had been doing the same thing for centuries. But not this time. Ivona would make sure that would not happen.

How lucky he was to have her.

But he had to be careful. Poland remained a deeply Catholic country. While divorce was legal, the church frowned on it. Separations, though, were tolerated. But neither would be acceptable for the president of the country, and open adultery would be politically fatal.

What was the only legal grounds for divorce?

The irretrievable and complete disintegration of matrimonial life.

Along with a lack of any spiritual, physical, or economic bonds.

Which all applied to his marriage.

Thankfully, there were no children involved. His wife had steadfastly refused to have any, making that clear from the start. So he could not complain. But he'd be as big a liar as the Americans if he said that he did not regret that decision. Instead, the nation had become his child. He'd dedicated himself to Poland. Nearly forty million people depended on him making the right decisions. And he was not going to let them down.

His cell phone rang and he was glad to see it was Ivona.

"Where are you?" he asked her.

"Making preparations."

Back at the monastery she'd explained her plan and how she intended to deal with Cotton Malone. He'd sensed there was a history between them and, for a moment, he had been jealous. He'd not felt that emotion in a long time. It had actually felt good. Made him alive once again. He realized he had no right to be jealous about anything that had happened prior to their relationship. It was none of his business. But it still bothered him. He loved Ivona, and he firmly believed she felt the same. She was doing everything she could to help him, and he appreciated that more than she would ever know.

Or maybe she might.

"Thank you for doing this," he felt compelled to say.

"My pleasure, Mr. President."

He loved it when she called him that.

"I'll expect a more proper thank-you, though, in person," she noted.

He chuckled. "And I'll be more than happy to supply that."

"First, I have to deal with an old adversary. He's good. Really good. So this has to be done with precision."

"We only have one chance."

"I agree. And I intend to make it count."

CHAPTER
TWENTY-EIGHT

COTTON GLANCED UP AT WAWEL CASTLE. HE STOOD ON A BUSY sidewalk, facing the fortress's east wing, the golden-stone walls rising nearly a hundred feet to a steeply pitched roof. The exterior seemed a carefully choreographed collection of galleries, piers, columns, and balconies. Many called it the Polish Acropolis, towering over Kraków, once the seat of secular and ecclesiastical power. On the upper floor he spotted a columned loggia that, according to the information he'd been provided, led to where the Spear of St. Maurice was currently being stored.

Ordinarily, the spear was kept on permanent display within the John Paul II Cathedral Museum, located just inside the castle's main gates. The museum housed one of the most valuable collections of art and artifacts in Poland. Hundreds of thousands of people visited every year. So many that the building had been closed for the past few months, undergoing an extensive renovation, its treasures stored away for safekeeping in several different locations. The spear had been moved inside the castle, currently locked away with a few other valuables in an upper-floor room, the windows of which he was now studying from ground level.

The time was approaching 5:00 P.M. Whoever had performed the recon for Stephanie had learned a wealth of excellent information. The castle itself was open for another twenty minutes. What was once the bakery and infirmary, a building fronting the inner courtyard, had long ago been converted into administrative offices. An interior door from that building led into the castle, for staff use only. It was locked but not impenetrable. Guards patrolled all of the floors at intervals and there were cameras, but not that many. The recon report advised that they were avoidable, if one was careful.

A photocopy of the second-floor layout had also been provided. It appeared to have come from a book on the castle, the entrance from the administrative offices circled along with the room where the spear was stored, near what was known as the loggia atop the Danish Tower. To get from one to the other meant navigating a dozen rooms along the north wing before turning into the east side of the building. That made for lots of opportunities to be discovered, but the intel advised that if he stayed to the interior side walls he could avoid all three cameras along the way.

He crossed the street and made his way up Wawel Hill along a brick-enclosed passage to a massive Renaissance gate. Humanity wheezed and murmured all around, more people flowing out than in, as the site was preparing to end another day.

He bypassed the exiting tourists and entered the castle grounds. The cathedral museum rose to his right, its entrance barred by a rope barrier and a sign noting the building was closed. The cathedral stood to his left, few people moving in and out its iron gate. He'd bought a ball cap in town, which was now firmly planted on his head and should help with anonymity. The recon report noted that there were cameras all across the exterior of the buildings. He had to assume the Poles were watching, so he needed to move fast.

He angled left, toward the administrative building. A manicured lawn spread out between the buildings within the inner sanctum. Towers were everywhere, offering excellent vantage points. They all had names. Labels like Sigismund, Thieves, Bell, Senators', Danish, and Hens. A large legend of the castle grounds, framed from the elements, stood off to the right. Visitors were studying the map. He took a moment and gave it a glance, too, noting the local geography, keeping a watch on the double doors. A crowd walked past and he used them for cover as he approached and slipped inside the admin building, which had not been locked for the day. Inside were offices. Whoever prepped this mission had provided a rough sketch of the corridors, showing exactly where he needed to go.

Being a field agent entailed doing things that most people shied away from. Like trespassing and breaking and entering. He'd grown accustomed to those violations as a means to get the job done. But they represented a path, he'd had to remind himself, that was no longer readily available now that he was retired.

An inner staircase led up, which he avoided. Instead, he followed a whitewashed corridor and turned right. A carpet runner lined the stone floor, and closed doors at periodic intervals on both sides led into offices. No cameras here. Nothing to steal. This was a workplace. He followed the drawing etched into his memory and found a vestibule, where a wide stone staircase led up at right angles.

At the top of the first rung of risers a small wooden door, encased within a stone frame, led from this building into the castle. He climbed to the landing and noticed that the entryway was protected by two locks. One was a simple keyed tumbler, easy to pick, the other a piece of braided wire threaded through two holders, one on the door, the other the jamb, the ends twisted together and sealed with a clamp. A simple and effective way to know if the door had been opened.

Now the hard part.

He had to disappear for a few hours.

He descended the stairs back to ground level.

The intel he'd reviewed offered little in the way of hiding places. He assumed there were people still in the building, though he hadn't seen anyone as yet. They would soon all be gone but for the guards. He could not just hang around in the halls. The vestibule before him was empty, save for a huge rosewood chifforobe. He walked over and opened it. Empty. The inside plenty large enough to accommodate him.

Why not?

He'd hidden in worse places.

He wiggled his way into the space and settled his spine against one of the side walls, his knees folded up but not all that uncomfortable. He'd be fine for a few hours. He closed the doors. Hopefully, no one would inspect inside.

He found his phone and made sure it was set to silent.

A text had come from Cassiopeia.

WHERE ARE YOU?

He knew she wasn't going to like the truth.

IN POLAND, HIDING INSIDE A CABINET, WAITING TO STEAL A 1000-YEAR-OLD ARTIFACT.

So he opted to not reply.

CHAPTER
TWENTY-NINE

JONTY WAS BACK INSIDE THE WIELICZKA SALT MINE. VIC HAD arranged for another special tour, this time for three people. Eli had supplied some of what he knew, and their guide had brought along another map that, hopefully, would lead them where they needed to go.

"This is an old drawing," Konrad said. "From when the communists ran this place."

They stood inside the magnificent Chapel of St. Kinga, a hundred meters underground. Twenty thousand tons of salt had been removed to create it. Thirty meters long, fifteen wide, nearly twenty tall, its floor spanned five hundred square meters of polished salt. One of the largest underground churches in the world, it was laid out in the late 19th century with loving devotion.

He admired its lavish decoration and iconography.

Once, when miners lived underground for weeks at a time, exchanging sunlight for lamps and candles, religion played a big part in their lives. Hymns accompanied their descent. They greeted each other with a reverent *God bless.* Eventually, to pass the time, some of them became artisans, carving in the salt, molding larger-than-life statues and dioramas scattered across the mine. Forty chapels were eventually created and, since the 17th century, Catholic services had been routinely held in many of them. St. Kinga's was the crown jewel. More a cathedral than chapel, decorated by five massive chandeliers made of elaborate salt crystals, numerous sculptures, and three-dimensional bas-reliefs of breathtaking detail, all inspired by New Testament themes, a tribute generations of the miner-sculptors left to their Christian faith.

Jonty studied the map.

Nazis occupied the mine during the war and tried to use it as an underground factory, employing slave labor. But the Soviet advance thwarted the effort. After the war the communists assumed control and kept possession until 1990. Then the new Polish republic took over and had operated it ever since.

"I've worked here for a number of years," Konrad said. "We've all been told stories of when the communists were in charge. We were still extracting salt then. I've heard that they also used this place as a storage facility. There's a huge chamber down on Level IX, in a part of the tunnels that's off limits. But I've seen it."

Eli seemed intent on what he was hearing.

"It's filled with wooden shelving," Konrad said. "The iron frames are all corroded, though. The salt has eaten them away. Why they used iron, I have no idea. It doesn't last down there." With his finger, Konrad traced a route on the map. "That chamber is here."

"How far down?" Eli asked.

"Over three hundred meters."

His competitor clearly was not pleased with that information. "You don't like closed spaces?"

"I don't like prisons," Eli said.

"You're welcome to wait here," Jonty said.

"I appreciate your concern for my comfort. But I'll suffer through it and come along."

"What are we after?" Konrad asked.

Jonty wanted to hear the answer to that question, too, as did Vic, who'd stood silent.

"A chamber named Warszawa," Eli said.

A puzzled look came to Konrad's face. "There is such a chamber. It's the grand ballroom, not far from here, where banquets, parties, and conferences are held. You can't mean that."

"This one would be secreted away."

"I know of lower-level chambers named Modena, Weimer, Florencja, Toskania, and other locations in Europe and Poland, but none named for Warsaw."

As before, they were each dressed in coveralls with a helmet and light, ready for a special tour. They'd descended from the Regis Shaft, then walked half a kilometer over in a Level II drift to the main tourist areas. Jonty had wondered about the change in procedure, as they usually descended straight to Level IX in the Regis Shaft elevator.

"Why did we come here?" he asked. "And not go directly to Level IX?"

Konrad pointed. "Because this map is for Level X."

He caught the look on Vic's face. He was thinking the same thing. "I didn't know there was anything that deep."

"It was opened in the 1950s, expanded in the 1960s, but closed in the mid-1970s."

He caught the significance of those dates. "All during the time of communist control."

Konrad nodded. "There's no elevator to that level. Only a wooden staircase, that's not in good shape, from Level IX. No tour groups are ever taken down there. The elevator to get us closest to that staircase is not far from here."

"How accurate is this map?" Vic asked.

"I have no idea. I know of a few miners who've been there. They say the tunnels are fairly clear, but there's a lot of water seepage. No maintenance has been done there in decades."

He caught the unspoken warning. Danger existed.

"We have no options," Jonty told Konrad. "We have to take a look."

"The good part is that there are only a few tunnels. Lots of offshoots, but only three main drifts. As you can see on the map, nothing is labeled. No names on anything. But that could be different down there."

Jonty stared at Eli. "Are you sure about this? It seems a lot of risk for something that could be pure fiction."

"We'll never know unless we look."

He stared around at the incredible church. Its pulpit at one end imitated Wawel Hill with its fortifications and dragon. The opposite end was dominated by a salt statue of John Paul II. A sign in several languages advised that this remained a living place of worship as mass was still said here every Sunday. Visitors were busy admiring everything.

He glanced at Vic, whose good sense and patience he'd come to rely upon. His associate had not been happy when told about the budding partnership with Eli Reinhardt. Nor had he been eager to release their prisoner, who was now waiting up at ground level in the car that had brought Reinhardt north into Poland. Their past experiences with Eli had all been competitive, but this deal was different in scope and magnitude. Hundreds of millions of euros were at stake. They were juggling the competing interests of seven sovereign nations, most of which cared little to nothing for the others. All seven possessed the resources to wreak havoc, if they so chose. Now another element had interjected itself. If the Pantry proved real, the potential could be enormous. If not, then this was a colossal waste of time and an unnecessary risk.

But what the hell.

He'd not become one of the world's most successful information brokers by being timid. Besides, Eli Reinhardt was coming with him, so both their asses were on the line.

"You're right," he said, motioning that they should leave. "There seems to be only one way to find out if we have something."

CHAPTER THIRTY

COTTON CHECKED HIS WATCH.

8:20 P.M.

He'd been inside the chifforobe almost three and a half hours, catching a little bit of rest, but staying alert in case there was any movement outside. So far, he'd heard nothing. All quiet. He could wait until later in the night, or the early-morning hours of tomorrow, but if his hunch proved correct the time of his visit would not matter.

His intel had noted that the castle was cleaned three nights a week, and this wasn't one of those nights. So there would be no janitorial staff about.

Was Ivona expecting him?

Probably.

And if she was here, what outcome did she want? Him to take the spear? Most likely. Why else play along with Fox and Bunch? Best guess? Their alliance with the Russians was tenuous at best. Sure, neither Russia nor Poland wanted missiles. But Poland would want the information being offered destroyed, while Russia would love to have it. For the future. Just in case. He realized that the Poles could not just give the spear to him. It was a national treasure. Too many questions would be raised. Ones with difficult answers. All of the other relics had been stolen. Their thefts suppressed. But the fact that something had happened where they were kept had made it to the media, and all of those relics were no longer on display. The same had to happen here, with a verified "incident," minus the actual theft, to report.

Time to get this party going.

He pushed open the chifforobe's door and climbed out. The exterior windows in the vestibule were darkened, signaling that night had begun to arrive. Only a few lights burned inside, illuminating the staircase that angled its way up to the next floors. Stephanie had thought ahead and left him two lock picks in the manila envelope he'd pocketed earlier. For a long time he used to carry them in his wallet, but he'd dropped the habit a while back. After all, his primary profession was now bookseller, and nothing in that job involved illegal breaking and entering.

He checked the corridors one last time. Empty. Before heading up the stairs he noticed a large 3-D model of the castle grounds that filled one side of the vestibule. He took a moment and examined the exterior layout, particularly the east façade, where the intel had said the spear was being stored in a top-floor outer room. He noticed the same columned loggia he'd spotted before entering the castle and the buttresses that helped keep the wall upright. A solitary exterior window, adjacent to the loggia, had to open into the room he sought.

He climbed the stone risers and approached the closed wooden door at the landing. A small metal plate read 122. He assumed with so many doors the only way to distinguish among them was to assign numbers. Before opening the lock he worked the braided wire that formed a seal on the door back and forth enough that heat snapped it. Then he picked the lock and freed the tumblers, turning the handle.

He stepped inside and quickly reclosed the door.

Before him stretched a dimly lit exhibit area, the space filled with glass cases displaying some fine Persian carpets, many stitched with blooming trees and fairy-tale animals. Others had lions, bears, gazelles, pheasants, and unicorns. He hustled toward the open portal in the far wall and entered another room displaying battle flags, swords, and saddles, all Turkish, surely acquired during the many invasions. He turned left, following the floor plan ingrained in his memory, seeing it as if it hung before his eyes. Through three more chambers he came to another stairway, which he bypassed, entering what was identified as the Senators' Hall, the walls decorated with figural tapestries, all with biblical themes.

And the first with a camera.

It hung in the corner to his right with a diagonal view of the checkerboard floor. Hard to know for sure how wide a lens it sported, but the intel recommended staying close to the south wall, the tricky part at the end, where another open doorway awaited.

He hustled forward, hugging the wall, moving sideways, staying as flat as possible. Ten feet from the end he sucked a breath and rushed through the doorway, disappearing on the other side to the left, using the wall for protection. If he was going to be spotted, this was the moment.

He hesitated and listened.

Footsteps were approaching from ahead. A steady click of leather heels on stone. He spotted a tall chair and sought refuge behind it, but the footsteps stopped before reaching him.

A door opened, then closed.

The footsteps faded.

Had to be a guard making rounds.

He held steady for a moment, then kept going, moving through the Eagle Room, the Bird Room, and ending up in the Battle of Orsha Room, each festooned with coats of arms, crossed swords, and dark-aged beams. An ethereal glow came from amber night-lights. Several had walls of cordovan and were decorated with period paintings, portraits, wall friezes, floral motifs, glazed ceramic stoves, sculptures, and heavy period furniture. Coffered ceilings stretched overhead with carved and gilt rosettes.

In the Orsha Room he spotted the double pedimented doors in the east wall that he'd been told were there. They should be unlocked, and he quickly discovered that was true. They led to a small anteroom atop what was known as the Danish Tower. The space was lined with faux-painted walls, the coffered ceiling gilded. There were a few inlaid chairs, a desk, a chest, and a large copper mirror. Two side tables were draped with a green wool cloth. Once it had surely been a small study that opened out to the columned loggia. A perfect place for a king to relax and enjoy some fresh air. A closed door led outside. Paintings dotted the walls, more stacked upright on the floor, five and six deep. Three heavy oak tables were covered with vases, clocks, statues, and busts. The room seemed to be doubling now as a storage chamber. He turned to the right and tried another door, one that he knew led to an even smaller space.

His destination.

Locked.

Damn.

That was not anticipated.

And the lock was not one he could pick. Old style, accepting only a skeleton key. The door itself was solid and opened inward, the hinges on the other side. No way to break it down.

Damn. Ivona was making him work for it.

He remembered the castle model.

He'd come this far. Finish it.

He opened the outer door that led onto the loggia and stepped into the night. Kraków stretched below, beyond the castle wall, people moving about on the sidewalks, cars in the street. The long side of the columned terrace was open air with pillared arches, its two ends closed. The night deepened by the minute, hopefully heading toward enough darkness to shield him for a few minutes. He climbed the railing and tested the small stone ledge that extended outward. Solid. He levered himself over and held on to the short wall, adjusting his balance and peering around the loggia's short side.

The window was there, just as on the model.

He glanced down. Maybe seventy-five to eighty feet to the ground. That fall would leave a mark, if not kill him. No way in hell Cassiopeia would ever be out here. She hated heights as much as he hated enclosed spaces.

He pressed against the ledge, hands high, searching for fingertip grips in the stone, and turned the corner. Thankfully the old castle was full of footholds, and he used the shallow ledge to move along, finally stopping at the window. Double-paneled, sixteen-paned, opening in the middle, to the inside. Not good. He pushed on the panels and felt a tiny give. He kept one arm on the sill, toes tucked into a crevice above the ledge, and pushed harder with the flat of his hand, hoping the panels might release.

No luck.

He spied the catch through the glass. He could not stay dangled out here much longer before someone on the street spotted him. Luckily, this side of the castle was not lit to the outside, all of the lighting confined to the picturesque north and west sides that faced the river.

He balled his fist and popped one of the panes hard, quickly withdrawing his hand. It cracked, but did not break. Two more blows and it shattered. Carefully, he reached in and freed the latch, swinging the sash inward, then he climbed in over the sill.

Wooden crates filled the small space wall-to-wall, each labeled in Polish and English. GILDED BOWL AND JUG. MONSTRANCE. CROSIER OF ADAM. CORONATION MANTLE. Precious artifacts from the cathedral museum, stored for safekeeping. Exactly as the intel stated. The fact that there were also English labels made him smile. Ivona knew he did not speak Polish. She'd thought ahead, as always. On another oak table sat several smaller wood boxes, each also labeled. FUNERARY OBJECTS OF BISHOP MAURUS. SARACEN-SICILIAN CASE. ZUCCHETTO AND SASH OF JOHN PAUL II.

Then, the jackpot.

SPEAR OF ST. MAURICE.

He lifted the pine box. About two feet long and six inches wide. Secured with screws. No way to open it and make sure it contained what he'd come for. But it was heavy.

Another good sign.

That it was here, right where the intel indicated, a better sign.

He cradled the box and hustled back the way he'd tried to come, through the locked door, which opened from his side, and back into the larger Battle of Orsha Room. An impressive frieze depicting the Polish victory over the Muscovites wrapped the room. Some tall portraits of important people dotted the walls. To the right was the route back to where he'd started. To the left was an open portal into the next room, another doorway farther down, then another, through all the rooms in succession, the doorways connected in an uninterrupted enfilade. A perfect line of sight from one end of the east wing to the other, nearly two hundred feet long. About halfway down he saw a black figure moving his way. One of the guards? In a flash of light, as the shadow moved from one room to another, he caught a face.

Ivona.

With a gun.

Up and level.

Aimed his way.

CHAPTER
THIRTY-ONE

JONTY DID NOT LIKE THE LOOK OF THE WOODEN STAIRCASE LEAD-
ing down into blackness. Konrad had led them off the main tourist routes
of Level III to an elevator used exclusively by the miners, where they'd
descended to Level IX. Not the same area they'd visited last night. That
was nearly a kilometer away. But the tunnels here were similar. They then
wound a path through them, following Konrad into one of the offshoots
where they found the old staircase.

"It doesn't appear it can handle our weight," Jonty said.

"Stay to the outside on the rungs and we should be fine. I'll go first."

Konrad began to descend. Slow and deliberate, hugging the interior
side where supports helped hold the load. Eli went next, Jonty followed,
with Vic assuming the rear. The wooden rungs were battered, the saw
marks still evident at their ends, many of the nailheads corroded away,
causing the risers to rattle loose. The only light came from their helmets,
the beams herky-jerky with their slow, cautious descent.

The staircase seemed to go forever at right angles down. It took a few
minutes to make it back to solid ground. Level X was a mess, the tunnel ahead littered with salt blocks, the walls and ceiling crystallized with
dripstones, more precipitated salt icing the walls and timbers.

"I told you this was dangerous," Konrad said. "If it's any comfort, we
haven't had a cave-in anywhere in decades."

That wasn't much solace. Added to the problem was the fact that no one above knew they were even here.

"Salt makes for a really good support," Konrad said as he found the map and studied it again. "This tunnel goes for about half a kilometer. There are several offshoots. We're going to have to explore them to see if there's a chamber named Warsaw."

Vic noticed something in the floor and bent down to examine it. "A rail line?"

Jonty also saw the iron embedded into the salt floor, mostly corroded away. He'd seen them before in the upper levels, but those were in much better condition.

"They installed tracks to haul out debris," Konrad said. "It's typical for the mine."

"But it also could have been used to haul things in," Eli noted.

Konrad nodded. "That's true. This level is unique. It was not opened by miners centuries ago. It's only fifty to sixty years old."

And not all that reinforced, Jonty noted.

Something else caught his eye.

It wasn't the gray-green salt rock that dominated. This was more crystallized, clear, with hints of yellow. He bent down and lifted a small chunk, examining it in his helmet light.

"The miners call it *szpak,*" Konrad said. "Starling, like the bird. It's fibrous salt and rare to find on the upper levels. Down here, it's common. When the miners' picks broke it, the pungent smell of sulfur leaked out. Quite a surprise to them. They thought themselves close to hell when that happened."

Jonty examined the chunk with his fingers, the crystals sparkling in his lamp.

"Go ahead," Konrad said. "Keep it. I do, when I find some of it."

Jonty grinned and pocketed the small rock.

They crept ahead, negotiating the debris, heading deeper into the drift. The tunnel width and height were less than on Level IX, but the ventilation seemed the same. And for that he was grateful.

Konrad stopped the parade, his headlight focused on one of the white signs common in the levels above. This one not affixed to the wall, but propped on the floor at a junction with one of the offshoots.

TARNÓW.

A city in southeastern Poland.

"We need to check these offshoots," Konrad said. "There's one here, and another farther down. Two of us take this one, two take the next. Just keep in a straight line, don't venture off, and let's see if there's a chamber called Warsaw down either of them."

Konrad and Eli walked ahead.

Jonty and Vic turned into the offshoot marked TARNÓW. The passage stretched about twenty meters, where it opened into a small chamber about ten meters square, one side protected by wooden cribbing, leached with moisture.

"This could have once been a place for storage," he said to Vic. "Crates stacked. That sort of thing."

"Nothing here now."

They headed back and learned that Konrad and Eli had found nothing, either. So they kept going down the drift, passing two more offshoots marked KIELCE and RADOM.

More Polish towns.

"There seems to be nothing down here but empty chambers," he noted.

Eli waved off his pessimism. "Which were once surely filled."

"When Vic called earlier about coming here," Konrad said, "I asked around. Most of the guides working now came long after the Soviet downfall. Some of the retired workers might know about this level. I've heard stories that things were stored deep back in the 1960s and 1970s."

Jonty was concerned about those inquiries. Bad enough they had to involve Konrad, they certainly could not afford any more nosy eyes and ears. The good part was that they were in the home stretch.

"From now on," he said, "let's keep this between us."

"Of course. I understand. Vic made all that clear. You don't have to worry about me. I was careful with my questions."

They kept following the drift, passing another offshoot labeled ŁÓDŹ. Not every offshoot was labeled. Only a few here and there. Farther on they came to two more bearing signs.

BYDGOSZCZ and GDAŃSK.

Then the drift ended at an unexcavated rock wall.

"We'll need to explore each of those offshoots we just passed," Konrad said.

But Jonty had been thinking. "Maybe not."

He wasn't entirely sure that he was right so he asked, "Am I correct that Tarnów is in southern Poland, east of Kraków?"

Konrad nodded. "That's right."

"And Gdańsk is in the north, on the Baltic Sea. Tell me where Kielce, Radom, and Łódź are located."

"They run south to north from Tarnów to Warsaw," Konrad said. "I've been to all of them."

"And I assume that Bydgoszcz is north of Warsaw?" he asked.

"It is. About two hundred kilometers," Konrad said. "As is Gdańsk."

The Soviets were, if nothing else, simple in their thinking. Why complicate matters when something easy could accomplish the same goal?

"The towns tell us where to go," he said.

He turned and headed back to the offshoot marked BYDGOSZCZ.

"This town is north of Warsaw. Which one is immediately south?"

"Łódź," Konrad said.

Jonty pointed. "Which is back there about thirty meters. What we're after is in between."

It had to be.

He walked down the tunnel about twenty meters until he came to an unmarked offshoot. He motioned to Vic, who hustled ahead and stopped at the next offshoot.

"Łódź?" he asked his associate.

"It is."

Jonty pointed. "This has to be Warsaw."

He did not wait for a reply, simply headed down the tunnel, which ended at a partial cave-in similar to the one he and Vic had seen last evening. A barrier, but passable. He squatted his stout frame down and squeezed under the ledge.

The others followed.

Their lights revealed another empty chamber, similar to the one Jonty saw at the end of the other offshoot.

A dead end?

Konrad, though, seemed intrigued, studying the far wall, his light tracing a path up and down.

"What is it?" Jonty asked.

CHAPTER THIRTY-TWO

COTTON DARTED LEFT, MOMENTARILY OUT OF THE LINE OF SIGHT for the doorway. Then he rushed toward the open portal, slamming its heavy paneled door shut and engaging the iron latch. That should stop Ivona's advance long enough for him to make his escape back the way he came. He noticed, though, that all the rooms on this level faced an inner courtyard, with a covered arcade wrapping the entire upper floor. A closed door to his left opened out to the loggia, as did two mullioned windows. It would not take Ivona long before she readjusted her path and came at him from that angle.

At least his instincts had been right.

Czajkowski had been playing Tom Bunch.

The Poles knew he'd come.

So make it look good.

He ran ahead, heading back through the assortment of rooms on the castle's north side, refinding the Senators' Hall, then the two exhibition halls and the wooden door that led into the adjacent building, the one whose lock he'd picked.

He stopped and heard voices.

A quick glance around one of the glassed exhibit cases and he spotted two security guards examining his handiwork at breaking the wire seal. No way he could escape there without some carnage. He decided to backtrack and find another way out. But he had to avoid Ivona. Hopefully all the doors leading from the inner loggia were locked, and her search for a way in would give him time to bypass her.

He hustled through the north wing.

Windows lined both sides of the rooms, all mullioned with watered glass. No way to see through. A blurry shadow moved past them on the outside, from room to room, stalking him from the exterior.

Ivona.

Had to be.

At some point they were going to come face-to-face, probably at a far exit point where she'd come up to this floor. The same exit he would need to leave. Perhaps she knew he was trapped and was simply biding her time, waiting for him to figure things out. He was still toting the heavy wooden box, which made the going a bit awkward.

He reentered the Battle of Orsha Room.

His mind wound through the possibilities, and only one made sense. On his trip through the north wing he'd noticed that the rooms were all roped off, keeping visitors from getting too close to the furnishings. The rope used was sturdy nylon, threaded through iron pedestals. He headed back and retrieved three lengths, obtaining a good hundred feet.

He heard glass shatter.

Apparently Ivona had grown impatient.

He carried the rope and the box back to the small study that jutted off the Orsha Room and locked the door from the inside, engaging an iron latch. He headed back outside onto the loggia, laid the wooden box down, and tied the rope to one of the stone pillars. He tossed the rest over the side and saw that there was enough slack to make it to the grass below. He quickly reeled the rope back up and tied the end to the box, then maneuvered it to the ground.

He heard the door back in the study being forced. Ivona or the guards were trying to make their way in. But the iron latch was holding. He wrapped the rope into a loop and stepped into it.

He heard muted gunfire.

They appeared to be trying to shoot their way past the door. He recalled that its wood was not all that thick, more just an interior door for privacy, not security.

Go. Now.

He hopped over the rail and began his descent, releasing the coil around his waist in short bursts and keeping his feet planted to the castle's stone. He'd purposefully located the rope so he could use one of the buttresses as a path, avoiding the walls themselves as they were dotted with obstacles. He was also careful with the slack at the bottom, keeping plenty there so as to not jostle the wooden box.

The descent was relatively easy and he was nearing the grass when he looked up and saw Ivona and two guards staring down at him. Her gun came up into view and she nestled the end of the barrel to the rope.

And fired.

His support severed, he fell the remaining twenty feet, pounding into the hard turf. Which hurt his nearly fifty-year-old body. He glanced back up and saw her aim the gun down toward him and fire, stitching the grass to his left with two rounds. He ignored the pain in his legs and snatched the box from the ground, lunging into an open arcade to his left, out of her line of fire. He had to leave the castle grounds, so he ditched the rope wrapped around him and freed the box, running ahead, down another covered arcade that led to a passage opening on the far side of the castle at the inner lawn, near where he'd first entered the administration building.

No one was in sight.

He assumed the guards themselves knew nothing about what was really happening. To them, this was real.

So he had to avoid them.

Exterior lights atop the buildings began to spring to life, dissolving the darkness and making him much more visible. He turned right and bolted back toward the main gate, passing the cathedral and the museum. Beyond the archway he found the same brick-lined passage that led down to street level. Lights burned here and there illuminating the path. At the end of the incline he saw that the heavy wooden gates were now closed. They were also tall, as were the surrounding walls. No way to scale either and no telling what type of lock secured the exit.

He had to find another way out.

And fast.

He could not go back inside the castle grounds. The guards would be on the move. To his left a rough cobbled path ran along the base of the castle's outer wall. Another smaller wall paralleled the outside, overlooking the river a hundred feet below. This had surely once been a path from which men and artillery could be shifted around the outer walls without risk. He ran down the path, visualizing in his mind the map of the castle's grounds he'd seen earlier outside the administrative offices.

There was another way down.

A popular spot, too.

The Dragon's Den.

He knew the story.

King Krak had lived in a castle atop Wawel Hill. A village lay below, beside the river, on fertile lands, and would have been rich and prosperous if not for a fierce fire-breathing dragon that occupied a cavern below the castle. The dragon liked to roam the countryside, eating sheep, cattle, and people. It particularly delighted in the taste of virgin flesh, as what dragon didn't. The beast devoured virgin after virgin, until only the king's daughter was left. It was then that King Krak declared that the brave hero who could slay the dragon would receive half the kingdom and his daughter's hand in marriage. Knight after knight tried to kill the dragon, and all were devoured. Then a poor young cobbler's apprentice wanted to try his luck. A mere boy. No warrior. No armor or sword.

But he had a brain.

He took a dead sheep and stuffed it with sulfur, then sewed it back together and left it at the mouth of the cave. The dragon swallowed the stuffed animal whole and soon developed a dreadful bellyache. The suffering creature crept down to the River Wisła and began to drink. He drank so much water that he eventually burst into pieces.

End of dragon.

Earlier, back at the main gate, Cotton had noticed the three large bones hanging over the entrance, suspended on chains. For centuries these were believed to be the remains of the dragon. In reality, they belonged to a mammoth, a rhinoceros, and a whale. But the cave under the castle was real and, ahead, through the darkness, he spotted the narrow turret at the top of a brick tower that held a spiral staircase. An iron gate barred access, but when he approached he noticed that it was secured by a modern keyed lock.

He glanced around and saw no one.

He was now on the castle's far west side, facing the river, which was over the wall to his right and a hundred feet down. He heard people below out walking the riverbank, enjoying the summer night. Lots of them. Just what he needed. He laid the wooden box down and picked the lock, quickly passing through the portal and relocking the gate behind him.

He descended the iron rungs in a tight circle and finally found himself standing in a limestone cave, nothing but blackness ahead, the attraction closed for the night. An electrical box was attached to one wall, and using his phone for light he tripped the breakers. The rocks came alive with back glow, exposing the Dragon's Den in all its shadowy detail. He hustled through the first chamber and into the next, the walls narrowing and heightening, the ceiling thirty feet high.

He heard a noise from above.

Voices.

Most likely the exterior security cameras had revealed his presence. He kept going and headed into another chamber, this one with a stone vault supported by a set of brick pillars and decorated by rock projections, chimneys, and fissures, the ambience trying to evoke thoughts of the mythical dragon that supposedly once lived here. The two-hundred-foot-long cave attracted hundreds of thousands of visitors each year, a place where superstition had evolved into folklore.

He spotted the exit.

A pointed-arch portal with another iron gate blocking it. Beyond, on the street that faced the river, a sculpture of the dragon stood. People congregated around it. He approached the gate and saw another lock, which was easy to pick. He emerged at the foot of Wawel Hill, the castle towering high above. He dissolved into the crowd, box in hand. A host of stray constellations circled overhead. He recognized the tangled silver chain of the Pleiades.

He kept walking.

And resisted the urge to turn back and glance up at the outer walls, where Ivona Novak was surely watching.

Mission accomplished.

CHAPTER
THIRTY-THREE

JONTY WALKED OVER TO KONRAD, WHO WAS STILL STARING AT THE salt wall.

"What is it?" he asked.

"There's something odd here."

He stared at the wall, too, comprising individual blocks mortared together, rising from the floor up five meters to the ceiling.

"These were built by the miners to block off unused tunnels. It was a safety measure against fires."

He reached out and stroked the rough gray-green surface.

"They cut the blocks themselves," Konrad said. "The mortar is salt mixed with water. It makes a good cement. The thicker the mortar lines, the newer the wall. The oldest used little to no mortar. But they were strong. I know of walls that are still standing after four hundred years. This one is different."

The others walked over.

"How so?" Eli asked.

"The blocks are too perfect, and the mortar is thin."

Jonty waited for more.

"The miners used anything and everything to build the walls. Trash, lumber, even horse manure. When they chipped the salt blocks into rough rectangles, no two were ever the same. They built fast, with little regard for craftsmanship. The idea was to get it up and done. So the mortar lines would be wavy, the layers all different. Nobody but them was ever going to see it, so it didn't matter what it looked like."

Jonty began to notice what Konrad was saying. The individual rectangles here were all remarkably similar, many of the edges impeccably straight. The mortar joints varied in width, but still crisscrossed in a defined pattern. "The mortar is thin, which would mean this is old. But the blocks are too perfect to be old?"

Konrad nodded.

"What are you saying?" Eli asked.

Konrad drew closer to the wall. "Vic, could you go back out to the main tunnel and get some of the iron pieces we saw lying around."

Jonty caught his acolyte's attention and nodded yes. *Do it.*

Vic left the chamber.

"You think there's something on the other side?" Jonty asked Konrad.

"I've seen it before where chambers were walled up. It's not unusual. But whoever did this wasn't in a hurry. They cut the blocks from the salt and made sure they were all close to the same. If we're assuming this is the Warsaw Chamber you are looking for, then there could be more to it on the other side."

Vic returned with several pieces of rusted iron. Konrad grabbed one of the bars and started to work the thin mortar in one of the side joints, where the blocks met the main salt wall.

"This isn't mortar. It's just part of the wall collapsed into the block. They definitely built this in front of an opening."

Konrad kept scratching the joint away, using the thin edge of the iron as a chisel. Salt dust sprayed away as a crease began to form. He then used the bar as a fulcrum and forced the iron farther into the seam, angling it away from the block, trying to pry it free.

Then he stopped.

"What?" Jonty asked.

"It moved."

Was that a problem? Did it mean danger?

Everything was illuminated by the motion of their headlights, but Konrad settled his beam down and used it to trace a path about two meters up the block wall. A meter-long crack had formed. Konrad used the iron to deepen it into a valley. Vic worked with another piece to clear away more mortar from the crack to the floor, revealing the crude outline of a doorway.

"Can we get through?" Eli asked.

"We shall see," Konrad said.

Jonty watched as the doorway was finally cleared. Vic and Konrad had used the iron bars to strip away the mortar, then extract the blocks, one by one. He'd cautioned them to be careful, because the blocks might need to be replaced. They left the last two rows at the bottom, as they could be stepped over. Beyond was a short tunnel that ended at a wooden door.

They all approached.

No lock. Only a rope handle. The salt wall had apparently been deemed enough protection.

Vic opened the door, which had been hung on wooden dowels. Beyond was another chamber. Racks of wooden shelves stood in five lines like a warehouse. None of the lumber was nailed. More dowels. The shelves were packed with black plastic bins, each container sealed at the top with heavy black tape.

"Somebody has a sense of humor," Eli said. "The Pantry. That's what this is, tucked safely within walls of salt. You see, Jonty. It is real."

That it was.

He noticed the floor. A layer of crystallized salt, wall-to-wall, that had not been disturbed in a long time.

He pointed it out.

"That was done to help with moisture," Konrad said. "The miners would crush the salt and spread it out on the floor to absorb humidity."

For someone who dealt in information, the value of a cache like this could be immeasurable. True, the vast majority was probably unimportant and meaningless. But somewhere amid all this information there was surely something of value.

They stepped inside.

He motioned and Vic lowered one of the plastic containers to the floor, peeled away its tape, and snapped off the top to reveal stacks of paper. Some bound together with string, most loose. Hundreds of pages. All in excellent condition thanks to the climate in the mine, ideal for pulp preservation. He and Eli each grabbed a handful of the pages and examined them, most written in Polish, many in Russian. Polish he was okay with, but Russian was not part of his repertoire.

"These are surveillance reports," Eli said, motioning with the stack he held. "From the Służba Bezpieczeństwa."

He saw that Eli was right. Some documents were statements from SB field agents and informants, most of them originals. Others were carbon copies of reports filed up the chain of command. Lots of names, dates, and places. Where people went. Who they met with. What they said. What they saw and heard. If this one box was representative, there were tens of thousands of documents in this archive.

"The possibilities could be endless," Eli said.

"Or useless," he added. "All of this is from a long time ago."

"That's probably what someone else thought, too, and look what happened there."

He knew exactly who Eli was referring to. Czajkowski. Good point.

Eli started to speak again, but Jonty cut him off with a wave of his hand. "Let's you and I walk back to the other side of the wall and speak in private."

He caught Vic's glance and indicated that he wanted Konrad occupied and kept out of hearing range.

He and Eli left the chamber and retreated far enough away that they could speak in private.

"Keep your voice down," he cautioned.

"Don't trust your guide?"

"Would you?"

"Of course not. I appreciate your precautions. But come now, Jonty. You and I both know the odds—somewhere in all that old paper is information that people in positions of power and influence today would not want revealed. There's value here. I can feel it. Look at what happened with Lech Wałęsa. He had a past that he did not want revealed. He tried hard to deny and disclaim it, but it stuck to him like a rash. There could be others just like him. And those people may be willing to pay to keep their secrets."

From preparing for the auction he knew that the SB had utilized tens of thousands of informants. What they reported had to be documented, since the Soviets loved to write everything down. Also, somebody went to a lot of trouble to conceal this cache, and that could not have been for nothing. And Eli had a point about both Czajkowski and Wałęsa. But going through all this would take time.

"I've been thinking," Eli said. "Let's not offer this for sale tomorrow. Let's hold it and study what's here, finding the ones that are actively negotiable today. I know of at least one buyer who would pay to have it all, intact."

He did, too.

Poland.

"We either need to come back here ourselves, or hire people to do it for us," Eli said. "Those containers have to be searched."

"That could take years, and this is not a public place."

"We'll do it slowly. No rush. It's not going anywhere. And you have access through your guide in there. I realize you don't trust him. But keep that relationship viable and we can study this at our leisure."

Everything he was hearing made sense. "You're cutting me in on this cache?"

"Absolutely. We made a deal. And this is too big for either of us. But together we can handle it. I also need your man to gain access. Sure, I could cultivate my own, but why start over when you already have everything in place? Less people to worry about. Let's do this. You pay me what we agreed for my silence on tomorrow's auction, and we'll split what we make from this, fifty–fifty."

He was instantly suspicious. "Why so generous?"

Eli smiled. "What choice does either of us have? I can ruin your auction tomorrow and you can ruin this for me. Why don't we be reasonable and both profit? There's plenty here."

He loved a good deal. Nothing better.

"All right, Eli. That's what we'll do."

CHAPTER
THIRTY-FOUR

Czajkowski stood in his suite at the Sheraton and stared at Wawel Castle. The ancient edifice was lit to the night in all its glory, five hundred meters away, high above the River Wisła. Crowds gathered at its base along the wide walkways that paralleled the river, enjoying another magnificent June night. He felt a pride knowing that, as president, he was the natural successor to the many kings who'd ruled Poland from that castle. Men like Bolesław the Brave, Casimir the Restorer, Sigismund the Old. What names. What legends. Their right to the throne was first acquired by conquest, then retained through heredity. Eventually, though, it evolved into something uniquely Polish.

Free election.

What a mistake.

The whole thing was hard to imagine. Ministers, archbishops, vaivodes, castellans, and nobles gathered on vast meadows near Warsaw and arranged themselves into a circle. Contenders would send envoys who made presentations as to why their particular man should be king. Promises were extended. Lots of them. Disputes arose. Physical violence was common. Eventually a vote would be taken and the man with the highest count won.

Few other nations in the world chose its ruler in such a bizarre way.

It reflected the Poles' strong belief in individual freedom and hatred of central authority. But the whole thing turned out to be disastrous. Kings, by definition, were meant to be independent and rule absolutely. But Polish kings were totally beholden to the nobles who elected them. Even worse, they had to abide by the promises they made to get elected. If they reneged, the nobles had the right to withdraw their allegiance.

The results from such insanity were predictable.

Monarchs became weak and ineffective. Most were not even Polish, as the tendency became to choose a foreigner with no local roots or connections. Those strangers cared little for the Polish nation, which led to countless unnecessary conflicts both foreign and domestic. Civil wars raged. The time between the death of one monarch and the election of the next eventually evolved into years, which caused even more unrest. In turn the power of the landowning nobles increased. They worked hard to keep the country rural, stifling the growth of cities and preventing the emergence of a middle class. None of which proved productive.

Corruption became institutionalized.

The Sejm, Poland's lower house of parliamentary representatives, grew in strength and stature, all at the further expense of the king, retaining for itself the final decisions on legislation, taxation, and foreign policy.

Nothing became law without their approval.

Then the liberum veto delivered the coup de grâce.

I freely forbid.

One member of the Sejm could stop any piece of legislation.

All votes had to be unanimous.

Even more incredible, if they were unable to reach a unanimous decision on an issue within six weeks, the time limit of a single session, their deliberations were declared void and all previous acts of that session, even if passed and approved, were annulled.

What insanity.

The liberum veto brought Poland to near collapse.

Good judgment finally prevailed and it was abolished in 1791. But far too late, as the Polish nation itself was dissolved four years later.

Thank goodness things had changed. But some of the bad tendencies remained. Poland still had a hard time moving forward. And still faced constant interference from foreigners.

Jak cię widzą, tak cię piszą.

How they see you, that's how they perceive you.

An old Polish saying that still rang true.

The door in the suite's outer room opened. It was manned by two of his BOR men, on guard in the hall. The hotel had been most accommodating with his last-minute booking. Luckily, the Royal Wawel Suite had been available and sat on an upper floor, at the end of a long hall, away from the elevators, an easy matter to secure access. He stepped from the bedroom and saw Ivona, who'd returned from the castle.

"What happened?" he asked.

"It went perfectly. Cotton took the spear and made his escape."

"Anyone alerted?"

She shook her head. "I personally handled it, with the guards none the wiser. They thought he was an intruder. I gave him just enough resistance to move him along, and he eventually fled the grounds through the Dragon's Den."

He chuckled. "How appropriate."

He stepped over to the small bar that had been set up for his visit and poured two generous measures of Irish whiskey. They'd discovered a mutual admiration for the beverage, so he'd asked that a bottle be made available, hoping she'd be here at some point.

"Now the question is, will we learn the location of the auction?" he asked, offering her a glass and sipping from his own.

"We will. Cotton will make sure of that."

They wanted Malone to take the spear. They'd implanted a GPS marker in the wooden box that protected it, which should lead them straight to the auction site.

"What do you mean, he'll make sure we know?"

"Janusz, Cotton is no fool. He certainly realizes that we allowed him to take the spear. He might be a little upset over the fall he took, but he'll get over it."

"If he knows, why take it?"

"It's America's ticket in, and he wants us to follow. He's headed into a blind situation, and he's being used by Tom Bunch and President Fox. He stayed in this because of Stephanie Nelle. It's the only reason he would. They used that loyalty to get him to steal the spear and they'll use it to force him to go to the auction with Bunch. But he knows the Russians are not happy. That was made clear in Bruges. There could be trouble, so he's going to need some help. That's where we come in."

"Sounds like you know this man well."

"He's a pro. He'd also dealt with Ivan before. So he knows the man is not trustworthy. Cotton has to assume that the Russians are not telling us everything. Especially the auction location. So he'll lead us there."

"You have great respect for him."

"Still jealous?"

"And what if I were?" he asked her.

"I'd say it's a strange reaction from a married man."

He appraised her with a cautious gaze, the whiskey warming his chest. "Why are you with me?"

He genuinely wanted to know.

"I work for you."

"That's not an answer, and you know it. Do you love me?"

He'd never asked her that question before.

"I do."

Her admission pleased him. "I love you, too."

She enjoyed more of the whiskey. "Was any of that in doubt?"

"Not doubt. But this whole thing is complicated."

She smiled. "That it is. But isn't the problem of this auction a bit more pressing than our personal lives?"

"They're both important to me."

He'd not felt so vulnerable to a woman in a long time. Yes, he was still married and the country would disapprove. The church would disapprove. His wife? Only if the press discovered any of it would she care. Thankfully, his security team was discreet and understanding. And now he found himself inside a magnificent suite, with a beautiful woman he loved, night firmly embraced outside, the day over.

Another saying came to mind.

Nie chwal dnia przed zachodem słońca.

Don't praise the day before sunset.

First, though, he wanted to know, "Will there be any mention of the theft?"

She nodded. "The castle is releasing a statement about the break-in, saying they are still determining what, if anything, may have been taken.

The director was told this is a national security matter and secrecy is necessary. He's the only one who knows that we planned it all. I assured him the spear would be returned within two days."

"If we lose it, there's going to be trouble."

"I know. I'll get it back."

"Along with what's being auctioned on me?"

"That too."

He finished his drink and laid their glasses down. "Where is the box being tracked?"

She nodded. "Only on my phone."

"And nothing more will be happening tonight?"

She shrugged. "I doubt it. But we'll keep an eye on it."

He took her into his arms.

"How about we both do that."

CHAPTER
THIRTY-FIVE

COTTON FOUND THE U.S. CONSULATE, LOCATED ON A SIDE STREET
not far from Kraków's main square. A message on his phone indicated he
was to go there after leaving the castle. He still carried the wooden box
containing the Spear of St. Maurice, the walk over through the night
crowd uneventful.

Two marines stood guard at the main entrance. Three American flags
hanging from the stone above waved an indolent welcome. The soldiers
opened the door as he approached, obviously briefed to expect him. Inside, he was ushered past the metal detector and up a steep flight of stairs
to a second-floor office where Stephanie and Bunch waited.

He laid the box on a desk.

"Well done," Bunch said, a smile on his face.

Stephanie did not appear to be as pleased.

Bunch called for a screwdriver, brought by an eager young man, which
he used to remove the top. Inside lay a dull-pointed iron spearhead,
about twenty inches long and three inches wide. Its color reminded Cotton of battleship gray. The tattered remnants of a copper sleeve wrapped
its midsection, partially covering an aperture chiseled from the top third
of the blade. He knew it once harbored a nail, like the Spear of Destiny
in Vienna, but the spike was gone. At its lower end were two wings, above

which stretched a crisscross of wire. Below that was the round receptacle that once attached it to a lance.

Bunch lifted out the artifact. "You think it might actually be the spear that pierced Christ?"

He couldn't resist. "Does a big white bunny bring candy to kids on Easter?"

Bunch wasn't amused. "I take it you are not a religious man."

"I'm a practical man. No piece of iron, two thousand years old, would have survived this intact."

"Why not? It's possible."

Actually, it wasn't. But he decided not to argue.

He did notice the clear disparity between this spear and the one on display in Vienna. Though similar in size and shape, that Spear of Destiny had a more pronounced oval aperture chiseled from its center where a forged iron pin still rested. Supposedly a nail from the crucifixion. A bright-gold sheath protected it. Lots of testing had been performed on the Vienna spear, which had revealed that it definitely had been forged, not molded, and its size was a bit large for those used by the Roman army at the time. Metallurgy testing dated the iron to long after Christ.

But who knew?

It was all a matter of faith.

Something he'd never had much of.

Bunch replaced the spear in the box. "That's the safest place for it."

On that Cotton agreed.

Bunch sat at the desk, faced an open laptop, and began typing. He then hit one final button and said, "I just RSVP'd to the auction."

The laptop immediately dinged, indicating an incoming message.

That was fast.

Had to be an auto reply.

Bunch read it, then turned the screen around so Cotton and Stephanie could see.

THANK YOU FOR PARTICIPATING. PLEASE
EMAIL AN IMAGE OF YOUR ARTIFACT TO
THIS ADDRESS. THEN HAVE YOUR TWO
REPRESENTATIVES AT THE MAIN BRANCH OF

THE TATRA MUSEUM IN ZAKOPANE AT 11:00 A.M.
TOMORROW. THEY WILL BE RETURNED THERE
AFTER THE AUCTION IS CONCLUDED. NO CELL
PHONES, WEAPONS, OR ANY ELECTRONICS ARE
ALLOWED. NO TRANSLATORS, EITHER, AS THE
SALE WILL BE CONDUCTED IN ENGLISH ONLY.
YOUR REPRESENTATIVES SHOULD BE FLUENT.
PAYMENT VERIFICATION WILL BE MADE ON SITE.
CONFIRMATION OF PAYMENT MUST BE RECEIVED
BEFORE THE SALE IS CONCLUDED. PLEASE
ENSURE THAT ALL NECESSARY ARRANGEMENTS
FOR PAYMENT HAVE BEEN MADE. ANY
VIOLATIONS OF THESE RULES WILL RESULT IN A
DISQUALIFICATION TO BID.

Cotton thought about Ivan and his warning for the United States to stay out of this. He'd passed that on to Stephanie, who'd surely shared the information with Bunch.

"The Russians don't care about any of that," he said. "They're going to either win or stop that auction, no matter what."

"We've dealt with that, too," Bunch noted. "President Fox has spoken with the Kremlin and related the same thing we told the Poles. He assured them we are not participating in the auction."

Cotton pointed to the box. "What happens when they find out that the spear has been stolen?"

Bunch shook his head. "None of the other thefts have been made public. We've kept a lid on them."

Incredible. These people really were stupid. "None of the other thefts happened on Polish soil. That spear is not a Catholic relic, stolen from a church. It's a national historical artifact. What's to stop President Czajkowski from telling the world it's gone? He has to know, by now, that you double-crossed him. Ivona Novak was there, waiting for me."

He omitted the *why* from that statement.

"Who cares? What can Czajkowski do about it?" Bunch asked. "Not a damn thing. Same with the Russians. We're the United States of America, for God's sake, and we're going to that auction with it."

Cotton glanced at Stephanie, who kept her face stoic, but he could read her mind. The Russians and the Poles were working together. To what degree? Hard to say. If it was all that close a relationship, then the Poles would have simply stopped the theft of the spear. Instead they allowed it to happen. That confirmed they were, to some degree, in the dark. How far?

Another unknown.

"You and I will be at that museum in the morning," Bunch said to Stephanie. "I assume Malone is done. Right?"

"You assume wrong," Cotton said.

And he saw the surprise on Stephanie's face.

"I'll go with you," he said.

Bunch smiled an irritating grin. "That's what I like to hear. A team player. Loyal to the good ol' US of A. We appreciate your dedication."

He decided to not take that bait and instead said what was probably expected, "And my $150,000. Let's not forget that. Paid in advance."

"No. Of course not," Bunch said. "A man has to make a living, right? We can appreciate that. I'll arrange the transfer of funds."

Better for Fox to think him a greedy mercenary than a loyal friend. No way he was going to allow Stephanie to walk into that quagmire of an auction alone. And that was precisely what Tom Bunch represented.

No help.

Cotton considered himself an expert in only a few things. One was the ability to deal with a tight situation and think on his feet. The old cliché was true. Desperate people did desperate things. And this scenario seemed the precise definition of the word.

"Are you sure?" Stephanie asked him.

He nodded.

"Absolutely."

Cotton and Stephanie stepped from the office while Bunch talked on the phone with Fox, motioning that he wanted to speak to the president in private.

"I wonder if there are classes in ass kissing that idiots like him go to," he said to her. "He has no appreciation for what's going on here."

"Not a drop."

"My guess is the box is GPS-tagged," he said, "and they're tracking it right now. We'll need to take a look."

"I know. We'll deal with that when he's done with his important call." He caught the sarcasm.

"Ivona set it all up, with just enough resistance to make it look good. Though shooting that rope was a bit much," he said. "I owe her for that one."

Stephanie smiled.

"It all means that the Poles didn't get an invite," he said. "The Russians must have tipped them off to the whole thing. That would explain their partnership in Bruges. But it was a limited engagement. The Russians would not want anyone else involved after that."

"Unless they force themselves in, or allow us to lead them to it."

He agreed. "They'll put out a story on what happened tonight. They have to in order to stay consistent with the other thefts. And they can't allow the Russians to think they are cooperating with us in any way."

He could see she agreed.

"Czajkowski will probably call Washington and raise hell at the lies," he said. "That would be expected. Our problem is that the GPS marker will never make it to the auction. Based on the email we just saw, our transport tomorrow will check for tags and, if discovered, the U.S. will be disqualified." He smiled. "We could leave it in and this will all be over quickly. Bunch would even have to take some of the blame."

"I wish. But that information would still go on sale."

"I'm actually a little curious as to what's being offered. It's got to be pretty big. The White House didn't tell you?"

She shook her head. "Not a word. And I'd be a liar if I said I wasn't curious, too. It has to be both personal and politically fatal. I say we keep going and see how it goes."

He was okay with that. "The Russians are not going to lose that auction."

"I know. But maybe it would not be a bad thing if they won."

He caught the twinkle in her eye.

"I like the way you think."

CHAPTER
THIRTY-SIX

JONTY CLIMBED INTO BED.

He'd chosen the largest chamber in Sturney Castle for his own, the one used long ago by the castle's lord, the room fully furnished with period pieces, all representative of Slovakia's past. Eli Reinhardt was down the hall, since he'd thought it a good idea to keep his newly acquired partner close.

They'd left the cache of documents in the mine, replacing the salt wall and disguising their invasion as best they could. Konrad had assured them that Level X was rarely accessed, since it was not actually part of the working mine. More a reminder from the past when the Soviets were in control, one few today cared to recall.

So the secret should be safe.

He'd promised Konrad some additional money, both to assure his silence and to cement his loyalty. They would need more visits to Level X in the weeks ahead as they determined what, if anything, there was to find. Unfortunately Jonty would be of little help, since his Polish was weak and his Russian nonexistent. Eli, of course, was fluent in both. But he was not about to allow his "partner" unfettered access. That would only end with Eli keeping the most valuable information for himself. No. He'd hire a surrogate and pay him or her enough to ensure that person stayed loyal. To further cement the relationship, Vic would accompany them at all times, since a little fear was a good thing. Both for Eli and for the hired help.

Eli had kept Art Munoz as his own personal protection. The Bulgarian was ensconced in the bedroom next to Eli. Why the need for a bodyguard? Who knew. But he'd decided to allow Reinhardt whatever he wanted. The important thing was to get through tomorrow and conclude the auction. The twenty million euros he would owe Eli was a small price to pay for no drama.

Yesterday's enemy can be today's friend.

How true.

Vic reported that six teams had been dispatched to various points in Poland, Slovakia, the Czech Republic, and Austria. All within a few hours' driving time. The Germans would not be participating. Eli had assumed their place and provided the Holy Nail from Bamberg Cathedral, which would be sold with the rest of the holy relics. He'd been worried about the Americans, but now they were in. Finally. He'd received both the RSVP and an image of the Spear of St. Maurice. Their presence was essential. During their phone call a few weeks back, Warner Fox had assured him that they would not only bid but actually win the auction, and that meant lots of U.S. dollars coming his way. Fox had been quite supportive of the endeavor, congratulating him on his enterprising ingenuity. More of that former businessman coming through, where money talked and more money talked louder.

He settled between the four posters, the firm mattress a wonder. The castle was wonderfully equipped. No expense had been spared in making it comfortable. For what he was paying for only a week's worth of use, the whole place should be lined with gold.

Normally, he liked to read before falling asleep. A habit he'd acquired as a teenager, and one he'd maintained his entire adult life. He loved the classics but, if truth be told, a good mystery intrigued him, too. Something about the puzzle. Much like his own life, which at times seemed straight out of an international suspense thriller.

He was comforted to know that Vic was keeping an eye on things during the night. He doubted he'd be able to sleep otherwise. His man was also monitoring the six teams, ready to begin transportation of their charges in the morning. He'd chosen the middle of the day for the auction on purpose. Easier to spot trouble coming, and easier to get away. He trusted none of the bidders, but was counting on their parochial self-interests to ensure that all proceeded as planned.

The Pantry still bothered him. There were tens of thousands of documents there. It could take a long time to go through them and there was no guarantee there'd be anything of value. Repeatedly going in and out of that mine could eventually draw attention, though Konrad had informed them of a way down where there was little to no monitoring, used exclusively by the miners. Still, one lesson he'd learned from years of careful bargaining was *never press your luck*. Take what was there and get out. Nothing good ever came from prolonging things, and everything about that cache screamed *long-term*.

Eli had been right about one thing.

Why not make a deal with the Poles and sell it all, intact.

That would surely be worth millions of euros and he'd derive half, per his deal.

He was hungry. Perhaps he should have the staff bring him a snack. Maybe a fruit bowl. Nothing heavy. He'd always found sleep hard to acquire after too much of a good thing.

More of that never pressing your luck.

He rested a little easier knowing that all communications in and out of the castle were now being jammed. They'd stepped up that precaution before leaving for the mine earlier. So there was no way Eli could speak to anyone beyond the castle walls. He was mindful, though, of Eli's threat about what would happen if he did not report in every few hours, so Vic had been told to allow those calls, but monitor every word. He was counting on his competitor's greed to ensure that nothing went wrong.

He decided to pass on the snack and the reading.

His mind was already racing, and any more stimulants should be avoided.

He switched off the light.

Time for sleep.

Tomorrow would require his best.

CHAPTER
THIRTY-SEVEN

COTTON HAD SLEPT FITFULLY, CONCERNED OVER WHAT WAS ABOUT to happen. He'd spent the night at a Kraków hotel, but not before performing some vital housekeeping chores. He and Stephanie had managed to convince Tom Bunch that the spear should not be transported in its wooden box. *Too informal,* he'd explained. *Not appropriate,* Stephanie had added. So they'd located another decorative container of sufficient size, lacquered and hand-painted in the Polish style, and stuffed it with the foam and velvet cloth from the original box. Bunch had seemed satisfied, never realizing what was actually happening. Sure enough, they'd found a GPS tracker embedded into the original box's bottom, which Cotton had removed and now carried in his trouser pocket, still bouncing a signal to Ivona Novak.

Stephanie had called earlier to tell him that a story in Warsaw's morning *Gazeta Wyborcza* reported a burglary last night at Wawel Castle that was being investigated by the local police. Few details had been offered and no determination had been made, as yet, on what might have been taken. That seemed more than enough to make the point, but not enough to give away the farm.

He hadn't been able to eat much breakfast, just nibbling on some toast and sipping orange juice before they left Kraków in Bunch's vehicle and drove sixty miles south to Zakopane, a town of about thirty thousand that sat on the Poland–Slovakia border. The city occupied a valley at the foot of the Tatra Mountains and billed itself as Poland's sports capital, catering to summer mountaineers and winter skiers.

The Tatra Museum seemed like a big deal. There were eight different locations, all featuring the history, culture, nature, and ethnography of the Polish Tatras. The main branch was located at the city center, the building a perfect example of the brick-and-stone variety that seemed typical in the area. Bunch had been buoyant on the drive, excited to be a part of the auction. It was clearly his first venture into something like this, and he seemed to have a twisted view as to how things were played.

It's like Mission Impossible, Bunch had said. *We're heading in on an assignment, on our own, and if either of us is captured or killed the secretary will disavow any knowledge of our actions.*

The moron spouted out nonsense as if all that were a good thing. Who the hell liked to be *disavowed*? Agents were not suicidal. And killed? None he'd ever met had a death wish.

They found the main branch of the museum at 10 Krupówki Street and parked on the curb. They exited the car and stood on the sidewalk, outside a waist-high iron fence that encircled the building. Cotton glanced at his watch and saw they were in place with five minutes to spare.

"When whoever arrives," he said, "it would be better if I did the talking. This has to be played carefully, and I do have some experience in this area."

"I don't see the problem. We're here to go to an auction. There's nothing to play. I'm the senior official. I'll do the talking."

Exactly what he thought Bunch would say. Perfect. He needed a little diversion and this guy could certainly provide it.

He figured whoever was coming would run an electronics sweep, so he had to be rid of the GPS marker before that happened. But he also needed to paint the way for Ivona, who was surely watching from afar.

The day was clear, sunny, and warm. At precisely 11:00 A.M. a black Mercedes coupe came to a stop on the street before the museum. The driver and one other man sat in the front. Both young, with a look and demeanor reminiscent of the Three Amigos in Bruges.

Cotton walked toward the new arrivals and greeted the men as they emerged. He also noticed that the car windows were down. Perfect. All he needed now was for Bunch to be Bunch, who stepped up and said, "I'm the White House's deputy national security adviser and deputy assistant to the president of the United States."

"Where's the relic?" one of them asked.

"What's the deal here?" Cotton asked.

"It doesn't work like that. We ask the questions, you provide the answers, and we don't have time to debate things. Where is the relic?"

Cotton pointed to their car. "In there."

He'd managed to convince Bunch to leave it inside until they knew what was happening. *It's our only ticket into the auction,* he'd told Bunch, who readily agreed.

The two men headed for the car.

Bunch did not hesitate. "Hold up there. That's ours. Not yours. If you need to see it, I'll handle it."

The moment provided Cotton an opportunity to remove the GPS tracker from his pocket and flick it through the Mercedes' open window. Where it landed didn't matter, only that it was inside, preferably toward the backseat. The device was the size of a Tic Tac and hopefully would go unnoticed.

Bunch and the other two men made it to the car at the same time.

"Stand back," one of them said.

"You will not speak to me in such a manner."

"We've been instructed to leave you here if there is any objection or resistance to our instructions. Of course, we'll take the relic with us."

"You will not," Bunch made clear. "That is property of the United States of America."

The guy chuckled. Cotton wanted to join him but knew better.

"It's actually stolen property," the other man said. "Please step aside and let us do our job."

Bunch tossed over a look that asked *should he do that* and Cotton nodded. Amazing that he wanted some guidance considering all his "expertise" with such matters. Bunch moved away and the man removed the lacquered box from the rear seat. The other found a 9V powered signal detector in his pant pocket, the kind that can be bought almost anywhere for under $200. Small, portable, simple, and effective. He switched on the unit and scanned the box. Then he opened the top lid and scanned the lance.

Nothing registered.

They then scanned Bunch.

Clean.

And finally they walked back to where Cotton stood and determined he harbored no electronic devices, either. He and Bunch had left their cell phones back in Kraków with Stephanie. He was betting they would not scan their own car and they did not, satisfied it was already clean. One disadvantage to a proximity scanner like they were using was that it needed to be close to any detectable source.

"All right," one of their escorts said. "You need to get inside our vehicle and ride quietly."

The other man took control of the spear inside its box.

Bunch offered no argument.

"We have a long drive ahead of us, and there are further precautions that must be taken."

They rode for about half an hour, over the border into Slovakia, through the Tatra Mountains. No one spoke. Cotton tried to grab his bearings, knowing they were headed due south. He was not familiar with northern Slovakia, so it was hard to say where their destination lay. Ahead, he spotted a tunnel cut into the mountain allowing the highway to keep on a straight course, unobstructed.

They entered the tunnel, which was artificially lit, and he saw that it was a long one, the other end visible about a quarter mile away. Cars were coming from the opposite direction in the other lane. One passed, then a second. A third car slowed, then did a U-turn in the road, falling into line behind them.

A black Mercedes coupe.

Identical to theirs.

Which sped past and headed for the tunnel's end.

Their car came to a stop in the small service lane. The driver switched on his emergency flashers.

"Why have we stopped?" Bunch asked.

Cotton realized what was happening. "Drones."

Bunch seemed puzzled.

"They're afraid we're watching from overhead," he said to Bunch. "So they bring in an identical car that will now take any eyes in the sky off on a wild-goose chase."

The guy in the passenger seat turned around. "I said no talking."

He'd had enough. "Then do something about it."

He was banking on the fact that Jonty Olivier wanted America in this show so much, he was willing to waive just about anything. Including the rules. But if this guy wanted to go toe to toe that was fine by him.

The guy turned back around.

"We'll be waiting here a few minutes," he said to Bunch. "Long enough to give the decoy time to do its job."

The guy in the front seat turned around and tossed two black cloth sacks their way.

"Once we get moving, put those on your head."

More old school. But an effective way to keep someone from learning where they were headed.

He decided not to argue.

Hoping Ivona stayed on the trail.

CHAPTER THIRTY-EIGHT

CZAJKOWSKI DECIDED TO STAY IN KRAKÓW FOR THE DAY, WANTING to be nearby so he and Ivona could communicate quickly in person. Michał Zima, the head of the BOR, had not been pleased with the decision, preferring to have the president of the nation within the controlled environs of Warsaw. He realized that Zima wanted to know what was happening, and why an agent of the Agencja Wywiadu was so directly involved with the president. That was unusual, to say the least, but he'd rebuffed all of Zima's renewed overtures to learn more.

His night with Ivona had been wonderful. He was beginning to miss not having her around. But feelings like that could be dangerous, so he quelled any notions of emotional attachment. Those could be dealt with later. At the moment, the auction was all that mattered.

Ivona had shown him the tracking device on her phone and that the Spear of St. Maurice had spent the night at the American consulate. Her last report was that the spear had left Kraków and been taken south to the Poland–Slovakia border. But that had been nearly two hours ago. No telling what was happening now. He could only hope that Ivona stayed with it. They'd discussed all the options, and in the end he told her to use her best judgment as to what had to be done.

He trusted her implicitly.

But he also had to be prepared to deal with the situation, if she failed.

He realized there was no way he could deny any of the documents' authenticity, since they were all either in his handwriting or signed by him. The one showed to Ivona by the Russians seemed representative of what he recalled providing to the SB. He'd worked as a paid informant for seven years, from mid-1982 until late 1989. Dilecki had been his main contact point, though others had, from time to time, been involved.

All informants were required to provide regular reports. If not, they were subject to being rounded up and "interrogated." For him, that had meant contact with somebody in the SB every couple of months. Something. Anything. Once someone came onto the SB's radar, it was nearly impossible to get off. You either provided what they wanted, or you ended up like that math professor, strapped naked to a stool and beaten savagely.

Or worse.

Defending himself now was going to be next to impossible. The documents themselves would be damning, and to his knowledge only a handful of people had known the truth. Not even Wałęsa, who'd headed Solidarity, had been aware of all that had been happening.

And it all started that day in Warsaw, when he left Mokotów Prison.

A few minutes before he'd been watching a man being tortured, the implications clear that he would be next unless he cooperated with the SB.

Then the next—

The clamor of a car horn brought him back to reality.

He'd stepped into the street without looking. Thankfully, the driver was paying attention and had stopped. He stared through the windshield at an older man who continued to pound the horn. He tossed him a wave and kept going, finding the sidewalk on the other side. The image of that professor, a learned man entitled to respect and dignity, crawling across the filthy prison floor, bleeding and naked, would never leave his mind.

Nor would the defiance.

He hated Dilecki. He hated the SB. He hated the communists. The government. And anyone and everything that opposed a free and independent Poland. Nothing and no one would ever change that belief inside him. But he'd been afraid. More so than anytime in his life. He did not want to be strapped to a stool, then beaten and kicked. He did not want to be tortured or defiled. He did not want to crawl across the floor. But he also did not want to be the eyes and ears of the oppressors.

He walked down the sidewalk, busy with people. There was a meeting of the local chapter of Solidarity in two hours, one that Dilecki knew all about, demanding a full report of what was said.

"Your first test," the irritating bastard had made clear.

He turned a corner and kept heading away from the prison.

Three men blocked his way ahead, standing shoulder-to-shoulder on the sidewalk, waiting for him to approach. He knew them, and the look on their faces was anything but cordial.

"Come with us," one of them said.

He'd already been intimidated by the state. He was not about to allow his own people to do the same thing.

"Go screw yourself," he said to them.

He turned to walk away and one of them grabbed his arm.

He wrenched it free.

"Please," the man said to him. "Somebody wants to speak with you."

He'd thought all that over. Finished. Never to be heard of again.

But that was not the case.

Far from it, in fact.

He sat alone in the hotel suite.

He was in constant communication with his staff in Warsaw, dealing with everyday problems. A lot was going on. A dispute with the European Union over local self-government seemed to be heating up. Preparations for the upcoming national budget had begun. Measures were being discussed to lessen inflation, which had recently been creeping higher. All issues that required his undivided attention. Yet he *was* divided, with the past intruding on the present. He'd resisted making the telephone call as long as possible. But it had to be done. His personal secretary had found the contact number two weeks ago, but the time had not been right then.

Now was the moment.

He reached for the cell phone.

Ivona had provided him the unit, noting it would be untraceable. He punched in the number and waited while it rang in his ear. When it was finally answered he realized that the voice had changed little in nearly thirty years. A voice he'd heard for the first time that fateful day, after Mokotów Prison, in a conversation that changed his life.

"I need your help," he said into the phone.

"Interesting how time has shifted our positions. Once it was I who needed your assistance. What can I do for you, Mr. President."

"We have to discuss the Warsaw Protocol."

CHAPTER
THIRTY-NINE

JONTY EXCUSED HIMSELF FROM HIS GUESTS AND LEFT THE GREAT
hall, walking back to the castle's main foyer where, he'd been told, another
pair of bidders was arriving. The Iranians, French, and Chinese were already on site, their escorts assuring Vic that everything seemed fine.

No tails. No problems.

He'd dressed for the day, wearing a new suit specially made by a tailor in Paris. Usually French high fashion for men centered on Balmain,
Saint Laurent, and Dior. But he preferred the newcomer labels. Places
like A.P.C., AMI, and Maison Kitsuné. His girth made for a challenge
in crafting an acceptable look, but he genuinely loved the berets, waist-
coats, and lapel pins, a mix of classic with more comfort-driven attire, the
whole look more English than French. Today's ensemble was a perfect
example. Smart, with a tweed jacket, the fleck of the sturdy wool offset by
a pale-blue cotton shirt, bow tie, and leather shoes.

He thought it important to personally welcome the bidders, showing
them courtesy and hospitality. Each, so far, had appreciated the gesture,
offering their part of the Arma Christi as a welcome, depositing it onto
the oak table upon entering the great hall. The site seemed to be working
its magic, all of the arrivals impressed by the surroundings and the array
of uniformed staff toting trays of fresh hors d'oeuvres and drinks appropriate to each nationality.

His expert was also on site, brought in earlier by Vic, to verify the authenticity of each relic. So far everything had seemed in order. All deemed authentic, including the Nail from Bamberg. Now a fourth participant was arriving.

He stepped from the foyer out into the bright morning sun. The Slovakian weather was cooperating with another glorious late-spring day. A black Mercedes coupe motored into the courtyard and came to a stop. Two men emerged from the backseat. Tall, dark suits, broad-shouldered, Slavic features. Russians. And neither man looked happy to be there.

"Welcome, gentlemen," he said to them in English.

One of them answered with a few lines of Russian. He did not need a translator to know the meaning.

He waved a finger. "As advertised, this auction will be conducted in English."

Neither said a word.

He continued, "I apologize for the insistence, and I mean no disrespect. But please know every effort has been made to make you as comfortable as possible. We have some lovely pelmeni, wrapped in light, paper-thin dough." He patted his midsection and laughed. "As you can see, I've enjoyed a few. I chose the filling myself, a combination of beef, lamb, and pork, spiced with pepper, onions, and garlic. I assure you, they are quite delicious."

Both Russians broke into a smile.

"How can we refuse such generosity," the one said in English that tended to thicken the consonants and round the vowels. "I have not had a good pelmeni in some time."

He noticed that the other man held a small wooden box.

"Is that the Holy Blood from Bruges?"

"It is, indeed." The man handed it over. "Our ticket to enter."

He led his new guests into the castle and down a wide corridor to the great hall. He watched as, like the others already there, the new arrivals surveyed the room to ascertain who else would be bidding. He excused himself and caught the attention of the headwaiter, who immediately marched over.

"Please make sure the Russians have whatever they desire to drink. Mention the Tovaritch vodka we have on hand. And bring out the pelmeni."

The man hurried off.

He, too, glanced around the room.

Four teams there.

Two to go.

Both were en route.

He glanced up at the second-floor railing and spotted Eli taking in the scene. Beside him stood Art Munoz, looking as dour as ever. Jonty had tried to apologize for the wire-down-the-throat business, but the Bulgarian had not been receptive. He'd even offered some generous monetary compensation for the pain and suffering, which was also refused. Apparently, this Bulgarian was not the forgiving type.

Eli tossed him a casual wave, as if to say that he was pleased things were progressing. Germany's two chairs in the great hall had been removed, and Eli would watch the proceedings from the second floor, out of sight. They'd already agreed to make another trip into the mine in two days' time to begin a cursory inspection of the containers. He was on the prowl for an expert, one with the historical knowledge along with the discretion to work quickly and quietly. He still liked the idea of selling it all, en masse, to the Poles. But that would be a discussion for another day.

The auction was all that mattered now.

Vic entered the hall and approached.

"The other two teams will be here within the half hour."

"Is everything okay?"

"So far, no problems. But that doesn't mean there won't be any."

He agreed.

The Iranians and the Russians would be the most dangerous. Both had a lot to lose from American missiles in Poland. Both had few to no scruples and were capable of almost anything. He was betting on them to use money instead of violence, maybe even join forces to raise their bid to astronomical levels, forcing America to counter even higher.

The possibilities seemed endless.

He checked his watch.

Everything would start soon.

CHAPTER FORTY

COTTON SAT IN THE BACKSEAT WITH THE BLACK CLOTH BAG OVER his head, feeling like a fool. Bunch didn't seem to mind, as he'd not said a word over the past twenty minutes. They'd waited in the tunnel for the decoy Mercedes to lead away any drone that may have been observing. A bit overdramatic in scope but, he had to admit, effective. Obviously, a lot of planning had gone into this.

They'd stayed on a smooth road for most of the way, maintaining a constant rate of speed south, with no stops. That meant a major highway, as there'd been few curves. Then a turn to the west and a curvy path that first ground its way up, then leveled off.

"You can take the hoods off," one of the men said.

He yanked the cloth off his head and it took a moment for his eyes to adjust to the sunlight.

And he saw a castle.

The Mercedes motored beneath a heavy, iron-studded gate, protected by a portcullis, which had been raised to admit them. A stonemason's sign on the rough wall bore the inscription 1564.

They entered a graveled courtyard. Five-sided. Towers rose to the bright sky, each crowned with a cupola. Some kind of Slovakian fortress. A rotund man in a tweed jacket and bow tie waited near a pedimented door.

"That's Jonty Olivier," Bunch whispered.

The Mercedes came to a stop.

Cotton gave the rear floorboard a quick once-over trying to find the tracker, but saw nothing. He could only hope no one ever noticed it.

"You can get out," the driver said.

He glanced at Bunch who never hesitated, grabbing the black lacquered box with the spear and opening his door. So much for coordinating how they would handle things.

"Gentlemen," Jonty Olivier said, his arms spread wide. "Welcome."

Bunch extended a hand, which Olivier shook.

"You work with President Fox?"

"I do," Bunch said. "He sent me personally to handle this. I believe you and the president spoke?"

Olivier raised a finger to his lips and shushed Bunch quiet. "That's a secret. Between us. Not everyone received such personal attention."

Cotton tried to gauge their host. Fashion-conscious? It certainly seemed so. Self-assured? Definitely. In control? That was the impression the man was trying to convey.

"This is for you," Bunch said, offering the box.

"The Spear of St. Maurice. How utterly exciting. Please, bring it inside."

Olivier motioned for them to follow.

"We have a special place for it."

Cotton studied the castle as they were led into what appeared to be its grand hall. Stout black pillars bore the weight of a flattened vaulted ceiling. A huge open hearth at one end bore the coat of arms of a former owner. Glass windows in black iron frames, high up, allowed in the late-morning sun. Four massive, electrified, gilded-bronze chandeliers provided ample illumination. Eight people milled about, chatting among themselves. Servers offered food and drink. Six pairs of chairs were arranged at the far end, facing a single high-backed chair and a large video screen. Olivier led them to a long oak table supported by legs the size of tree trunks. A portrait of Christ embossed into a copper plate, displayed on an easel, decorated the center. Four other artifacts lay about. The Holy Sponge, the Pillar of Flogging, the True Cross, and the Holy Blood. That meant the Russians were here, but he did not recognize any of the people in the room.

Bunch laid the box on the table, opened the lid and withdrew the spear. Olivier seemed impressed, which was surely Bunch's intention.

"Quite wonderful," Olivier noted. "Thank you for bringing it."

"Like we had a choice," Cotton said.

Olivier chuckled, merriment in his watery eyes. "No. I don't suppose you did. But I thank you nonetheless. Now, if you'll excuse me, I have other guests arriving."

Two more pairs, in fact.

Who would bring the Holy Nail and the Crown of Thorns.

Olivier waddled off.

Bunch seemed pleased with himself. "So far, so good. Right, Malone?"

That all depended, but he wasn't about to discuss those possibilities with this idiot. Hopefully, somewhere out there Ivona Novak was coming this way. He'd seen little security, but that did not mean none existed. No cameras ringed the great hall, but again they could be concealed. He'd noticed an older man on the second floor, peering down from the stone balustrade, watching with great intensity.

Just one more odd thing to add to the list.

Bunch captured a flute of champagne from a passing tray and motioned to ask if he should take another. Cotton shook his head and walked over to a table where ice water was being offered and poured himself a glass. He assumed they were about forty to fifty miles inside Slovakia. He hadn't been able to see any of what was beyond the castle as the courtyard had totally blocked his field of vision and the windows here, in the great hall, were too high up. Olivier had made sure that there would be little to nothing that could be used to pinpoint a location. That should not hinder Ivona. But what exactly would she do?

Good question.

He glanced across at the delegates and wondered if any of them had also managed to lead the way for someone else. Or was he the only bird dog on this hunt? Bunch sauntered over and approached the Chinese delegation. One of the serving staff removed the Holy Lance from the table and carried it off. Most likely to confirm authenticity. But this auction wasn't about sacred relics. They were merely icing. The cake was damaging information on the current president of Poland.

"Malone," Bunch called out. "Come over here. I want to introduce you."

The man was oblivious to anything and everything beyond himself. But something about this whole setup screamed trouble.

And he still wondered about the older guy in the second-floor gallery.

Who was he?

And why was he there?

CHAPTER
FORTY-ONE

CZAJKOWSKI LIKED THE FACT THAT NO ONE RECOGNIZED HIM. HE'D
dressed in casual clothes and blended in easily with the hundreds of
people that surrounded him. Most were foreign tourists, many pilgrims,
their presence understandable given he was entering Poland's spiritual
capital.

An abbey had stood on the hill beneath him since the 13th century,
manned continuously by the Pauline Fathers. It grew into a fortified
complex of thick stone walls that had withstood multiple sieges, the most
notable from the Swedes in 1655. The nearby town of Częstochowa,
along the River Warta, had always been a center for trade, and now was a
major industrial center for metals, textiles, and chemicals.

He'd left Kraków in an unmarked car with two of his security detail. The drive north had taken a little over an hour through a picturesque stretch of limestone hills called the Jurassic Upland. Many of the
mounds, which stretched for hundreds of miles in both directions, were
crowned with castle ruins in what had come to be labeled the Trail of
the Eagle's Nest. Another popular destination. Buses flooded there every
day, offering tourists some amazing photo opportunities of sites that
once protected Poland from invaders.

He followed the crowds and climbed the wide stone steps, passing
beneath the first of four gates that led into Jasna Góra Monastery. They

were not only highly ornamented and strikingly beautiful, but practical, too, since they presented an invader with multiple challenges to gain entry. The rest of the monastery was surrounded by thick bastions with ramparts at each corner, all defensive in nature.

Every day, from dawn to dusk, streams of pilgrims approached the monastery via a long tree-lined avenue that led into town. He'd passed today's visitors on the drive in, the groups deep in prayer and singing hymns. Many of the pilgrims wore badges with the name of their hometown and a number showing how many times they'd come before. Fitting that he, too, was making a pilgrimage, only of a different kind, with a different purpose.

He passed through the last gate and entered an enclosed area surrounded by buildings. Waiting for him was a stout, white-robed man with a neck and chin covered in a thick, matted beard. The man had aged in the years since he'd last seen him, the belly a bit fuller, hair thinner, the jowls drooping. Interesting that this man—whom he knew to be clever, tough, resourceful, and completely without conscience—had become a monk.

"So wonderful to see you again," the man greeted.

It had been two decades since their paths had last crossed.

"Stanis, or I should say Father Orlik. It's wonderful to see you, too."

His old friend extended a hand, more like a paw, which he accepted and shook. The grip remained hard and firm. His two security men stood a few feet away, trying to blend in. People streamed in and out from the nearby ticket office. He knew that all of the tours were guided by monks.

"Not working today?" he asked Stanis.

"I was. Until you called."

He caught the glint in the older man's eyes. Just like the old days.

"Shall we go inside," Stanis said. "Where we can have some privacy."

He turned to his security men and told them to wait in place. Neither was happy about that decision, but no arguments were offered.

Above him rose a tower, over a hundred meters, one of the tallest in the country, topped by a cross. About a third of the way up the cream-colored brick façade a clock face read 11:50 A.M. He could not linger long. Ivona would be dealing with the auction soon and he had to be available when she called.

But this had to be done.

Stanislaw "Stanis" Orlik once served a high position within Solidarity. Of course, he was also much younger, as they all were back then. Orlik's job was not one that the organization had ever publicly recognized. His name had never appeared in any of the countless books that had been written about the movement. Only a few had known of his existence. But he was a man with a razor-sharp mind and a vast repertoire of talents. Czajkowski only learned of him after his unexpected visit to Mokotów Prison, when he was confronted on the street by three men and led away to an apartment in a crowded Warsaw neighborhood.

Stanis had been waiting there.

"Please, Janusz. Have a seat."

"How do you know my name?"

"It's my job to know those things."

He remained standing. *"What do you want with me?"*

"We need your help."

"Who is we?"

"Your country. Your brothers in the fight against the oppressors. Solidarity. Choose one."

"You know where I've just been."

Orlik nodded. *"That is exactly why we need your help."*

He was so confused. First the government had coerced him, wanting from him that which he could never deliver. Now his own people were doing the same thing.

"What do you want?" he asked again.

"Are you still forcing people into doing what you desire?" he asked Stanis as they walked.

"There's not much call for my services within the order. I dedicate myself these days to more selfless endeavors."

He doubted that, since this man had headed Solidarity's most secret intelligence and counterintelligence units. For more than ten years Stanis had wreaked havoc with the SB, disrupting the security services at every turn, turning their own tactics against them, creating nothing but chaos.

They entered the Basilica of the Assumption of the Blessed Virgin Mary and Founding of the Holy Cross, an enormous brick-and-stone structure elongated toward the north. Its vaulted ceiling was covered in rich stucco frameworks, everything colorful and airy. Frescoes abounded, as did polychrome paintings, all geared to the Virgin Mary—appropriate, since the entire monastery was a Marian shrine. Groups of people milled about admiring the spectacle, all accompanied by white-robed guides.

Stanis had stayed within Solidarity until 1991. Once Wałęsa had been elected president, there was no further need for his services. He'd then moved into the government and worked there for a while, but eventually faded away. About ten years ago he resurfaced as a Pauline monk.

"Why did you turn to the church?"

Stanis shrugged. "God called me. I simply answered."

Short. Concise. To the point. Classic Stanis.

"I never thought of you as religious," he said. "Not ever."

"Faith is a personal matter. One we keep to ourselves. But with what we did, faith seemed the only way for me to stay sane."

That was true. Faith among those who once fought the communists had been strong. The church had played a key role in all that happened, aided by the fact that the pope at the time was Polish. Many took that as a sign from God that they were on the right track.

"Now it is my life," Stanis said.

And he believed that. Stanis, if nothing else, was a pragmatic man, and whatever he did, he did well. Their first encounter in 1982 had been both unexpected and confrontational. But after that, they became more than colleagues. Perhaps even friends. Until 1991 they worked closely together, behind the scenes, implementing what they called the Warsaw Protocol.

Stanis stopped, standing beside him. "It's interesting, is it not? The two of us, here, and no one seems to know who we are. Me? That's understandable. I was always anonymous. But you. Once anonymous, but no longer."

Several hundred people roamed about around them, many headed toward the Chapel of the Miraculous Image, the main reason why pilgrims traveled to this holy spot.

"This is about as anonymous as my job ever gets," he said.

"What's happening?" Stanis finally asked in a whisper, his old friend's gaze still out into the basilica.

"The past is coming back."

"Did you ever think it gone?"

"I'd hoped so. I was wrong."

"A wise person once said that the past cannot be changed. Only the future is in our power."

"I prefer what Napoleon said. *If we open a quarrel between past and present, we shall find that we have lost the future.*"

Stanis chuckled. "And the election is fast approaching."

"Precisely."

"Is it that bad?"

"Enough that you and I have to deal with it."

"Just you and I?"

"No. Thankfully, I have other resources and they, too, are dealing with it, as we speak."

Stanis motioned ahead.

"Then let us visit with Our Lady and see if she can help us find wisdom."

CHAPTER
FORTY-TWO

JONTY SURVEYED THE GREAT HALL FOR THE FINAL TIME.

Everyone had arrived, and now all six delegations were milling about enjoying food, drink, and conversation. Even the Iranians and North Koreans, who seemed far more cordial than he'd envisioned. Frequent visits of the servers offering fresh trays of food and drink attested to the growing ease among the bidders. His expert had verified that all seven of the Arma Christi were authentic—which was good news—and they were safely tucked away in a car, just beyond the inner courtyard, awaiting him after the auction. The expert had been paid and was gone. He and Vic would leave as soon as the business was concluded. He'd deal with Eli tomorrow from long distance.

Reinhardt and his sidekick were behaving themselves, disappearing from the second-floor gallery, prepared to listen to the auction from an open, upper bedroom door, out of sight. He was certain that everyone was nervous, considering they would be bidding against one another, each wondering if the other might do something stupid. Vic's latest report was that all remained quiet both inside the castle and beyond.

He checked his pocket watch.

A Breguet. Eighteen-karat gold. Hand-engraved on a rose engine. Nearly $750,000 U.S. A gift to himself after another lucrative deal. He'd have to reward himself big after today.

Outside, a sonorous bell unleashed a cascade of peals.

Noon.

"Shall we get started," he called out.

COTTON HEADED FOR THE TWO CHAIRS ADORNED BY AN AMERICAN
flag. He noted that the other bidders were likewise denoted by their respective national colors. France, Iran, Russia, China, North Korea. He
wondered why Great Britain and Germany were not involved, but perhaps they'd declined. He recalled that the Arma Christi consisted of
seven relics. But only six had been on the oak table. Where was the Holy
Nail? And who was the older man that had been staring down from the
second-floor gallery? He hadn't seen him the past twenty minutes.

Not knowing the players, the room, the house, or even where he was
located was unsettling to say the least. But he'd been in worse situations.
Tom Bunch remained oblivious, busy socializing with the French. It
seemed everyone here had heeded the warning in the email instructions
regarding no translators—they all spoke English.

"This is all so exciting," Bunch said as they took their seats. "We're
right in the middle of the storm."

"You do realize that the eye of a storm is the worst place to be, since
that means trouble is raging all around you."

"Ah, quit being such a pessimist. Here we are, representing our country. About to buy some information that will allow us to stick it to the
Russians and the Iranians at the same time. How many chances at that
do you get? Not many, Malone. Not many at all."

On a small wooden table before them were two notepads and pen-
cils, a carafe of ice water, two glasses, and a sealed manila envelope upon
which was written DO NOT OPEN UNTIL INSTRUCTED. Cotton noticed
that the servers had all withdrawn and the room's heavy oak doors were
closed.

Jonty Olivier stepped to the front of the assemblage, beside a big-
screen television supported by a thick wooden frame. "I want to formally
welcome everyone and thank you for participating. I know you're anxious

but, prior to conducting the bidding, I have some documents to show you. Each of you was provided a sample at the time of your invitation. Now I would like to share a bit more, as a good-faith offering to demonstrate the wealth and value of the information that is for sale here today."

"We appreciate that," Bunch called out. "Nobody likes to buy a pig in a poke."

Cotton caught the curious look on the faces in the hall. Probably not a phrase many outside of America had much familiarity with.

"No, Mr. Bunch," Olivier said. "No one ever likes to do that, and we will make sure no one buys a problem today. Everything I have for sale is authentic. Now, some further instructions before we begin. I want everyone to conduct themselves with courtesy and respect. Civility is expected. As you can see, I have not employed any security personnel to keep order. I am trusting each of you to maintain a proper decorum. Are we clear?"

"We not children," one of the Russians said.

"Certainly not," Olivier replied. "But you are all passionate people, here on a mission, with differing goals and objectives. That can lead to . . . irrational thinking. Let us not have any of that."

No one else chimed in.

"All right, please open the envelope before you. Remove the clipped stack of documents and place them on the table."

JONTY STEPPED OVER TO THE BIG-SCREEN TELEVISION FACING HIS twelve guests, black at the moment, but about to come alive thanks to the laptop connected to it, resting on a shelf behind. The agenda was simple. Tantalize them with more of what he possessed, then, once their appetite had been whetted, open the bidding. Everyone had already been notified that the auction was with reserve, which meant he could reject any offer prior to accepting the final bid.

And for good reason.

He had no intention of selling what he had cheap.

What would the ultimate price be? Hard to say. He'd make a decision on what to accept as things progressed.

He resisted the urge to glance upward at the second-floor gallery, not wanting to draw any attention that way. He'd told Eli to stay out of sight and it appeared his nemesis was heeding that directive. Vic knew to keep an eye on things and would alert him of anything out of the ordinary. Everyone else was gone from the premises, as previously arranged, including all of the drivers and staff. They would be recalled when the proceedings were over. His focus now turned to the people in the great hall.

He switched on the screen. "Please remove the top blank sheet on the stack before you."

He punched a key on the laptop and brought a document up.

A crisp, high-resolution image.

"Let me explain what we are seeing."

CHAPTER
FORTY-THREE

CZAJKOWSKI ENTERED THE CHAPEL OF THE MIRACULOUS IMAGE, a tight, compact space topped by a ribbed, Gothic vault. Cordovan protected the lower walls, a gold-plated leather decorated with ornaments and impressions. At the far end, just past the ebony-and-silver altar, set amid a background of Baroque, hung the image that millions of pilgrims came from all over the world to adore.

Our Lady of Jasna Góra.

A Black Madonna.

Not all that large. Its ornate wooden frame about one hundred centimeters tall and eighty wide, resting under a canopy, as if on a throne. The image was of a half figure of Mary, with the Child Jesus in her arms, both figures dark-skinned in the Byzantine style, their faces lost in reflection, gilded halos filled with gems wrapping their heads. Mary wore a blue cloak dotted with golden lilies, the baby a carmine robe. His left hand held a book and the right extended outward in a gesture of blessing, symbolic of the way to salvation. The Lady's face was beautiful, piercing the onlooker with deep piety. People called her a *hodegetria*.

She who knows the way.

Legend proclaimed that it was painted by St. Luke the Evangelist upon a plank from the table at which the Holy Family ate. Reality was far different. It was a Balkan image created during the Middle Ages, tempera on canvas, attached to three lime tree boards, claimed as a war prize by a Polish prince and presented to the monastery. Miracles had always been associated with the image, particularly physical healing. That drew pilgrims, who'd come for centuries, many bringing votive gifts in return for a miraculous intercession. Many of those gifts now adorned the chapel walls as a testimony of thanks. After Hussites raided in the 15th century and vandalized the image it was restored, but the parallel slashes on Mary's cheek were left, impregnated with red cinnabar, the marks another symbol of Poland's constant scars.

Today the chapel was full of worshipers searching for consolation and deliverance, many approaching the image on their knees, as was customary, a sign of humility and respect. Even Hitler had shown Our Lady deference, taking the monastery but not touching the image, only forbidding anyone from worshiping. But that did not stop the Poles, who continued to come in secret all during the war.

Stanis performed the sign of the cross and he followed suit. His faith remained strong and he firmly believed that the Virgin Mary's presence was here. He knew several people who'd been healed from a visit. They stood at the rear of the reverent crowd, beyond a stout railing, the room in utter silence, only the scrape of cloth from the knees to stone disturbing the silence. A nearby showcase featured canes, crutches, and other medical devices left behind by people who'd been cured.

Quite a testimonial.

His old friend seemed to be in deep prayer, so he joined him in the traditional plea.

Holy Mother of Częstochowa, Thou art full of grace, goodness and mercy. I consecrate to Thee all my thoughts, words and actions—my soul and body. I beseech Thy blessings and especially prayers for my salvation. Today, I consecrate myself to Thee, Good Mother, totally—with body and soul amid joy and sufferings to obtain for myself and others Thy blessings on this earth and eternal life in Heaven.

He muttered an *amen* and hoped it helped, as his troubles were mounting by the moment. Every minute he spent here was another minute he would not hear from Ivona. Cell phones were not allowed inside the monastery, and that prohibition included the president of the country. So any contact was going to have to wait.

Stanis finished his prayer, crossed himself again, then whispered, "Come with me."

They left the chapel and headed back into the basilica, bypassing its opulence and finding a series of rear passages that led to a room marked BIBLIOTEKA. Inside was a magnificent paneled library, heavy with Baroque, lined with wooden cases. Decorative cartouches above each defined its subject matter. Two massive tables stood on the checkerboard marble floor, their tops a puzzle of polished wood in remarkable patterns. The shelves were lined with illuminated medieval manuscripts, all safe within gilded leather cases. One after the other. Thousands of them. The vault overhead was a sea of bright frescoes praising life and learning, the room illuminated by bright chandeliers. On the vaulting above he noticed a painted phrase. SAPIENTIA AEDIFICAVIT SIBI DOMUM. Wisdom hath built her house. He breathed in the rich aroma of aged leather and took some solace from the phrase.

"Shall we sit," Stanis said.

They each slid out a wooden chair from one of the tables.

"The time may have come to publicly discuss the protocol," he said to Stanis. "So much time has passed. It doesn't matter anymore."

"But it does. We took an oath and that means something to me. It should mean something to you."

"Remaining president of this country for another five years means more to me than any oath we took decades ago."

His old friend gave him a puzzled look.

So he explained what he was facing.

"Do you ever think about those times?" Stanis asked when he finished. "When we changed the world."

"I prefer to concentrate on the future. Part of that is keeping this country safe. American missiles will make us a prime target for Russia and Iran. I cannot allow that to happen. The United States wants to force me either to resign or to lose the coming election. If my people cannot contain that auction, the whole country will see me as a traitor. Only you and I will know different."

"But, Janusz, that was the whole idea. Secrecy is what made it all work. Nothing could have been accomplished otherwise."

He knew this was going to be difficult, but he had to try. "Stanis, if the Americans acquire those SB documents, they will use them to force me to accept missiles inside our borders."

"Would you do such a thing?"

"I would be placed in an untenable position. If I resign, the marshal of Parliament will become acting president and he will definitely allow them to be placed here. If I refuse, they will expose me as some sort of traitor. I prefer better options than that."

The older man sat silent.

He'd never been able to gauge this enigma's thinking.

"During the Second World War, Polish resistance fighters met here, inside this library, to plot strategy," Stanis finally said. "They assumed they were safe in a monastery and, for the most part, they were. Those brave men and women did a lot of damage. They disrupted German supply lines, provided military intelligence, and saved more Jews than any Allied government. All part of the great Polish Underground State. Which we inherited when we began the fight against the Soviets. We were the new Polish Underground State."

"And those sacrifices have not been forgotten. We celebrate them every September 27. The Day of the Polish Underground State. The Nazis and the Soviets are gone, Stanis. The enemies today are much different. Many times they are your friends. The world has changed. I'll say it again. I need your help."

"I want to show you something."

Stanis rose and approached the shelves, removing one of the tall leather cases, from which he freed an old tome.

"This is the first volume of the *Miraculorum Beate Virginia Monasterii Czestochoviensis,* a record of 498 miracles attributed to Our Lady from 1402 to 1642."

He was amazed. "They actually kept records?"

"Oh, yes. The Pauline monks were quite meticulous. They handwrote and documented each one of the miracles with facts about how it occurred, along with witnesses to the event. Two handwritten and five printed registries still exist that inventory the miracles over a four-hundred-year period. Whether those accounts are true is impossible to determine. All we know is that they exist."

"I assume there's a point to this."

Stanis smiled. "Definitely. I, too, have a record."

He waited.

"Of the Warsaw Protocol."

CHAPTER FORTY-FOUR

COTTON STARED AT THE BIG SCREEN, WHICH DISPLAYED AN IMAGE of a handwritten document, the page filled with a heavy masculine script, all in Polish. At the bottom was a signature, a bit smeared but readable.

Janusz Czajkowski.

Along with a date.

August 9, 1982.

"As you can see, in the lower left corner is a seal, one used by the Służba Bezpieczeństwa from the 1970s until 1989 to certify its records. There are hundreds of thousands of these SB documents in existence with the same seal. Many are archived at the Institute of National Remembrance. The documents at issue today were kept by a former SB major, a man named Aleksy Dilecki, who recruited a young Solidarity activist, Janusz Czajkowski, as a government informant. You have a copy of this document in the stack of papers before you. Please take a closer look."

Bunch was already reaching for the sheet.

"Do you read Polish?" he asked Bunch.

"Hell, no. If it's not English, it's not important to me."

Why was he not surprised.

Languages were easy for him, thanks to an eidetic memory he inherited from his father's side of the family. Unfortunately, Polish was not in his repertoire.

"For those of you not proficient," Olivier said, "I have provided a translation in your native tongues on the next sheet."

Cotton reached for that page ahead of Bunch.

Together they read the English.

Olivier pointed at the screen. "This document states that Janusz Czajkowski agrees to work as an informant and provide good and valuable information to the SB. You might ask, why was such a record created? Why not just keep everything informal? It was done to ensure the absolute loyalty of the informant. At the time, to be an informant was perhaps the worst thing a Pole could do. Releasing the signed document to the public would have been a way to disgrace the signer. Informants were terrified of being exposed, as there would be repercussions from both sides. So informants did what was expected of them, mostly as a way not to be exposed." Olivier paused. "You can also see that Czajkowski was given a code name to be used in the future. And not all that flattering either. *Baran.* Sheep."

Cotton studied the handwriting on the Polish copy.

"The signature has been authenticated," Olivier said. "I employed three world-renowned experts who reviewed comparative material in the form of 142 documents that were either drafted or signed by Janusz Czajkowski in the time frame from 1987 to last year. These included, among others, his former identity card, driver's license, proof of vehicle registration, documents from his time serving in Parliament, documents related to his purchase of land and a home, personnel files from two employers, pages stored in the Office of the President of the Republic of Poland for the last five years, and passport files, all of which I obtained. The handwriting experts' findings will be provided to you. They all agree, with no reservation, that the documents at issue here are all in Czajkowski's hand."

"And what if they are wrong," one of the French called out. "And these are fakes."

"I assure you, I have no intention of selling fakes. Or a pig in a poke, as Mr. Bunch put it earlier. If any of them are deemed a forgery or fake within fourteen days of this sale, I will return your money. After that, they are yours with no reservations. That should provide you plenty of time to authenticate. How much more of a guarantee do you want?"

"But you will already have our money?" one of the Iranians said.

"True. But all of you can hunt me down in a matter of hours. I recognize that fact and have given it the respect it is due."

Smart play, Cotton thought. Address the issue of credibility up front and acknowledge that the bidders were in a superior position. Everyone in the room seemed satisfied with both the concession and the condition.

"In the stack before you are more examples of the writings that will be for sale today. I will give you a few moments to study them. There is also an inventory sheet in your stack that provides an overview of all of what you will be buying."

Cotton studied the list.

1 handwritten commitment to cooperate with the Security Service of 9 August 1982;

37 handwritten confirmation notes of receipt of money transferred by security service officers in return for information, all created between 12 August 1982 and 29 June 1989, totaling PLN 11,700;

49 handwritten reports of a secret collaborator, drawn up and signed with the code name "Baran";

18 reports of a secret collaborator, not bearing the code name or any other signature, but definitely in the handwriting of Janusz Czajkowski;

26 handwritten reports of a secret collaborator prepared by Janusz Czajkowski, code named "Baran," as outlined by the appointed security service officer (Aleksy Dilecki);

5 handwritten reports consisting of 34 pages prepared by the appointed security service officer (Aleksy Dilecki), bearing the codename "Baran";

11 handwritten reports by the secret collaborator drawn up and signed with the code name "Baran" by the appointed security service officer (Aleksy Dilecki).

One hundred and forty-seven pages.

That was a lot for Czajkowski to deny as a forgery.

The sheer volume spoke to their authenticity, as did Olivier's confidence in his experts and his money-back guarantee, secured, of course, with his life.

"I'm convinced," Bunch whispered.

Again, no surprise.

"To be labeled a former communist informant today in Polish society retains the same stigma as it once possessed. Maybe even more so. But to be the president of the nation and have such a label stamped on you? That is unthinkable," Olivier said. "Look what happened to Lech Wałęsa. Documents surfaced showing he, too, may have been an informant. Handwriting experts verified their authenticity. Wałęsa declared the documents fake, created by the communists to discredit him. Eventually, a Polish court declared that he had *not* been a collaborator. But the stink would not go away. Finally, Wałęsa admitted to signing the documents, but said he was playing the SB, trying to learn what he could about them." Olivier shrugged. "What's the truth? Who knows? What we do know is that the taint remains. Here the situation is much clearer. Czajkowski was one of millions who joined Solidarity in the 1980s. He was no Lech Wałęsa. He was a nobody. No one would have created any false documents to discredit him."

"Unless they are a more recent forgery," one of the Chinese said.

"Which will be an easy matter to expose. My experts tell me that the originals you will be buying are from the 1980s. The paper. The ink. Everything is consistent. Czajkowski's SB handler apparently kept many documents relative to various informants. Czajkowski was just one of many. I personally viewed his cache."

"He's still alive?" one of the Russians asked.

"Long dead. But the information survived. There were two filing cabinets full of paper. One drawer was special. Documents on people who had achieved prominence since 1990, people whom the SB major had once been familiar with. He kept those files separate. One of those dealt with a young Solidarity activist named Janusz Czajkowski, who went on to achieve great things."

Olivier went silent, seemingly allowing his words to take hold.

Bunch appeared thrilled at the prospects.

Cotton remained concerned.

Nothing about blackmail ever turned out good.

CHAPTER
FORTY-FIVE

CZAJKOWSKI STARED AT HIS OLD FRIEND.

Had he heard right?

"You have a record of the protocol?"

"I was mindful that one day history might need proof. After we are all gone."

Thank God for obsessive-compulsive behavior. It was what made Stanis such a superb intelligence officer, though he knew that his old friend hated the label. He'd much preferred *Sowa,* which was what Lech Wałęsa had privately called him, while always adding a sly smile.

"Are you still the Owl?" he asked.

Stanis smiled and nodded. "Solitary, nocturnal, with perfect vision, incredible hearing, and sharp talons. But I'm not much of a hunter anymore for people's weaknesses. Thankfully, the people we dealt with back then had plenty to exploit."

"Where is your record of the Warsaw Protocol?"

"Safely hidden away."

"Right now, as we speak, an auction is occurring where documents that are 100 percent authentic are being offered for sale to foreigners intent on using them to blackmail me. If that happens I would then have two choices. Concede to their threats or be publicly ruined. I could even be tried for crimes against peace and humanity by the Commission for the Prosecution of Crimes Against the Polish Nation. What we did may certainly qualify. And I emphasize the *we* there. Many who we dealt with are still alive. Men and women who would testify against us."

"You're not the first who has come to me."

He was surprised.

"Wałęsa came and asked the same thing you are asking to deal with his own troubles."

He was surprised. "Why would he do that?"

"It's simple, Mr. President. He was the one who tasked me with running the Warsaw Protocol." Stanis paused. "He was also its first participant."

Now he was shocked.

The idea of the protocol had been simple. Turn SB's informants into counter-informants. Not all of them, of course, as there were far too many. But enough to cause havoc within the security services. A small cadre of men and women who routinely made reports to their handlers—except those reports were Stanis's creations. Some were innocuous, meaningless information that kept the informants in the SB's good graces. Some were deliberate lies, sending the SB off chasing ghosts with false leads. Wasting time and resources.

But eventually the program traveled into darker territory.

The imposition of martial law changed everything. Where before everyone had hope that things were changing, that Solidarity was making progress, the strong arm of the government eventually crushed all political opposition and sent the freedom movement underground. Thousands were arrested and jailed. People fled the country by the hundreds of thousands. The SB expanded its reach and worked hard to pit Poles against Poles.

Spies were everywhere.

So Stanis devised a way to deal with those spies.

He used his army of counter-informants to turn the SB against their own. A perfect way to clear the opposition ranks. And it worked. Hundreds were arrested. People who thought themselves safe since they'd made a deal with the government to inform on their neighbors disappeared, never to be seen again. Most likely they were now rotting away in the ground somewhere, shot for their supposed duplicity. The communists were never tolerant of betrayal.

The Warsaw Protocol allowed Solidarity to continue to function without some of the prying eyes of the government. Was it 100 percent effective? Absolutely not. But it was effective enough to ensure that the movement survived.

And Wałęsa himself created it?

"What are you saying?" he asked Stanis.

"In the 1970s Wałęsa was recruited as an informant. Of course, at the time he was just a young electrician at the Gdańsk Shipyard. A nobody. But he was tough and scrappy. He hated the communists and everything they had done to Poland. He wanted to know more about them. So he allowed himself to be recruited. It was quite an education, one he put to good use years later when he helped lead a revolt."

When all of the furor arose over any supposed complicity, Wałęsa stayed silent for a while, but eventually stated that he was never an agent, never spied on anyone, took no money, and would prove it all in court. He also boldly stated that if he had to repeat his life, he would not change a thing

Now Czajkowski knew why.

"Wałęsa came here," Stanis said. "We sat at this same table. He wanted me to testify before the court and prove his innocence. He knew of my record of the protocol and wanted it made public. I refused."

"He took quite a public beating."

"That's true. But he survived. As you will, too."

"This is much different. He did not have to face an electorate. The safety of the Polish people was not at stake. Those missiles make us a target on Moscow's radar. They threaten our existence. We would have chosen sides in the conflict between East and West. My opponents will skewer me with those documents, if they are made public. Then the weak will bow down to the United States."

"You have little faith in your government."

"I have no faith. I believe only in me."

Stanis smiled. "You always were the tough one. I saw that the first day we spoke, and you proved it every day thereafter. You were a fighter."

He appreciated the kind words.

"I sympathize with your situation," Stanis said. "I truly do. But it doesn't change things."

No, he supposed not.

"I took Wałęsa's idea and expanded it from one person to hundreds, to eventually over a thousand. Not only did we learn about our enemy, we were able to mislead them, all made easy since they were too stupid and too anxious to be careful. In the process, yes, Poles were killed. But I have no regrets over those deaths. We had to weed out the traitors, and what better way to deal with them than allowing the government to kill its own. But what we did must remain secret. To reveal anything now would only taint what we accomplished."

"I have no regrets, either," he said. "Those people chose their fate when they became spies against their neighbors."

"That is exactly what Wałęsa said. I'll tell you the same thing I told him. I swore upon the Bible, to God, that I would take that secret to my grave. I kept a record only to clarify history, if that was ever needed, after I was gone. What happened to Wałęsa, what's happening to you now, requires no clarification. This is not my problem."

He shoved the chair back and came to his feet. Anger surged through him. "Not your problem? You coerced me into your scheme. Me and all of the others. We had no choice. Then I helped you recruit so many others. They, and I, worked for you so we could justify in our minds the weakness we'd shown to the SB." His voice kept rising. "We convinced ourselves we were doing the right thing playing both sides. And we were, Stanis. It helped win the war. We took down a government. We threw the communists out. We gave courage to all of Eastern Europe to follow our lead. We changed the world."

The white-robed prelate never moved, his face set in stone. He allowed a moment for his words to take hold. Finally, Stanis said, in barely a whisper, "That does not alter what we all agreed to."

"I can go public and expose it all." He pointed. "You included."

Stanis looked up at him. "You can. But the taint upon you will still be there."

"So what? I'm destroyed at that point. There are others, still alive, who participated. They can speak out, too."

"Not a one of whom would ever admit to being an informant, much less a counter-informant. None of those people want to relive any of that. Why would they? And if they do, it is merely their word. There is no proof. You will stand alone, Mr. President. Just as Wałęsa stood alone. Be strong, as he was."

"If I do nothing, I will be ruined. Poland will be infested with foreign missiles, and, if aggressions ever escalate, we'll be the first target Moscow will destroy. We'll be nothing but a puppet to the West. Beholden to it for our safety. Our existence. History has shown that nobody gives a damn what happens to Poland. But I do."

"You can draw comfort from the fact that you know the truth. That we did what was necessary and changed the world. In fact, what we did allows you to be in the position you now are in. It was glorious, Janusz. Glorious."

He headed for the door.

This had been a waste of time.

He turned back and faced Stanis, his expression cold, his eyes conveying the rage he felt. "That glory doesn't mean a thing anymore. It only counts within the mind of the pathetic coward who hides behind these walls."

And he left.

CHAPTER FORTY-SIX

COTTON NOW UNDERSTOOD WHAT ALL THE FUROR WAS ABOUT. Somehow Jonty Olivier had managed to acquire 147 documents, most in President Janusz Czajkowski's own hand, that directly implicated the president of Poland as a former communist informant.

He had to admit, it definitely looked bad.

"President Fox is going to love this," Bunch whispered. "It's everything he needs to make those missiles happen."

"And you think Poland is just going to roll over? Give you what you want? Without a fight?"

"Get real, Malone. What can they do? If Czajkowski wants to stay president, he'll work with us. It's that simple."

No, it wasn't.

Far from it, in fact.

The Poles were a tough, resilient people who had survived both the Nazis and the Soviets. That was no small feat. They were now, once again, a free nation and Cotton doubted they would relinquish that independence without a fight. Actually, he was counting on a fight. A part of him knew that his duty was to aid his country. But another part told him that his country was dead wrong.

"Are there any questions?" Olivier asked from the front of the gathering.

"Will we have the documents today, when we leave? You've insisted that payment has to be verified and completed immediately. When will we get what we paid for?" one of the French asked.

"The documents are not here. I have hidden them away in a place that is fairly inaccessible. I'm sure you can understand that precaution. I am the only one who knows that location. But again, all of you possess a vast multitude of resources, so obtaining them will be easy. I will inform my assistant, Vic DiGenti, of the location after the auction, and if you desire he can be your guide. I'm hoping that gesture is a further demonstration of my good faith."

"And your distrust of us," one of the Russians added.

"What is there to trust?" Olivier said. "Each of you is here for differing reasons, most of which conflict with the other. I realize that none of you are above using violence to get what you want. So no, I trust none of you. As I'm sure none of you trust me. This whole endeavor is not about trust. It's about power."

"It's about blackmail," Cotton said. "And coercion."

Olivier faced him. "I suppose it is. A most unpleasant business."

"But profitable," he said, adding a smile.

"That it is. Or at least, I'm hoping so."

Olivier extended his arms in a welcome embrace.

Everyone looked back in silent anticipation.

"Shall we begin?"

CZAJKOWSKI RODE IN THE BACK OF THE CAR DRIVEN BY HIS TWO security people, still unnerved by the meeting with his former boss. Stanis had always been a hard man, difficult to know, even harder to like. But the nature of the job had demanded a certain degree of detachment. Of all the recruits, only a few managed to get close. He'd always thought himself one of those. How many counter-informants had he personally recruited for Stanis? Fifty? More like a hundred. People who'd placed their lives on the line. Some even gave their lives. Others had them taken. Which would all come out if the protocol became public. The good and the bad. How would the people react? Would he face charges? Had what he'd done been a crime against peace and humanity? Hard to say. And that indecision troubled him.

His cell phone vibrated.

He found the unit and saw it was Ivona.

"I hope you have good news," he said, answering.

"The tracker worked," she said. "The auction is occurring at Sturney Castle, inside Slovakia. Not that far away."

No, it wasn't. "Where are you?"

"Positioned about half a kilometer away, among the trees. I've watched as three cars drove inside, all similar to the cars that brought Cotton and Bunch."

"You still think Malone knew you would be following?"

"Absolutely. You have to think that whoever transported Malone and Bunch to the castle guarded against being followed. Yet Cotton made sure that tracker stayed active. I was able to stay a long way back. Now I just have to figure out how to get inside, undetected."

"What do you plan to do, once there?"

"Improvise."

"Be careful."

"You sound like you care."

"I do."

He heard the smile in her voice.

"Which is wonderful to hear. I'll check back when I have something to report."

The call ended.

He considered having Mirosław "Father Stanis" Orlik arrested and a full-scale search instituted for his so-called proof. Maybe tie him naked over a stool? He hated himself for even thinking such a thing. Was that desperation? What else could it be? It drove the communists, but it would never motivate him. He was the duly elected president of the Republic of Poland. Entrusted with looking after the welfare of the nation. His job was to make smart, informed decisions that advanced the greater good. Only this was personal. No other way to view it, since everything was being directed his way.

"Do you wish to go to the airport?" one of the security men asked.

They were headed south back toward Kraków and would pass the airport on the way. But he could not return to Warsaw.

Not yet.

"No. To the hotel, please."

CHAPTER FORTY-SEVEN

ELI REINHARDT STOOD JUST INSIDE THE OPEN BEDROOM DOOR, listening to what was happening past the second-floor railing, down in the great hall. It seemed everything was about to begin.

He turned to Munoz. "Are you ready?"

His associate nodded and walked over to the bed. A black Louis Vuitton duffel bag lay on the woven spread. They'd brought it with them when they arrived last night at the castle. Jonty had been overly accommodating and not searched anything. Eli had been counting on a drop in guard, hoping Olivier would be trying as hard as he could not to antagonize anyone. That was why he'd made such an inviting offer to seal their "partnership," conceding away half of the hidden cache and defraying any financial interest in the auction save for a relatively small cash payment. Of course twenty million euros was not necessarily "small," but he had to display some semblance of opportunism. Otherwise, Jonty definitely would have become suspicious. Now here he was, exactly where he wanted to be.

He listened as Jonty called for the first round of bids. He heard fifty million euros. Then sixty. Seventy.

"We need to deal with Mr. DiGenti," he said to Art. "While things progress below."

Munoz reached into the duffel bag and removed two Uzis with extended forty-round clips. An old-school weapon, but proven and reliable. He laid them on the bed, then found two pistols, with sound suppressors attached to their short barrels, inside the bag. Eli grabbed one of the pillows and handed it to Munoz. They slipped from the room, staying close to the inner wall, the second-floor railing three meters away. No way they could be seen from below. They left the gallery and found a corridor at one end that led deeper into the castle. DiGenti was holed up in one of the second-floor bedrooms in a makeshift command post, monitoring the closed-circuit cameras that watched the main gate and other points beyond the walls, waiting for the auction to conclude. The jammer was located there, too, which cut off all communications in and out. A single laptop was the exception, hot-wired to a direct internet line to be used shortly to verify the high bid and transfer funds. Jonty had seemed quite proud of all the preparations when he'd shown them off earlier.

They approached the closed door.

He signaled for Art to position himself to one side while he grabbed the knob. His minion gripped the gun, nestling the suppressor's end into the pillow. What was about to happen would be irrevocable. No turning back. But he'd known that would be the case when he agreed to all of this in the first place.

He gripped the knob and slowly turned, pushing the heavy panel inward. DiGenti reacted to the intrusion by springing to his feet, where he sat before video monitors, and turning toward the door, reaching for a weapon in a shoulder holster. Art never hesitated, firing the 9mm twice and sending the thin, wiry man to the floor. They entered and Eli closed the door. Art fired one last time through the pillow, planting a third round into DiGenti's skull.

Little sound had escaped.

Perfect.

He approached the monitors and studied the images, each a different swath of the outer walls and the road into the castle. Leaves on the birches and oaks hung motionless in the midday sun.

DiGenti was all Jonty had for protection inside the castle. The staff had left just before the auction began, as had all the chauffeurs. No chance for any prying eyes or ears to see or hear anything. A wise precaution, but it also provided the perfect opportunity.

He found the signal jammer and switched it off.

Then he sent a text message out over his phone that all was clear.

One more thing.

He stepped over and searched DiGenti's pockets, hoping. Jonty had told the participants that his man would be available to lead the winner to the prize, saying that his associate was not yet aware of the information's location.

That had to be a lie.

Jonty would never have done that all by himself.

Perhaps there was some written record of that location? And in the front pocket he found a folded sheet of paper. On it was written 9 BOBOLA.

Was this it?

Could be.

He pocketed the paper.

"Let's return to the auction and see where it goes," he said, his voice low. "And finish this."

COTTON WAS IMPRESSED.

The latest bid was 120 million euros from the Iranians. The French and the Chinese seemed to have hit their limit, as they'd not upped the ante once it topped one hundred million. The North Koreans also were beginning to go silent. It seemed to be a battle between Russia, Iran, and the United States, the three with the most skin in the game.

"One hundred fifty million," Bunch said in a firm, decisive voice.

Quite a jump.

Thirty million euros in one swipe.

"One hundred sixty," the Russians bid.

Olivier was directing traffic in a calm, collected manner, keeping things moving, not allowing a lot of time for the participants to hesitate. He could, at any moment, bring things to a close, and none of the three still in the game would want that to happen. Not unless, of course, one of them was the high bidder.

"One hundred seventy-five," the Iranians said.

"Two hundred million," the Russians countered.

"Two fifty," Bunch called out.

A quarter of a billion euros. Cotton wondered if any piece of information was worth that much.

But apparently so.

"You do realize," one of the Russians said, "that we have lots of money, too."

"Then spend it," Bunch said. "Two hundred and fifty million euros is America's bid."

"Three hundred," the Russian said, his face defiant.

"Three fifty," Bunch countered.

"Four hundred," the North Koreans said.

Which momentarily jarred the room.

Cotton wondered where the Democratic People's Republic of Korea would get nearly half a billion euros. That was a substantial sum for anyone.

No one countered.

"What's the problem?" he whispered to Bunch.

"It's getting out of hand."

"You think?"

"Four hundred and fifty million," the Russian said in a calm voice.

Something was wrong. The bidding was progressing in unusual leaps. No one was interested in inching the price upward. Instead they all seemed intent on preempting the others with outrageous numbers. He stared at the participants hoping to transmit some of his own suspicions to them.

"Five hundred million," Bunch said.

Silence reigned.

The two Russians stood from their chairs. "We are done. Have a car brought for us."

"I must conclude this auction first," Olivier said.

"This auction is over for us."

"What's the matter," Bunch said. "Sore loser?"

The taller of the two Russians glared at Bunch, then said, "Mr. Malone. You met a man in Bruges. Did he not tell you what our intent would be."

We not know where auction will occur. But when we do, we will act. Tell Stephanie Nelle that I do not bluff.

Ivan's words right before he fired the Taser.

"That intent has not changed," the Russian said.

Cotton caught another pinprick of trouble in the man's cutting black eyes, a spark that flared a warning.

Not good.

"We wait outside."

The two Russians marched from the hall.

"Are there any more bids?" Olivier asked.

No one replied.

"Last chance."

More silence.

"Then I declare the United States the winner."

"Hot damn, Malone," Bunch said. "We did it."

But what exactly had they done?

ELI HAD LISTENED TO THE ENTIRE PROCEEDING.

Half a billion euros.

Jonty must be ecstatic.

There was talk coming from below as the auction wound down. He glanced out the doorway and saw the two Russian bidders who'd exited the hall appear at the top of the staircase.

He motioned for them to wait there, out of sight.

He and Munoz lifted an Uzi from the bed, then fled the room, staying away from the railing and easing toward the staircase, where they handed over the weapons. The two Russians then stepped across the second-floor gallery to the balustrade—

And opened fire.

CHAPTER
FORTY-EIGHT

CZAJKOWSKI REENTERED THE SHERATON GRAND KRAKÓW
through a back door that the hotel had made available for his exclusive
use. Two of the hotel's security men staffed the entrance and opened the
metal door for him as he approached. He was taking a huge chance lingering. His ruling coalition teetered on collapse almost every day, one faction
or another always demanding something. His job was to keep them all
happy and his chief of staff had already told him that people were asking questions. His answer was that he was working on the next election,
cementing what would be needed to carry Kraków and Małopolskie province. Which was not far from the truth. That should hold them off for
another day, which was all he needed. This would be over, one way or
another, soon.

He took an elevator up and walked back to the Royal Wawel Suite,
his two BOR security men in tow. Once inside, he'd have privacy, which
he'd need if Ivona called. His watch read nearly 1:00 P.M. and he wondered what was happening at that auction. Frightening that his entire
future was being decided by strangers trying to outbid one another for
the chance to destroy him. He flushed all that negativity from his mind,
reentered the suite, found his phone, and called Ivona.

"I only have a moment," she said. "I'm inside the castle."

"What's happening?"

"Trouble. A car arrived a few moments ago. I could not see who it was, but I followed it in on foot."

"Have you seen the auction?"

"Not yet. But I'm going to find it now."

He heard *rat-tat-tat* through the phone.

Then more.

"Is that gunfire?" he asked.

"I have to go."

Jonty's emotions went from a mountainous high of five hundred million euros, and how his life was about to irrevocably change, to the horrifying fear that his life could be over.

Gunshots.

From the upper gallery.

A deafening volley raked the hall.

He looked up and saw the two Russian bidders, who'd left, firing automatic weapons below. The people remaining in the great hall reacted to the attack and sprang from their seats, scattering, but with no cover they were simply cut down. One after another. The bodies of both Chinese erupted in splattering wounds, their muscles contorting in a drunken dance that ended with them smashing facedown to the stone floor. A similar fate met the French and Iranians.

Jonty stood, frozen with indecision, a nauseous feeling of panic surging toward his throat. Running seemed stupid.

But he should do something.

Fright welled in his throat and forced his breath to come in choppy gasps.

He dropped behind the big-screen TV and its wooden support, seeking cover.

COTTON REACTED WITH REFLEXES THAT HAD BEEN TRAINED AND conditioned long ago, springing from the chair and reaching for Tom Bunch. They were totally exposed in the center of the hall, at least fifty feet between here and where they'd be beyond the shooters' angle above. He yanked Bunch toward the right side of the hall, beneath the upper gallery.

But Bunch resisted and pulled away. "Olivier. We have to get to him."

Two new sounds entered the hall.

Gunshots from a different weapon.

A pistol.

Which momentarily stopped the Uzis.

His head whipped to the right and he saw Ivona rush into the hall, firing upward. He took advantage of the moment she'd bought him and lunged left, through an arch beneath the overhead gallery, out of the line of fire. The gunmen above resumed their attack, cutting down three more of the auction participants. Bunch foolishly moved toward Olivier, who was nowhere to be seen.

Above, Cotton caught sight of the two gunmen, at the railing, their weapons aimed downward.

The two Russian bidders.

"Halt," one of them yelled out.

Bunch froze.

He heard clips being ejected and fresh ones inserted. Everyone else who'd been part of the auction lay dead in ever-growing pools of blood. Only he and Bunch were unharmed. Along with Jonty Olivier, whom he now saw was crouched behind the TV. Ivona was across the hall, with no shot upward as the gunmen were directly above her. One of the Russians above let him know they were watching by unleashing a short barrage of rounds that obliterated the stone supporting the arch he was using for cover.

He managed to steal a quick peek around the edge and saw the older man from earlier staring down at him, another younger man standing beside him. Both gripped pistols. He also noticed that Ivona was no longer on the far side, most likely headed up to deal with the problem.

So stall them.

"Could you explain the point of all this?" he called out.

"The point obvious," a new voice said from above, with a Russian accent.

One he recognized.

Cotton glanced up to see a new face standing at the railing.

Ivan.

Who'd apparently found a way here, too.

"You were warned, Malone. Clear. Emphatic."

"We don't take orders from Moscow," Bunch yelled. "Not now. Not ever."

"Shut up, Tom," Cotton said, hoping the use of the first name would strike home.

He needed to buy Ivona more time, so he said, "Okay, Ivan, I get it. Point made. What now?"

"That depends on Olivier."

Cotton shifted positions to the other side of the pillar so he could see Olivier and Bunch more clearly. They both stood near the large-screen TV, their heads cocked upward. Concern filled Bunch's face.

"I should have known better," Olivier said. "You're no good."

"I rather think my performance was masterful," the older man holding the pistol said.

"What do you want, Eli?" Olivier said.

"I have what I want."

That didn't sound good.

"You had your people run the price up during the auction, didn't you?" Cotton asked, interrupting, calling out to Ivan. "Since you knew they were all going to die, why not bid hundreds of millions of euros?"

"Americans think money solves everything," Ivan said.

He caught Bunch's gaze with his own and motioned for him to stay quiet.

"Your president told Kremlin that you would not even be here," Ivan said. "All lies."

"It was necessary," Bunch said. "To deal with you."

One of the Uzis erupted in a brief rattle of fire.

Bunch's body jolted from the impact of the rounds, his face frozen in shock, his arms flailing, trying to maintain balance.

Then he collapsed to the floor.

Dead.

"That necessary, too," Ivan said.

Cotton shook his head.

Dammit.

CHAPTER
FORTY-NINE

ELI STARED DOWN INTO THE GREAT HALL.

Odd how thinking like a villain both worried and stimulated him. He faced the Russian named Ivan. His benefactor was short, heavy-chested, with grayish-black hair. He wore an ill-fitting suit that bulged at the waist. The deal had been to not only smuggle in the weapons but also lead the Russians to the site. That had been accomplished yesterday when Ivan had tracked the car he and Munoz had used to get to the castle. Again, Jonty had been far too accommodating. Then, once DiGenti had been eliminated, a text told Ivan the coast was clear for him to arrive.

"Malone, my friend," Ivan called out. "We must talk."

The American remained hidden behind the arch.

"You waiting for Ivona to act?" Ivan asked.

No reply.

"Ivona," Ivan called out. "Ivona."

More silence.

"Come out," Ivan said. "We must talk, too. You not suppose to be here, and you know that."

COTTON HEARD IVAN'S WORDS.

Not suppose to be here.

What was Ivona doing?

He looked around the stone arch. Five hostile faces stared down at him with silent menace. He glanced at Jonty Olivier who again crouched behind the big-screen TV, near Bunch's body.

"You killed a deputy national security adviser of the United States," Cotton called out.

"Who not be missed," Ivan said. "We have many deputies in Russia. Many more who want job. I'm sure you do, too."

"It will not go unanswered."

Ivan laughed. "Your new president not so tough. He thinks himself tough. But he just a liar. Unlike him, you know us, Malone. You would have listened and stayed away. I have no problem with you."

What had he gotten himself into? Obviously the Russians had been serious back in Bruges, but the carnage around him seemed a bit much even for them. So much risk. Taken against people who had the means and resources to retaliate.

And would.

He was bare ass to the wind, and there was little he could do. Five men stood in the gallery above him, two armed with Uzis, two with pistols. Stinking cordite filled the air, along with the coppery waft of blood.

"Come out, Jonty," the older man named Eli said. "There's no need to hide. If we wanted you dead, you would be already."

"Who are you?" Cotton asked.

"My name is Augustus 'Eli' Reinhardt V. I am an acquaintance of Jonty's, though I doubt he'd claim me any longer."

Olivier slowly revealed himself.

"Are you working with the Russians?" Cotton asked Reinhardt.

"Of course he is," Ivan answered. "We stay in front of this from the start. He lead us straight here."

"You'll never find those documents," Olivier blurted out. "They are hidden away. I'm the only one who knows where they are."

"I would not underestimate me again," Reinhardt said.

The comment came quick and Cotton read something in the older man's tone. Confidence. Like a man who knew something. His warning senses cautioned that Reinhardt could represent the greatest threat, even over Ivan. Olivier was surely hoping that what he knew would keep him alive. And perhaps it might. But Olivier was clearly worried, as the pudgy man's hands shook and a vein on his right temple squirmed with each beat of the heart, like a fat blue worm. He was probably trying to assess things, too. But nothing about this situation made sense.

Two plus two here added up to nine hundred.

Especially considering the wild card.

Where was Ivona?

JONTY HAD NEVER EXPERIENCED THE SEETHING CONFLICT OF EMO-tions that rushed through him. An unsettling combination of a burgeoning excitement, a chilly dread, and irrational anger. The extent of the horror that surrounded him was beyond words. Never had he imagined such an outcome. His business was hardly ever violent. But this was clearly a different scenario. Thankfully, his hatred of Eli Reinhardt transcended his fear and brought him strength.

"Where is Vic?" he asked.

"Dead," Eli said. "You're on your own, Jonty."

"There was no need to do this. None at all."

"So you would have turned everything over?" Eli asked. "Just like that. All I had to do was ask?"

"This was my deal, but you couldn't leave it alone. What was the Pantry? A diversion. Just a way for you to get close?"

"Exactly. And it worked. You were so accommodating. But this is business, Jonty. Nothing more. Though I will say for my associate here, Mr. Munoz, it's a bit more personal. He truly wants to kill you."

Jonty could see that was the case. The Bulgarian's weapon was trained straight at him.

"Sadly for him," Eli said, "he can't. That was not part of the deal."

Which begged the question.

What was?

ELI WATCHED HIS ADVERSARY STAND FIRM. IMPRESSIVE, CONSIDER-ing Olivier's dire predicament. The Russians had simply asked that they be led to this location and that weapons be provided so all of the participants could be killed.

Save for Jonty.

He'd not questioned that condition since he was being paid an obscene amount of money. Then fate had smiled upon him and provided the folded piece of paper in his pocket. Was it the key to where the damaging information was hidden? He intended on finding out just as soon as he was away from the castle.

Truth be told, Russians made him nervous. Slavs in general made him nervous. They were an unpredictable lot, whose motivations were most times impossible to decipher. Overall, they were well educated and well read. They loved theater, opera, concerts, and ballet. He'd learned long ago that the power of an individual was not nearly as important as family, friends, and acquaintances. You had to know people to get things done, which was why Russians had lots of friends. What was happening here seemed proof positive of that maxim. Know the right people, you could arrange almost anything. Like crashing a secret auction and killing everyone there.

But Russians were difficult.

Many elements of their character he found unsavory. They had few principles, rejected tradition, and were overly cynical. Flashy, too. Gender still meant something there, the roles of men and women clearly defined. Overall, they were a blunt, serious people. Chain smokers and habitual drinkers. Superstitious to the point of annoyance. But he was an accessory to mass murder, so who was he to judge? He'd hated dealing with them, but had out of necessity since Moscow's money was as good as everyone else's.

But none of that answered the most important question.

What now?

COTTON HAD BEEN IN SOME TIGHT SPOTS, BUT THIS ONE RANKED near the top of the list. He was trapped in the lower arcade. Across the great hall, fifty feet away and ten feet up in the opposite upper gallery, trouble stared down.

Apparently Olivier had been kept alive purposefully.

And he'd managed to dodge the bullets.

"I want to know," Ivan said, pointing at Olivier. "Are you truly the only one who knows where information is kept?"

"Only me and my associate, who is now dead." Olivier's tone had returned to businesslike. "I'm the only route left to it. Kill me, and it's gone."

Which surely explained why Olivier was still breathing.

Cotton watched as Reinhardt considered that information, too.

Pitting him against Ivan seemed like the smart play.

But he was interrupted when the doors banged opened and Ivona re-entered the hall.

CHAPTER FIFTY

Czajkowski stared out the window at Wawel Castle. He was nursing his second whiskey, propped in the bed, the same one he and Ivona had shared last night. The last thing he'd heard was gunshots through the phone. What was happening? Was Ivona all right? Her reputation was legendary, and her superiors spoke of her in glowing terms. But that didn't mean trouble could not find her.

He savored another sip, allowing the alcohol to trickle down his throat and burn away the anxiety.

Out the window, the view to the castle was across a busy street, up a rocky slope populated with cafés and restaurants. Crowds occupied the path that encircled Wawel Hill, particularly off to the right at the exit for the Dragon's Den, where an enormous bronze effigy of the famous dragon stood atop a limestone boulder. Seven-headed, with one that breathed fire thanks to an ingeniously placed natural gas nozzle. It had even been modernized so that a text message from a phone could trigger the fire, which people did hundreds of times each day.

Modern technology.

The bane of his existence.

The entire reason he was in this mess.

The Aegis Ballistic Missile Defense System.

Designed to provide protection against short- to intermediate-range ballistic missiles, and to intercept incoming missiles above the atmosphere, prior to reentry, long before they could do any damage, with a fragmentation warhead. Right now they were deployed on U.S. warships and land-based in Japan and Romania.

But were they reliable?

Nobody knew.

Most times they worked, but most was not all.

Russia hated them, saying they were merely fueling a new arms race based on nonexistent dangers, since Iran had never threatened Europe with missiles. The last time the idea was proposed Russia announced that it would deploy short-range nuclear missiles along its NATO borders. A new Cold War had been predicted. Putin even stated that Russia would withdraw from the Nuclear Forces Treaty of 1987 and that the chance of Poland being subject to attack, in the event of war, was 100 percent.

He had no reason to think that this time would be any different.

Nearly 60 percent of Poles had been opposed to the missiles. He imagined that percentage would be higher this time. So far, the outcry had been minimal, but the debate had not yet begun.

Oddly, years ago, the Polish government's response to the first cancellation of the program had been mixed. Some had been glad the missiles were gone, but a sizable bloc voiced concern that the country would lose its special status in Washington—that Obama had canceled the project to appease Moscow at Poland's expense. One proposal in Parliament had been to spend the equivalent of $10 billion U.S. in zlotys to build their own missile defense system.

Talk about insane.

He recalled one party leader lamenting that the decision to withdraw the initiative had been made *independent of Polish sensitivities.* Lech Wałęsa had been openly critical of the cancellation, saying *Americans have always only taken care of their own interests and they have used everyone else.* One front-page headline he recalled quite clearly. *ALE BYLIŚMY NAIWNI. ZDRADA! USA SPRZEDAŁY NAS ROSJI I WBIŁY NAM NÓŻ W PLECY.* WE WERE SO NAÏVE. BETRAYAL! THE U.S. SOLD US TO RUSSIA AND STABBED US IN THE BACK. Oddly, the ending announcement came on September 17, 2009, a date of great symbolic value, as it had been on September 17, 1939, that the Soviet Union invaded Poland.

234 | STEVE BERRY

Irony? A message? Or just a coincidence?

Who knew.

Ever since the announcement by President Fox the foreign ministry had been working on both responses and alternatives. Ways to try to appease both sides. No formal request for the missile base had yet been made. He assumed Fox was waiting to acquire the ammunition he would need to make sure that there was no meaningful opposition from Warsaw. And certainly the Americans knew they had a friendly ear with the marshal of Parliament, who would temporarily assume the presidency if a resignation was forced. That's when things would escalate out of control into a wild national debate.

He needed to handle this.

One man.

Quick and decisive.

Thankfully, the constitution gave him the power, which could not be overruled.

Why had Ivona not called back? He wanted to call her, but knew better. He had to trust her to handle it.

He finished his drink.

And knew better than to have another.

The door to the outer room opened. He stood and stepped from the bedroom. Michał Zima occupied the entranceway. Odd. He wondered why this cold, calculating man had traveled south from Warsaw.

"I've come to see if I can help," Zima said.

"With what?"

"Sturney Castle."

Apparently the head of the BOR had become well informed. "What do you know about that?"

"I know that a Russian foreign intelligence operative named Ivan is there. He was detected in Bruges, where he came into contact with a former American agent named Cotton Malone. Interestingly, Malone was here, yesterday, in Kraków, where four of the AW's intelligence agents brought him to you."

"You've been busy."

"I've been doing my job."

He appraised Zima with a critical eye. "You've been doing exactly what I told you not to do."

"I'm not your enemy."

"But you're not my friend, either."

"I am here to protect the president of this country. Being your friend was never part of that duty. But if you must know, I actually admire your leadership."

That was a surprise.

And welcomed.

"Something is happening that affects the security of this nation," Zima said. "Something that involves our foreign intelligence agency. I'm aware of your relationship with Ivona Novak. The BOR has accommodated your requests in that area. Again, I am not here to judge. Only to help."

"Michał, I appreciate your concern and your offer, but I cannot involve the BOR. This is a personal matter."

"That somehow concerns a man who once directed the secret intelligence services for Solidarity."

Zima surely knew of the trip to Jasna Góra, since two of his men had been there. But he was surprised about the reference to Stanis Orlik's past life experience.

"Is that a well-known fact?" he asked.

"To some it is. But it's a select few. Does whatever is happening here relate to what happened back in the 1980s?"

He decided to be honest. "It does."

"And Major Dilecki was likewise involved? I could tell when we were at his house that you knew the man. I can only assume that since he retained records on others, he did so on you. Records that are now out in the open."

"That would be a safe assumption."

"And Sturney Castle is where they have surfaced?"

"In a manner of speaking. They are being auctioned to the highest bidder."

He caught the moment of concern on Zima's face. Perhaps this man did genuinely care.

"Ivona is there," he said, "trying to stop that from happening. But there were gunshots during her last call to me. I'm concerned."

The door leading out of the suite opened. Usually, the security detail knocked first before allowing an intrusion.

Then he caught site of his visitor and understood.

His wife.

Who did not look happy.

CHAPTER FIFTY-ONE

COTTON KEPT HIS EYES LOCKED ON IVONA AS SHE CROUCHED NEAR another of the arches, thirty feet away.

"There she is," Ivan called out. "You not suppose to be here."

"And yet, I am," she said.

The Russian laughed. A rumbling, indolent guffaw, half real, half forced, and totally unfriendly.

Now he got it.

She was disarming these people. Creating confusion. Doing what she did best. Playing them.

"Who are you?" Jonty Olivier asked Ivona.

"The one who brings you greetings from the president of the Republic of Poland. Did you really think we would just let this auction happen?"

Olivier said nothing.

"What now?" Cotton asked them all.

"As Olivier says," Ivan noted, "only he knows where information is hidden. We need him to tell us."

"Not going to happen," Olivier declared.

"Forget about the Americans for a moment," Cotton said. "Do any of you think the Chinese, the North Koreans, the French, the Iranians are not going to retaliate?"

"Maybe you a good person to blame," Ivan said. "Former spy. Here.

Your reputation will work against you. Of course, you will try and convince all that you did nothing. Then we could blame Poles. They would certainly want all this stopped. Like I say, Ivona, you not suppose to be here."

"There are a lot of witnesses here," Cotton pointed out.

"Good point," Ivan said.

The big man reached beneath his jacket, removed a pistol, then turned and shot both of the other two Russians, with Uzis, in the head.

Cotton had witnessed all kinds of depravity and transgressions, his job usually to exploit those sins to his advantage. But he was appalled by the killing. Death occurred in his profession. No question. He'd pulled the trigger himself more than once in the heat of battle. But this was different. Compulsion seemed to be replacing reason. Protest burned his throat, but he knew better than to say a word. He glanced across the hall at Ivona, then turned his attention back to the second floor.

"Just you left, Malone," Ivan said. "And you, Ivona."

But there was one other loose end, and it was standing a few feet away.

He had little sympathy for Jonty Olivier. The man had tried to pet six rattlesnakes simultaneously. What had he expected? That they would lie docile? And like it? No surprise that one had reared up and bit him.

The Fox administration had been fools to try to manipulate this scenario. On what planet would the deployment of medium-range missiles only a few hundred miles from the Russian border not be met with a show of force? Bunch and Fox thought that lies and deception would work. Maybe in the business world. But this was the big leagues, where you played for keeps. You just didn't lose a deal, or some money. You lost your life. The participants here had played the game for a long time. Warner Fox was a rookie. And an arrogant one at that. Tom Bunch had been a blind follower, intent only on pleasing his boss, ignorant to the risks he'd taken. Now he was lying in a pool of his own blood in a remote Slovakian castle.

He studied both Ivona and Ivan, trying to decide what was next. The best he could determine was that their interests diverged. Ivan would want the information Olivier had to sell as insurance against the Poles. It could provide an effective way to keep American missiles out of Poland, and a means of control over a foreign head of state. Russian interrogation techniques would be more than enough to break Jonty Olivier. The man would eventually tell them anything and everything he knew.

Ivona would want the information destroyed, so it could never be used again. It was essentially destroyed now, hidden away where only one person knew its location. Olivier would surely have chosen a spot that would remain secret. Could it resurface? Possible. But not likely. Or at least not likely within the relevant time frame of the next five years of Czajkowski's second term as president. After that, whatever Olivier had to peddle would be worthless.

"You seem to have a problem," he told Ivan.

The big Russian shrugged. "I do my job. But Ivona not suppose to be here. Olivier is mine."

"I'm not telling any of you anything," Olivier blurted out.

Ivona stayed behind the arch but raised her weapon and pointed it at Olivier. "Where is the Spear of Maurice?"

"Now, *that* I can tell you. It's in a car, just beyond the courtyard, with the other relics, awaiting my departure."

She lowered her gun. "I came for that. That's why I'm here."

Made sense. A national treasure had to be returned, especially one that she'd allowed to be stolen.

Ivan shrugged. "You now have. Go."

Two shots tore the air and echoed through the hall.

His head whipped to the right. Ivona had fired. But not upward. He looked left. Olivier stared in astonishment at the spreading red stain across his shirt that clutching fingers could not contain. Air gasped from his mouth, followed by more blood, then the eyes rolled skyward and the stout body thumped hard to the floor.

"Now this is over," Ivona called out. "There will be no missiles and nobody gets that information. It stays wherever it is."

He stared at her.

"The Polish government had unfinished business with Jonty Olivier," she said. "That matter is now resolved."

"Not good," Ivan said. "This is a problem."

"Let it go," she called out.

"That may not be possible. I wanted Olivier. Alive."

"Cotton."

He turned toward Ivona.

She slid a gun across the polished stone floor straight to him. He grabbed the weapon, checked the magazine, then chambered a round.

Ready.

"There's two of us now," he told Ivan. "You can walk out of here, or be carried out with a bullet in you. Take your pick."

Silence reigned.

He risked a look and saw that the three men above him were looking at one another, Reinhardt surely waiting for Ivan to make a decision.

"I didn't come here to die," Reinhardt finally made clear.

"All right," Ivan said. "We be done."

He watched as the three men withdrew from the railing and began to leave the second floor. He'd need to stay alert until they were gone from the building.

He turned back toward where Ivona had been hidden.

But she was gone.

CHAPTER FIFTY-TWO

CZAJKOWSKI FELT THE TENSION THAT ENTERED THE HOTEL ROOM with his wife. He'd married her twenty-one years ago when they were both much younger and far less political. They'd since led public lives and, for a time, they'd been a team. Not anymore. They were now two separate entities. Intertwined only by ambition.

"Please excuse us," he said to Zima.

The head of the BOR nodded and left the suite.

"Make sure we're not disturbed," his wife added.

This was not going to be good. "Why are you here, Anna?"

"That was going to be my first question to you."

He wondered how much she knew. Or was this a fishing expedition?

She settled herself onto the sofa. She'd dressed for the occasion in an expensive Chanel suit. Pearl gray. Little jewelry. Low heels. Perfect for the First Lady of the nation.

"I'm told you've been here two days, after canceling appointments and clearing your schedule. Then I'm told your girlfriend stayed here last night."

No surprise she would know any of that. She had a BOR security detail, too, and those agents surely talked to one another.

"I want to know what's going on," she said.

"I'm dealing with the coming election."

She laughed. "And I'm the Virgin Mary. Come now, Janusz, I came for answers." She paused. "Truthful answers. Something unusual is happening."

"What makes you say that?"

"I know you."

Which was a problem. Hard to fool somebody who's been there nearly half your life. So he decided not to even try. "The Warsaw Protocol has come back to haunt us."

He'd told her the truth a long time ago, back when they were more like husband and wife.

"That sorry excuse for a human being, Dilecki, kept documents on me. How? Why? I have no idea. I only know that he did and they still exist."

"And your girlfriend is trying to retrieve them?"

He nodded. "An effort is being made."

"How wonderful that you have her in this time of need."

He caught the sarcasm and wondered about jealousy. That emotion had long left them both. Part of their *arrangement.*

"This has international implications," he said. "The security of this nation is at risk. If a foreign government obtains that information, it could be used against me. I may be forced to resign or, worse, do what they want. I don't want to do either of those."

She appraised him with a gaze he knew all too well. "It's that bad?"

He nodded. "You know what I did back then. You know what we all did."

"I know what you told me."

He was shocked at her reservations. "Am I to understand that you think I *was* an informant for the communists? That I sold out my fellow citizens? That I took their filthy money to help them keep us under their thumb? Do you really believe that?"

Her pale-blue eyes cast one of her trademark stares. "You and I both know what you did, Janusz. How many died?"

He'd thought about the past a lot lately. "Forty-six."

"Excuse me?"

"That's how many of my recruits I know were killed."

She sat up. "Now, that's new information. All these years and you never mentioned how many actually paid the price."

All were men and women who willingly took money from the SB in return for willingly providing information on their family, friends, neighbors, and acquaintances to the Security Service. The worst possible traitors. No one forced them to do a thing. No one coerced them. They had not been beaten or forced to crawl across a prison floor.

So what he and a few others had done was easy.

Find active recruits of the SB who were *not* working willingly. Who had been forced to spy. Then turn them into double agents and feed the government controlled information. Just enough of a spark of truth to keep the informants out of trouble and the SB busy chasing shadows.

And it worked.

Big time.

Eventually, they took it to the next level. Feeding more strategic and damaging information, designed to totally discredit some of those *willing* informants and make the SB question their loyalty. Enough that, in some cases, the SB permanently eliminated those informants.

Forty-six, that he knew about.

"Every one of those people deserved their fates," he said. "They sold us all out for greed. I don't regret a single one of those deaths."

"I doubt the Polish electorate will see it the same way," Anna noted. "Hence the reason you're here, right?"

"Precisely. Of course, no one who matters will acknowledge the Warsaw Protocol ever existed, much less the good it did. The end result will be that I will be branded a traitor. A spy for the communists. I will take the fall for everyone."

"Father Orlik was not cooperative?"

"Not at all. And you are well informed."

"I learned a long time ago to stay at least one step ahead of you, Janusz. Two, preferably."

He'd once loved this woman, and a small part of him still did. She understood him like no one else, not even Ivona. He'd decided to come to Kraków on an impulse, with only the vaguest idea of what he expected to accomplish. He'd flown south from Warsaw in a cold sweat, chewing at his lip, all thoughts frozen in the past. He'd hoped that, once here, he might figure it all out. A futile hope, for sure, as he remained in a deep turmoil. But he imagined his wife found herself in a similar quandary.

"This is the most serious threat we've ever faced. My political career could be over." He pointed. "Your career will be over."

She shrugged. "It seems we constantly face one challenge after another. Why should this be any different?"

"Because it is different. The Americans and Russians are involved. A lot is at stake."

"Does she love you?"

The question caught him off guard. Never had they discussed their mutual diversions.

"She does."

"That's good. You may not believe this, but I want you to be happy."

"As I do for you. I have no desire to harm you in any way."

She was still his friend, and always would be.

"I was there, Janusz. I was born into that horrible communist society. I know its mind-set. You don't have to convince me that times were tough. Survival depended on following the rules and avoiding attention. I remember it all, quite clearly. And I agree, I shed no tears for those traitors. So I've come to help. But I have to know what we're facing. I need the truth."

So he told her everything that had happened over the past few days.

"I understand," she said when he finished. "We cannot allow foreigners to dictate how this country is governed. Never again."

She might be an estranged spouse, but she was first and foremost a Pole.

And a proud one at that.

"You and I do not see eye to eye on many things," she said. "But on this issue we're united. Why are you waiting here?"

"For Ivona to report in. The last thing I heard was gunfire."

"Should you send people south to that castle?"

He'd been considering just that, but he'd promised Ivona not to interfere and let her handle it. "I can't. Not at the moment."

She seemed to understand why and said, "What would it hurt to get your men close, ready to move at a moment's notice?"

Not a thing.

He stepped to the door and summoned Zima back inside, telling him what he wanted to happen. "Stay back a few kilometers, but close enough to move quickly, if needed. How fast can you have people there?"

"I have six already at the Slovakian border. I was hoping you'd give this order."

He smiled. "Take care of it."

Zima left.

Anna stood from the sofa. "I have a mission, too."

He was curious. "Can I ask what?"

"It's time I pay a visit to Jasna Góra. Father Orlik and I need to have a talk."

"You might find that a bit one-sided."

She shook her head. "Come now, Janusz. You know how persuasive I can be."

CHAPTER
FIFTY-THREE

COTTON STEPPED AWAY FROM THE ARCH, SURROUNDED BY CAR-
nage. Ivona had executed Jonty Olivier in cold blood. What better way
to protect both Poland and Czajkowski than by eliminating the source of
the problem. Clearly, she hadn't known the location of the auction. The
Russians had shared no intel with her. And why would they? The last
thing they wanted was Olivier dead. So she'd set the trap with the spear
and allowed him to spring it. That way Olivier, the Russians, or whoever
might be watching would not be spooked, and she'd get a clear shot.

He was still concerned about Ivan and Eli Reinhardt. They could be
lying in wait. So he carefully made his way toward the front of the castle,
finding a room from which he could gaze down at the courtyard. There
he watched as Ivan, Reinhardt, and Munoz left in a black sedan. He then
saw Ivona as she calmly walked across the cobblestones and out the main
gate, with the boxed spear in her grasp.

There was still the matter of Eli Reinhardt. Something wasn't right
there. He wished he knew more about the man. Why was he involved?
Why would he agree to take the risk of participating in the murder of
government representatives, several of which were anything but friendly?
And make a deal with the Russians? Olivier's comments only confirmed
that he and Reinhardt had been somewhat working together, Olivier lamenting how foolish he'd been to trust the man. A double cross? Maybe.

THE WARSAW PROTOCOL | 247

And when Ivona gunned Olivier down, Reinhardt had seemed far more relieved than shocked.

Was this over?

Was the information truly gone?

Ivona apparently had been unconcerned with Reinhardt, leaving without giving him another thought. Satisfied the situation had been contained.

Had she made a mistake?

The castle loomed cemetery-quiet.

He left the front room and headed back to the great hall. Bullet holes scarred the walls and floor, while pools of blood framed out the casualties. He walked to Olivier's body, the face a waxen mask, the eyes closed but distended. He searched the pockets, finding nothing except a small chunk of yellow-white rock crystal. Odd that Olivier would be carrying it. He wondered about its significance. He pocketed the chunk and recalled Olivier asking about an associate—a man named Vic—and decided the second floor would be a good place to look. So he found the stairs and climbed, passing the two dead Russians, then searching rooms until he located a bedchamber that had been converted into a command post. Another body lay on the floor with bullet holes. He was about to search that corpse when he noticed the right-hand pants pocket.

Turned inside out.

As if somebody had already been looking.

He searched anyway and found only a wallet, a set of car keys, and a cell phone. A British driver's license identified Victor DiGenti. Vic. The video monitors were still working, displaying images of the outer walls and the forest beyond, especially the road near the main gate. All quiet. One of the split-screen images was of a vehicle parked inside the walls, probably down one of the alleys he'd noticed when he'd exited the car that had brought him earlier. The one Olivier had mentioned. Ready for his exit. Harboring the Arma Christi.

He noticed a laptop hot-wired from the wall. Surely the means whereby the high bid would have been authenticated and a wire transfer verified. He assumed that Reinhardt had killed DiGenti first, giving his co-conspirators an open run to everyone else. All of the staff had apparently been ordered from the premises, leaving everything overly vulnerable. Foolishness on Olivier's part, but just add that to the list of improbable chances the man had taken.

He wondered, had Reinhardt come here first and found something? Olivier had said that only he knew the location. During the auction he'd also said DiGenti would lead the highest bidder to the information. Which made sense. A man like Olivier did not seem the type to do the heavy lifting. No. He'd pay for that service, and what other person besides the one man Olivier had specifically inquired about with Reinhardt.

Had this guy known the location?

Of course, he was speculating. Like the lawyer he used to be.

But it all seemed reasonable.

He opened DiGenti's cell phone but it was password-protected, so he tossed it back on the body and decided to search the remainder of the castle to find Olivier's room, which he did farther down the hall. It was elegantly furnished with a heavy wooden table, a four-poster bed, a carved chest, and a dark wood wardrobe filled with clothes that were clearly Olivier's size. It all smelled of polish, soap, and fresh flowers. The afternoon sun threw in a reddish glow, exposing patches of dust on the furniture. Save for some toiletries and a couple of novels, there was nothing else. He left there and the second floor, exploring the ground level, eventually finding what had once been the castle's library.

No books lined the shelves. A large piano occupied one corner, a few choice lithographs adorned the walls, a rug lay underfoot. French doors opened to a stone terrace. He searched for anything that may have been compromised. Curiously, there was a vacuum-seal machine, the kind used to preserve food, sitting on a small table. Not much littered the top of the Victorian-style desk except for three cell phones, all password-blocked. He wasn't going to learn anything fast from those, so he walked back to the great hall.

How long would it be before the respective governments of the dead learned what had happened? Not long. A matter of hours. The response? That would be a challenge, considering the illegality of the entire venture.

He approached the big-screen television. Olivier lay nearby. He recalled the documents that had been displayed and glanced behind, noticing a laptop connected to the screen. He scrolled through the five images displayed on the left side, which Olivier had shown the assemblage. Nothing else was loaded on the machine.

Then he noticed something.

Resting beneath the machine on a wooden shelf was a large manila envelope, like the ones that had been used during the auction. He slipped it free and tested its weight. Heavy. He tore off the flap and opened it to find an oversized coffee-table book.

Miasto w Soli: The City in Salt.

He only knew that since there was both English and Polish on the cover. Inside was the same, the text in both languages, all of the glossy colored images of the underground salt mine at Wieliczka. He thumbed through the pages and admired the extraordinary pictures.

On the end page was writing.

In blue ink.

9 *Bobola*

He thumbed back through the book to see if there was any more writing, but found none. On page 145 one of the full-page images caught his eye. Yellow-white crystals clung to a gaping fissure in the mine shaft wall. No caption identified the photo, but he found a legend at the end, the book's author stating, *Lower level IX. A fragment of roof of the upper grotto covered with large halite crystals.* He found the piece in his pocket that Olivier had been carrying and compared it with the photo.

Identical.

He brought it to his lips and cautiously tested the outer surface with his tongue.

Salty.

The tantalizing fragments of a pattern formed in his brain and the math was anything but fuzzy.

This two plus two had to equal four.

CHAPTER
FIFTY-FOUR

ELI WAS GLAD TO BE AWAY FROM THE RUSSIANS. HE AND MUNOZ had ridden north with Ivan, back into Poland, with their mouths shut. His deal with them had worked out perfectly. They'd paid him five million euros to work his way into the auction, direct them to the location, then facilitate the elimination of the participants. The Russians wanted every delegate dead. They also wanted Olivier alive. But that had not worked out. The Poles had intervened. Malone had survived. Luckily, Ivan did not hold either of those unexpected occurrences against him.

Ivan deposited them near the main square in Kraków, surely on his way to the nearby Russian consulate and home soil. He wondered how long it would take for the carnage at Sturney Castle to be discovered. Surely the staff had returned by now. But perhaps the Poles had cleaned up the mess and disposed of the bodies. That would make more sense. The last thing they would want was public attention.

The time was approaching 3:00 P.M. and he was hungry.

But he also needed information.

He knew that Jonty had visited the nearby Wieliczka Salt Mine twice in the past forty-eight hours. Once to find the Pantry, but the other visit, the first one, had been all Olivier's call. Munoz had told him about the torture with the electrical wire down the throat and how he'd finally coughed up a name. Ordinarily he'd be upset with such weakness. But here it told him that Jonty had returned to the mine *after* learning that a competitor was watching.

Had he hedged his bets?

Perhaps.

And Vic DiGenti would have been right there with him.

In his pocket he found the paper that he'd lifted off the corpse.

9 *Bobola*

What did it mean? Was it relevant here? Or did it have nothing to do with any of this?

He believed Olivier when he'd said that no documents were at the castle. That would have been a wise precaution, one he himself would have taken. Was it possible that Jonty had decided the salt mine was the perfect place to stash his prize? Why not? It certainly was isolated and there were endless possibilities for secreting something away. He should at least investigate before dismissing the thought entirely.

Kraków was not unfamiliar to him. He'd visited many times, and one of his favorite places to eat was Pod Aniołami. It sat about halfway between the main square and Wawel Castle, on a busy pedestrian-only side street. It served traditional Polish cuisine, using the old recipes, all cooked on a charred beechwood grill. The ambience was lovely, too, reminding him of places he'd visited in the countryside, its décor the kind of knickknacks you'd find in people's homes.

He led Munoz to the restaurant. They took a table in the cellar, surrounded by rough stone walls and arches straight from the Middle Ages. Nobody else was enjoying a late lunch, so they had a measure of privacy in the dimly lit chamber.

"I want you to find a man who works at the Wieliczka Salt Mine," he whispered to Munoz. "He's a guide named Dawid Konrad. I met him last evening. Go there. Ask around. Find him. I must speak with him immediately."

Munoz had worked for him before, and Eli knew him to be dependable. Of course, getting caught by Olivier had not been one of the Bulgarian's finest moments, but it all worked out in the end. He prided himself on being adaptable. Being here, right now, seemed proof positive of that.

He'd managed to eliminate a competitor and secure an unobstructed path to information that could prove quite valuable. But he would not make the same mistake Jonty had made. If found, he'd sell directly to the Russians for a fair price, taking every euro earned as icing on the cake of the five million he'd already pocketed. Of course, the Poles might pay more. Either way, the information would be suppressed and no missiles would be deployed.

Right now he wanted food.

He and Munoz discussed a few more details, then his acolyte rose and climbed the steep stone steps back to ground level.

For the first time in the past few days he relaxed.

No one was left to interfere. All of the parties had either been killed or placated.

He again found the paper with the writing on it.

9 *Bobola*

He needed to know if it was relevant, especially before speaking with Konrad. He still had control of the Pantry, now his alone to sell. But what he wanted was the information on Janusz Czajkowski. Olivier's fate had offered a glimpse at the disaster that came to those who tied themselves to limited capabilities. He wanted to be freer. More flexible. He felt a panicky need for some assurance that he could escape the path he'd just taken with his life. What he should do was walk away. Leave it alone. He had more than enough. But that was not his nature. He was a broker. Buying and selling every day. Taking risks. And out there, right now, waiting to be found, was something of great value.

And not only in money.

But also to his reputation as a dealer.

So go for it.

He found his phone and typed BOBOLA into a search engine.

What appeared both surprised and intrigued him.

COTTON APPROACHED THE LIGHT-COLORED BMW THAT HE'D SEEN on the monitor upstairs in the room where Vic DiGenti had been killed. He'd retrieved the keys from the body, hoping they were for the vehicle, and was pleased when the fob opened the door locks.

On the rear seat he spotted various containers that held the relics of the Arma Christi. He noticed that there were six. When he subtracted the one Ivona had taken, it made for seven. Where had the seventh come from? Earlier, one had been missing on the table in the great hall.

Another mystery.

No matter, though, he now had the relics and he was certain that the churches from which they'd been taken would be grateful beyond measure for their return. It would be quite a feather in Stephanie's cap to be able to make restitution. He needed to call her, but had no way at the moment. It would have to wait until he was back in Poland. Right now he just needed to get as far away from here as possible before the crap hit the fan.

He was still playing a hunch.

One he knew Stephanie would want him to pursue.

And though he no longer had any dog in this fight, he was intent on finding out if the information on Czajkowski was still out there, capable of being located.

Was the threat still active?

The silence around him was broken by the cawing of a crow.

An omen?

He hoped not.

He was alive thanks to Ivona's intervention, and what he was doing by keeping in pursuit might be deemed a problem by her.

She'd wanted this to be over.

But something told him there was still a way to go.

CHAPTER FIFTY-FIVE

CZAJKOWSKI WANTED THIS DAY TO END. IT HAD BEEN ONE OF THE most nerve racking of his life—and he'd experienced some pretty harrowing ones. Speaking with Anna had brought back memories he preferred not to relive.

It happened so fast on the night of December 12, 1981.

When the Polish military swept in and imposed martial law.

Most of Solidarity's leaders were rounded up and herded to freezing detention centers, cast on the mercy of brutal guards. Over forty thousand people. Neither he nor Stanis Orlik was part of that roundup. Orlik because he constantly stayed in the shadows, and himself as a nobody.

It had all been horrible.

But people had debated for years whether Poland, without martial law, would have made it through that winter.

Widespread famine seemed imminent. The health care system was about to collapse. The economy was gone. Anarchy loomed, and neither the government nor Solidarity possessed the ability to develop workable solutions. With power came responsibility. Leaders had to get along. Put petty differences aside. Avoid division over trivial matters. But Solidarity had constant problems with unity. At least it wanted to compromise, but the Red Bourgeoisie, who would have had to relinquish many of their class privileges, refused to budge.

No deals.

By then, all that remained of the Polish Communist Party was the complacent, the incompetent, the corrupt, and the evil. Thankfully, the army stayed at bay. Polish soldiers refused to fire on Polish workers. But the militia, the SB, and the special forces were another matter. They did the dirty work, one person at a time.

He recalled the sense of defeat that dominated throughout that winter.

Poles seemed to know that Poles always lost.

It had been that way for centuries. Doomed by geography and ideology, they had never effectively governed themselves. The whole idea of martial law had been to isolate and neutralize any obstructive groups and deprive the people of knowledge, save for what the government decreed. For years Solidarity had existed out in the open, keeping the people informed. Now it was gone. Subverted. Made illegal. There was no more information network. Phone lines were cut, television shut down. Everything required a permit. Even typewriters had to be registered.

So implementing the Warsaw Protocol had been easy.

Feeding the SB false information had been easy. Turning one against the other, setting up traitors, even easier.

Their deaths just the price to be paid.

And the last holdouts?

Two thousand coal miners in Silesia, barricaded underground in protest, cooped up in low, dark, clammy shafts, thick with winter dampness. No ventilation, no light. Just days before Christmas. To get them out, the government engaged in its own form of the Warsaw Protocol by feeding down false stories of ill family or wives in labor. Women impersonated their loved ones begging them to surrender. Anything to break their resolve. But the coal miners knew a lie when they heard one. They were tough. They'd always been regarded with high honor. The aristocrats of Polish labor. They'd not joined in previous labor unrest actions and were among the last to go on strike.

But strike they did.

With the result being just another stalemate.

And the only way out of a stalemate was to change the rules.

Which was what the Warsaw Protocol had done.

Attacking the SB at its core.

His limousine glided to a stop and he prepared himself to step from the car. He'd been driven fifty kilometers southwest of Kraków to Wado-wice, population twenty thousand, a fairly unremarkable town beyond the fact that it was here, on May 18, 1920, that the future St. John Paul II had been born. That event turned an otherwise sleepy municipality into a place of pilgrimage, complete with all of the tacky tourist trappings. Everything of interest revolved around the central square, appropriately named Plac Jana Pawła II. The main attraction was the Wojtyła family house. Twelve hundred square meters of exhibition space over four floors that charted the great man's life. Family photos, heirlooms, manuscripts, even the gun used in the 1981 attempt on the pope's life were on display.

A renovation of the site had just been completed and he'd come to see the work and bestow his presidential blessing. The trip had been sched-uled yesterday as camouflage on the pretext that since he was nearby, why not drop in for a quick visit.

Ivona had called two hours ago and said she was on her way back from Slovakia. He'd told her about the detail of BOR agents he'd dispatched, and she told him what had happened. They'd agreed that the agents would scrub the castle clean and dispose of the bodies, removing and destroying all the written materials distributed to the participants, along with the computers on site. Michał Zima would oversee it all. The hope being only they, the Russians, and Eli Reinhardt knew about what had happened.

Then there was Cotton Malone.

He doubted the Americans would make trouble. If so, they'd have to explain how one of their own made it out unscathed. Unlikely the Chi-nese, Iranians, or North Koreans would accept any explanation. Not to mention the French, a supposed ally. More likely, they'd all think that the United States had the information and Washington's denials would fall on deaf ears.

He checked his watch. 3:20 P.M.

He exited the car into sunshine muted by clouds rapidly dominating the afternoon sky. Some of the local politicos were waiting to greet him and he took a moment to shake hands and chat with them, assuming a patrician but warm smile of welcome. Off to his right he caught sight of

Ivona with a black box in hand. He grabbed the attention of the head of his security detail and motioned. He entered the house, greeted by the curator. They exchanged pleasantries and he asked if there was a room where he might have a moment. The man offered his office and he followed him there, where he was left alone. A soft knock came to the door, then it opened and Ivona entered. She laid the box on the desk. He took her in his arms, hugging her tightly.

"What's that for?" she asked.

"Do I need a reason?"

She smiled. "No. I suppose not."

He was glad she was all right. "I'm told the location has been sanitized. No trace of the carnage remains, save for a few bullet marks in the floor. Everything found there was burned."

"Only Jonty and his man DiGenti knew the hiding spot for the information," she said. "I made sure of that before I killed him. He was going to use it as a bargaining chip. The Russians definitely wanted Olivier alive."

"It's still a risk—with that information out there, in the open."

"We could not allow Olivier to walk away."

"Yet we allowed Malone to walk away."

"Because there was no reason to kill him," she said. "He was drawn into this, not of his own accord. He has no idea where that information is located, so he poses no threat. It was bad enough that all of the others had to die. And Olivier. I'm in the intelligence business, not murder-for-hire."

He caught the sharp tone in her voice. "I understand. You did what you had to do, and I appreciate it."

They'd discussed it at length. He'd never asked or ordered her to kill Olivier. But she'd known what to do.

She pointed at the box. "I'll return the spear to the castle."

"That definitely needs to be done. Let's make sure there are no loose lips there, either."

A buzz disturbed their privacy.

His phone. He checked the display. His chief of staff back in Warsaw. He answered the call, listened, then said, "Do it."

Ivona stared at him.

"The president of the United States wants to talk to me. Now."

CHAPTER FIFTY-SIX

COTTON RECALLED A STORY HE'D HEARD WHILE GROWING UP IN middle Georgia on his grandfather's onion farm. A local man ran for county sheriff and garnered only seventeen votes. The day after the election he paraded around town with a gun strapped to his waist. Someone asked him why and he said, *With as few friends as I apparently have, I definitely need one.*

He felt the same way.

He was back in Kraków, surrounded by strangers, walking straight for the American consulate. Sunshine filtered through broken pewter clouds. He had no idea where Stephanie might be, but this seemed like the best place to start. The time was approaching 4:00 P.M., the shops and eateries busy for late afternoon. He was stopped at the doors by the uniformed marines. This time they weren't expecting him. He asked if Stephanie Nelle was there, and a few moments later he was allowed inside. He found her on the second floor, eyes dull and red-lined with fatigue, and made a full report, including Bunch's death.

"Where's the car?" she asked him.

"Parked down the street. With six of the most precious relics in the religious world locked inside." He paused. "All yours."

"I appreciate the gift. But I doubt it's going to buy me any political capital with Fox. He wants missiles here and he's not going to stop."

"We don't get everything we want."

"What is it you're not telling me?"

"Do you have your Magellan Billet laptop?"

She nodded.

He felt numbed, confused, and bewildered by all that had happened. He needed time to sort things out, to categorize, compartmentalize, make sense of the confusion. "Can I use it?"

"Is it about that book?"

And she pointed.

He'd brought the volume that he'd found at the castle. *The City in Salt. The Wieliczka Salt Mine.*

"That's what I want to find out."

She handed over her computer and he opened it to a search engine. He typed in the word BOBOLA and found a reference.

On May 16, 1657, Cossacks surprised a holy Polish Jesuit in the town of Pińsk. Father Andrew Bobola, aged sixty-five, fell to his knees, raised his hands toward heaven, and exclaimed, "Lord, thy will be done." The Cossacks stripped him of his holy habit, tied him to a tree, placed a crown of twigs upon his head, then scourged him, tearing out one eye and burning his body with torches. One of the ruffians then traced, with his poniard, the form of a tonsure on the head of the priest and the figure of a chasuble on his back. Finally, all of the skin was stripped from the body. During this indescribable torture the priest prayed for his tormentors until they tore out his tongue and crushed his head. Father Andrew Bobola was declared Blessed on the 30th of October, 1853. He was made a saint by Pope Pius XI in 1938.

At least he now had a Polish connection to the name.

One more inquiry.

He typed in BOBOLA and WIELICZKA SALT MINE and found several hits, one that explained the relationship.

The deep Christian faith of the Wieliczka miners comes from their Catholic upbringing, as well as the difficult work conditions in the mine. They faced threats from fire, leakages of underground water, and collapse. Holy patrons were supposed to protect them from such dangers. For centuries, the miners cultivated a group of saints whom they worshipped with particular devotion, believing in their powers of intercession. Many were honored with carvings made in the salt, the miners themselves the artisans.

One of those carvings was of Father Andrew Bobola.

He found an image of the salt sculpture, created in 1874, still there in the mine. A little crude and eroded from time and water, it sat alone in a square-shaped niche. A caption indicated that the figure had once been colored white, red, and black, the same paint used for marking the mine's work sites. It had been carved by a miner, in his spare time.

Located on Level IX.

He showed Stephanie the chunk of salt crystal.

"That was on Olivier's person when he died," he told her. "And he had that book, all ready to go in an envelope. It all adds up. 9 Bobola. That information is hidden in the mine, where that statue is located, on level nine."

He thumbed through the oversized picture volume, finding a schematic of the mine's various levels. Not a lot of detail, but enough to get the idea that it was a huge underground complex.

He placed a period on his line of thoughts. "I think that Eli Reinhardt knows this, too."

"He's going after it?"

"You tell me. Do you know him?"

She nodded. "He's an information broker, just like Olivier, but his reputation is not the best. He and Olivier were active competitors, and that information on Czajkowski is still worth a lot of money. So yes, if he can, he will go after it."

"He may already be on the way to that mine, trying to find a way in."

They were inside the same office used yesterday, with the door closed. The afternoon sun, still hazy, slanted through the blinds.

"We ought to preempt him," he said.

He could see she was intrigued by the possibility.

"And what do we do if the information is there?" she asked.

"Let's cross that bridge when we get to it."

Neither one of them was comfortable with any of this. Stephanie was defying her employer. He was offending Ivona. But the thought of allowing that information to fall into the hands of Reinhardt seemed repugnant. No telling what would happen then.

"You think Ivan knows?" she asked.

He shook his head. "He seemed genuinely pissed when Ivona killed Olivier."

The phone on the desk rang.

Stephanie answered, listened, then pressed a button activating the speakerphone, hanging up the receiver.

"Mr. Malone, this is Warner Fox."

Cotton sat up on the edge of his chair.

"What happened?" the president asked.

"Exactly what you should have anticipated. The Russians killed everyone."

"Including Tom?"

"He's not here, is he?"

"You're telling me everyone, including Olivier, is dead? Except you?"

"That's exactly what I'm saying. And before you ask, I'm only here because I got lucky. The Poles were working with the Russians, and both of them were one step ahead of you the entire way. Your lies only infuriated both Warsaw and Moscow."

"I did what I thought necessary."

"You have no idea what you're doing, and a lot of people are dead now thanks to you."

"You won't be paid a dime for your work here," Fox said.

He shook his head. "You know where you can stick that $150,000."

"You have no respect for this office, do you?"

"Actually, I have a tremendous respect for the presidency. What I lack is any semblance of respect for you."

"Stephanie, what about the information on Czajkowski?" Fox asked, ignoring the jab. "Any idea where it might be?"

She glanced his way and he shrugged, signifying it was her call.

"None at this time," she lied.

"I'm about to speak with the president of Poland," Fox said.

262 | STEVE BERRY

"Who knows you lied to him," Cotton said.

"Can anything be salvaged?"

"Maybe some pride, if you apologize to Czajkowski," Cotton said.

"Your impertinence knows no bounds," Fox muttered.

"Did Tom Bunch have a family?"

"A wife and two children."

"Give them the $150,000."

And he meant it. Bunch had been a blind fool, but his wife and children were another matter.

"Stephanie, please answer my question," Fox said.

"Nothing I'm aware of can be salvaged. This is over."

"Then explain to me why the Russians think otherwise."

Damn. Fox had practiced the old adage that every good trial lawyer knew. Never ask a question you don't know the answer to, unless you don't care what that answer may be.

And he clearly had not.

Truth or lie, he had her.

"The NSA detected a message from a Russian SVR agent named Ivan Fyodorov, currently in Kraków, confirming to the Kremlin that the information may still be in play."

Neither of them said a word.

"I'm going to assume that you both know more than you're willing to share," Fox said. "That's fine. Doesn't matter. You're both off this operation. It will be handled by others, who are on their way to Kraków now."

Stephanie shook her head.

Cotton knew what was coming.

"Stephanie, you're relieved of duty, pending termination. I'll leave it to the attorney general to decide your fate."

"Like that decision is in doubt," she said.

"No. It's not. Unlike you, he understands loyalty."

"He's an idiot," she said.

"I won't miss you," Fox said.

"Nor me you."

And she ended the call.

CHAPTER
FIFTY-SEVEN

CZAJKOWSKI ALLOWED HIS CELL PHONE TO KEEP RINGING. IVONA smiled at his impertinence toward the president of the United States.

Finally, he answered.

"What can I do for you, Mr. President," Czajkowski said on speaker.

"You're not going to win this," Fox declared.

"I wasn't aware that we were in competition."

"Tom Bunch is dead. Murdered in cold blood."

"I'm sorry to hear that. What a terrible tragedy. But that concerns me how, Mr. President?"

"You will not get away with this."

"I'm at a loss. What are you referring to?"

"I'm referring to whatever you had or allowed to be done. Malone reported that everyone was killed and that you and the Russians were working together."

"Our interests do align relative to this issue."

"I'll have every dime in foreign aid cut off to Poland in retaliation."

He laughed. "Really? All ten million euros' worth? Go ahead. We shall not miss it."

The United States had never been generous with Poland when it came to foreign aid. True, they considered the country of strategic importance and were always willing to provide military assistance, but that always came with some ceding away of pride or possession. With the constant looming threat from Russia, previous Polish administrations had been willing to make that deal. He was not.

"I was referring to the $150 million in military sales we allow to Poland," Fox said.

He'd been warned about Fox by other European leaders who'd already dealt with him and made their own assessment. Rude. Pedantic. Arrogant. Willfully uninformed. Quick to anger, especially when challenged. Big on threats. Like now.

"May I ask what would be the basis for cutting off those military sales?"

"Your refusal to cooperate with an ally. If our missiles aren't good enough for you, then our military hardware should be treated the same."

"That would be unfortunate," he said. "But we will just buy those arms elsewhere. I'm sure the Chinese, or the French, would appreciate the business."

"That's not the same as made in America, and we both know it. Our weapons are the finest in the world."

Another assessment he'd been told about Fox was an irrational belief that all things American were best.

"I'm sure the Chinese and the Europeans would disagree with your statement. No matter, I will not be coerced by you, or anyone. There will be no missiles on Polish soil. None at all. You are putting this country at risk, and that will not be allowed."

"Nor will I suffer the insult of a refusal from a second-rate, barely-above-a-third-world nation. If it weren't for us, all of you would be speaking German."

His gaze met Ivona's and her eyes signaled for him to keep his temper. *Play this out.*

Calmly.

He nodded, then said, "As I recall, Mr. President, it was the Soviets who liberated us. Then your country, and England, allowed Stalin to steal our nation and subject us to forty-five years of brutal oppression."

"Ungrateful. That's what you are, Czajkowski. Ungrateful. You, and all Europeans. We saved your ass. All we ask is a little loyalty. We have

a serious situation here. Representatives from several sovereign governments were murdered today—"

"Trying to buy information with which to blackmail me, yourself included."

"Don't interrupt me."

"The last I looked, Mr. President, I was the duly elected head of a
sovereign government. We are equals."

"That is the one thing we are not. Tom Bunch was gunned down.
That's not going to go unanswered."

"I was there," Ivona said.

"Who is that?" Fox asked.

"The person who killed Jonty Olivier," she said. "The rest were killed
by the Russians. Good luck answering that insult, Mr. President. Are you
prepared to start World War III?"

"Killing Olivier was stupid," Fox said.

"No. Trying to blackmail the president of Poland was stupid. We just
countered that."

"I have agents on the way there," Fox said. "This will be dealt with.
Decisively."

He'd had enough. "And if those agents violate any law of this country,
they will be arrested and imprisoned."

"I'm sure the Slovaks would love to know what happened within their
jurisdiction today. My next call will be to them."

Interesting that Fox did not seem to have a full grasp of the situation,
unaware that the site had been sanitized. He could see that Ivona had
come to the same conclusion. She mouthed *Malone.* He nodded. Made
sense. He'd made a report, but Malone would not have known what sub-
sequently happened, either.

"I would encourage you to do whatever you deem necessary," Czajkowski said. "After all, you are the president of the United States, and
who am I to argue. I'm just the leader of a second-rate, barely-above-a-
third-world nation."

"I'm going to have those missiles in Poland, one way or another.
Either you're going to do it, or your successor. There's something you
don't know."

They both waited.

"You failed. The Russians say the information on you may still be in play. And they're going to get it. But not if I can help it."

He was instantly concerned but knew better than to let on. "Good luck with that, too, Mr. President."

And he ended the call.

"Is that possible?" he asked Ivona.

"Olivier said repeatedly he was the only one who knew the location. And that made sense. Why would he trust it to anyone else? He said that not even his man, DiGenti, knew the location. But DiGenti is dead."

"Did that man talk before he died?"

"I have no idea."

"Could the Russians be bluffing just to keep Fox off guard? They could manufacture documents. They've done it before."

He could see she was thinking, her mind racing.

"I need to make a call." She found her phone, punched in a number, spoke for a moment, listened, then said goodbye. "Cotton and Stephanie Nelle left the American consulate together twenty minutes ago. We watch the building daily. And we caught a break. Cotton used the car I found at the castle with the spear and the other Arma Christi relics inside. After I retrieved the spear, I tagged the car with a tracker. I thought we might want to know where the remaining relics ended up."

Ivona's phone buzzed.

She answered, then muted the call.

"The car is moving out of town, east toward Wieliczka. I need to head that way."

He nodded.

She unmuted the call and told her man to keep her posted. Then she turned for the door to the small office.

"Wait," he said, "I'm coming with you."

CHAPTER
FIFTY-EIGHT

COTTON DROVE, WITH STEPHANIE IN THE SEAT BESIDE HIM. HE sympathized with her untenable position. Of course, none of it mattered any longer since she would soon be unemployed. True, he did not know her exact age, but it was definitely past sixty-five. So she could retire, travel, enjoy herself. Visit more with her son, Mark, who lived in southern France. Build on her relationship with Danny Daniels. But he knew none of that was going to happen. Stephanie was an intelligence officer through and through. Her husband had died long ago and her career had become her life. Was that a good thing? Maybe not. But it was a fact, and she seemed content with the choices she'd made. He knew of countless situations where her cool head and hard decisions had made all the difference. Where the United States owed her a debt of gratitude. Hell, she'd even been shot in the line of duty. And what had she received?

A pink slip.

"The good thing," he said, "is that Fox's people have no idea about the possibility of a connection to the salt mine. The bad thing is someone's tailing us."

"I assumed that would happen," Stephanie said, her gaze fixed out the front windshield. "Fox will want to know what we're doing."

"I'm going to drive past the mine. I'll lose them on the other side of town. Then we'll double back." He paused. "I'm sorry this is happening to you."

"I've always wondered how my career would end. Nothing goes forever, and God knows I've had a great run and lingered far longer than I should have. So maybe it's time to walk away. Move on."

"Who are you kidding?"

He caught the grin on her face as she went silent and he checked the rearview mirror. The same car he'd noticed in Kraków remained three back. He assumed it was someone from the embassy. Maybe one of the marines, responding to an order from the White House. Fox had surely wanted Stephanie and him watched. But in his rookie arrogance Fox had not even considered that two experienced intelligence officers would anticipate that move and be ready to counter.

"I'm kidding myself," she finally said. "You and I both know that. I'm not ready to leave."

Her world had always been about secrets. Nothing was as it seemed. Every word, every act, suspect. That was how an intelligence officer lived life, and it was tough to readjust.

Which he knew from his own experience.

"This isn't over," he said. "If we find that information, the value of your stock just rose."

He entered the small town of Wieliczka. It lay in a valley between two ridges, ten miles southeast of Kraków. Its old architecture blended perfectly with the greenery of its parks and charming alleys. It had historic churches, a market, and a monastery. But its claim to fame was the salt mine beneath it, which he specifically avoided, easing through the center of town, then out the other side, still headed southeast.

Traffic thinned.

Their pursuer stayed about five hundred yards back, no cars between them now.

Enough cat and mouse.

On a flat stretch of pavement he eased off the gas and allowed the other vehicle to come close. It approached the left rear quarter. He swerved into the opposite lane, slowed a bit, and allowed the car to draw parallel.

A gun appeared.

He and Stephanie slumped down.

"That's no marine," she said.

He agreed and played the steering wheel, slamming the right side of his car into the left of the other, momentarily preventing any shooting. Then he pumped the brake and allowed the car to skid to a stop, the other vehicle speeding ahead, where it executed a smooth U-turn and headed back in their direction.

He stamped the accelerator and yanked the steering wheel hard left. A quick roar of an engine came before the skid of rubber as the rear wheels caught the pavement. The car spun, the rear end swinging to change places with the front. He straightened out the hood, giving the engine more gas. He reminded himself that the backseat was loaded with precious relics, which were bouncing around unimpeded.

"Like a damn roller-coaster ride," Stephanie said. "Good to see your skills are still sharp."

He grinned. "We're just getting started."

The gun from the castle lay on the console between them.

"Get ready to fire," he told her.

Stephanie grabbed the pistol.

They were now headed back toward town down two lanes of asphalt. Their pursuer shot out of his lane and crossed the double line into a hole in incoming traffic, trying to get to them.

Horns blared.

The car swept back into their lane, now directly behind them. Cotton was doing nearly 120 kilometers an hour. They would run out of highway a few miles ahead when they reentered Wieliczka.

But their pursuer seemed without fear.

Or brains.

The car closed straight on and popped them in the bumper. Cotton's right foot slammed the brake, which caused another collision. But he was ready for it, spinning the wheel left into the other lane and braking again, allowing the other vehicle to draw alongside. Stephanie rolled down her window and fired twice. Once into the driver's-side window. The other into the front left tire.

Which burst.

Cotton floored the accelerator, knowing what was coming. The other car veered hard left, off the road, into the trees.

"Nice shooting," he said to her.

"I still have some talent."

That she did.

He parked in a paved lot specifically for visitors to the Wieliczka Salt Mine, in a space that provided quick access out. They crossed the street and headed for the Daniłowicz Shaft, which a placard informed them was the only way down for general visitors. The mine complex, at ground level, stretched for acres, its various buildings incorporated into the town, which had been built centuries ago to accommodate the miners and their families. They'd left the consulate in a hurry, speaking to no one. But Stephanie had made one call before they fled the building.

One she hadn't elaborated upon until now.

"I spoke with our ambassador to Poland before we left," she said as they walked. "He's one of Danny's holdovers. Fox has not filled the post yet. Needless to say he's not a fan of our new president. I had him make a call. He knows the right people to get us inside, unnoticed."

The time was approaching 5:00 P.M., and there was still a modest crowd waiting to gain entrance. Maybe a hundred people. Just past where the line to buy a ticket ended a short, petite blonde stood, dressed in official-looking coveralls. She seemed to be waiting for them and stepped right up, introducing herself as Patrycja. She said, "I was told you want access to Level IX."

"Can we do that, and fast?" Stephanie asked.

"I've been instructed to do whatever you want. Let's get you changed and we'll head right down. You're going to need some equipment. That level is not like the tourist areas, it's on the miners' route."

He was not looking forward to this. Tight spaces were not his favorite. Stephanie seemed to sense his anxiety and said, "I'm told the tunnels are wide and there's plenty of ventilation. Is that right?"

Their guide nodded. "It's not cramped down there at all."

But he wasn't comforted.

He'd heard that disclaimer before.

What concerned him more, though, was the Russians and Eli Rein-

hardt. One or both could be headed here, too. The guy they'd just encountered was employed by one of them.

He glanced around, seeing nothing that caused alarm.

But that didn't mean trouble wasn't nearby.

CHAPTER FIFTY-NINE

ELI STEPPED FROM THE CAR.

He'd hired a cab to drive him from Kraków to the salt mine. Not a long trip, though costly at a hundred euros. But the driver was an entrepreneur, too, just like him, so he couldn't blame the man for predatory pricing. His entire business hinged on taking advantage of others.

He stood before the graduation tower, an enormous castle-like structure crafted of larch branches and blackthorn, upon which salt brine flowed twenty-four hours a day. The microclimate created within the gaudy wooden structure worked like a natural inhalator, the salt air able to penetrate the mucous membrane of the respiratory system, good for lungs, sinuses, intestines, even the brain. Salt baths had existed in the area for hundreds of years, the mine below producing an abundance of concentrated brine that had to go somewhere. So toward the end of the 19th century the locals started pumping it to ground level and created a spa.

He paid the price for an admission ticket and strolled into the tower, heading up a walkway that wound a path deep into the twenty-meter-tall wooden structure. Its working principle seemed simple. Take salt suspended in water, pump it to the top, then allow the brine to thicken as it flows down the branches, breaking up as it hits each twig, partially evaporating, saturating the air with a curative saline aerosol.

He sucked in a few deep breaths.

Which felt good.

He should take better care of himself, especially now that he was five million euros richer. Munoz had called and told him to come here, near the top of the tower, which sat within sight of the salt mine's main entrance. He caught glimpses of the afternoon crowd, many headed to their cars to leave, through breaks in the outer walls. Not many people were partaking of the curative effects today. Which was good. He needed a little privacy.

He rounded a corner and saw Munoz and Konrad ahead.

"What is this about?" Konrad asked, with concern. "And how did you know where I live?"

"My business is information."

"Where is DiGenti?"

He knew better than to tell the truth. "We're handling matters now."

"Mr. Olivier made it clear that all of this had to be held confidential. He said nothing about you being a part of that."

"I was here last evening. I am a part of this." He decided to soothe the man's clear anxiety. "I require your assistance. For that I'm prepared to pay you one hundred thousand euros."

Konrad's face froze in surprise. "That's far more than DiGenti ever paid me."

"Unlike Mr. DiGenti, I believe that people should be adequately compensated for their services. Is that amount satisfactory?"

Konrad nodded.

He'd long ago learned that everyone had a price. The trick was finding it, then being able to pay. Luckily, neither was a problem here.

"What do you want me to do?" Konrad asked.

"Take us to the statue of St. Bobola, on Level IX."

He watched as the request was considered. He'd learned of the connection between the saint and the mine from the internet.

"I think I know where that is," Konrad said. "It's inside a small chapel."

"Excellent. How fast can you get us there?"

"Half an hour. Maybe faster. When do I get paid?"

"When we return from the statue. Of course, we need discreet access, with no attention whatsoever. The more anonymous the better."

"I can take care of that. DiGenti wanted the same thing."

"But I'm paying much more than he ever did, so I expect more."

"As do I," a new voice said.

He turned and saw Ivan waddle his way toward them, like a plow horse, bulky, bony, with black, oily eyes like a crow. He felt his head spiral upward toward a different reality, one where he wanted to stay. But he couldn't. He had to maintain control of the situation, though he could feel the confidence draining out of his fingertips.

"Konrad," he said, "could you go arrange for that access. Mr. Munoz will come with you. Art, come back and get me when all is ready."

Munoz and Konrad started to leave.

"Add one more to tour," Ivan said.

Konrad stopped.

Eli realized there was no choice. "Do it."

Konrad nodded and headed off with Munoz. Eli faced Ivan. "How did you know?"

"I been doing this long time. Reading people is talent I have. And, besides, I not trust you ever. So I watch close." Ivan motioned to his eyes with his fingers. "You find something at castle. I saw in your face. Why you think I let Malone go so easy?" Ivan pointed. "You know what I want to know. I want information on Czajkowski."

"I had hoped to sell it to you."

Ivan chuckled. "Sure you did. But I have better deal. I let you live, in return for information."

He'd known that was coming. "Why don't you just go down without me and find it yourself. There's no need for me to be involved any longer."

"I disagree. You most important. We go down together. Cotton Malone is on his way here."

Great.

"I have man trying to stop him."

"Seems this whole venture is becoming crowded."

"My thought, too."

He definitely had a problem. Going down into that mine could be a one-way trip. But he doubted this Russian had come alone. So there was nowhere to run. No. Go down. Deal with things below, where the darkness and solitude might give him an edge.

"All right," he said. "We go together."

A disdainful smile worked at the corner of Ivan's mouth. "You were paid much money. More than enough to cover information, too."

"That information is worth far more than five million euros."

"Not for you. Call it price of lying."

Again, he had no choice. "Let us conclude our business and be done with each other."

"Be grateful, Mr. Broker, I don't kill you."

"You don't know where the information is hidden."

"See how far that got Olivier. Not much. Don't push me. I want information and I want to be done with this."

But he was not buying a single word. Russians lied with uninhibited ease. A talent that came with them from the womb. He had to go down with this devil. That was the easy part.

But getting back up in one piece?

That was going to take some effort.

CHAPTER SIXTY

CZAJKOWSKI FELT A MEASURE OF FREEDOM. FOR THE FIRST TIME IN
five years he had no BOR security people in tow. No media. No aides. Only
Ivona. It had taken Michał Zima's direct order to have his bodyguards
stand down. Having Ivona with him helped soothe Zima's concerns—if
anything happened, it would be Zima who'd take the fall. But the head
of the BOR had assured him that he was prepared for any consequences.
He was reevaluating his opinion of Zima. The man seemed a team player,
sensitive to the gravity of a delicate situation and its political effects, recognizing that everything, quite literally, seemed at stake.

A call had come a few moments ago to Ivona's phone telling her that
the car ferrying Cotton Malone and Stephanie Nelle was now parked in
a lot adjacent to the Wieliczka Salt Mine. A strange place for two American intelligence officers to head. They were not tourists. He'd been down
in the mine several times over the years for concerts and ceremonies. The
whole place cast a surreal air, like being inside a shopping mall a hundred meters below earth. Still, the tourist areas were but a tiny part of
the massive complex. He wondered if there was more hidden down there
than new salt deposits.

"Why are they there?" he muttered.

Ivona drove the car she'd been using all day. He sat in the passenger seat, his tie and suit jacket gone, the collar to his white shirt open, his sleeves rolled up.

"I don't know," she said. "It is peculiar."

"It has to relate to the Russians. What Fox said. The information is still in play, and somehow Malone got ahead of them."

"Or maybe just even with them."

She kept speeding down the highway, headed toward the salt mine. He imagined himself no longer president, his second term over, free of all political and personal entanglements, able to do as he pleased.

That would be a first.

His entire life had been one responsibility after another, working his way up until he achieved the pinnacle of Polish success. He recognized that the presidency was in many ways more ceremonial than practical, but there were areas where he possessed true power. One of those was in approving agreements with foreign governments.

This would be so much more difficult if Parliament had the final say. Good luck getting them to agree on anything. Not much had changed in the three centuries since the liberum veto was finally abolished. True, everything no longer had to be unanimous, but achieving a simple majority vote could prove equally vexing.

I freely forbid.

Poles took that declaration to heart—both then and now.

Thankfully, the decision to place missiles on Polish soil was his alone. There would be a great many within Parliament who would look favorably on an increased American presence, as was evident years ago when the first effort was abandoned. But there were others who would resent any and all foreign interference. He suspected they would be in the majority, though not by much. The missiles would be viewed as a slap to Moscow—there was no other way to view it—and that had never been taken kindly by Poland's neighbor to the east. He doubted anyone in Europe or America would ever go to war to protect an independent Poland. NATO or no NATO. Poland had always been expendable.

And would remain so.

"This all rests in our hands," he said in barely a whisper. "We can't allow the Russians to get that information."

"I won't," Ivona declared.

Her phone vibrated and she answered the call, which lasted only a few seconds before she ended it. "They're headed into the mine. We need to delay them."

He found his own cell phone and called Zima, explaining what he wanted. "Delay, but don't stop them. We need another fifteen minutes."

No surprise that Zima said he could handle it.

"What are we going to do, once there?" he asked her, after ending the call.

"Try to stay close without them noticing."

He glanced down at his left hand and the ring he'd worn for decades, fashioned by a long-dead Warsaw jeweler. Not gold, as that was a rare commodity in Soviet-controlled Poland and remained so in the years thereafter. Instead pewter had sufficed in a simple statement of patriotism.

Back in the 10th century, Bolesław the Brave had been the first to use the white, single-headed eagle as the symbol of the king. He was also the first to call the area Polona, after a local tribe that had occupied the land for a millennium. The display of the eagle was now mandated by the Polish Constitution in precise terms. White, upon a red field. The crown, eagle's beak and talons, gold. The wings and legs outstretched, its head angled to the right.

He'd worn the ring every day for the past thirty years.

A reminder of his life's dedication.

But for the first time in a long while he was afraid. Not since that day in Mokotów Prison had he felt so helpless. Only after, when he first met

Stanis Orlik and realized that he actually had a choice, had his anxiety waned.

Here was the same.

There were choices.

But none seemed good.

CHAPTER SIXTY-ONE

COTTON ZIPPED UP THE GREEN COVERALLS THAT HE'D DONNED over his clothes. He and Stephanie were inside a locker room, part of a building that accommodated one of the shafts used only by the miners. The tourist shaft was in another building, still busy ferrying visitors up and down. Another set of elevators was located farther away, where special groups for a miner's experience made their way below. Their guide had avoided those hot spots and led them to this employees-only area. The gun from the castle was now safely tucked at his waist beneath the coveralls. He assumed bringing weapons into the mine was not allowed, so he'd kept its presence to himself. But after what happened on the road, he was not about to leave it up here.

"Not much in the way of fashion," he said to Stephanie. "But functional."

She donned her helmet with light. "We look like the Mario Brothers."

He grinned.

That they did.

Stephanie sat on a bench and slipped on the boots their guide had provided. He'd already laced his up, which fit snugly.

"Here we are," she said. "We have a trunk full of sacred relics out in the parking lot, and below may be some extremely damaging blackmail on the president of Poland. The people I've dealt with for the past few decades, the people I worked with to protect the country, the vast majority of them would have never placed me, or themselves, in this untenable situation. Yet here I am."

"You have to play the cards you're dealt. And you know that."

"That's the problem, Cotton. I don't even have a pair of twos here."

"If we find those documents, you'll have a royal flush."

"To do what with?"

"Maybe Senator Danny Daniels can use them to make a move on Fox. I'm sure trying to blackmail the president of a foreign nation qualifies as *high crimes and misdemeanors*. Perhaps he could encourage the House to impeach the idiot."

She shook her head. "That only amplifies the problem. Everybody loves to scream impeachment. But that's not a tool to undo elections. The people chose Warner Fox. The fact that he may be incompetent is really not at issue. They've already decided they want him to lead them."

"You've become quite the fatalist."

"Just a realist."

He had to say, "I assume you wouldn't wait here while I go below?"

She smiled at him. "You've always looked after me."

"I could say the same to you."

"Back that first day we met," she said, "in the Duval County jail, I wasn't quite sure I'd made the right decision going there. The reports on you were all glowing. But that first impression? You shot a woman."

"Who murdered her husband, then tried to kill me."

"I know. You handled yourself well in that situation. As you did in that first assignment. I knew then I had a winner." She finished tying her boots. "For the record, I'm not interested in having Danny fight my battles."

"You'll have a hard time keeping him out of it."

"I know. And I love him for it. But this is my problem to solve."

"Fox has wanted you gone from the start. The only bargaining chip you have may be waiting below."

"Which isn't saying much, since I think this whole thing stinks."

The door to the locker room opened and their guide returned.

"Arrangements are all made," Patrycja said. "We can head down in a few minutes. I brought a map of Level IX."

She laid out a large sheet of heavy paper that detailed a labyrinth of twisting tunnels and chambers.

"St. Bobola's statue is one of hundreds scattered around the entire mine," Patrycja said. "It was carved in the 19th century. I'm told it's not in a good state of repair. Strange that it seems so important."

He realized they needed to maintain this woman's cooperation while revealing as little as possible. But there was also an element of danger here, especially if the Russians or Eli Reinhardt decided to show up. He could only hope that he was ahead of them, as he did not want to place this woman in jeopardy.

"Let's just say that it might be what's near it that's important," he said. "That's why we need to have a look."

"The statue is located here." She pointed to a spot on the map, inside a small chamber along a secondary drift on Level IX. Several tunnels led in and out.

"It's a junction point," Patrycja said. "Many of the chapels were placed where tunnels joined."

"How did Jonty Olivier get those documents down there?" Stephanie asked. "I assume that's not a spot someone could just wander into."

Patrycja nodded. "Only the guides can get there." She unzipped a pocket in her coveralls and removed a small plastic fob. "This unlocks the elevators for the lower levels. About fifty of the guides carry these on a daily basis. We have to turn them in at the end of each day."

He glanced at Stephanie. That meant Olivier had arranged for a way down, too, one that included a guide. And if the Russians wanted down, they'd have to do the same. That might work in their favor and provide them enough time.

"Let's deal with that later," he said to her, knowing she was thinking the same thing.

She nodded. "You do know, in 1978, this was one of the first places ever given the distinction of being a World Heritage Site."

He caught the significance of her humor. "I'll try to be careful."

And he thought of Ivona. Was she aware of this latest development? The Agencja Wywiadu ranked as a first-rate intelligence agency. If Warner Fox knew the Russians were still in the game, the AW would know that, too. And Ivona would not be confined by rules or fobs.

He needed to stay alert.

The plan? In and out. Fast. Clean.

No mistakes.

CHAPTER
SIXTY-TWO

Czajkowski walked with Ivona.

They'd first found the car Malone had used, parked in a public lot, minus the sacred relics Ivona had said were lying on the rear seat back in Slovakia. He didn't really care about those. Poland's national treasure had been recovered, the rest were somebody else's problem. He was worried, though, about being recognized. No street clothes this time like at the monastery. One good thing was that the vast majority of people around him were tourists who had no idea what the president of Poland looked like.

But he'd feel better once they were inside.

After locating Malone's vehicle, they drove farther into the royal free mining town of Wieliczka, to Żupny Castle, where Zima had directed them. Named for the żupnik, the royal administrator of the salt mine, who once lived inside, it had stood since the 13th century but like much of Poland was destroyed during the war. Surprisingly, it was rebuilt during the time of the communists. The attractive Gothic castle now came with a fortified wall, tower, and outbuildings that housed mining exhibitions where visitors discovered the history of both Wieliczka and its mine.

But they'd not come for the sights or an education.

They parked in another public lot and walked up a tree-lined, cobbled path to the castle entrance. Waiting for them was a short, stumpy man in a suit who introduced himself as the mine manager. Apparently Michał Zima had some serious connections and had gone straight to the top, conveying the appropriate instructions about not making a big deal over what was happening.

"I appreciate your assistance," he said to the manager. "We need to know the exact whereabouts of two people who are here, on site."

"That was explained to me by your security people. We have full video surveillance of the entire facility."

He was not in the mood for chitchatting.

"Then please, take us to the monitoring station."

The central security office sat within the castle walls and looked like something out of the space program with one wall sheathed in high-definition screens. Each displayed a different slice of both the exterior and interior of the mine.

"There are three main ways down," the manager said. "We've been watching them all." The man motioned to one of the attendants. "We found the car when it arrived."

On one of the screens the crisp image of Malone and an older woman came into view as they exited the vehicle they'd just seen, stopping only to remove the relics from the backseat and place them in the trunk.

"That's Stephanie Nelle," Ivona said. "Head of the Magellan Billet."

The two Americans then walked from the parking lot onto the grounds and approached the building that housed the Daniłowicz Shaft. They were met by a petite, blond woman, dressed in tan coveralls, then all three headed away from the tourist area.

"I've learned that the American Polish ambassador was in contact with our communications office," the manager said. "He arranged for Patrycja, the woman you just saw, to meet the two visitors. She's one of our guides. She took them to the miners' entrance where they dressed and descended about five minutes ago. I delayed them as long as I could without drawing suspicion."

"Where are they in the mine?"

"Level IX. There are no cameras there, but all guides carry trackers that we can monitor. Mr. President, can I inquire as to the nature of this?"

"You can. But it's a matter of state security. The two people on Level IX are American intelligence agents. It's imperative they do not wander out of your electronic sight. And we need to go down there."

Ivona motioned for them to step aside together.

They left the room and stood alone out in a hallway.

"Are you sure about this?" she asked.

He looked at her puzzled.

"*We?*" she said. "Why don't you let me handle it."

"It's my life that's at stake."

"You're the president of this country. Act like it."

Her tone was sharp.

So he made no attempt to hide his frustration, either. "You told me this was over. You told me it was handled. It wasn't."

"We have no idea what's going on here. Yes, it bears investigating, then a decision can be made once we know the facts. Right now we're speculating. Even worse, we're guessing. What you're doing smacks of desperation."

"I am desperate. I've worked my whole life to get to this point. I won't allow that opportunity to be taken from me. Not without a fight."

These were the first cross words that had ever passed between them, and he hated they were being said. But he meant every one. He'd worked too long and too hard to be cut short now. If salvation waited below, then salvation *he* would find.

Her eyes softened. "You're in my charge. There's a clear danger here."

"From Malone? I didn't think he was a problem."

"We have no idea who's here. The Russians could be around. I can't be cavalier about your safety. We should inform the BOR."

"There's little they can do."

She reached out and touched his arm. "All the more reason to proceed with caution."

He stared at her and saw she could read his thoughts.

"All right," she said, resignation in her voice. "We'll go together."

She turned for the door.

He grabbed her arm. "I'm sorry for blaming you. I know you only did what you thought necessary. Killing Olivier could not have been easy."

"I did what had to be done." She paused. "And if I'd thought for a moment we'd end up here, right now, with this dilemma, I would have handled it differently. I genuinely thought this was over."

"I know. Again. I'm sorry."

They stepped back into the control room.

"We're ready," he told the manager. "We'll need a way to track the guide, Patrycja, from down there."

"We have handheld monitors."

Ivona's gaze was locked on the screens. Hard to tell which one had grabbed her attention.

"What is it?" he asked.

"Look there, on the fourth one down from the top, right side."

He did and saw four men, dressed in coveralls, walking toward an elevator. All wore hard hats with lights.

"That's Eli Reinhardt and his man Munoz."

He knew the names.

"The big one is Ivan."

He knew that name, too. Fox's declaration about the Russians had not been idle chatter. He pointed at the screen and asked, "Where is that?"

"The Regis Shaft. Not far from here."

"They can get to Level IX from there?" Ivona asked.

The manager nodded. "Of course. But it's a walk."

He pointed at the screen. "Who's with them?"

The manager studied the screen. "It's one of our guides. Dawid Konrad."

"We'll need to track him, too," Ivona said.

But he doubted that was going to be a problem.

Since they were all headed to the same place.

CHAPTER SIXTY-THREE

ELI RODE IN THE ELEVATOR, WHICH PURRED IN A STEADY, CON-trolled fall to three hundred meters belowground. With Ivan around, he was glad to have Munoz with him. They were both armed with the weapons from the castle. Good thing, too, as surely there were Russian reinforcements waiting above. It was doubtful he'd make it away from the mine in one piece if Ivan was challenged. But he was no fool, either. Once the information on Czajkowski was located, no reason existed to keep him alive. On the contrary. Every reason existed for him to die. Ivan had shot two of his own men with no hesitation. He'd already told Munoz to stay alert, and at the first opportunity they'd make their escape, getting lost in the mine and finding another way out. Ivan could have the information for free. He just wanted this to end. What had, at first, seemed a profitable idea had turned into a disaster.

At least he still had five million euros and the Pantry.

Which the Russians apparently knew nothing about, as there'd been no mention of its existence.

The elevator came to a stop and the metal doors opened to a lit foyer and an unlit tunnel beyond. They stepped out into chilly air. The solitude of the uninviting blackness swallowed him as they entered the tunnel, their headlamps illuminating about ten meters ahead.

"Where you want to go is a long walk from here," Konrad said.

"Then let us start," Ivan said. "I don't move so fast."

Eli had always imposed a rigorous discipline on himself. He'd dealt with Israelis, Americans, French, Congolese, Chinese, South Africans, you name the buyers, anyone and everyone had been a customer. Unlike Olivier, who had an abhorrence for killing, he'd never harbored any such reservations. But killing this Russian would come with dire consequences.

And Ivan knew that.

Eli tried to dismiss the disturbing thoughts swirling through his brain, but couldn't. Like fat on a man who'd always been lean, they slowed him down. But he forced himself to focus and kept following their beams down the wide tunnel.

"Amazing place," Ivan said.

"It shows what forty generations of hard work can do," Konrad noted. "They just kept digging, making money for the king."

Eli was not ignorant of the salt mine. Though there were larger and older caverns in both Poland and Europe, they paled in comparison with this vast labyrinth, hundreds of kilometers long, so like the Minotaur's lair. Everything about it screamed *monumental*. Mines had always fascinated him, particularly how the Nazis used them in Germany and Austria in the last war as secret vaults. Here the treasure had been far more practical.

Salt.

What a thing.

A rock, hard but fragile. But also a symbol, a measure of wealth, a spice, and a raw material. Once entire kingdoms depended on its trade.

Not so much anymore.

If he'd lived centuries ago and worked the mine, he would have wanted to be a treasurer. They ruled the underground. Miners simply called them He. No name. Just He. It was the treasurer who rewarded hard work and punished the lazy. The treasurer who delivered a harsh slap across the face to any miner who cursed. The treasurer who warned against danger, scampering through the tunnels, examining the ceiling and walls, blocking the path to places where trouble lurked.

They kept walking down the drift.

Konrad led the way, Ivan next, then himself, with Munoz in the rear. He wanted to keep the Russian ahead of him where he could see his every move. For whatever good that would offer. He could hear the fat man's heavy breathing, obviously unaccustomed to a brisk workout. Maybe Ivan would have a coronary.

He could only hope.

Eli had not made a name for himself by being either bashful or cowardly. And he wasn't going to embrace either weakness now.

Be smart and patient, he told himself.

The tunnel forked.

The right side was blocked by a sign.

WSTĘP WZBRONIONY. No entry.

Dripping disturbed the silence from down the blocked path. Past a rope barrier, in the combined beams of their lights he saw water seeping from the ceiling. A respectable puddle had formed on the floor beneath. Not a recent leak, either. Crystallized salt, white as snow, painted the walls.

"Is that okay?" he asked Konrad.

"It happens all the time. We come down and make repairs."

"What would happen if you didn't?"

"The water would slowly eat it all away. One salt crystal at a time. But don't worry, that would take about 150 years. We're okay."

"How far to go?" he asked Konrad.

"Another few minutes."

He turned to leave and his helmet slipped from his head, clattering down the salt wall and finding the floor, the light beam dancing in the darkness.

"My apologies," he said, retrieving the headgear.

Ivan stood facing him. Beneath those coveralls was a gun, too. Probably the same one used to shoot two of his own men back at Sturney Castle. Normally Eli stayed in control. At the head of the parade. Here he was nothing more than a spectator. He tried not to think of the darkness around him and what it might contain.

But one thing he knew for sure.

Nothing could be as threatening as a Russian.

CHAPTER
SIXTY-FOUR

COTTON FOLLOWED STEPHANIE AND THEIR GUIDE DOWN THE
tunnel on Level IX. The trip into the bowels of the mine had required
two elevators, one to Level III, then a second from there to Level IX.
Patrycja had used her fob to activate both elevators, confirming her previous observation that not just anyone could descend this deep. She'd
also noted that a count was kept of everyone who entered the mine, including every tourist. At the end of each day the ins and outs were rec-
onciled so that nobody could remain. Cleaning crews worked during the
day on the upper levels, so at night the mine was essentially shut down,
the last tour switching off the lights, everything left in blackness until
the following morning.

The time was approaching 6:00 P.M., another hour and a half before
the site officially closed. They needed to work fast, staying ahead of not
only the tourists but also the Russians, the Poles, and any new Americans who might show up.

A chilly, salt-laced breeze blew in his face, helping dissipate any feelings of claustrophobia. It wasn't enclosed spaces that drove him nuts. It
was enclosed, *tight* spaces he hated. He had to keep telling himself to ignore the fact that over nine hundred feet of rock lay between him and
daylight. Patrycja told them that following the direction of the air served
as a means of navigation, one the miners still used. The rough floor was

full of obstacles and slippery in places. The silence pressed onto him as if the tunnel were collapsing. He imagined the sounds from a former time, when horses moved the heavy salt blocks, their hooves clunking on the hard floor. Railcars eventually replaced them, which came with the screech of metal on metal.

"You know your way around these tunnels?" Stephanie asked as they walked.

"I bring groups down here all the time. They grind salt like the miners once did."

The whole place had an air that did not speak of things neglected. Offshoots appeared with regularity leading into more absolute blackness.

"I assume it would be easy to get lost," he noted.

"More misdirected," Patrycja said. "At some point you'll come to stairs or an elevator leading up. It's big, but it's a finite world."

He smiled at her sarcasm.

"Keep an eye out for the White Lady, though," she said.

Had he heard right? A Dame Blanche? Obviously not a chocolate sundae. So he asked what she meant.

"The miners called her Bieliczka. Supposedly a spirit that roams the tunnels looking for a miner she'd once loved."

Good to know.

The tunnel spanned about six feet wide and eight tall, and the steady breeze kept bringing a measure of comfort. The darkness seemed omnipotent and impenetrable, but not frightening. No sunrises or sunsets happened here. No midnights or middays. For those long-ago miners who worked here for weeks at a time, only the light from their lanterns had brought a reprieve.

He thought of those miners and how they probably heard down here, for the first time, the sound of their own breath, their own heartbeat. How odd that must have been. But the silence was also threatening since it lulled the brain into a false sense of security. He had to constantly tell himself to stay alert. Trouble could be around the next turn. Or behind them? Hard to know anything for sure.

If Cassiopeia could see him now.

She would not be happy.

But at least he'd be done and back in Copenhagen by tomorrow evening. They'd have a great weekend. Dinner at Nyhavn. Then Tivoli on Saturday or Sunday. They both loved the amusement park. She'd stay until Tuesday or Wednesday, then head back to southern France. Her castle reconstruction project kept going forward. No surprise. She was a determined woman who could do anything she set her mind to.

He focused on thoughts of her as a way to avoid the obvious discomfort around him. How she painted her bread with butter in short, even strokes covering every square inch until the knife was shiny clean. Salt was always poured into her open palm before being dispensed. Never did she eat ice cream in a cone—too much pressure to perform before it melted. She hated apple juice, but loved apples, green ones especially. And potato chips. She loved them with only spicy mustard.

Everyone had their quirks.

God knew he had a long list of them.

He'd have to come clean about all that had happened this week, and she wouldn't be happy to have been left out. But she'd understand, like always. That was their way. They both tended to find trouble. And they both always tried to handle it—by themselves. Admitting they needed help seemed a weakness.

But he trusted no one more than Cassiopeia.

She'd never let him down.

Nor would he disappoint her.

The tunnel drained into a chamber.

Several shadows, large and fast, detached themselves from the darkness and assumed form in their lights. Two weathered statues, whose florid features had fallen into a portrait of despair. They framed the entrance to a nave cut into the far wall through the salt.

"St. Peter of Alcantara on the left. St. Casimir on the right," Patrycja said. "Not in good shape, as you can see. Leached by humidity and water leaks. Everything on this level has succumbed to some degree."

With his headlamp he studied the rest of the chamber.

"The chapels were strategically placed," Patrycja said. "Near wells and shafts, where new salt deposits were found, so prayers could be conducted. They were also landmarks. Lamps burning inside them were source points for workers, a place where they could safely congregate and reignite their own when it extinguished."

Stephanie stayed quiet and he saw the concern on her face. Here they were. Underground. One gun between them. Were they alone? So far, so good. He found her gaze and said with his eyes, *Why don't you stay here? Let me finish this.*

She shook her head.

My problem. My fix.

"St. Bobola is that way," Patrycja said, pointing to an exit off to the right.

He gestured for Stephanie to go first.

Something echoed in the distance.

A clattering sound.

Far off, like a stone down a deep well.

And the hair on the back of his neck bristled.

CHAPTER
SIXTY-FIVE

CZAJKOWSKI WORE COVERALLS, AS DID IVONA. THEY HELPED WITH anonymity, all provided by the mine manager. They were back in the security office with the video screens.

"I'm told," the mine manager said, "that Malone and Ms. Nelle, along with the Russian you identified and two others, are now all on Level IX."

"Are they aware of each other?" Ivona asked.

The man shook his head. "Unlikely. The trackers on the guides show them far apart, but heading in the same direction."

"We need to get down there," he said.

Ivona shook her head. "I've been thinking on that."

He was curious. "What do you suggest?"

"At some point, they have to get out," Ivona said. "So let's keep them underground and force them to the upper levels, where there are lights, cameras, and people. We can take them down there."

He saw the wisdom in the move.

She faced the mine manager. "Can you shut down the elevators that go all the way to the bottom and leave only the one up from Level IX to Level III working?"

The man nodded.

"Then all we have to do is wait at Level III," she said. "They'll come to us."

He really wanted to head for Level IX. No telling what was going to happen. But there was nothing to be gained by rushing into the unknown, especially when nobody knew they were even here.

They had the advantage.

So wait.

He nodded.

"The tours are winding down for the day," the manager said. "Fewer people will be on the upper levels, as they head for the surface. Most of the people there will be in line, waiting for an open elevator up. Those lines are long this time of day."

"Can you stop the tours for the day?" he asked. "Close early."

"It's most unusual."

"This whole thing is unusual."

And he saw the manager understood.

"I'll do it."

"Then," Ivona asked, "can you get us to Level III unnoticed?"

They descended a wooden staircase.

Strong and sturdy.

Built to last from solid timbers.

Tourists could choose walking down to Levels I and II, or take the elevators. Most rode. He and Ivona walked. He noticed that few were making the climb up, and no one was heading down. Surprisingly, after nearly four hundred steps, he wasn't all that winded. He just hoped he didn't have to use them to get back up. The manager had stayed above to keep an eye on what was happening on Level IX, saying he would meet them below shortly.

They came to the bottom and stepped off onto a salt floor. No cold, dark, damp passages awaited. Instead everything was well lit, with an arid but comfortable temperature and a steady breeze of fresh air. He assumed the mine had to be kept as dry as possible to prevent humidity from dissolving the salt. The manager had told them to head for the Copernicus Chamber, which was not far away. They followed the signs and passed within sight of the elevators up, spotting lines of people waiting to leave.

"Let's keep going," Ivona said to him.

They followed a corridor into a spacious chamber that housed a larger-than-life-sized statue of the famous astronomer. Timber frames supported masonry blocks along three walls. Logs stood at attention, one after the other forming a fourth wall behind the statue. A simple, almost modernistic representation, the arms outstretched, the open palms holding a celestial sphere. A handful of people loitered about, snapping a few final pictures before leaving.

"He studied in Kraków and lived in Frombork," he said, pointing at the salt carving. "What courage it took to say that the earth was not the center of the universe. That simple idea fundamentally changed humanity forever."

"You're an admirer?"

"Absolutely. He was an astronomer, with a doctorate in canon law. He was self-taught as a physician, polyglot, translator, diplomat, and economist. He spoke five languages. He's the father of the scientific revolution. And most important, he was a Pole."

A placard near the statue stated that, in 1493, while a student in Kraków, Copernicus visited the mine. Perhaps the first tourist ever to do so, the text suggested. The statue was carved in 1973 to commemorate the genius' 500th birthday.

"I don't like being helpless," he whispered.

"You're not. We have the situation under control. Let Malone and the Russians fight it out below. Whoever emerges we will deal with. They have no idea we're here, and there's only one way out."

The others left the chamber.

The manager appeared at the far side and walked their way.

"We have everything contained. All of the tour groups that were in the lower levels are now topside. Level IX is empty except for the two groups we're watching. We have all the exits guarded, with the only way out through here."

"I assume there's a place where we can watch that elevator?"

The man nodded. "There is a spot. Not far away, down on Level III.

The passageways here move between the three levels. We'll continue to ferry people up, and, as you asked, we've stopped selling tickets for the day. I've had all of the guides instructed to keep their groups near the elevators, or in the café and the adjacent dining hall."

He'd never been one to solve problems from the bottom. Smart people started from the top. And he'd always considered himself smart. Never had he done anything legally wrong or corrupt in his life. The Warsaw Protocol? That was war. Different rules. But if he was forced to defend himself and reveal the truth to counter the documents, how many would agree with him?

Not enough.

Most would see him as a spy for the communists, providing information on his friends, family, and acquaintances. That he sold out his country. Few would believe the Warsaw Protocol ever existed. Those who did might think him a murderer. A classic lose–lose. And the resulting firestorm would not be survivable. Candidates had been destroyed with far less damaging slander. Things like being called insensitive to war veterans. Labeled narcissistic. Elitist. Bragging about their education. Poor health. Even staring too long at a video monitor during an interview. All had been used in attempts to destroy campaigns. But an even greater danger existed, one that history cautioned should not be ignored. The possibility of dividing Poland.

Something similar had happened before.

Not here, but in France.

He knew the incident well.

In 1894 a traitor was discovered within the French army. A spy, passing information to the Germans. An investigation revealed the potential culprit. Captain Alfred Dreyfus, a French artillery officer of Jewish descent, who was found guilty and sent to solitary confinement on Devil's Island. Two years later an investigation unearthed the real culprit, who was tried. But officials suppressed vital evidence and the man was acquitted. The army then accused Dreyfus of more charges with more falsified evidence. Dreyfus was retried and found guilty again, but was pardoned and set free. Eventually it was proven that all of the accusations against Dreyfus were baseless.

But the whole thing bitterly divided France.

One half defended everything. Pro-army, mostly Catholic, screaming absolute loyalty to the nation. Dreyfus was a Jew who could not be
trusted. He had to be a spy. The other half, anti-clerical, pro-republican,
wanted justice for all, regardless of religion.

Political parties chose sides. Families split, sometimes for more than
a generation. The debate continued for decades and remained even today
with the "France for the French" nationalism clashing with a more global
vision of the rule of law and a nation for everyone.

Incredible.

One court case created unresolvable divisions between people who
never knew they disagreed with each other. It also revealed two vastly
different views of what people thought was France.

The same would happen in Poland.

Revealing the Warsaw Protocol would open wounds that had never
healed. What happened from 1945 to 1990 remained as fresh as yesterday in the minds of many Poles.

Divisions already existed.

Attacks on foreigners were steadily increasing.

Just recently, a fourteen-year-old Turkish girl was beaten on the street
while her attackers shouted *Poland for Poland.* Anti-Semitic demonstrations had become commonplace with Jews burned in effigy. Jokes about
the Holocaust were no longer unacceptable. Pro-fascist rallies happened
monthly. Crimes committed from racial prejudice were on the rise.
There'd even been a massive neo-Nazi march during last year's celebration of Polish independence.

It would be easy for the populace to add one more divide to that mix.

Some would agree with the protocol's radical tactics. Traitors had it
coming. Solidarity did what it had to do. Others would find the lies and
deaths no different from what the communists did, Solidarity nothing
but hypocrisy.

The debate would be endless.

There'd be political shifts. Ones, as in France, that would split families and friends, cut across social classes, and rearrange long-standing alliances.

Old wounds would bleed again.

Ivona was staring, allowing him his thoughts. He wanted to talk to her, to explain, seek her help, but knew better. This was better kept to himself.

At least for now.

One of the curses of being president.

But the fact remained that much more was at stake here than just his political career.

CHAPTER SIXTY-SIX

COTTON RAN HIS HAND ALONG THE WALLS. PARTS WERE SMOOTH, like glass, others sharp and rough, easily capable of slicing skin.

"Why is it gray?" he asked Patrycja.

"The salt is impure. It has some magnesium and calcium mixed with it, which is good for you. That's what once made this salt so highly valued."

They walked in the center of the tunnel, over grooves made long ago by heavy carts. All around were stalactites and stalagmites in the irregular shapes salt crystals adopted from water intrusion. One wall was totally sheathed in bright-white cauliflower-like formations.

"Do a lot of people come down here?" Stephanie asked.

"Oh, yes. It is a busy place. When the Austrians controlled the mine in the 18th century, they set up the first tourist routes. The price of a ticket then depended on the quality of the light provided. Torches were a basic fee, but fireworks were expensive."

"They actually set off pyrotechnics down here?" he asked.

"As crazy as that sounds, they did. And the price depended on the color used."

The sound from earlier continued to bother him, but Patrycja explained that it was probably just another tour group. Many ventured to

Level IX during each day, but, as she explained, they all stayed closer to the elevators. None ventured this deep into the tunnels.

Their path drained into another chamber, larger than the ones they'd already encountered, and different in that pillars had been left across it from floor to ceiling. He counted eight, along with spotting two other exits.

"Is this some sort of junction?" Stephanie asked.

Patrycja nodded. "The miners would use this as a starting point, then dig to the next deposits. That's why there's a chapel here."

Her light revealed a small room, separate and individual, that jutted from one wall into a square-shaped cavity. Heavy timbers framed out its entrance, a set of beams securing the opening on all four sides, supported by a thick center post. Across the top, scrawled in white chalk, was KAPLICZKA ŚW. FRANCISZKA.

Patrycja pointed at the words. "Chapel of St. Francis. *Kapliczka* means 'small chapel.'"

Cotton stepped across to the framed opening. Past it, in his headlamp, he spied a crucifix relief chipped from the wall. Beneath, a thick salt shelf rested on two projecting wooden dowels. A few feet away a wooden pew had been constructed of plank boards and faced the altar. Neighboring walls held small niches with crude statues, one he recognized from the book back at the castle.

St. Bobola.

Stephanie and Patrycja came up beside him and added more illumination.

"This is it," he said.

ELI STOPPED.

Both Konrad and Ivan had halted, too, along with Munoz behind him.

"I heard voices," he whispered.

"It could be another tour group," Konrad noted.

Perhaps. But *caution* was the word for this day. "Let's go slow and make sure it's not a problem." He stared at Ivan. "You said Malone was in the vicinity."

"I never received report on what happened," Ivan breathed out. "You think he's here."

"I don't know what to think. But we need to be careful."

The Russian broke into a toothy grin. "Good advice, comrade. I agree. We be careful."

"How much farther?" Eli asked Konrad.

"Around the next two bends and we're there."

"Lead way," Ivan said to Konrad, who began heading off into the darkness.

Ivan unzipped his jumpsuit, removed a gun, and kept it down at his side, finger on the trigger but shielded from view by the big man's thigh.

The Russian headed off.

Eli turned back to Munoz, who'd done the same thing with his weapon. His acolyte nodded.

Ready.

COTTON STEPPED INTO THE CHAPEL. SIMPLE AND AUSTERE, EVERY-thing stained white by humidity. Graffiti decorated the roof bars that had been inserted along the rear wall for strength. Random words and letters. Initials. Numbers. Dates. A layer of crushed salt lay across the floor like sand.

"What's with all the writing on the wood?" he asked.

"From the miners, over the centuries. We don't eliminate what they left."

"What exactly are we looking for?" Stephanie asked him.

"One hundred and forty-seven pages of documents. So it should be about that thick."

His index finger and thumb showed three-quarters of an inch or so of space.

He stepped over to St. Bobola and saw that, like the crucifix, the distorted sculpture was not a separate piece. Instead it, and the niche itself, had been chipped from the wall in bas-relief. No way anything was either behind or under. The same was true with the other images.

Everything pointed to here.

But where?

Think.

ELI HEARD THE VOICES AT THE SAME TIME EVERYONE ELSE DID, AND they all stopped. Ivan motioned and they extinguished their lights, Konrad the last to catch on to what was happening and follow suit.

They stood in absolute darkness.

"Is our destination just ahead?" he whispered.

"Around the next bend," Konrad breathed out.

"Somebody already there," Ivan said.

Both Ivan and Munoz were armed, the darkness now concealing that fact from Konrad. Eli knew what had to be done.

"Konrad, stay here," he said to the blackness. "We have to investigate."

"We go ahead with one light, pointed to floor," Ivan added.

"Agreed."

COTTON NARROWED THE CHOICES AND DECIDED THERE COULD only be one solution.

The wooden pew.

It was the only thing not built of salt in the makeshift chapel.

Crude and simple in construction, fashioned from rough-cut one-by-six and one-by-eight planks nailed together. About four feet wide. With a bench for sitting and an angled platform for resting hands or a hymnal while kneeling.

He stepped over and lifted the structure, setting it to one side. Beneath, the salt floor was solid and undisturbed. He brushed it with his shoe. Little to no give was returned. Like concrete. He looked at Stephanie. Who nodded. They were thinking the same thing. Nothing buried.

He tipped the makeshift pew over.

Nothing.

Its base was composed of one-by-eight boards fashioned into rectangles. One was set at the rear beneath the bench where a penitent could sit, while the other formed a kneeler. They were tacked together with headless nails.

"There's a compartment formed in both of those," he said.

The trick was opening them.

He threw his weight and gave two swift kicks with his boot. The thin wood split and parted from the frame. He pushed through the splinters and saw he was right. There was a compartment. But it was empty. He turned his attention to the other base support and pounded it, too.

Inside, taped to the boards, was a vacuum-sealed plastic pouch. Now the machine he'd spotted back at the castle made sense. It contained a manila envelope, similar to the one in which he'd found the book back at the castle.

He wrenched it free. "This is it."

And a gun fired.

CHAPTER SIXTY-SEVEN

CZAJKOWSKI SAT AT A LONG WOODEN TABLE INSIDE A SPACIOUS HALL adorned with salt chandeliers, the room available to rent for large cultural and business events. He'd once attended a concert here—the Wrocław Philharmonic, if he recalled right, with a wonderful cello concerto—a treat at 125 meters underground, the acoustics near perfect. Adjacent to the hall was the miners' tavern, hacked from more gray salt, which served an excellent array of Polish food. Two years ago he hosted a dinner here for participants in a European energy summit. He especially recalled the chocolate tart served that day. What a delight. Nobody was in the hall, or the café, at the moment, as business was clearly winding down early thanks to the mine manager.

Incredibly, there was cell phone service courtesy of hard lines from the surface and repeaters stationed throughout the tourist levels. Which made it possible for him to speak with his wife, who'd called.

"I just left Jasna Góra," she said to him through the phone. "Brother Orlik and I had a lovely chat."

He could only imagine. "Is he still refusing to cooperate?"

He kept his voice low and a hand up, covering his mouth.

"Once he knew that I knew the truth, his attitude changed. Of course, he berated you for telling me and simply denied everything. What he didn't know is that while we were chatting, I had the BOR search his room."

He smiled. Nothing about her was subtle or sublime. "Find anything?"

"A thick file."

He was shocked. "You have it?"

"I do. And by the way, you two are a lot alike. But I assume you already realized that fact."

Long ago, in fact. He was perhaps one of the few people in Poland who could call the Owl a friend. But that had seemed to count for little.

He decided to keep to himself what was happening in the mine. There was nothing she could do about any of it. But if things went wrong here, having a record of the Warsaw Protocol could prove helpful.

"You did good," he told her. "I appreciate it."

"Just doing my part."

And she ended the call.

He stared around at the hall and its stage at the far end. What an amazing place. A huge cavity, carved entirely from salt. A hole in the earth, which reminded him of Bolesław the Brave and the legend of the sleeping kings. Every schoolchild knew the tale. Once a year, at midnight on Christmas Eve, the mighty Sigismund bell rung, and the Polish kings woke from their eternal sleep and gathered in a grand underground hall. A place with plenty of light, like a cathedral. Some say it lay beneath Wawel Castle, but others said it was much farther south, in the Tatra Mountains. Or maybe it was here, in Wieliczka?

Who knew?

They came dressed in their coronation robes, sitting before a round table, discussing the fate of the country. Bolesław himself presided, holding the famous Szczerbiec, Poland's coronation sword.

What a sight that would have been.

But they were not the only ones who arose that night.

The Sleeping Knights of the Tatra also roamed on Christmas Eve. They would leave the mountains on their white horses and ride off in search of the kings. Once found a loud knock would come to the hall's door. Then again. And one more time. Always three. The kings would fall silent as Bolesław opened the door, telling the knights, *No. The time has not yet come.*

He smiled at the drama.

And irony.

Men there, ready to fight, ready to serve Poland.

But the time had not yet come.

Before the kings resumed their council they would listen to the fading hoofbeats as the knights rode back to their icy caves. Once there, the knights fed their animals then fell asleep, leaning against their saddles in readiness.

For when the time comes.

What a glorious tale.

His phone buzzed.

A text.

From his private secretary.

He'd left instructions with his BOR detail to return to the Sheraton in Kraków and pretend he was back inside the Royal Wawel Suite. He'd called his private secretary and told him that he was going to rest for a few hours and did not want to be disturbed.

Unless vital.

He read the message.

UNITED STATES ISSUED STATEMENT THAT DEPUTY NATIONAL SECURITY ADVISER THOMAS BUNCH IS MISSING SOMEWHERE IN POLAND. HE WAS HERE ON OFFICIAL BUSINESS, UNDER DIPLOMATIC IMMUNITY, AND WASHINGTON HAS CALLED ON WARSAW TO ACT IMMEDIATELY AND ASCERTAIN HIS WHEREABOUTS. THE FOREIGN MINISTRY WANTS TO KNOW OUR RESPONSE.

Fox had tossed the first salvo, shining a light. But the statement's wording allowed room to maneuver.

He typed his reply.

TELL THE AMERICANS WE ARE SYMPATHETIC TO THE SITUATION AND WILL INVESTIGATE. ALSO, HAVE THE FOREIGN MINISTRY INQUIRE AS TO THE EXACT NATURE OF THE "OFFICIAL BUSINESS" THE DEPUTY WAS ENGAGED IN. WE REQUIRE DETAILS TO AID IN OUR INVESTIGATION.

He smiled.

That should slow Fox down.

Enough, so that what was about to happen—

Could play itself out.

CHAPTER
SIXTY-EIGHT

COTTON REACTED TO THE SUDDEN BANG THAT REVERBERATED OFF the salt, throbbing his eardrums.

Which hurt.

The sound surprised him, so out of place given the constant silence. Patrycja screamed and his gaze shot to the outer chamber as a large form materialized from the darkness, seeking cover behind one of the pillars. They were sitting ducks in this confined space, their headlamps beacons upon which to aim. So he reached for the battery pack at his waist and switched off the power. Stephanie followed suit, but Patrycja lagged. He lunged and brought her down to the floor, switching her light off, too.

Darkness now engulfed them.

He heard movement in the outer chamber, feet scuffing across brittle salt. He reached out for the overturned pew to use for cover. Their assailants' headlamps were also off. But nothing would prevent them from strafing the chapel with gunfire. The pew could offer some cover, but not much.

"Nowhere to go, Malone," a voice said from the blackness.

Ivan.

Hard to tell exactly where, thanks to the echo and the black ink, both of which disoriented the senses with a lack of reference points.

"Get over here," he whispered to Stephanie and Patrycja. "And stay low."

He reached out into the blackness, guiding them behind the pew.

"We meet again, Mr. Malone," an older voice said.

Reinhardt.

"You know what I want," Ivan said. "I saw what you found."

But he wasn't ready to concede just yet. The darkness worked both ways, though it was a long way from where they crouched to the exit tunnel in the outer room, and their assailants' lamps, if switched on, would illuminate them like a deer in headlights.

"I could kill all you," Ivan said. "Then come get it myself. Be reasonable, Malone. I really not want to shoot you."

Like he believed that one. Ivan would do whatever he had to do in order to get what he wanted. All those dead bodies back in Slovakia were proof of that. He and Stephanie were pros. They knew the risks. But Patrycja was another matter. He owed her safety.

"All right, Ivan. Here it is."

And he tossed the packet toward where he thought was the chapel entry.

A light went on.

He shielded his pupils and saw a black form beneath a headlamp retrieve the packet. In one hand he spied a pistol. A quick flash of the face showed the form to be Munoz, Reinhardt's man. Shapes hard to discern moved in the darkness.

The light extinguished.

"We leave now, Malone," Ivan said. "Stay where you are."

Obviously there was another way to this point through Level IX, since they'd encountered no one on the trip here. He assumed Ivan and company would utilize that path back out.

So he was surprised when four lights came on, then disappeared into the tunnel through which Patrycja had led them.

"Why that way?" he asked her.

"Much quicker to an elevator. They probably came down from the Regis Shaft, which is about a kilometer away."

They continued to sit in the dark.

"I'm going after them," he said. "Stephanie, you and Patrycja head back the way we came."

"Like hell," his old boss said.

"I agree," their guide added.

Stephanie he could understand, but the young Pole was being foolish. "Patrycja, this is about to get real messy."

"And you don't have a clue where you're going without me. I saw the face of one of the men who just left. He's a miner who works as a guide. They have help. You need it, too."

She had a point. And he admired her bravery.

"All right, let's go. One light only. Mine."

Which would make him the first target.

"They should be far enough down the tunnel that we can head after them. You don't happen to know another way back to that elevator that doesn't involve the tunnel they took?"

"Actually, I do."

ELI FOLLOWED IVAN.

Thankfully, the Russian had volunteered to stay in front of him. The big man carried a gun in one hand and the sealed packet in the other. Munoz had handed it over back in the chamber.

He debated whether to kill the fat Slav and take his chances with anybody waiting above. But the Russian foreign service, the SVR, was every bit as ruthless as its predecessor, the KGB. Its staff and resources were endless, and there would literally be no place to hide anywhere on the globe. Not to mention the Americans, French, Iranians, North Koreans, and Chinese who would want to exact revenge for their losses, too. The smart play, the only play, was to allow Ivan his moment and get out of this mine, and away, with his five million euros. The Pantry was still one level below him and he could barter it to the Poles.

Personally, he would have killed Malone and the others back in the chamber. But Ivan had made it clear that was not to happen. He did not want to antagonize the Americans any further by generating another martyr they could rally behind. Better to let Malone and Stephanie Nelle be embarrassed over their failure to secure the information.

They kept walking, following Konrad down the dark tunnel, their lights illuminating the way. The chilly breeze in their face felt good and brought the anticipated comfort of fresh air above.

Around two bends and they came to the elevator.

Konrad stopped before the closed doors. "When do I get paid?"

"That not my problem," Ivan said.

Konrad pointed at Eli. "It's his problem. One hundred thousand euros. And no one said anything about guns and shooting. Weapons are not allowed here. We could all be in trouble if anyone heard that shot."

"But apparently no one did," Eli said.

"You said I would be paid once I led you to that statue. It's done. Where's my money."

Ivan raised his gun and fired.

COTTON HEARD A SHOT.

From somewhere in the echoing darkness.

"How far to the elevators?" he asked Patrycja.

"Just ahead."

ELI MOTIONED AND MUNOZ DRAGGED KONRAD'S BODY BACK DOWN the tunnel and into one of the offshoots they'd just passed.

"Was that necessary?" he asked Ivan.

"We can't afford that witness."

But he needed Konrad to get back to the Pantry. Now another way would have to be found.

Damn Russians.

"Can you afford me as a witness?" he asked.

Ivan chuckled. "I was told to leave you be. You have friends in Kremlin who like doing business with you. No worry." Ivan motioned with the packet. "We have what we want."

Some comfort, but not enough, since Russians lied.

Munoz returned.

He wondered how long it would be before the body was found. Hours? Unlikely. Days? Probable. Which was fine. He'd already thought it all through and saw Munoz had been thorough, handing over Konrad's fob that activated the elevator.

"We go up to Level III and blend in with the tourists leaving for the day. That way"—he motioned with the fob—"this gets recorded as having been used to leave from down here. We remove these coveralls and walk right out with the rest of the visitors. Nobody the wiser."

Ivan smiled, then reached out and clamped a paw on his right shoulder. "Good plan."

CHAPTER SIXTY-NINE

CZAJKOWSKI STILL SAT AT THE TABLE IN THE MEETING HALL. A FEW people had wandered in and out, but no one had paid him any attention, thinking him a mine employee thanks to the coveralls. Ivona was dealing with the mine manager, checking out the situation and determining how they would proceed. She'd thought it best he wait here, which had given him time to speak with Anna.

Interesting how his fate might rest in the hands of two women, one his estranged wife whom he'd once loved, the other a woman whom he now loved. Both working in concert, their goal the same.

To save his ass.

Some men might see that as emasculating. Not him.

His entire life he'd tried to do the right thing. But defining *right* had sometimes proven tricky. Dealing with the communists had required extreme measures. Both offensive and defensive. Back then they'd lumped it all under the label of "resistance." An easy thing to describe. Difficult to understand, since its actions took many differing forms. Eventually, he'd come to learn the difference between revolution and resistance. Revolution looked ahead to what could be. Resistance dreamed of the past and a restoration of what once existed. Both, though, were paid for in exile, prison, torture, and death. He, and millions of others, had *resisted* the communists, wanting nothing more than a free Poland restored.

It had been a war.

Exactly how the communist government described it, declaring that *there will be no turning back from socialism*. And the government supported that declaration with fifty thousand SB internal security forces deployed throughout the country, who broke strikes, coerced, and intimidated the people with death, violence, and fear. Spies played an integral part on both sides.

It truly *was* war.

And there were casualties.

On both sides.

Sitting here now, over three decades later, within the cocoon of an underground hall, it all seemed like yesterday. But lately, his mind had stayed deep in the past. The government had been so stupid. So foolish. Adhering to what Stalin had practiced. *The people who cast votes decide nothing. The people who count votes decide everything.*

Which, luckily, evolved into a disaster for them.

He could not repeat those mistakes, nor allow others to do so.

In truth, he was replaceable. He could be gunned down at any time, in any crowd, and the police would have his blood hosed from the pavement and traffic flowing again by nightfall.

Sad.

But not a lie.

In Poland, no one person controlled much of anything.

Everything was a consensus.

Nothing good would come from revealing the Warsaw Protocol. Any defense he might mount would be drowned out by a screaming opposition. There was no internet in the 1980s. No social media. No Twitter. Information could actually be contained. The backlash today would be relentless. A multitude of Polish political parties, who could not agree on a single thing, would unite under one common theme.

Removing him from office.

And they would succeed.

His entire ruling coalition revolved around the other side staying fractured since, sadly, creating unity within Poland always seemed easier when confronting a common enemy.

This time that would be him.

He shook his head.

What a quandary.

Made worse by another reality. Hastily planned operations nearly always came with problems. He had a bad feeling that some detail, now tiny, could later reveal itself and grow into something fatal. Something out of his control. But he realized that doubt always accompanied responsibility. So he sucked in a few deep breaths and steeled himself.

Ivona appeared at the entrance and walked toward him across the parquet floor. "The elevator is coming up from Level IX."

He stood. "I'm not waiting here. So don't tell me to."

"I wasn't planning on it."

"You have any idea who's coming up?"

She shook her head. "Let's hope whoever they are have what they came for."

"And if they don't?"

"Then we'll go find it."

He loved her determination. Never an ounce of pessimism. "I think I need a divorce."

She smiled. "That's the anxiety talking."

"It's a man who loves you talking. Why can't I be happy, too?"

"Because you're the president of this country and Poland will never tolerate a leader who divorces while in office. You know that."

"I'm tired of living a lie."

"It seems you've been doing that for a long time."

She knew nothing about the protocol, only fleeting references here and there. He needed to tell her, but now was not the time. So he only said, "There's more to this than you think."

"That's always the case."

"We'll talk. Once this is done."

"Janusz, I don't care what you did. I'm sure, whatever it was, you did it out of necessity. I was ten years old when the Soviet Union collapsed. Those were tough times. People did whatever they had to do in order to survive. Me, you, no one can judge them by today's standards." She paused. "And who am I to judge anyone. I shot a man in cold blood today. And he was not the first. So I really don't give a damn what you did."

He smiled.

So practical, too.

"Come with me," she said. "There's a place where we can watch that elevator when it arrives."

And he followed her from the hall.

CHAPTER SEVENTY

COTTON STOPPED AT A CORNER IN THE TUNNEL. REMNANTS OF incandescent light leaked around the edge, signaling that the exit foyer was on the other side, which was lit earlier when they arrived. He heard nothing save for the whine of the elevator as it rose. A quick glance around the edge and he saw three sets of coveralls lying on the floor, along with three helmets.

"They're gone," he said.

Stephanie and Patrycja came up from behind.

He knew from their previous descent that this elevator only went to Level III. They'd switched to it earlier from another that rose to the surface. He pointed at the clothes. "They intend to blend in with the crowd up on the lower levels and just walk out."

But there was still the matter of the gunshot.

He stepped around the corner, approaching the pile of clothes and helmets. He studied the floor and noticed streaks in the fine layers of ground salt, leading away, toward a dark tunnel to his right. He followed the trail into the blackness, which continued about twenty feet to an offshoot, where he found the body of a man dressed in the same color coverall as Patrycja. Surely, the other guide either forced or bribed into cooperation and the source of the gunshot. Ivan was not the type to leave loose ends.

He headed back to the elevator.

"There's a body," he said. "Has the name KONRAD stitched to the coveralls."

Shock filled Patrycja's face. "Dawid Konrad. I know him." She paused. "Knew him."

So far this attractive young woman had handled herself like a pro, asking few questions. Even when the shot rang out in the chapel, she'd only momentarily panicked, then regained control. Now a murder. That might be too much. He needed her to keep thinking.

"Call the elevator back down," he said to her.

She stepped over to the control panel and used her fob to activate the UP button, which lit to her touch.

"What are you going to do?" Stephanie asked.

"Cut them off."

"Should we not have some help sent down? Surely this place has security people."

He shook his head. "We can't risk losing that information. This one's on us."

He saw she agreed.

The elevator returned.

He unzipped his coveralls. "We have to blend in, too."

CZAJKOWSKI STOOD ON A STURDY WOODEN STAIRCASE THAT ANgled up from Level III to Level II, blocked off for use by the mine manager. From the first stoop it was easy to watch the elevators that led both up and down, unobserved. The chamber that accommodated them was tall, spacious, and well lit with a polished salt floor, white timbers fronting two of the walls forming an impressive latticework of support. Lines had formed behind a rope barrier, the crowd a bit noisy and anxious to end their visit and head up to ground level. Ivona stood beside him as they waited for the lower-level elevator to open its doors. Thanks to the angle of the stairs and their location, none of the crowd could see them.

"It will take time for all those people to leave here," he said.

"The less attention the better."

She held a small walkie-talkie that was connected to an ancillary security center on Level I. He'd already noticed cameras, attached to the walls high up and aimed down at the elevators.

"They have this place under video surveillance?" he asked.

She nodded. "That's a plus for us. There's nowhere for any of them to go."

"I want those cameras shut off."

She stared at him.

"We can't have a record of this. Surely you can see that."

And he saw that she did.

She spoke into the radio and told the manager to shut off all cameras. On order of the president of Poland.

The elevator that led down to the lower levels opened and three men walked out.

"The older one is Reinhardt," she said. "The younger is his hired help, Munoz. The big man is Ivan. The Russian."

"I assume the plastic pack he's holding is what we're after?" he asked.

"Has to be. Safe and sealed."

They watched as the three men casually turned right, away from the stairs, and stepped over a rope barrier, dissolving into the crowd, waiting their turn for the up elevators.

"Bold," he said.

"They have no idea we're watching."

"Do we allow them to go up first? Or deal with them here?"

She did not immediately answer. He assumed she was weighing the risks.

"Ivan is a killer," she said. "He'll do whatever he has to do to get out of here. Better not to challenge him and allow him to go up. We can be there waiting when the elevator arrives."

That made sense.

"We'll watch them a little longer, though," she said. "To make sure they stay here."

He reached over and grabbed her hand, squeezing hard. She returned the gesture and added a smile. For the first time, he believed this might be containable.

The elevator from the lower levels opened again.

Cotton Malone, Stephanie Nelle, and another younger woman dressed as a mine guide stepped out. Malone gave the crowd behind the rope barrier a quick survey.

A gun appeared in Ivan's hand.

Which was fired.

CHAPTER
SEVENTY-ONE

ELI SAW MALONE AT THE SAME TIME IVAN HAD, AND HE'D NOT DIS-
agreed with firing a shot toward the ceiling.

It generated the desired effect.

People scattered in all directions, oblivious to the barrier that had
held them back from the elevators. Like a stampede of cattle they formed
a surging wall toward where Malone stood, allowing him, Munoz, and
Ivan to join the crowd fleeing in the opposite direction.

They hustled down a wide, lit corridor, their walk alternately on salt
and on wooden planks. These paths were nothing like those deep below,
the walls polished smooth, the floors even smoother, with plenty of light.
The route drained into a medium-sized chamber that displayed wooden
chests, carts on iron wheels, and buckets used long ago in mining. The
tourists kept going out the other exit, into the next tunnel.

But Ivan stopped.

And assumed a position behind one of the iron carts, gun in hand.

"We deal with Malone here."

He motioned to Munoz, who crouched behind another of the old
carts, armed too. He was about to find his own cover when Ivan said to
him, "Stay there."

Out in the open?

Which meant he was bait.

COTTON HEADED IN THE DIRECTION THAT IVAN AND HIS TWO CO-horts had gone. All of the people had fled, leaving the wood-lined corridor clear. He held the gun in his right hand, retrieved from beneath his coveralls. Stephanie and Patrycja waited back near the elevators. The path was a straight line for about fifty feet, where it drained into an open doorway with darkness beyond.

He approached the entrance and decided, as he had back in Bruges, that rushing in was foolish. Instead he hugged the salt wall on the left side of the portal and risked a look beyond.

He saw Reinhardt standing in the middle of a dimly lit chamber.

But no Ivan or Munoz.

CZAJKOWSKI HAD WATCHED THE MAYHEM THAT ENSUED AFTER THE Russian fired into the ceiling. Ivona had radioed the mine manager again and told him to shut off all the elevators going up. Too much chaos was happening to take a chance that their quarry might escape. This way, they were sealed belowground, along with everyone else.

Malone had gone in pursuit.

But Ivona had not insisted they follow.

And he understood.

So far their presence was unknown and it seemed better to keep it that way. But he did not want anyone hurt. Enough blood had been shed already.

He and Ivona had quickly climbed the stairs to Level II and, following the manager's radio instructions, made their way to where the tunnels began a steady descent back down to Level III, hopefully on the opposite side of where Ivan had gone.

With luck, their target would come straight to them.

ELI FROZE.

He'd seen a shadow approaching from the brightly lit tunnel beyond, which had abruptly stopped. Then he'd seen a head take a quick look past the portal's edge. Munoz and Ivan were ready with their weapons.

Malone was obviously being cautious.

He caught Munoz's gaze and motioned for him to shift positions, placing his man closer to the doorway, on this side of the opening.

"I'm here, Malone," he called out. "Why don't we discuss this?"

COTTON SMELLED A TRAP, BUT DECIDED TO NOT ALERT REINHARDT. "All right. Let's talk. Come on out."

He waited.

Reinhardt appeared from the darkness.

He stayed to his side of the doorway, offering no one on the other side a clear line of sight. If they wanted him, they'd have to come get him.

"I'm a bit surprised to see you here," Reinhardt said. "How did you know?"

"Lucky guess."

Reinhardt smiled. "A funny man? This is quite a serious situation. Yet you think humor in order?"

He shrugged. "It's only serious for you. I'm on the side of might and right."

"Come now, Malone. Can't we be reasonable?"

"Where's Ivan?"

"Doing what Russians do best."

And Reinhardt added a sly smile.

Then dropped to the floor.

Shots rang out from inside the chamber.

Rounds whined past and found the salt and timbers farther down the tunnel, ricocheting off. He hoped Stephanie and Patrycja had taken cover. He stayed glued to the wall at the side of the opening.

Reinhardt crawled back inside.

He heard movement in the darkness beyond the doorway. A quick glance showed an empty chamber.

"Stephanie," he called out behind him.

"We're here."

"I'm going after them."

"The elevators are not working," Patrycja told him. "They've been shut off from above."

Which meant something more was happening here.

Stephanie and Patrycja appeared and hustled his way.

"Where does this route go?" he asked.

"It winds back around to the main areas, past the lakes," Patrycja said. "To the stairs."

"You two head up, any way you can. Keep these bastards down here. Don't give them a way out."

Stephanie nodded and she and Patrycja retreated toward the elevators.

He headed the opposite direction.

CHAPTER
SEVENTY-TWO

Czajkowski stood inside a chamber filled with lit display cases that exhibited salt crystals in all colors, shapes, and sizes. He'd taken refuge here while Ivona assessed the unexpected situation. He wanted to be in charge, as always—he was president, after all—but realized that he had to keep a low profile. If they managed to contain this he could not afford to be exposed any more than he already was. Bad enough that the mine manager was aware of his presence, and that he'd pulled rank with the order to shut off all the cameras. So the fewer people who knew anything, the better.

"There's more shooting below," Ivona said as she hurried into the room. "Visitors have scattered. They're trying to get them all up to Levels I and II. The mine manager says he can't keep this quiet much longer. There are safety concerns and his security people are pushing hard."

He caught the message. *This has to end. Now.*

"We need to get down there," he said.

"Janusz."

He loved when she used his name. Which was rare.

"I can't risk anything happening to you," she said. "Don't put me in that difficult situation. I need to get down there. Will you wait here?"

"I'm the president of this country and your boss. This is not open to discussion."

She tossed him a quizzical look. "You're going there? Pulling rank?"

"I am."

"Big surprise."

She shook her head, then unzipped one of the pockets in her coveralls and removed a semi-automatic pistol.

She handed the weapon over.

"I assume you know how to use it."

"Absolutely."

Eli followed Ivan and Munoz.

They'd laid down gunfire trying to hit Malone, but failed. It had provided them, though, with enough cover to flee. Now they were in a long traverse that led toward another low-ceilinged chamber displaying ancient mining equipment. They kept moving, unsure of their destination, only that they had to get back to ground level. But how? Malone was on their flank and none of them knew what lay ahead.

Ivan waddled along, heavy-legged but spry for a big man, a gun in one hand, the plastic pack in the other. Good thing Jonty had thought ahead and properly protected the information. Malone had to be proceeding with caution given that he, too, had no idea what was waiting for him.

They entered an open corridor that ran twenty meters straight ahead, sloping upward, a tall salt wall to the right, a wooden railing on the left overlooking a small lake beyond.

A strange sight so far belowground.

The clear water lay still like glass, the bottom illuminated by underwater lights that cast an eerie emerald glow. Obviously there had to be somewhere for all the water that seeped down to go, so lakes seemed a reasonable solution.

Ivan stopped. "We cannot keep running."

"What do you suggest?"

The big man pointed down at the water and a short set of stairs that led to a tiny dock, where two boats were tied. Eli studied the lake and saw that there were several exits where the water flowed out into black yawns.

"You're assuming one of those will get us away from Malone?" he asked.

Ivan nodded. "Not us. Me. We need split up. Give Malone choices. I go in boat. You two keep moving ahead."

"And do what?

"Find way out. Get away. Disappear. Enjoy your money. Our business is done."

There was wisdom in the strategy. Particularly from his standpoint. Malone had to be after the information, but he'd have no way of knowing who possessed it. Best guess? Not the broker. The Russian. The one who fired the shot.

And he'd not killed anyone, either.

That bullet came from Ivan's gun. His own gun was still tucked at his waist, beneath the coveralls.

"*Do svidaniya,*" Ivan said, waving with the gun he held.

And goodbye to you, too.

Ivan stepped over a low gate in the railing, descended the stairs, then climbed into one of the skiffs. At its stern hung an electric motor, which he switched on and used to ease toward the tunnels.

"What do we do?" Munoz asked.

"What he said. Get out of here."

And they headed off.

COTTON MADE HIS WAY THROUGH THE CHAMBER TOWARD ITS other exit, careful as he sidestepped the old mining equipment on display. At the other exit he saw Reinhardt and Munoz, fifty feet away, rushing down a railed corridor. Then darkness blotted them from sight as they entered another chamber. He turned toward the lit underground lake and saw Ivan puttering away in a small skiff, entering a black tunnel.

They'd split up.

He was betting that what he was after lay with Ivan.

He noticed a padlocked gate. Then stairs and another skiff floating atop the still water. He jumped the low rail and descended, hopping into the boat.

Following Ivan.

CZAJKOWSKI KNEW HOW TO HANDLE A WEAPON, BUT IT HAD BEEN A long time since he'd held one. Solidarity had never been about violence. Weapons had been forbidden, as had been drinking. Never was anyone allowed to participate in official functions under the influence. Never was a knife or a gun allowed at a demonstration. Not that some didn't appear, but at no time had anyone in any position of authority ever sanctioned their presence.

Quite the contrary, in fact.

Visuals had been vital to the movement. What you said and what you did mattered. But what it looked like mattered more. They'd been trying to win the world over to their cause, and no better way existed than for their protests to be nonviolent. They'd not been 100 percent successful, but they'd come pretty close. Solidarity had always then, and now, been perceived as good. The government bad.

But what would the Warsaw Protocol do to that legacy?

Hard to say.

Definitely nothing good.

Quietly he followed Ivona down a wooden staircase, the boards strong and firm under his feet. They were headed for Level III. The mine manager was working to evacuate everyone to the surface from Levels I and II. Last he saw, Malone had taken off in pursuit of Reinhardt and his man, Munoz, along with Ivan, all of them surely still on Level III. Ivona was armed with a map supplied by the manager. But it might not be needed. As they turned on the landing, preparing to head down the last flight of stairs, they spotted Eli Reinhardt, thirty meters away, leaving the brightly lit chamber where the stairs ended and entering another dark tunnel.

They headed in the same direction.

CHAPTER SEVENTY-THREE

COTTON NAVIGATED THE BOAT ACROSS THE LAKE AND HEADED FOR the tunnel where Ivan had gone. He left the lit surface and entered blackness. If not for another illuminated lake about fifty feet ahead his visibility would have been zero. Things were also a little too close for comfort, as the ceiling was less than a foot away. The small electric motor provided nothing in the way of speed, so he puttered along at a snail's pace.

He exited out into a lake smaller than the first, the salt walls at its edges rising up fifty-plus feet. Another wooden railing lined one side and bordered another walkway that led past the water. Only one tunnel opened out, so he kept going into another dark abyss. This one tighter, the ceiling barely a few inches above his head as he sat in the skiff. He navigated with one hand on the motor and the other holding the gun. For a guy who hated enclosed spaces he seemed to find himself in them more often than not. This place was bearable, though, given the ventilation and the lights he could see at the far end of the tunnel.

He also caught shadows on the water.

Movement.

He switched off the motor and allowed only momentum to send him toward the exit. With no idea what waited beyond, he lay flat on his spine making for a low profile, one hand on the motor, the other holding the gun. The boat emerged into another lit lake, this one bordered with more steep walls on three sides, the same wooden railing stretching from one side to the other.

He saw the other boat at the same moment Ivan fired a shot his way.

Which whined past overhead.

He was far enough away, and low enough, that Ivan had no clear angle without standing, which the big Russian apparently realized.

Cotton turned the motor on and sent the moving skiff straight at Ivan, who was having trouble maintaining balance while standing in the unstable platform. He bumped his bow into the side of Ivan's boat, which sent the Russian down. The boat wobbled but remained upright. Ivan lost his grip on the gun, which clattered into the boat and discharged. Cotton's skiff proved Newton's third law—that with every action there was an equal and opposite reaction—as he recoiled back across the still surface.

He rose up and sat again on the center bench.

Ivan worked to regain control of both himself and the boat.

He allowed his adversary a moment.

Then pointed his gun.

ELI KEPT MOVING FROM ONE CHAMBER TO ANOTHER, EACH ADORNED with a variety of exhibits from the days when all this had been a working mine. He'd come across no one, which was odd.

Where had they all gone?

He entered another of the junction rooms, this one full of more lime-washed timbers supporting the towering walls and accommodating a staircase that led up to the next level. Ahead, past the stairs, metal doors blocked the tunnel out, which explained where the visitors had gone.

Up.

He should follow them and disappear into the crowd. But something told him there might be danger up there. Security personnel could be waiting. Too late to use that route for escape. Years of dealing had taught him a lot about people. That's how he'd been able to seduce Jonty into allowing him to become part of the deal. Find what someone wants. Get control of it. Then bargain. He'd made a fortune doing just that. The whole point of him being here had been in the hope of achieving that objective once again. But he'd never suspected that the Americans or the Russians would figure things out. If he'd had even an inkling of their suspicions, he never would have come near this mine. Nothing was worth that risk.

He and Munoz avoided the stairs and headed for the metal doors, which were merely closed and not locked. Made sense. Never would routes be locked off, made inaccessible, restricting movements.

Except maybe with a fire.

Which was not the case here.

He heard what sounded like a gunshot.

From beyond the doors.

Ivan?

He opened one of them.

And they slipped into the dark on the other side.

CZAJKOWSKI AND IVONA STAYED ON ELI REINHARDT AND ART Munoz's tail. Their quarry had no idea they were being followed.

They came to a chamber that ran upward in a wide shaft to the next levels, filled with cribs of round timber logs fitted to support the walls and ceiling, all whitewashed. Between clusters of beams rose a staircase.

Did they go up? he mouthed to Ivona.

She shrugged and told him to wait there.

He watched as she hustled up the wooden risers two at a time, making not a sound. At the landing where the stairs right angled upward, she stopped and listened, staring up into the shaft in which the stairs rose.

She slipped back down.

"No one is up there," she whispered.

Ivona motioned, and they headed for the metal doors.

COTTON WATCHED AS IVAN SETTLED HIMSELF BACK INTO THE BOAT. The gun had fired, but nobody had been hit. He wondered about the packet, but assumed it lay safely in the boat.

"You're not getting out of here," he said.

Ivan again held the pistol.

He displayed his, too.

"Neither of us is getting away." Ivan chuckled. "You almost got me. I not able to swim."

"That won't matter here. The lake is loaded with salt brine. Nothing sinks. You could walk on this water."

"Great comfort to know. But I still not like water."

"And yet here you are. On a lake."

Ivan shrugged. "Do what we must."

"I want that packet."

"Let's be reasonable, Malone. Your president not reasonable. You're not him. We use this information to do what Poland wants. No missiles. What's the harm?"

"You killed a lot of people to get your hands on that packet."

"I do job, Malone. We all do job."

"I just don't commit mass murder while doing mine."

"You feel sorry for those people? They not your friend. They not America or Russia's friend."

He was trying to decide if Ivan was stalling or just unsure as to his next move. He'd only dealt with the man once before, but he'd never known any Russian foreign intelligence officer to be either stupid or cowardly. Especially not one of Ivan's age and stature, surely starting young with the KGB then, once the Soviet Union fell, gravitating to the SVR. At best the man was immoral, more likely amoral, which only compounded the threat.

A lot was at stake here.

As Ivan had told him back in Bruges, Moscow did not want to spend billions of rubles deploying missiles of their own just to counter the American move. Not when the problem could be dealt with quickly and quietly with some good old-fashioned blackmail.

But all that was now in jeopardy.

ELI HEARD A NOISE FROM BEHIND.

The metal doors had squeaked open.

He stood inside a chamber exhibiting a variety of salt sculptures, all artfully lit with floodlights casting an eerie glow.

Was it some of the frightened tourists coming their way?

"We need to see who this is," he whispered to Munoz.

Then he heard voices.

From the opposite direction.

Ahead.

Trouble in both directions?

"You see what that is," he whispered to Munoz, finding the weapon he'd brought along in his coveralls. "I'll check what's behind us."

Munoz headed off.

He assumed a position in the shadows, gun ready.

And waited.

CHAPTER SEVENTY-FOUR

CZAJKOWSKI FELT A SURGE OF EXCITEMENT, BUT NO FEAR. HE wasn't a rookie to danger. For years back in the 1980s he'd walked a fine line where the government could have turned on him at any moment. Playing both ends against the middle was not something for the faint of heart. So he'd learned how to handle himself under extreme pressure. Here, nothing less than his whole life was on the line.

He'd been a damn good president of Poland and wanted to finish what he started with five more years. They would be his last. After that, he'd become an ex-statesman and join the ranks of the irrelevant, making speeches and accomplishing nothing. But before that happened, he wanted to leave a mark on his homeland. Change things for the better. Bring Poland closer to the West and make it warier of the East.

Thankfully, the government had matured. No longer could fringe groups, like the Polish Beer-Lovers' Party, achieve much political success. The days of ridicule were over. Luckily, the economy was strong. He'd been fortunate to be elected during an economic upturn, and the people were far more forgiving when more money lay in their pockets. He'd taken advantage of that prosperity and introduced new, generous family benefits that helped the poor. Such a notion had once been foreign to Polish politics. But the concepts had been embraced. He'd worked hard to make Poland a regional leader in political, social, and economic development. An important member of the EU and NATO. But there were many who wanted a much more nationalistic stand, a return to isolationism. Poland for Poles. Some of which he did not disagree with. Like stopping American missiles, aimed supposedly at Iran, from being planted on Polish soil. Missiles that could easily be redirected toward Russia. Missiles that endangered every citizen.

That was madness.

Talk about poking the bear.

He and Ivona stepped past the metal door and headed through another lit chamber, finding the exit on the far side. He was grateful for the cool air, his brow beaded with sweat.

Nerves?

Surely.

The gun Ivona had provided was tucked into one of the thigh pockets of his coveralls. Better to keep it there until truly needed. Hopefully, that moment would never come. The image of the president of Poland toting a weapon around a national historic site would not play well in the media.

Ivona was armed.

And that seemed protection enough.

ELI STOOD CLOSE TO THE ROUGH WALL, AWAY FROM THE FEW LIGHTS that backlit the rest of the chamber. No artifacts adorned this room, only another chapel with an altar and figurines, which was in much better shape than the one he'd seen below. He stood in blackness, watching the entrance from which he'd arrived to see who was coming.

A woman entered.

Ivona Novak.

Armed.

Behind her came a man.

No, not any man.

Janusz Czajkowski.

Finally.

Providence had smiled upon him.

COTTON STARED OVER AT IVAN. "DO YOU KNOW ABOUT AN EGG-sucking dog?"

"Sounds highly American."

"Not at all. They're everywhere. Even in Russia. Every once in a while a farm dog will acquire a taste for fresh eggs. They'll kill the chickens to get them, too. They don't really suck the eggs. More eat them whole. But once a dog gets a taste for egg, there's no breaking him of it."

"Sounds like greedy dog."

"Obsessed. Bewitched. That dog lives to get into other people's hen-houses. And nothing will stop it," he paused, "short of killing."

Ivan chuckled. "Your president is the egg-sucking dog."

He shrugged. "Maybe so. But right now you're the one I have to deal with. You're in my henhouse. And *if you don't stop eatin' my eggs up, though I'm not a real bad guy, I'm goin' to get my rifle and send you to that great chicken house in the sky.*"

He sang the words to a mournful tune he recalled from long ago.

"It's a Johnny Cash song," he said to Ivan. "My grandfather used to sing it when he worked."

"You stalling, Malone?"

"I am."

"Hoping help will come."

"That is the plan."

"Maybe I have help, too."

"I saw Reinhardt and Munoz heading off. I suppose they could find their way here."

The gun rested in his right hand, his finger on the trigger, his eyes locked on Ivan's body, watching for any move.

"You say this lake thick with salt?" Ivan asked.

"Pure brine. But clear and pretty, I'll say that. They keep the brine here, then pump it to the surface and extract the salt."

Ivan reached down and, with his free hand, gently stroked the water. "Cold. Like Arctic Ocean."

It seemed a little nuts to be floating a few yards from his enemy, shooting the breeze, while they were both armed, waiting for the other to act. But he was only going to challenge this demon when he was sure of the outcome. Right now, that was in doubt.

Like everything else.

So be patient.

ELI WAITED UNTIL IVONA AND CZAJKOWSKI WERE IN THE CHAMBER, past him, subdued by the silence, near the chapel on the opposite wall. Then he stepped out of the blackness and nestled the barrel of his gun to the back of Czajkowski's head.

The president froze.

"Stay still," he said to his captive

Ivona whirled, her gun coming level.

"Drop the weapon," he ordered.

And he clicked the hammer of his gun to emphasize the point. She stared at him, probably trying to decide if she could take a shot before he pulled the trigger.

"I assure you," he said, "you can't."

She seemed to agree and lowered the gun.

"Drop it to the ground and kick it away," he told her.

She did as instructed.

"Keep your hands where I can see them," he told her.

CHAPTER
SEVENTY-FIVE

COTTON SPLIT HIS ATTENTION BETWEEN IVAN AND THE SURROUND-
ings. They floated in their respective skiffs, about fifty feet apart, the
emerald-tinted lake so clear it appeared as if they were drifting on air.
Around a huge wall pillar wrapped a walkway with railings, a wooden
gallery running along the upper chamber wall. Ivan had been right. He
was stalling, hoping Stephanie was able to convince the locals that she
needed their assistance. If anyone could make that happen, she could.
But there was still the matter of Reinhardt and Munoz who were loose
somewhere on this level.

"What we do?" Ivan asked.

A good question.

Retrieving that packet would go a long way toward easing Stephanie's problems with the White House. Yes, he disagreed with the entire
tactic Fox was trying to employ, and he'd deal with that quandary later.
What he could not do was allow Ivan to leave the mine with that information. Sure, Moscow wanted the missiles gone. But as with Fox, there
was no telling what else they would want from Warsaw. With that degree
of blackmail, which several countries had been willing to pay huge sums
to possess, anything could be possible.

"You could give me that packet," he said. "And we'll call this whole
thing over."

Ivan laughed. "I could say same to you about your gun."

Portions of the lake were lit, portions were not. Between those two extremes were areas that gravitated from bright to dark, the flat surface like a mirror. In one portion to the right of Ivan's boat, he caught the reflection of the wooden railing that spanned one side.

And Munoz.

Who was lurking behind where he floated, higher, on the path that extended from one side of the lake to the other, part of the walkways and tunnels that visitors traversed to admire the lakes. Apparently Ivan's allies had found them faster than his own. Munoz was staying low, using some of the stonework between the railings as a shield. He assumed the man was armed, and the good thing was he'd have to stand up to make a move.

But there was still the matter of Ivan.

Who had no such hindrance.

ELI PRESSED THE GUN CLOSE TO CZAJKOWSKI'S HEAD.

"Where's Ivan?" Ivona asked.

"Nearby."

He needed to keep this woman off guard. She was formidable. And dangerous. She'd shot Jonty with no hesitation. She now knew he was working with Ivan, which meant he could have backup.

"I'm getting out of here," Eli told them.

"Then leave," Ivona said.

"It is not that simple."

He wished it were.

What was happening with Munoz?

Where was he?

CZAJKOWSKI THOUGHT OF THAT MATH PROFESSOR WHO'D BEEN kicked and prodded across the filthy floor of Mokotów Prison. He always did when he needed strength. That man, in the face of death, had showed nothing but courage.

And he intended to do the same.

"You're done," he said to Reinhardt.

"Brave words from a man with a loaded gun to his head."

"I've lived my life with one right there. Every day."

"Don't push him," Ivona said.

But he intended to do just that.

COTTON SAT STILL IN THE SKIFF, NOT LETTING ON HE WAS AWARE they had company. Ivan was trying hard not to glance toward the wooden railing, but it was clear that he was aware of Munoz's presence, too.

Interesting the situation he found himself in. Floating on a frigid lake of pure salt brine, hundreds of feet underground, amid total silence, two men intent on shooting him. He held the gun, and the reflection continued to offer him a viewpoint that showed Munoz trying to maneuver himself into a better position. He had to take them both out, complicated by the fact that he was sitting in an unstable skiff. The one saving grace was that one of his opponents was likewise handicapped. Reaction time would suffer. Which meant the guy on dry land represented the greater threat.

He needed a distraction.

Something to provide him a few precious seconds to react.

ELI HAD TO FIND MUNOZ AND LEAVE.

Staying put seemed like a bad idea. Though he had the situation under control, Ivona Novak represented a problem.

"Move toward the other exit," he ordered her.

She hesitated.

"Do you really want to test me?" he asked.

"Do as he says," Czajkowski said to her.

The tone clear and direct.

"This gun is pointed at my head, not yours," the president said. "Don't play games with my life. Remember, you work for me."

He saw that she did not appreciate the rebuke. But the man had a point. She did work for him. It was not her place to take such risks.

"Are you ordering me to do as he says?" she asked.

"That's exactly what I'm doing. Move."

He tapped Czajkowski's head with the gun. "Follow her."

Czajkowski added a wink to his command, a gesture only Ivona could see that signaled she should play along. There was no way Reinhardt knew of any connection between them other than employer–employee. Of course he had to be wondering why the president of Poland was here, but that could easily be explained because it was his ass on the line. He did catch a moment of concern in Ivona's eyes before she backed toward the exit, surely wondering what he was going to do next.

She would not like the answer.

He stopped walking.

"Keep going," Reinhardt said.

"I'm not going anywhere."

Ivona stopped.

"What are you going to do?" he asked Reinhardt. "Shoot the president of Poland? How far do you think you will get. I doubt you'll make it off this level alive."

Ivona's eyes asked, *What are you doing?*

His hands were down by his side, his right hand close to the side pocket where the gun she'd given him rested. When he'd first challenged Ivona, delivering the order of retreat, with Reinhardt focused on her, he'd managed to unzip the pocket.

Now he had to reach in.

But too much movement could be fatal.

CHAPTER SEVENTY-SIX

COTTON SAW THAT MUNOZ HAD FINALLY DECIDED ON A VANTAGE point. Even worse, his boat was drifting closer to that point, about eight feet above the lake's surface, closing the distance between him and trouble.

"I leave now," Ivan said.

He held up his gun. "I don't think so."

"I think different."

Ivan motioned with his free hand and Munoz stood, gun aimed.

"He make sure I leave."

The motor on Ivan's boat came to life.

CZAJKOWSKI DUG IN. "YOU'RE A DEALER IN INFORMATION. LET'S deal."

"What do you offer?" Reinhardt asked.

"A way out of here to begin with. What did the Russians pay you?"

"Five million euros."

"All right. I'll pay five times that for you to deliver what Jonty Olivier was going to sell. Do you have it?"

Ivona knew they already had the answer to that question, which he hoped would alert her to pay attention and be ready. Her gun lay three meters away on the floor.

"I have it," Reinhardt said.

"Really? The Russian allowed you to keep it," he said. "That was quite generous of him, considering Moscow would love to use that information against me, starting with no American missiles in Poland. Where is the information?"

"My associate, Munoz, went to retrieve it."

He doubted that, too. But—

"Let's get him back. Mr. Munoz," he called out. "Please come here."

COTTON HEARD MUNOZ'S NAME CALLED OUT.

So did Munoz.

He turned his head for barely a second toward the source of the summons, but long enough for Cotton to raise his gun and take the man down with one well-aimed shot.

Not bad for twenty feet away, eight feet up, in dim light.

He immediately turned his attention to Ivan, who was disappearing into a dark tunnel that allowed the water to flow toward the next reservoir.

Too late.

He fired up his own electric motor.

And headed after him.

CZAJKOWSKI HEARD THE GUNSHOT.

And used that instant to wrap his fingers around the pistol in his pocket and grope the trigger. But he did not withdraw the weapon. Ivona could see what he was doing, but Reinhardt could not. Luckily, the pocket had been stitched to his front thigh high enough that he did not have to overextend his arm.

"Don't call out again," Reinhardt said, pressing the gun into his hair to emphasize the point.

"I don't take orders from you," he made clear.

Reinhardt's gun kissed his scalp again. "Brave words. Mr. President."

"True words."

Ivona stared at him, now knowing exactly what he was doing. Her eyes pleaded for him to stop, but she kept her features frozen, revealing nothing to the threat that stood behind him.

"It's time to decide," he said to Reinhardt, his eyes locked on Ivona. "Time for you to make a choice."

"I'm not interested in selling anything to you. And twenty-five million euros is not even close to what it is worth."

"What if Munoz is dead?" he asked. "Was that the shot we just heard? If so, then you're on your own. You going to shoot us both? Then walk out of here? You do realize that's impossible. We have you trapped on this level."

He was pushing. Doing what he once did with the SB. Playing off fears and insecurities, aggravating paranoia, making adversaries doubt themselves, which was the fastest way to cripple them.

"Shut up," Reinhardt barked.

His right hand stayed on the gun, the semi-darkness of the chamber helping shield his intent. Reinhardt was focused more on Ivona, since he felt he had one threat contained while the other was still loose, capable of striking.

"Just put the gun down," he said to Reinhardt. "Cut your losses before this gets totally out of control."

"I said, shut up."

Movement disturbed the darkness at the exit.

A man stumbled into the chamber, one hand clutching a gun, the other his chest. The gait was short and strained. A face dissolved from the darkness.

Munoz.

Ivona turned her attention to the new arrival. Czajkowski used the moment of distraction to remove the weapon and, though he could not see to aim, he stuck the barrel behind him into Reinhardt's belly and fired.

He felt the vibration as the round tore through flesh.

To be sure, he pulled the trigger again.

Reinhardt collapsed.

Munoz tried to raise his weapon, but Ivona kicked it from his grasp.

Finish it.

And what the foreign force has taken from us, we shall with sabre retrieve.

He fired a third round into Munoz.

COTTON HEARD MORE SHOTS ECHOING THROUGH THE MINE AND wondered who else was shooting. Some help? Maybe. There'd been no way to determine if Munoz was dead, but he'd definitely hit him.

Ivan was the focus now.

He kept motoring through the dark tunnel, this one longer than the others, as the light at the other side was still another fifty-plus feet ahead. Ivan had enough of a head start that he could be lying in wait, so it seemed foolish to just pop out the other side.

He'd spoken the truth when he'd told Ivan about the salt brine. Once, years ago, he'd taken a dip in the Dead Sea, floating easily on the thick water. He'd had to shower right after, so as not to leave a layer of salt on his skin for too long, which would burn thanks to the heat of a Middle Eastern day. Signs had warned about protecting faces from the water and not to swallow it.

The same dangers were here, compounded by freezing temperatures.

Ivan was surely waiting to see what the whine of an electric motor was bringing his way. Munoz? Or trouble? With no choice, he slipped over the side and into the frigid water. Coldness wrapped him like a coat. He could only take this for a few minutes. But that was all he'd need. The pitch and timbre of the electric motor never changed as he clung to the boat's low side, floating high in the brine, unable to go down even if he wanted to. His right hand held the gun, which remained dry in the boat. There'd be a moment or so of confusion on Ivan's part when he first saw a pilotless skiff, then realized his target was in the water.

That would be his opportunity.

The boat kept moving, the lower part of his body numbing from the cold. He emerged from the darkness into the lit lake. Sure enough, Ivan was floating to one side, below another wooden railing, standing in the boat, gun aimed.

Ivan fired.

He dipped down below the skiff and got a little of the freezing water on his face. The bullet whined by as he continued to glide across the lake. The buoyancy now became his ally as he no longer resisted the push upward and relaxed his grip. He popped from the water like a cork, aimed, and fired, catching the big Russian right in the midsection.

Ivan winced.

One hand found the wound.

The other released his grip on the gun.

Balance faltered and Ivan dropped backward from the boat into the water, making a large splash that sent waves in every direction.

Cotton dropped his gun inside the boat and propelled himself up and over the side, reentering the skiff. His legs were freezing, but he grabbed the motor and turned the boat toward Ivan, who was thrashing in the brine. He swung around to one side and saw Ivan roll over, face to the water.

Then all movement stopped.

Blood continued to leak from the wound, staining the clear water with red clouds. The body flipped and Ivan floated high, on his back, eyes open, two black orbs boring into the ceiling.

He shut the motor off and caught hold of the other boat.

The plastic packet lay inside.

He relaxed and moved his head gently, trying not to disturb the spots before his eyes, clicking and clacking off one another in all directions, sending his brain spinning from the cold. His legs were stiff and throbbing, but seemed to work.

Ivan lay dead.

Like all the others.

CHAPTER
SEVENTY-SEVEN

CZAJKOWSKI LOWERED THE GUN.

Ivona rushed over to him. "You okay?"

He nodded. But he wasn't all that okay. He'd just killed two men. Add them to the list. He'd killed before. Not directly, but every bit as deadly with the Warsaw Protocol.

"It had to be done," she said to him. "You had no choice."

He stared at her, his grip on the gun still firm.

"Let's see if we can find Ivan," she said.

Before they could leave the chamber they both heard someone approaching from the direction Munoz had come from. Ivona motioned and they shifted to the shadows and waited.

Cotton Malone entered and stopped. One hand held a gun, the other the plastic packet. Two-thirds of his clothes were soaking wet.

They stepped forward.

"I heard the shots and your voices," Malone said before motioning at the bodies. "Looks like you have this under control."

"Ivan?" she asked.

Malone nodded. "Floating in the salt brine, which by the way is quite brisk."

Ivona smiled. "You must be freezing?"

"To say the least."

Czajkowski pointed at the packet Malone held. "Is that the information?"

"Yep."

"What are you going to do with it?"

"You get right to it, don't you? No wining or dining from you. Just wham, bam, thank you ma'am."

"I don't have the luxury of time."

"No. I suppose not. But, to answer your question, I'm still deciding."

"May I ask your options?"

"Keep it and do my job, giving it to the asshole who calls himself the president of the United States." Malone paused. "Or not."

"We could take it from you."

"You could try."

He smiled. "I like you, Malone. I liked you the moment I realized you hated Tom Bunch. Who was a liar, by the way."

The American shrugged. "More just a guy in way over his head. An amateur, playing with professionals, trying to make himself a big deal. Which got him killed."

"This is now an Agencja Wywiadu operation," Ivona said. "We'll take full responsibility for all of the deaths here. Including Ivan."

"That's fairly decent of you, considering you both had a part in that slaughter in Slovakia."

"That wasn't us," Ivona said. "We had no idea that was what they intended. We needed you to lead the way to that castle."

"So your warning in Bruges for us to stay out of their way was just idle chitchat? You knew what they were going to do. Maybe not in so many words. But you could add up the two and two." Malone faced him. "Did you order Olivier to be eliminated?"

"He did not," Ivona said. "That was my call."

"But," Czajowski said, "it is all my responsibility."

Malone shook his head. "It's not yours to take. This one is all on President Warner Fox. He started the whole thing. You just did what you had to do in order to survive. What Fox forced you to do. I just shot two men, and all because of Fox. Tom Bunch's children are fatherless thanks to the same idiocy. Reinhardt and Munoz here died for the same reasons. Fox owns this one." Malone motioned at the bodies. "By the way, who bagged these?"

"I did," Ivona said.

"Then why is the president holding the gun."

"Because I shot them both."

Malone gestured with his own weapon. "A little unpresidential, wouldn't you say?"

"Desperate times, Mr. Malone."

"Yeah, speaking of that. Here."

And Malone handed over the packet.

He was shocked. "Why are you doing this?"

"America should not have to blackmail somebody into doing something. Either they want to do it, or they don't. If they don't, we should respect that. It's who we should be."

"I don't disagree," he said.

"My report will be that Ivan found nothing. Neither did I. The information is lost. That will probably bring some American agents snooping around, but since there's nothing to find, who cares. I assume that the stuff in that packet will be torched."

He nodded. "President Fox won't be happy."

"Which is the cherry on the whipped cream here. Making it all worthwhile."

He heaved a euphoric sigh of relief, moved by the sweet purity of the moment. He'd been set free, granted a reprieve. Back from the dead.

Like Lazarus.

Now it was truly over.

"Everything that happened here will be stamped top secret by the AW," Ivona said. "We'll get the bodies out once the mine is closed for the night. We'll scrub this place clean like we did Sturney Castle. It will all have a tight lid placed on it. The Russians will be told there was a gunfight and Eli Reinhardt shot their man. I killed Reinhardt and Munoz. No mention will be made of anyone else."

Czajkowski realized that included not only Malone, but himself. Ivona was handling everything with dispatch and characteristic efficiency, like the agent she was.

"There's another corpse down on Level IX. One of the guides that Ivan or Reinhardt killed."

"I hate to hear that," Czajkowski said.

"Can I get out of here without a lot of hassle?" Malone asked.

Ivona grinned. "We can do that, and get someone to dry your clothes, too."

"Now, *that* I would appreciate."

Czajkowski stepped forward and offered his hand, which Malone shook, hard and firm. "Thank you. For what you did, and for your honor."

"It was my pleasure, Mr. President."

COTTON STEPPED OUT INTO THE BRIGHT EVENING, WHICH STRUCK him like a blow, his eyes struggling to focus after the gloom within the mine. Ivona had made good on her promise and had his clothes dried in the mine's laundry. They were a bit wrinkled, but felt a damn sight better than the previous salty cold. Stephanie waited for him outside.

"Patrycja okay?" he asked.

"She's good. Somebody else is calling the shots here. I tried to get the security people on board, but nobody was listening. The next thing I know, Patrycja is gone and I'm in the elevator and out the door, told to wait out here."

He reported all that had happened, leaving nothing out.

"Ivona's in charge," he said. "Czajkowski is there, too. Though she was working to sneak him out when I left. I gave the information to Czaj-kowski."

"I'm glad. If you hadn't, I would have."

"Your career is over."

"I know. But maybe it was time for me to leave."

He felt for her. But there was nothing he could do, and the last thing Stephanie Nelle would ever want was pity.

"Let's head back to Kraków," he said.

"Cotton."

He turned at the call of his name.

Ivona was exiting the building and approaching. "I wanted to say thank you. I appreciate what you did down there. All of it."

He'd noticed something while talking to the Polish president. "He's your new man, isn't he? Your love."

"How did you know?"

"The look in your eyes. The willingness to take all the blame."

She nodded. "He and I have been seeing each other for a while now. His marriage is over. I don't know where we're headed. But we're together."

"I'm happy for you, Ivona. Go for it."

And they hugged.

She gave him a soft kiss to his cheek. "Like I told you in Belgium, that girl of yours is a lucky woman."

But he wasn't going to accept that praise.

Not then.

Or now.

"I'm definitely the luckier one."

CHAPTER SEVENTY-EIGHT

Czajkowski stared at the fire.

He was back in Warsaw at the presidential palace, the events from three days ago in the salt mine still weighing heavy on his mind. He'd managed to leave Wieliczka unnoticed, making it back to the hotel in Kraków under cover of darkness. Ivona supervised cleaning up the mess. There'd been some press coverage about the gunshots since so many had been witnesses, but according to the reports the perpetrator had not been caught and no one had been injured.

God bless Ivona.

But he could not forget Anna, either. She'd obtained what Father Orlik had withheld from him. The proof about the Warsaw Protocol. Which was no longer needed, though it was still good to have, along with the documents that Jonty Olivier had wanted to auction. Which lay on the table beside him, free of their vacuum-sealed packet. He'd studied every one of them, recognizing his handwriting, his signature, and the disgusting code name Dilecki assigned him.

Baran. Sheep.

Many of the pages brought back memories of people and places. Of things that he'd done. Of fateful decisions that had consequences then and now. Would he do anything different?

Not a thing.

It all turned out as it should.

Poland was free.

He sat and watched the flames, enjoying a splash of whiskey, which seemed one of his more constant comforts of late.

The door to the room opened and Anna walked inside. He'd told the staff to send her this way as soon as she arrived. She'd stayed in the south all of yesterday, fulfilling obligations as the country's First Lady. That was the thing about her. She performed her duties with grace and dignity. A credit to the nation. Sadly, they were not as dedicated to each other.

But at least they were friends.

She came inside and closed the door. Over her shoulder hung a cloth bag that appeared heavy.

"Is that it?" he asked.

She nodded and removed a thick pocket folder stuffed with paper. "I went through some of it. Lots of names, dates, places. Payments made. Bribes. Orlik seems to have played the game well with the communists. One list details people who worked directly with him. A lot of names. Yours is on that list, near the top. Proof positive."

"Sadly, nobody would have cared. They would claim it all was a forgery, done to protect me."

"But there are surely many still alive who were part of the protocol. They can be found for corroboration."

"I doubt a one of them will want to talk about it. Like me, they prefer to leave it in the past."

She pointed to the stack of paper on the table. "Is that what they were going to sell?"

He nodded. "And if any of it were true, it would be quite damaging."

She sat in one of the high-backed chairs. He'd told her yesterday on a secure call about what happened in the mine, omitting only that he shot two people.

Better to leave that alone.

"What you did, Janusz, back then, was brave. I realized that while I was speaking with Orlik. You and he dealt with a horrendous situation that life had presented. Wałęsa and all the other Solidarity leaders had to work in the limelight. They were the face of the movement. But to be able to do that it was necessary that you, Orlik, and the others noted in that file work in the shadows. In secret. Doing what had to be done against an unrelenting enemy."

He sipped more whiskey. "Together we changed the world. But we also ended people's lives."

They both sat in the quiet, listening to the crackle of the fire, deep in their own thoughts.

"No matter where we end up," she finally said, "I'll always love you. Maybe not as a wife should love her husband, but as a woman feels for a man she respects and admires."

He smiled. "That's about the nicest thing you've said to me in a long time."

"I mean it. I truly do." She pointed at the hearth. "No one asked why you wanted a fire started in June?"

"I received some looks, but I told them it calms me down."

More silence passed between them.

"What of us, Janusz? What now?"

Her voice was low and soft.

"We run for reelection. If we win, we keep doing what we're doing. Once this is over, in five years, we'll end the marriage."

"Seems so hypocritical on our part."

He savored another short swallow of whiskey. "Maybe so but, as you say, we deal with what life gives us."

"I'm glad she loves you."

He'd not expected that. "She saved our asses."

"Tell her thank you from me."

He smiled at her graciousness. "You did good, too. And you searched Orlik's room? That was bold."

"I don't think he saw that one coming. The good brother probably thought his monastery more than adequate protection."

But he wondered. After his visit with Orlik, the Owl would have known that what he had was now in play, his room the first place anyone would look. So he should move whatever might be hidden there. No. Instead, he'd left it right there, ready to be found. Maybe his old friend had had a change of heart after their talk and used Anna's visit as a way to make amends?

Who knew?

"And the missiles?" she asked. "Is that over, too?"

"I informed President Fox yesterday that under no circumstances would I agree to their deployment on Polish soil. I've prepared an address to Parliament where I will state my case, and that refusal will become a cornerstone of my reelection platform. So they'll have to beat me at the polls to make it happen. My advisers tell me the issue will play well with the public, and a comfortable majority will agree with me."

"It's time the world learns that Poland is not their playground."

He concurred. "Too bad it cost so many lives to make that point."

He'd not told her anything about what had happened in Slovakia. That was a state secret, and would remain so. As would one other piece of information they'd learned. Apparently, Eli Reinhardt and Jonty Olivier had visited the salt mine together, had been taken down into the extreme lower recesses four days ago. Where? Nobody knew. Maybe it had to do with hiding away the documents for the auction? But if so, why had Olivier and his man DiGenti visited the mine the night before? Maybe there was something else down there? The matter had been referred to the Agencja Wywiadu, and Ivona would personally lead a search party to see if there was anything else to find.

He stared over at Anna. She was the perfect political wife. But his heart now belonged to another. He finished the whiskey and stood.

"Shall we?"

He lifted the stack of incriminating paper retrieved from the mine, and she grabbed the thick file. Together they approached the fire and fed both into the flames. The old paper smoldered, turned brown, then dissolved into the flames with a dull *whoomph*.

They watched as it all turned to ash.

"The Warsaw Protocol," he said, "is finally over."

Cotton sat with Cassiopeia at a window table in the Café Norden. It was a lovely Sunday evening in Copenhagen, the Højbro Plads cobblestones busy.

She looked wonderful, as always, dressed casually in a silk blouse, jeans, and heels. Little jewelry and makeup, just the bracelet he'd bought her at Cartier for Christmas. Pink gold, set with ten brilliant-cut diamonds, fashioned onto the wrist in a perpetual oval, removed only with its pink-gold screwdriver. It was meant to be worn constantly, and she had every day since December.

The café sat across the square from his bookshop, which was closed for the day. He never opened on Sundays, not for any religious reason, just because his employees deserved a day off. He lived above the shop in the fourth-floor apartment, which he'd been sharing with Cassiopeia since she arrived on Friday. He'd beaten her to town by about two hours. But he hadn't been an idiot, and had told her everything. Luckily, his unilateral, extracurricular activity had not affected their weekend.

The past couple of days had been wonderful.

"Have you heard from Stephanie?" she asked him.

"She emailed late last night. The attorney general notified her that she was suspended, pending possible termination. Fox was not happy with the outcome from Poland, and made good on his threat. But she's civil service, entitled to a hearing, and I imagine she'll get one."

There was also the matter of Tom Bunch's body. Fox wanted it found, but Cotton doubted that was possible. The Poles had sanitized Sturney Castle, all of the dead long gone, surely burned and buried, never to be found.

"You and Stephanie both did the right thing," she said to him.

"That's not much consolation, considering the fallout. If Fox could, there'd be ramifications for me, too. But I imagine my punishment will be no more freelance work."

"That's no real loss," she said.

"I like the money."

They were done with dinner, having eaten early, and were enjoying the evening, waiting on dessert. The café always sported an enticing array of sweets. The second-floor windows all hung open to the warm evening. She was scheduled to stay until Tuesday, returning then to her home in southern France. Next time, he'd travel her way for a visit.

"Hopefully," he said staring out the window to the crowd below, "Fox won't hurt me with any of the other foreign intelligence services I work for from time to time."

"I doubt it's going to be a problem. Those people have to see what's going on here, too. They know you're the best."

He smiled at her compliment.

"Cotton," she said in a tone that grabbed his attention.

His gaze met hers, and he could see she was focused on something behind him.

He turned in the chair.

Danny Daniels stood alone at the top of the stairway leading down.

Perhaps the last person he expected to see in Copenhagen.

Tall, broad-shouldered, with a head full of thick silver hair, the former president of the United States, and current junior senator from Tennessee, was dressed casually.

Daniels walked over to their table.

Cotton stood. "Is this about Stephanie?"

His friend held up two hands in surrender. "She's made it clear that's none of my business."

"So what are you doing in Denmark?" Cassiopeia asked.

Concern filled the older man's face.

"I need your help."

WRITER'S NOTE

This one involved some really unique journeys. The first was to Bruges, Belgium, a spectacular, living museum of medieval life. Then there were two trips to Poland that involved time in Kraków and the nearby salt mine. Both are world-class treasures. If you've never visited any of these three places, I highly recommend them as a trip you will not forget.

Now it's time to separate fact from fiction.

Mokotów Prison exists in Warsaw, the scene of many horrible things during both the Nazi occupation and the Soviet domination (prologue and chapter 16). The beating described in the prologue is based on an actual event, one of countless "interrogations" that occurred behind those walls. Many also died there, those deaths commemorated by a memorial now affixed to the outer walls (chapter 16). Spies were also sometimes recruited through demonstrations of extreme cruelty.

Bruges is full of olden houses, cobbled squares, and canals straight out of the 16th century. All of its locales—the fish market, central square, cafés, and streets (chapters 7, 9, 15) along with the canals and tour boats (chapter 3)—are faithfully described. One item, though, that I was unable to fully work into the manuscript was the swans. There is only a brief mention in chapter 10. Since 1448 swans have occupied the canals. Why? In the late 15th century the people of Bruges rose in revolt against the unpopular Emperor Maximilian of Austria. They managed to capture and imprison Maximilian along with his adviser, a man named Pieter Lanckhals. When Lanckhals was sentenced to death, Maximilian was forced to watch the beheading. Of course, the emperor eventually escaped and took his revenge, retaking the city and decreeing that, until the end of time, Bruges would be required to keep swans on all of its lakes and canals. Why swans? Because they have long necks, and Dutch for "long neck" is *lange hals*—a word so similar to Pieter Lanckhals' name.

Be aware that is just one of several versions of the legend I was told.

All of them quite colorful.

The Basilica of the Holy Blood stands in Bruges, and little about its fanciful exterior reveals the somber style within. The Veneration of the Precious Blood occurs each day. It's a quiet affair, held as depicted in chapter 1, including the dropping of money into a basket before being able to approach the relic. The reliquary itself is a Byzantine marvel. It's been there a long time, and remains one of Europe's most precious objects. Each year, on Ascension Day, the local bishop carries the phial through the streets in the Procession of the Holy Blood. The first one occurred in 1291, and it's still happening to this day.

Belgium is a wonderful place to visit. The Dame Blanche (White Lady) that Cotton speaks about in chapter 1 is a mainstay in every café. These are sundaes extraordinaire, made even more delicious by a liberal use of fine Belgian chocolate and real whipped cream. Each establishment sells its own version, and I must confess to enjoying more than a few.

Religious relics have a checkered and troubled past (chapter 9). A belief in something larger than life has perpetually seemed a human necessity. We also have an insatiable urge to preserve what we believe, regardless of authenticity. An excellent example is the infant Jesus' foreskin. Supposedly it was placed within an oil-filled, alabaster box following circumcision. It first appeared in the 9th century, said to have been gifted to Charlemagne himself by an angel. Eventually it ended up in the Basilica of St. John the Lateran in Rome. Stolen in 1527 by invaders, it reappeared in nearly twenty different places over the next four hundred years, stolen for the last time in 1984. Millions venerated it. Churches exploited it for untold revenue. Never mind that it rang contrary to the doctrine that Christ ascended to heaven intact.

The same is true of the Arma Christi, something else of long standing within Christendom. Not one, but a collection of relics of the passions of Christ, many depicted in countless religious paintings and art. An excellent treatise on the subject is *The Arma Christi in Medieval and Early Modern Material Culture*, edited by Lisa Cooper and Andrea Denny-Brown. Of course, no one knows which of the many objects, scattered around the world, are the true Arma Christi. Unlike in the novel, there is no official list from the Vatican. I randomly chose seven (chapter 9) from the many eligible for my weapons of Christ. But the story of the Empress Helena, and how the veneration of relics began, related in chapter 9, is true.

The European Interceptor Site was first proposed by George W. Bush and ultimately canceled by Barack Obama. The idea (as detailed in chapter 9) was to land-base interceptor missiles in Poland as a deterrent to Iran. Moscow hated the idea, as did most of Europe and a sizable amount of Poland. My resurrection of the concept is fiction.

The Aegis Ballistic Missile Defense System (chapter 50) would have been the weapon of choice, though there were issues then, and now, as to its effectiveness. The controversy over the canceling of the project, as described in chapter 50, happened, with many Polish leaders thinking it a sellout to Moscow at Poland's expense. Ironically, the end came on September 17, 2009, seventy years to the day after the Soviets invaded.

The Agencja Wywiadu (chapter 11), AW, exists as Poland's foreign intelligence service. The Biuro Ochrony Rządu, BOR, Government Protection Bureau (chapter 5), shields the president of Poland every day. The former Służba Bezpieczeństwa, the SB, the communist security police (chapter 12), wreaked havoc on Poles for decades, torturing, killing, and recruiting spies as detailed in chapter 38. Thankfully, it no longer exists. The Dreyfus affair, recounted in chapter 65, is part of history. And the qualifications to be eligible for the presidency of Poland (chapter 5) are accurate. Those elected serve a five-year term, with the possibility of only one reelection thereafter.

Kraków is also another place straight from the past. Rynek Główny, the massive central square, is impressive, as is the cloth market. The *hejnał* mentioned in chapter 20 is a legend of long standing, and you can still hear the mournful notes of the lone trumpeter daily.

Wawel Castle has dominated Kraków for centuries, once the center of Polish political power. Many kings and queens are buried within its walls. The castle's rooms and geography are both faithfully recounted (chapters 28, 30, and 32), including the armoire in which Cotton hides (which is there), the back entrance into the palace, and the outer loggia. The Dragon's Den exists and can be visited. It is one of the oldest continuously occupied sites in all of Europe, and the legend associated with the dragon (chapter 32) is part of Kraków's mythology.

The restaurant Pod Aniołami (chapter 54) is a terrific place to enjoy traditional Polish cuisine. The Sheraton Grand Kraków stands in the shadow of Wawel Castle, and there is a terrific view from its Royal Wawel Suite (chapters 27 and 34). The Monastery of the Camaldolese Monks sits on a hill outside Kraków. A truly unique locale. If possible, pay it a visit, but be warned, the monks are a bit traditional (chapter 22). One rumor says they sleep in coffins, which is ridiculous. But they do keep the skulls of their predecessors in their hermitages. Also, women are only allowed inside to visit a few days a year.

The Holy Lance exists in a world of doubt. There are many around the world that lay claim to being authentic, the major contenders described in chapter 20. The one in Kraków known as the Spear of St. Maurice remains on display in the cathedral museum atop Wawel Hill. Unlike in the novel, the real museum underwent its restoration a few years ago. The stories associated with the spear, how the Holy Roman Emperor bestowed it onto the king of Poland, how it survived multiple invaders, and how the Germans stole then returned it, are all true (chapter 20). The Spear of St. Maurice remains a Polish national treasure, and stands as a symbol of strength and unity, along with the single-headed eagle (chapter 60).

Lech Wałęsa was indeed accused of being a former communist informant (chapters 27, 45). There were many charges and countercharges. At first Wałęsa called it all a hoax created to discredit him. A court did exonerate him of any complicity. Years later, under renewed pressure, he admitted to signing certain documents that seemed to implicate him as an informant, saying he did so to gain the government's trust and learn what he could from the inside. That's where the idea for my Warsaw Protocol originated, though I took it to a more radical extreme (chapter 38). The documents described in chapter 44 are based on real ones. To be labeled a communist informer then, or now, within Poland is a horrible thing. There may be no greater insult, so Janusz Czajkowski's fears were well founded.

Memories of all that happened from 1945 to 1990 remain fresh. The Institute of National Remembrance, and its Commission for the Prosecution of Crimes Against the Polish Nation (chapter 12), are tasked with making sure those memories never fade. Both maintain a vast archive of documents from both the Nazi and communist times. Documents still turn up from time to time, many from private individuals who've held the information for decades. As in the story, one such cache was actually offered for sale by the widow of a former party official. The Pantry (chapter 25) is my invention, but it's not beyond the realm of possibility that such a thing might exist. And what better place to hide away lots of valuable old paper than in a salt mine?

Solidarity changed Poland. It was founded at the Lenin Shipyard on September 17, 1980, as the first trade union within Eastern Europe not controlled by a communist party. It was, as noted in chapter 16, a young person's organization, most of its leaders under the age of thirty. At its peak over ten million joined, one-third of the working-age population of Poland. It fought to effect political change, challenging the Red Bourgeoisie (chapter 16), ultimately succeeding when communist control ended in 1990. But unlike in the story, there was no Warsaw Protocol, or at least history has yet to note its existence.

Sturney Castle is a composite of several that exist across northern Slovakia (chapter 4). The torture Jonty Olivier utilizes in chapter 2, with the electrical wire down the throat, is not my invention. Košice, Slovakia, and Zakopane, Poland, are real, as is the Tatra Museum (chapters 23 and 37). The U.S. consulate in Kraków is there (chapter 35). The Wojtyła house museum in Wadowice can be visited (chapter 55).

The monastery at Jasna Góra is Poland's most sacred religious site (chapters 41, 43, and 45). The Black Madonna and Child have long been associated with miraculous cures. The monks who guide visitors wear white robes and look a lot like a pope. All of the locales within the monastery are faithfully described, including its magnificent library. Finally, the Edgar Allan Poe pen mentioned in chapter 23 is a true collector's piece, created by Montblanc. Many years ago, I was given one as a gift.

The salt mine at Wieliczka was one of the original twelve places first chosen in 1978 for a World Heritage Site designation. And rightly so. It is a spectacular accomplishment. Seven hundred years of salt extraction has left thousands of chambers and almost two hundred miles of tunnels. The story of Saint Kinga, and how the mine first started, is another tale that is ingrained in the local mythology (chapter 14). There are only nine levels. I created the tenth (chapter 31). Those familiar with the mine will see that the internal geography I used does not fit reality, but it was necessary to make changes.

The vast majority of visitors walk the tourist routes on Levels I and II. Access is through the Daniłowicz Shaft and its authentic caged elevators. Those levels are well lit and beautifully designed. There's everything from a restaurant to a conference center, souvenir kiosks, exhibits, shops, and even a health facility for asthmatics. For the more adventurous there is the miner's tour with a descent of the Regis Shaft to the much more rustic (though younger) lower levels. There the visitor experiences what it was like all those centuries ago to be a miner. It's dead silent, and the only light comes from your helmet. I tried to capture that ambience throughout the novel, but if you're given the opportunity, take the miner's tour. I'm not a big fan of enclosed spaces, but I had no issues while down there thanks to all of the shafts being properly ventilated. An excellent book on the subject is referenced in the novel (chapter 53). *City in Salt,* by Andrzej Nowakowski.

Most of the underground chambers are named (chapter 18), and many are supported by wooden cribbing (chapter 31) placed there centuries ago. The salt wall described in chapter 33 is one of countless that exist. I saw one that had been erected in the 18th century. Chapels are scattered across all nine levels, the most magnificent being Saint Kinga's (chapter 29). My Chapel of St. Francis (chapter 66) is a composite of several. Carvings and sculptures are likewise everywhere, all created by the miners. The image of St. Bobola, described in chapter 56, is my invention.

Outside the mine stands the graduation tower (chapter 59), which makes extensive use of salt brine pumped from underground. That brine is collected in a series of underground lakes (chapters 73–76) that are clear, cold, and artfully illuminated. The concentration of saturated salt is so intense that nothing can sink without an enormous amount of ballast. Tourism in the mine started many centuries ago when the Crown would bring royalty down to show off its wealth. They would eat and dance in the largest chambers, then row across the underwater lagoons. There's a story the mine guides tell of a time, in the 19th century, when one of the boats capsized, its occupants trapped beneath. Because of the brine, none were able to dive down and swim out from underneath to safety.

They all suffocated.

At its heart, this novel is about Poland, a nation that knows oppression. Invaders have come for centuries. The Swedes, Turks, Cossacks, Russians, Prussians, Austrians, French, and Germans all wreaked havoc. The nation was wiped from the map in 1795, the land divided among Russia, Prussia, and Austria, history rewritten to blot out all memory of anything Polish (chapter 12). Eventually Poland reemerged (chapter 16) only to be taken by the Nazis then handed away by the Allies after World War II to Stalin. In 1990, with the fall of communism, the nation came back to life. As is quoted in chapter 16, Poland is indeed *the Jesus Christ of nations.*

Martial law was imposed in December 1981 (chapter 55). Tens of thousands were arrested and imprisoned, the country placed on total lockdown. But, as noted in chapter 55, that horribly oppressive act may have saved the nation. First, it allowed Solidarity time to regroup. Second, it graphically demonstrated to the people the horrors they were living under. Life in Poland then was beyond hard (chapter 22). The government, in a foolish move, began to stock stores with food and merchandise, thinking the populace would be grateful. Instead, all it showed was that the government had been responsible for the shortages all along. Finally, it galvanized the world into action, which placed even more pressure on the communists (all of which I dealt with in my novel *The 14th Colony*).

But Poland bears some responsibility for its troubled past.

It has a volatile history (chapter 5). The absurdity of electing a king (chapter 34) led to centuries of political chaos. Then the single-man veto, the liberum, crippled government and allowed a few to dominate the many, making it even easier for invaders to triumph. For a long time Poland did not have weak government, it had no government at all, and that ultimately cost them everything.

Today the country is littered with political parties, the PO and PiS the most dominant (chapter 12). They constantly fight and bicker and try to glue together some semblance of a coalition. Sometimes it works, most times not. The Polska Partia Przyjaciół Piwa, Polish Beer-Lovers' Party (chapter 12), existed and is illustrative of how absurd things can get. Poland continues to struggle to find its place within the European and world communities. Sadly, though, all of the current violence and struggles discussed in chapters 65 and 74 are fact-based. Ronald Reagan said, *Poland is not East or West. Poland is the center of European civilization. It has contributed mightily to that civilization. It is doing so today by being magnificently unreconciled to oppression.* And a few lines from its national anthem say it all:

Poland has not yet perished,
So long as we still live.
What the foreign force has taken from us,
We shall with sabre retrieve.

Rana Faure

STEVE BERRY is the *New York Times* and #1 internationally bestselling author of sixteen Cotton Malone novels, four standalones, and several works of short fiction. He has twenty-five million books in print, translated into forty languages. With his wife, Elizabeth, he is the founder of History Matters, which is dedicated to historical preservation. He serves as an emeritus member of the Smithsonian Libraries Advisory Board and was a founding member of International Thriller Writers, formerly serving as its copresident.

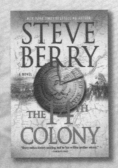
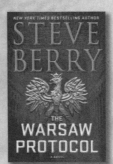
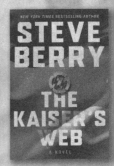
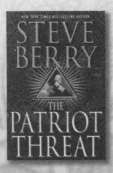
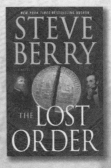
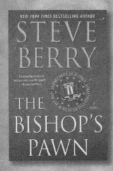